P9-EFJ-782

Praise for the novels of Barbara Freethy

Silent Run

"If you love nail-biting suspense and heartbreaking emotion, *Silent Run* belongs at the top of your to-be-bought list. Barbara Freethy writes romantic suspense that delivers on all counts—a terrific love story and suspense that begins to build on the first page and doesn't let up until the last."   —Mariah Stewart

Played

"An exciting page-turner. . . . This top-notch author delivers top-notch thrills."   —*Romantic Times* (4½ stars)

"The characters are very well developed, and reading this story was almost like going on one of those spooky rides as a kid: You expect something to happen, you think you know where it will occur, and then something jumps out at you from an unexpected area."
                                                —*Mystery News*

Taken

"Terrific and twisty intrigue makes this novel choice reading. . . . An amazingly gripping, fascinating mystery!"
                                        —*Romantic Times* (4½ stars)

"Another crowd-pleasing page-turner in the first of a tricky romantic suspense series."   —*Publishers Weekly*

"Romance sizzles between the wary protagonists in this riveting page-turner."   —*Library Journal*

Don't Say a Word

"Barbara Freethy at her best!"
                        —Carla Neggers, author of *Dark Sky*

continued . . .

"*Don't Say a Word* has made me a Barbara Freethy fan for life!"

> —Diane Chamberlain, author of *The Bay at Midnight*

"Dark, hidden secrets and stunning betrayal . . . potent and moving suspense. Freethy's storytelling ability is top-notch." —*Romantic Times* (4½ stars)

"Guaranteed to keep readers on the edge of their seats. Very highly recommended."

> —Romance Reviews Today

All She Ever Wanted

"A haunting mystery . . . I couldn't put it down."

> —Luanne Rice

"A suitably eerie atmosphere." —*Publishers Weekly*

"A gripping tale of romantic suspense. . . . Barbara Freethy is a master storyteller."

> —Romance Reviews Today

"Sizzling. . . . Freethy's expertly penned novel is a true page-turner." —*Romantic Times*

Golden Lies

"An absolute treasure, a fabulous, page-turning combination of romance and intrigue. Fans of Nora Roberts and Elizabeth Lowell will love *Golden Lies*."

> —Kristin Hannah

"A rich and compelling tale." —*Library Journal*

Summer Secrets

"Barbara Freethy writes with bright assurance, exploring the bonds of sisterhood and the excitement of blue-water sailing. *Summer Secrets* is a lovely novel."
—Luanne Rice

"Freethy skillfully keeps the reader on the hook, and her tantalizing and believable tale has it all—romance, adventure, and mystery." —*Booklist* (starred review)

"An intriguing, multithreaded plot, this is an emotionally involving story . . . sure to please Freethy's growing fan base. . . . Like Kristin Hannah's novels, [it] neatly bridges the gap between romance and traditional women's fiction." —*Library Journal*

Further praise for Barbara Freethy

"In the tradition of LaVyrle Spencer, gifted author Barbara Freethy creates an irresistible tale of family secrets, riveting adventure, and heart-touching romance."
—Susan Wiggs

"A fresh and exciting voice in women's romantic fiction." —Susan Elizabeth Phillips

"Superlative." —Debbie Macomber

"Barbara Freethy delivers strong and compelling prose." —*Publishers Weekly*

"If there is one author who knows how to deliver vivid stories that tug on your emotions, it's Barbara Freethy."
—*Romantic Times*

OTHER NOVELS BY BARBARA FREETHY

BARBARA FREETHY

SILENT FALL

AN ONYX BOOK

ONYX
Published by New American Library, a division of
Penguin Group (USA) Inc., 375 Hudson Street,
New York, New York 10014, USA
Penguin Group (Canada), 90 Eglinton Avenue East, Suite 700, Toronto,
Ontario M4P 2Y3, Canada (a division of Pearson Penguin Canada Inc.)
Penguin Books Ltd., 80 Strand, London WC2R 0RL, England
Penguin Ireland, 25 St. Stephen's Green, Dublin 2,
Ireland (a division of Penguin Books Ltd.)
Penguin Group (Australia), 250 Camberwell Road, Camberwell, Victoria 3124,
Australia (a division of Pearson Australia Group Pty. Ltd.)
Penguin Books India Pvt. Ltd., 11 Community Centre, Panchsheel Park,
New Delhi – 110 017, India
Penguin Group (NZ), 67 Apollo Drive, Rosedale, North Shore 0632,
New Zealand (a division of Pearson New Zealand Ltd.)
Penguin Books (South Africa) (Pty.) Ltd., 24 Sturdee Avenue,
Rosebank, Johannesburg 2196, South Africa

Penguin Books Ltd., Registered Offices:
80 Strand, London WC2R 0RL, England

First published by Onyx, an imprint of New American Library,
a division of Penguin Group (USA) Inc.

First Printing, April 2008
10 9 8 7 6 5 4 3 2 1

PUBLISHER'S NOTE
This is a work of fiction. Names, characters, places, and incidents either are the product of the author's imagination or are used fictitiously, and any resemblance to actual persons, living or dead, business establishments, events, or locales is entirely coincidental.

The publisher does not have any control over and does not assume any responsibility for author or third-party Web sites or their content.

If you purchased this book without a cover, you should be aware that this book is stolen property. It was reported as "unsold and destroyed" to the publisher, and neither the author nor the publisher has received any payment for this "stripped book."

The scanning, uploading, and distribution of this book via the Internet or via any other means without the permission of the publisher is illegal and punishable by law. Please purchase only authorized electronic editions, and do not participate in or encourage electronic piracy of copyrighted materials. Your support of the author's rights is appreciated.

To Dorothy and George and the Freethy family—
I couldn't have asked for better in-laws.

ACKNOWLEDGMENTS

Many thanks go to my brainstorming pals Candice Hern, Tracy Grant, Carol Culver, Monica McCarty, Jami Alden, Bella Andre, Anne Mallory, Kate Moore, Barbara McMahon, Lynn Hanna, and Diana Dempsey, who are always up for lunch, chocolate, Starbucks, and a good story idea. Thanks also go to my fabulous agents, Andrea Cirillo and Annelise Robey, and everyone at the Jane Rotrosen Agency, who help with all the big and small details. And thanks to Ellen Edwards and NAL for doing such a terrific job editing and publishing my books. And last but not least, thanks to the Fog City Divas and the hottest blog on the Net at www.fogcitydivas.com. For more information on my books, visit my Web site at www.barbarafreethy.com.

SILENT FALL

Prologue

Golden Gate Park, San Francisco

She was going to die. The terrifying thought made her stumble, her spiked heel catching in a crack in the pavement. She fell forward, breaking her fall with her hands. Tiny pebbles of cement burned into her palms and her knees. For a moment she was tempted to quit. She was so cold and so tired, but if she stopped now he'd catch her, and there would be no tomorrow, no second chance.

Forcing herself back to her feet, she pulled off her broken shoes and headed deeper into the park. The grass was wet beneath her feet, the midnight fingers of fog covering everything within reach with a damp mist. Her hair curled around her face as the wet spray mixed with the tears streaking down her cheeks.

She'd never been a crier, but this was too much. She'd never felt so alone or in such mortal danger.

Everywhere she turned, he followed. She couldn't seem to get away. How did he keep finding her?

Even now she could hear the footsteps behind her, the crack of twigs, the sound of a distant car. Was it him?

She probably should have stayed on the city streets, but she'd thought the tall trees and the thick bushes of the park would offer her protection, a place to hide. Now she realized how desolate the area was at night. There were no phone booths, no people, no businesses to run into. She was completely on her own.

She gasped and stopped abruptly as a shadowy figure came out of the undergrowth. Her heart thudded against her chest. The man walked toward her, one hand outstretched. His clothes were old and torn, and his face was covered with a heavy beard. He wore a baseball cap, and a backpack was slung over one shoulder. He was probably one of the homeless people who set up camp in the park at night. Or maybe not . . .

"Hey, baby, give me a kiss," he said in a drunken slur.

"Leave me alone." She put up a hand to ward him off, but he kept moving forward.

"I'm just being friendly. Come on now, sweetheart."

Turning, she ran as fast as she could in the other direction, hearing him call after her. She didn't know if he was following her or not, and she was too terrified to look, so she left the sidewalk and moved deeper into the park, looking for a little corner in which to hide. Her side was cramping and her feet were soaked. She desperately needed to find some sanctuary. Branches scraped her bare arms and face, but she kept going. It was so dark in the heavy brush that she could barely see a foot in front of her. Tall trees and fog had completely obliterated the moonlight.

Fortunately she had her hand out in front of her when she ran into a cement wall that rose several stories in the air. She must have hit the side of one of the park buildings. Pausing, she caught her breath and listened. She could hear nothing but her own ragged breathing. Maybe she was safe, at least for the moment.

Leaning back against the cold cement, she pondered her next move, but she didn't know what to do, how to escape. She was out of options.

How had she come to this? Running for her life and all alone? This was not how it was supposed to go. This was Dylan's fault. He'd put her in this situation, and dammit, where the hell was he?

But she couldn't count on him to rescue her. She had to find a way out on her own. She couldn't let things end like this. She'd fought for her life before, and she'd won. She would do it again.

Her heart stopped as a nearby branch snapped in two. A confident male whistle pierced the silent night. Whoever was coming didn't care if she heard him or not. The bushes in front of her slowly parted. Terror ran through her body. There was nowhere left to run.

Chapter 1

Dylan Sanders took a shot of Jack Daniels from the bartender, enjoying the burn as the liquor slid down his throat. After draining the glass, he immediately ordered another. He didn't like weddings and usually avoided them at all costs, but this one he hadn't been able to miss, because he was the best man. He was thankful that he'd finished his formal duties. He just had to get through the next hour before he could call it a night.

Glancing across the room, he watched his brother, Jake, and Jake's bride, Sarah, share their first dance on the back deck of the Woodlake Mountain Lodge. In the glow of candlelight and against the backdrop of the purple-blue twilight sky, they looked exceedingly happy, as if the past year hadn't tested their love in every possible way. But they'd come through the bad times. From here on out, it would be nothing but smooth sailing—at least he hoped so. He smiled as one of Sarah's friends brought his niece, Caitlyn, to the dance floor. Jake's eighteen-month-old blond angel was the hit of the wedding, but as usual she wanted to be part of the action. Jake swung his baby daughter into his arms, and the three of them danced together like the family they were.

Dylan tossed another shot down his throat, pushing back the ridiculous thought that he was jealous of their happiness. While he loved his brother, he did not yearn for marriage and a family of his own. He'd grown up in a broken home, and he didn't intend to repeat the experience. Although he hoped Jake and Sarah would make it, that they would beat the odds of divorce and that they would never fall out of love the way his own parents had.

A cool evening breeze blew through the open patio doors, drawing goose bumps down his arms, but it wasn't the wind that had put his nerves on edge. It was the beautiful redhead who slid onto the bar stool next to him.

"Are you drinking to your brother's happiness or to the demise of yet another bachelor?" Catherine Hilliard asked.

Dylan set his glass on the bar. Catherine had cleaned up pretty well since their first meeting two months earlier, when she'd helped him find Sarah. There were no paint spatters on Catherine's clothes today, and she'd covered her bare feet in a pair of high heels. She wore a gorgeous, sexy black dress with a low-cut halter top that showed off her beautiful breasts. He loved the way the freckles danced across her chest. He had the sudden urge to see if she had freckles all over her body.

He tugged on his tie, feeling tightness in his chest at the very bad ideas flooding his brain. Catherine was an old friend of his new sister-in-law, and as such was off-limits, not to mention the fact that she was more than a little quirky, with her passion for painting gruesome pictures and her claim that she was psychic. But despite her eccentricities, Catherine had a big heart and a fierce loyalty to her friends, which he found far too appealing.

"Hello," Catherine said pointedly. "You're staring."

"You're stunning," he replied, unable to stop the words from crossing his lips.

She gave him a quick smile. "That's a good start to the conversation. The wedding was lovely, didn't you think? Jake and Sarah make a good match. I think they have a chance."

"A chance, huh? That's an enthusiastic endorsement," he said dryly, hearing the same note of cynicism that echoed through his own head.

Catherine shrugged. "I haven't seen a lot of happy marriages in my time, but if anyone can make it, they can."

"So, how have you been? Painting a lot?"

"Every night. I even painted you. It's been quite a challenge."

He raised an eyebrow. "No kidding? Do I want to see it?"

Her smile widened. "Maybe I'll show you some-time."

"I don't get down the coast much." Catherine lived in San Luis Obispo, three hours away from his apart-ment in San Francisco, which provided a nice buffer zone. He had to admit she'd crossed his mind more than once in the past six weeks, but fortunately he had been busy with his work as an investigative reporter for KTSF Television News in San Francisco.

Catherine accepted a glass of champagne from the bartender. "I brought the painting with me. I wanted to work on it some more. I'm staying here at the lodge for a few days. I figured with a Friday-night wedding, it was only fitting that I get a weekend retreat in the woods."

"Who's watching your menagerie of pets?" he asked. "I can't imagine you leaving them alone." Catherine shared her home with two cats, two dogs, and a very annoying and talkative bird. In some ways he envied her little zoo. He'd never been allowed to have a pet growing up, and watching her with her golden retriev-ers on the beach behind her house had made him feel like he'd missed out. Of course, he'd missed out on a lot of things besides having a pet. That had been the least of his problems.

"My neighbor, Lois, watches them when I'm gone. I will miss them, but the mountains are beautiful, and I haven't been away on my own for a while. Besides, the lake has a peacefulness about it, a depth and a secrecy that appeal to me. I want to soak it all in for a few days."

Dylan didn't see the lake the way she did, but he had

always enjoyed Tahoe. For years he and Jake had come to the lake with friends or family members to escape the overbearing presence of their father, who luckily never left the city. Dylan wasn't surprised Jake had wanted to get married here. It was a good start to his new life, although Jake and Sarah wouldn't be staying long. They were taking a late-night flight to Hawaii to begin their honeymoon.

"What about you?" Catherine asked, interrupting his thoughts. "Are you staying through the weekend?"

"I leave in the morning."

"Are you sure?"

His gaze narrowed. "What does that mean?"

Her dark blue eyes grew mysterious. "Do you remember what I told you about the two women entering your life, one bringing danger, the other salvation? I think it starts here."

"What starts here?" he began, and then quickly backtracked. "You know what? I don't want to know. I don't believe in your psychic visions. I'm sorry. That's just the way it is."

"I understand," she said, raising her glass to her lips.

He didn't like the look in her eyes. He told himself to forget what she'd said. She was just trying to yank his chain.

Someone took the seat on the other side of him. A waft of familiar perfume made his head turn. The brunette gave him a big smile. Damn, he was in trouble.

Catherine leaned over and whispered in his ear, "Be careful, Dylan. She's one of them."

"Who's the other one?" he asked as she got up and

walked away. Catherine didn't reply. He had a feeling he already knew the answer. But it didn't matter. He wouldn't let her crazy words rattle him. His life was going great, and he didn't intend to let anything or anyone change that.

"We need to talk, Dylan."

Dylan turned his head and stared into the bright brown eyes of a woman he'd never thought he'd see again, Erica Layton. Six weeks earlier they'd shared a night—a rather drunken night, and one he preferred to forget. He didn't usually sleep with his sources, and he shouldn't have slept with Erica, but a late-night celebration had somehow landed him in bed with her. And now she was here with an expectant expression on her face. This couldn't be good, and he didn't need a psychic to tell him that.

Erica handed him a glass of champagne.

"What's this?" he asked.

"We're celebrating your brother's wedding. Cheers." Erica tipped her glass to his.

He reluctantly took a sip. "What are you doing here? You weren't on the guest list."

"I've been calling you for the past two weeks, but you haven't returned my calls," she complained.

"I was busy."

"You weren't too busy for me when you needed my help."

He sighed at the sharp tone in her voice. "I appreciate all the help you gave me, Erica, but if you were looking for something more, it's not going to happen." He was surprised that he even had to tell her that. Their one encounter had been mutually satisfying, but certainly not the beginning of a relationship. And Erica had understood that. He would have sworn she'd understood. He never got involved with women who didn't know the score.

Erica frowned, and her face went from pretty and edgy to hard and brittle. There was a wild gleam in her eyes that made him uneasy. Was she on something?

"We need to talk," she repeated.

His gut twisted at the purpose in her words. A quick mental calculation reminded him that when a woman you'd slept with six weeks earlier suddenly wanted to talk, there was a good chance it had something to do with a baby. But they'd used protection. He'd been stupid to sleep with her, but he hadn't been completely careless. Still, his niece, Caitlyn, was a prime example that condoms didn't always work. He gulped down another swallow of his champagne.

He did not want to have this conversation now. His career was flying. He'd just broken one of the biggest stories of his life. He was on the fast track to success. Everything was going as planned. The last thing he needed was a complication—a baby. His glance drifted down Erica's body. She looked as thin as ever in a short red cocktail dress that was now hitched up to midthigh. Her legs were bare, her skin tan, her feet strapped into a pair of red stilettos. A sheer red scarf was draped around her shoulders. She didn't look pregnant, but if she was, he might as well face it head-on.

"All right, talk," he ordered, never one to shy away from a problem. Whatever it was, he'd deal with it.

Erica hesitated, her gaze darting around the room. "Not here. It's too crowded. Take a walk with me."

He didn't want to go anywhere with her, but he also didn't want to have a private conversation in a public place. Nor did he want to worry his brother or upset the wedding reception by getting into what could be a volatile conversation with Erica. She wasn't exactly the calmest, most reasonable woman he'd ever met. Even now her fingers tapped nervously on the top of the bar, and she kept glancing around as if she were afraid someone was watching her, watching them.

Maybe he was off base. Maybe this wasn't personal. Erica had a way of getting herself into trouble without really trying. He'd learned that about her when she'd helped him link a state senator to murder. He owed her for that. The least he could do was listen to her now.

"Does this have to do with Senator Ravino?" he asked, lowering his voice.

She licked her lips. "Of course not. He's in jail, awaiting trial."

"I know, and you helped me and the police put him there. Has he tried to contact you? Are you feeling threatened in some way?"

"The police say I'm in no danger, but I know the senator better than anyone. He has a lot of connections outside prison."

"What do you need from me?"

"I need to talk to you," she said, sounding desperate. She slid off her stool. "Are you coming?"

"All right." He finished the rest of the champagne and stood up.

"There's a path we can take," Erica said as they walked out of the bar and through the lobby of the lodge. "It winds along the mountain, and there's a spectacular view of the lake."

"How do you know that?"

"I got here earlier. I had a chance to explore." She gave him a look he couldn't decipher and then led him out a side door.

Nestled in the High Sierras and surrounded by tall ponderosa pines, the Woodlake Mountain Lodge was perched on a steep hillside overlooking the glistening waters of Lake Tahoe. Adjoining the main building of the lodge were a dozen small, rustic cabins.

"That's my cabin over there." Erica pointed to a nearby building. "I didn't want to drive down the mountain after dark, so I got a room. Are you in the main lodge?"

"Yes. Why did you come here, Erica? You could have contacted me in San Francisco. You know where I live." It didn't make sense to him that she would have come all the way to Tahoe to talk to him.

"Let's go this way," she said, taking a path to the right. "I knew I would have to surprise you, or you'd find an excuse to avoid me."

"You should have waited until after my brother's wedding. This is a big day for him."

"You don't care about weddings, Dylan."

"When they involve my brother, I do."

She rolled her eyes. "Right," she said, a cynical note in her voice.

Dylan stopped abruptly, losing patience. "Look,

whatever you have to say, just say it. It's getting dark, and I don't feel like getting lost in the woods with you."

"Let's walk to the end of the path. There's a bench. We can sit." She proceeded without waiting for him to answer.

The cement walkway was lined with small lights every ten feet or so, but as the path turned into dirt the lights disappeared and dark shadows surrounded them. He tried to call out to Erica to stop, but she was moving at a good clip, and his tongue felt thick in his head. He must have had more to drink than he'd realized.

Where the hell was the bench Erica wanted to reach? His legs felt strangely fatigued, and the scenery began to spin in front of his eyes. It took everything he had to put one foot in front of the other. What was wrong? A sick, queasy feeling swept through him. He stumbled and almost fell, but he caught himself at the last minute. He put his hand on the trunk of a nearby tree to steady himself.

"Erica," he mumbled, forcing the word out.

She turned to stare back at him, but she made no move to come to his side.

"Help me." He tried to lift his arm, but it was too heavy.

"This is your fault, Dylan," she said. "I had no choice. I had nowhere else to turn."

No choice? What was she talking about?

"It always comes down to every man for himself. You said so yourself, Dylan. Now it's my turn to look out for me."

She took a few steps backward. She was getting awfully close to the edge of a very steep cliff. He wanted to warn her to stay back, but he couldn't get the words out. The landscape took another wild spin.

She'd drugged him, he realized, suddenly remembering the overly sweet taste of the champagne. Why? What the hell did she want? Before he could ask her, his legs gave way and the world went black.

Catherine Hilliard awoke in the middle of the night, her heart racing and sweat dampening her cheeks. The digital clock read four forty-four. Every night for the past two months she'd woken up with terror flooding through her body like a tidal wave threatening to take her under. The screams of the past ran through her head, a maddening refrain that she feared she would never forget and yet never fully remember.

The events of one night had been lost in her subconscious for twenty-four years. And every few years the nightmares came back, torturing her for weeks at a time and then disappearing as quickly as they'd come. But this time was different. The dreams were getting worse, and the fear was relentlessly increasing with each passing night, as if something were coming for her, something horrific.

Scrambling out of bed, she did the only thing she could do to take the fear away. She painted.

On the easel a blank canvas waited. She picked up her brushes and opened her mixed paints, finding comfort in the familiar actions. Dipping her brush into the paint, she paused for a second and then put the brush to the canvas. The nightmare in her mind took shape with bold, dark swaths of color, red, green, black, blue. She barely breathed as the fear seeped out of her with each swipe of the brush. She never knew what would come out of her subconscious. Finally, shaken and drained, she set down her brush and backed away.

The picture she'd painted would make no sense to anyone. It was a mess of lines and shapes, collisions of color, but in the abstract images she thought she could see a face haunted by fear, dark eyes filled with terror, a mouth pleading for help. And deep down she believed she was supposed to help, but she didn't know how.

Sitting on the edge of the bed, she let out a sigh as she studied her picture from afar. Calmer now, she tried to analyze what she'd done, the way she did every night, but the turmoil in her brain was as confusing as always.

She'd been six years old when her life had changed forever, when her reality had become a nightmare, when the bad dreams had begun. The police had wanted to know exactly what she'd seen that night, but she couldn't tell them. A therapist had given her paper and crayons and told her to draw, so she'd drawn, but the images hadn't made any sense then, nor did they now. And since that day she hadn't been able to stop drawing. Art had become her refuge, her passion, and her way of making a living. If she couldn't paint, she didn't think she could live.

During the daylight hours she could draw beautiful pictures, landscapes, flowers, happy people—but at night, after the dreams came, her paintings became monstrosities as she was driven to put brush to canvas in a desperate effort to free herself from the endless nightmares.

She'd tried changing her environment, but that hadn't worked. As a child she'd lived in eight different foster homes, and the nightmares had always found her. As an adult she'd tried three different cities and rented more than a few apartments before settling into her current beach cottage, but the dreams always returned.

Of course, there were months when she slept undisturbed. She wished for the relief of those dreamless nights. The longest she'd gone without a nightmare was six years. She'd thought they were over. Then they'd returned, and she'd realized she would never be free until she did something. . . .

She had the sense that she was meant to act in some way—only then would she be able to escape. But what was she supposed to do? She didn't know. Nor did she recognize the abstract faces of the people she painted. They called out to her, but she couldn't answer, because she didn't know who they were.

Although tonight she couldn't help wondering if the face in her picture belonged to the woman who'd approached Dylan in the bar. There was a faint resemblance, wasn't there? Maybe she was just imagining it. Or perhaps she'd painted the woman's face because she'd seen her in her head, when she'd had a brief glimpse into Dylan's future—a future that seemed to include her. Not that she wanted to be included. She had a feeling Dylan was heading for trouble, and the last thing she needed was more trouble in her life.

Getting up, she walked over to the window and drew back the curtain. Her room was located on the top floor of the three-story lodge and had a direct view of the lake several hundred yards below. The water shimmered in the light of a full moon. The tall pine trees that covered the hillside swayed in the breeze like giant monsters. A shiver ran down her spine. She believed in connections, in fate and destiny. Nothing happened by chance. There was always a purpose. A long-ago childhood psychiatrist had told her that sometimes bad things just happened, and she had to stop looking for reasons, but Catherine hadn't believed the doctor then, nor did she buy into that philosophy now. Which was why she couldn't ignore the fact that something was wrong.

Crossing her arms over her chest, she felt a cold draft through her thin camisole top and silky shorts. She hoped her sense of impending doom didn't have anything to do with Sarah. Her friend deserved to be happy after everything she had been through the past few years. And Jake and Sarah and their daughter were on their way to Hawaii, to the land of swaying palm trees, soft, warm breezes, and blue skies. They were fine. They had to be.

She drew in a deep breath and then slowly let it out. She repeated the action several more times. Usually painting her nightmares tired her enough so that she could sleep until morning. Tonight she still felt edgy, as if she were waiting for something else to happen. She walked over to the valise set against the wall and pulled out another painting, a portrait this time. . . .

Dylan stared back at her with his golden brown eyes that were a mix of mystery, pain, amusement, and cynicism. She'd worked hard to capture the complexity of his eyes, the proud strength of his jaw, and the hint of wariness that was usually present in his expression, as well as the cocky smile that could also be kind, but she didn't think she had it quite right yet. They'd spent only a few days together two months earlier, when Dylan had asked for her help in finding Sarah and Jake's daughter, but those few days in his presence had touched her in a way she didn't completely understand. She just knew that they were connected. There was a reason Dylan had come to her.

He'd say pragmatically that it was because she and Sarah shared a past, and that was the end of it. But she suspected there was more to come. If only she knew how the woman in the bar figured into things, that would be helpful, but her visions were never as complete or as forthcoming as she wanted. She would have to wait for whatever came next.

Setting the painting aside, she returned to the window. In the light of the moon Dylan's image flashed through her head once again. She saw fear in his eyes, an expression of shock and betrayal. She grabbed the curtains with both hands, swaying with the sudden and certain knowledge that Dylan was in trouble.

Glancing back at the clock, she realized an hour had passed since she'd first awoken in the grip of her nightmare. It was almost six. She just had to make it until dawn and then she would be fine. Once the sun came up she could relax. She could breathe again. And she could check on Dylan. She wanted to call him now, but she doubted he'd appreciate being wakened so early.

A red-and-blue strobe light caught her eye. She turned back to the window, stiffening as a police car pulled up in front of the lodge. She pressed her face against the glass, watching two uniformed policemen enter the building.

Her fear intensified. She was torn between wanting to go downstairs and find out what was happening and wanting to stay safely tucked away in her room.

This wasn't her problem, she told herself. She didn't need to get involved in a situation that didn't concern her. Keeping away from cops was second nature to her. They hadn't been able to protect her when she was a child, and as she'd grown up she'd learned that the only person she could trust was herself—certainly not uniformed police officers, whose nightly sweeps of the streets had made trying to survive only that much more difficult.

She moved away from the window and sat down on the bed, staring at the phone. She couldn't shake the desire to call Dylan and find out if he was all right. She hadn't seen him since she'd left him at the bar with that woman. She'd looked for him several times during the reception, especially when Jake and Sarah had wanted to say good-bye to him, but he'd been nowhere in sight. Jake had joked that his brother had probably gotten lucky. And she'd figured he was right. But now she wondered. . . . Dylan and Jake were so tight, as close as brothers could be. Would Dylan have really taken off with a woman at his brother's wedding? It seemed unlikely.

Giving in to impulse, she picked up the phone and dialed the hotel operator, asking for his room. The phone rang and rang, finally giving way to voice mail. She hung up, her hand shaking. He might just be a heavy sleeper. Or he could be spending the night with that woman.

Catherine crawled under the covers and pulled the blankets up to her chin. She stared at the clock, watching each minute tick away. She wanted to sleep, but she knew she couldn't, not until the sun came up and her fears went back into hiding.

Chapter 2

Dylan stirred, feeling something sharp stabbing the middle of his back. His head felt thick, a dull pain reverberating from the front of his skull down to his neck and shoulders. His lids were heavy, and it took him a second to get his eyes open, another minute to realize he was lying flat on his back on the ground. He reached under his body and yanked out a pinecone, the source of his discomfort.

The sun was just beginning to rise over the tall trees that surrounded him, the air still chilled with the icy cold of dawn. A few wispy clouds hung in the otherwise blue sky. It was morning, he realized, feeling half-witted. What the hell had happened? Why was he on the ground in the woods? Had he gotten drunk and passed out? He struggled to sit up.

There was dirt on his pants and on the sleeves of his charcoal gray suit. A cut on the top of his hand had swelled up, his skin now puffy and red. A glance at his watch told him it was seven fifteen in the morning. And the last thing he remembered was . . . what?

He drew in a deep breath and ordered himself to think. The view reminded him that he was in Lake Tahoe and that Jake had just gotten married. Dylan had been at the wedding reception, sitting at the bar. He'd spoken to Catherine, and then Erica had arrived. She'd wanted to talk to him. She'd given him champagne. They'd taken a walk—a long walk.

His pulse began to race as he jerked to his feet, suddenly feeling vulnerable. He looked around him, but he could see nothing but trees and the downward-sloping hillside that led to the edge of a cliff—a sheer drop to the lake below. Erica had brought him to this spot. She'd said something about having no choice, but the rest of her words were a blur. He remembered feeling sick, too weary to walk, as if he'd been drugged. That had to be what had happened. Erica must have put something in his champagne. But why would she do that?

He checked his pockets. His wallet was intact, along with a couple hundred dollars. She hadn't taken his money or his watch, and he had nothing else of value on him—unless she'd wanted something from his room. He patted down his pockets again, realizing he didn't have his car keys. Had he left them in the room? And speaking of his room, where was his room key? He'd brought his laptop with him to do some work. Some of his files and notes from the Ravino case were on it. Had Erica wanted some piece of information?

Was that why she'd drugged him and lured him out to the woods, so she could get into his room?

A stirring nearby made him turn his head. Was the rustle of leaves and branches the work of squirrels or birds, or was someone watching him? Was it Erica? Was she about to put another part of her plan into action? He needed to return to the lodge, but he was disoriented, so he took a minute to figure out which direction to go. Stumbling on the dirt and rocks, he made his way slowly through the trees, eventually finding a trail.

It took him a while to reach the lodge. He hadn't realized how far they'd walked the night before. Erica had obviously wanted to get him far enough away from the property so that no one would find him. Still, luring him out to the woods and leaving him there half-drugged didn't seem like a complete plan to him. There had to be more.

He realized what that *more* was when he saw two police cars in front of the lodge. Something had happened. Picking up the pace, he jogged up the front steps, a multitude of fears running through his head. He'd lost a dozen hours or more, and he had no idea whether Jake and Sarah had gotten off on their honeymoon. Had they wondered where he'd gone? Had they worried about him, called the cops? Or, God forbid, had something happened to them? Was that why the police were here?

As he entered the lobby he saw a uniformed police officer and a man in a dark gray suit standing by the reception desk. They were talking to the manager of the lodge while half a dozen employees looked on. One of those employees was the bartender who'd served him drinks the night before. When their gazes met, the bartender lifted his hand, pointing to Dylan.

"That's him," the bartender said. "That's the guy I saw leaving the bar with her last night."

Erica. This had to do with Erica.

"What's happened?" Dylan asked.

The man wearing the suit walked toward him. He appeared to be in his early forties, with light brown hair and a receding hairline. His tie hung loose around his neck, as if he spent a lot of time tugging on it, and his ruddy complexion bore testament to a man who lived outside as much as in. At the flash of his badge, Dylan's gut tightened.

"I'm Detective Richardson with the Washoe County Sheriff's Department," he said. "And you are . . . ?"

"Dylan Sanders. What's going on?"

"We're checking on the welfare of one of the guests, Ms. Erica Layton. Do you know her?"

His heart skipped a beat. "Yes. I know her. What happened to her?"

"That's what we're trying to find out. The bartender who worked the wedding reception last night said he saw Ms. Layton at the bar with you, and that you left together. Is that correct?"

The detective's gaze ran down his body, and Dylan was suddenly very aware of his appearance, the dirt on his shirt, the pine needles sticking to his sleeves. He resisted the urge to draw more attention to himself by shaking them off. "That's right," he muttered.

"When did you last see Ms. Layton?" the detective asked.

"Last night about seven thirty."

"Where were you?"

"In the woods. Erica and I took a walk. She said she wanted to speak to me."

"About what? Do you have a relationship with Ms. Layton?"

"Not exactly." Dylan hesitated, his brain beginning to work again. He didn't like the speculative gleam in the detective's eyes or the direction of his questions. "Why are you asking?"

"As I said, we're concerned about Ms. Layton's whereabouts. Did you accompany her to her cabin last night?"

"No. The last time I saw her was in the woods."

"Where she wanted to speak to you about what?"

"We worked together on a story I did several months ago. I'm a news reporter for KTSF Channel Three in San Francisco. I assumed she wanted to talk to me about that," Dylan replied. He had no intention of discussing his personal relationship with Erica until the detective told him what was going on.

"So Ms. Layton was a guest at your brother's wedding?"

"No, she wasn't a guest. She apparently came to Tahoe to speak to me."

"You said you assumed she wanted to talk about the

story you did together, but that wasn't her purpose, was it?"

"I'm not sure. We never actually got around to having a conversation."

"Why not?"

"She left."

"Did you argue? Was Ms. Layton upset?"

Dylan frowned. He didn't know what the hell had happened to Erica, but there must be some evidence of something, or the police wouldn't have been called and the detective wouldn't be interrogating him as if he were the prime suspect in a murder investigation. His pulse jumped at the thought. Was Erica dead?

No, the detective had said he was concerned about her welfare. That meant she was missing, not dead.

"Where did you go after Ms. Layton left you?" Detective Richardson continued.

As a reporter, Dylan had worked with the police on several occasions, and he knew it would be best to tell the truth, but his mind jerked ahead to what his explanation would sound like, and he knew it wouldn't be good. But what choice did he have? Lying would only delay the inevitable revelation of the truth.

The nearby elevator opened with the ring of a bell. Dylan was surprised to see Catherine step out. She wore a pair of blue jeans and an oversize cream-colored sweater. Her reddish blond hair was swept back in a loose ponytail. She stopped abruptly when she saw the police officer, her expression a mix of relief and wariness.

"Mr. Sanders?" Detective Richardson prodded. "I'm

going to need you to answer my questions. Where did you go after Ms. Layton left?"

"Nowhere."

"Excuse me?"

"I have to back up," Dylan said, realizing he needed to explain what had happened.

"All right." The detective folded his arms across his chest as he waited for Dylan to continue.

Dylan looked away from Catherine. He needed to focus on one problematic woman at a time. "Erica approached me in the bar. As I said, we'd worked together on a story a few months ago. I was surprised to see her at my brother's wedding, because we haven't had any contact in weeks. She handed me a glass of champagne and told me she needed to talk to me, but she didn't want to do it in the bar because it was too loud and too public, so we took a walk along the path that runs in front of the lodge. After a few minutes I started feeling ill, dizzy, as if I were drunk or drugged. But Erica kept walking, leading me deeper into the woods. I became disoriented. I didn't know how far we'd gone. I stumbled, and that's the last thing I remember until I woke up about fifteen minutes ago, and I came straight back here. I believe Erica slipped something into my drink."

"Hold on. You're saying that Ms. Layton drugged you? Why would she do that?" the detective asked, tilting his head to one side, his brown eyes sharp and thoughtful. "I thought you were friends."

"I thought we were, too. I don't know why she

would drug me. I vaguely recall her saying something to me about not having a choice, but the rest is a blur."

"That's quite a story," the detective said skeptically.

"It's the truth. That's what happened."

"So Ms. Layton was angry with you."

"I don't think I said she was angry."

"Didn't you?" the detective countered. "Why else would she slip something into your drink? That doesn't sound very friendly to me."

"She did not appear angry or upset when she approached me in the bar. The only emotion she exhibited was nervousness," he added, remembering how jittery Erica had been.

"Your relationship wasn't just business, was it, Mr. Sanders?"

Dylan licked his lips, feeling as if a noose were being pulled around his neck. He needed time to think, but he doubted the detective would give it to him. "Do I need to get a lawyer?"

"I don't know. Do you?"

"Look, I was drugged. I don't know what happened to Erica—if, in fact, anything did happen to her. If you don't believe me I'll get a drug test," he said impulsively. He needed to prove his innocence, and this was the perfect way to do it. "I'll get one right now."

"You'd be willing to do that?"

"Absolutely. I don't have anything to hide."

"If you didn't have something to hide, I doubt you'd be asking for your lawyer," the detective said with a wry twist to his lips. He paused for another second and then nodded. "I'll send one of our deputies with you to the local hospital. He can set up the tests. Excuse me for a minute."

Dylan let out a breath as the detective went to confer with the deputy. He hoped he hadn't made a mistake by agreeing to take a drug test, but he couldn't think of a better way to prove he had been incapable of hurting anyone. Turning his head, he saw Catherine watching him from across the lobby. He walked over to join her.

"Are you okay?" she asked with concern. "You have dirt in your hair, and you look like you've been up all night."

He ran his fingers through his hair, creating a shower of needles on the carpet. "Obviously I'm not all right. What do you know about Erica?"

"Was she the woman at the bar?"

"Don't play dumb, Catherine. You know something is going on. That's why you're down here. And you predicted Erica's arrival, remember?"

"Of course I remember. I never forget my visions," she said, her blue gaze meeting his. "I knew her face, but I didn't know her name."

"Didn't you?" he challenged. "You said we were all connected. Why do I get the feeling you're setting me up?"

"Why would I do that? You're Jake's brother, Sarah's brother-in-law. Sarah would kill me if I tried to hurt you." Her eyes narrowed. "Besides, what reason could I possibly have for wanting to set you up for something? I barely know you."

He couldn't think of a reason; he just knew he didn't completely trust her. "If you knew Erica would cause trouble for me, why did you take off yesterday? Why didn't you stick around to help me?"

"It wasn't my business, and you seemed to know her. I certainly didn't expect her to drug you and drag you off to the woods, if that's what happened. I heard what you told the detective," she added. "You weren't talking all that quietly. I'm sure everyone heard your story."

"Well, it's not a secret," he said with annoyance, although now he wished he'd spoken to the detective in a more private setting. The lodge employees were all looking at him with extreme speculation.

Catherine's gaze darted around the room as if she were waiting for something else to happen. Did she know what was coming? Had she seen something else?

He'd never believed in psychics or visions, and certainly Catherine's prediction that two women would enter his life and cause problems was vague enough to come true at just about any time. After all, a lot of women came into his life. But it did bother him that Catherine had identified Erica as the woman she'd seen in her vision, especially now that Erica was missing. Had it been just a lucky guess? Had Catherine seen Erica come up to him at the bar and decided to tell him that was the woman from her vision to make it look as if she really were a psychic? Or was there something to her supposed visions?

"So what's going to happen next?" he asked. "Since

you seem to have an insight into the future that the rest of us don't have."

"Obviously you don't believe that I do," she snapped back. "I don't know why I came down here."

"Why did you? Or are you going to claim you were just headed for breakfast?"

She hesitated. "I was worried about you. I saw the cop car from my room. I knew something was up."

"And you decided I was the one in trouble?"

"I had a bad feeling."

"Sure you did," he said wearily. "You can never give me a straight answer, can you?"

"That is a straight answer. I work off my instincts, Dylan. But you have bigger problems to worry about than why I'm here."

"You can say that again." He let out a sigh. "I wish I knew what happened to Erica, why the police were called."

"They arrived a little over an hour ago," Catherine said.

"That long? What were you doing up so early?"

"I couldn't sleep."

He could tell by her short answer that she had bitten off the rest of what she wanted to say, which probably had something to do with her bad feeling.

"I tried calling your room," she added, "but you didn't answer."

"Because I was unconscious in the woods, which won't be easy to prove without a witness. That's why I need a blood test to confirm that I was drugged." He shifted his weight, feeling restless and pissed off. He didn't like being taken unawares, and someone was definitely setting him up for something. "What happened with Jake and Sarah? Did they get off okay? Did they wonder where I was?"

"Sarah asked if I'd seen you, and I mentioned that you'd been having drinks at the bar with a woman. Jake laughed and said you always got lucky at weddings. I guess he thought you were having a good time somewhere."

"Lucky . . . yeah, I feel real lucky right now. But I'm glad they left. I don't want Jake involved in my problems." The last thing Dylan would do was ruin Jake and Sarah's honeymoon. He was glad they were safely away from this mess. He straightened as the detective and a uniformed police officer walked back to them.

"Deputy Barnes will accompany you to the hospital," the detective said. "And we'll talk later, when we have the results of your tests. I hope you don't have any plans to leave the area."

"I was going to return to San Francisco today," Dylan replied.

"I'd appreciate it if you'd stay in town until we have a chance to speak again. We're going to search the woods, but we may need your help pinpointing your last location with Ms. Layton."

The detective's voice was friendly, but there was steel in his words. If Dylan didn't agree to remain in the area, he suspected the detective would find a way to keep him here.

"All right. I'll stick around until we can clear this up."

"Good. Now tell me again where you went last night after you left the bar."

"We took the path in front of the lodge, and when it ended we went into the woods. We wound in and out of the trees, and when I woke up this morning I was about ten feet away from the edge of a rocky cliff."

"Could you find it again?"

"I don't know," Dylan admitted, knowing his answer wasn't going to help his cause. "I could try, but when I woke up I was still dazed, and I made a couple of wrong turns on my way back here, so it wasn't like I took a straight shot back."

"All right. We'll see what we can find. And we'll talk when you return from the hospital." Detective Richardson turned his attention to Catherine. "May I ask your name, ma'am?"

Catherine gave him a startled look, appearing not at all pleased to be brought into the conversation. "Uh, it's Catherine Hilliard," she said, stumbling a bit.

"How are you acquainted with Mr. Sanders?"

"My friend married his brother yesterday."

"So you were at the wedding?"

"Yes."

"Did you speak to a Ms. Erica Layton?"

"I don't know the name," Catherine replied.

"Ms. Layton left the bar with Mr. Sanders," the detective said. "We're concerned about her welfare, and we need to find her as soon as possible."

"I saw Dylan speaking with a woman at the bar, but I didn't see them leave, and I wasn't introduced to her," Catherine said.

There was an edge to her voice, but Dylan admired her short, succinct answers. Most people rambled on when questioned by the police. But Catherine wasn't giving away any more than she was asked. Nor did she appear eager to help the authorities. In fact, she looked like she was ready to bolt.

Why was she so nervous? Did she have something to hide?

"Thanks for your help." The detective gave Dylan another speculative look. "I'll speak to you later, Mr. Sanders. Deputy Barnes is waiting out front. He'll give you a ride."

As the detective left, Dylan turned to Catherine and said on impulse, "Come with me to the hospital."

"What? Why?" she asked in surprise. "You don't need me for that."

"I could use a friend."

"We're not exactly friends," she reminded him. "In fact, a minute ago you were accusing me of being involved in the trouble you're in."

"I didn't mean it," he said quickly. He didn't know why he wanted to keep Catherine near, but he did. "You're the closest thing I have to an ally, and maybe you can help me figure out what's going on."

Her lips turned down in a frown, and her eyes were more than a little reluctant when she uttered the words, "I guess I could."

"Good, let's go," Dylan said, grabbing her hand before she could have a second thought.

But as they left the lodge, heading toward the squad car, Catherine's steps began to falter. She stopped walking completely and pulled her hand out of his.

He glanced back at her, alarmed to see how pale her face had become. "What's wrong?"

"I can't get in that car," she said, putting up a hand as if to ward him off.

"The deputy is just giving us a ride. It's not a big deal."

"No, I can't. I'll meet you there." She shook her head as she backed away from him. "I can't get into that car, Dylan. Don't try to make me."

"Are you having another vision?" he demanded. "Is the car going to crash? What? What do you see?"

"I see blood, lots and lots of blood, and a little girl standing in the middle of it."

He drew in a sharp breath. "Catherine, what are you talking about?"

His question went unanswered as she turned and ran back toward the lodge. She'd been spooked by something, but a little girl in blood? What the hell . . . ?

"What happened to your friend?" the deputy asked as he opened the back door of the car for Dylan.

"She'll meet us there."

"Looks like you're on your own then."

"Yeah," Dylan muttered as he slid into the backseat.

It wasn't the first time he'd been on his own, nor was it the first time he'd been in a police car. That momentous occasion had occurred when he was seventeen years old. Back then he'd had Jake to bail him out. Back then he'd been a stupid, reckless kid. Back then he'd always known exactly what crime he'd committed. This time he was in the dark.

He had no idea what Erica had wanted with him, and the only person besides her who might be able to shed any light on the matter had just run away.

Chapter 3

As Catherine jogged around the front corner of the lodge, she paused to catch her breath. She shouldn't have left Dylan, but she couldn't face getting into a police car again. She could still taste the panic bubbling up in her throat and feel the beads of sweat dotting her forehead. The past she'd thought was years behind her was rushing back like a freight train intent on running her down. Why? Why now?

She didn't want to go back in time. She couldn't. She'd barely survived the first ten years of her life, and the second decade hadn't been much better. But she was thirty years old now, and she was happy. She had a job, a house, animals, friends, neighbors, and, most important, roots. She didn't need to mess it up by getting involved with a man who was little more than a stranger to her. There was nothing to tie them together except their mutual relationship with Jake and Sarah.

But even as the thought went through her head, she

knew she was lying to herself. She was tied to Dylan in a much deeper, far more personal way. He might not believe in her visions, but she knew they were real and that they always came true. She was a part of whatever was happening to him. But she didn't have to participate, she reminded herself.

She could get into her car and drive home. In eight hours she'd be far, far away from whatever mess Dylan was in. She could choose to leave. And she would. She'd just go down to the hospital and say good-bye. Dylan surely had other family and friends who had come to the lake for the wedding who could assist him. This was not her problem.

As she walked down the path toward the line of cabins adjacent to the lodge, she saw yellow tape strapped across the front door of one cabin. The detective stood in the doorway. Another officer worked inside, probably collecting evidence from what appeared to be a crime scene. But what exactly had happened in there?

The detective had said they were checking on the welfare of Erica, so that meant she was missing. The window near the front door was broken, shattered glass on the ground. Had someone broken in during the night?

Catherine's pulse began to speed up. She could hear glass breaking in her head along with the sound of a scream. But was it a scream from a few hours ago, or one of the screams that haunted her from the past? It was difficult to tell the difference.

The detective turned and caught her staring. She started moving quickly, not wanting to get trapped into answering more questions, but it was too late. He was already coming toward her.

"I thought you were going to the hospital with Mr. Sanders," he said.

"I'm taking my own car," she replied in a steady, unconcerned voice, although inside she was shaking. She didn't like cops; she never had. And even though this man wasn't wearing a uniform, she knew he could make trouble for her. But she also knew that the surest way to arouse attention was to be uncooperative. She had to at least make it look as if she wanted to help. "Is this where the woman was staying?" she asked. "The one who disappeared?"

The detective ignored her question and asked one of his own. "Tell me something, Ms. Hilliard—does your friend have a temper?"

"Dylan?"

"Yes."

"I don't know him that well."

"But well enough to go down to the hospital and stand by his side?"

"He's my friend's brother-in-law. I know she would want me to help him if I could, especially since she's not here." Catherine paused. "What exactly do you think Dylan did?"

"I'm not sure. That's why I'm asking questions."

"Dylan is a good guy. He wouldn't hurt anyone."

"I thought you didn't know him that well."

Catherine realized how easily the detective had tripped her up. "I don't know him well, but my friend speaks highly of him. I trust her judgment. I should go."

"One second," Detective Richardson said. He held up a plastic baggie. Inside was a gold cuff link. "Do you recognize this?"

Catherine had seen such a cuff link before, when she'd helped one of the groomsmen put it on. Jake had given cuff links to all of his ushers, including his brother. Had Dylan been in the cabin with Erica? Had he hurt her? He was the only one who had a connection to Erica. And what did she really know about the man?

Maybe her vision had pointed the danger to the wrong person. Maybe she wasn't supposed to help Dylan; perhaps she was supposed to help Erica.

But that thought didn't ring true. She needed to stop thinking and go with her instincts.

"Ma'am?" the detective prodded.

"I don't recognize it," she said, realizing that with the lie she'd just taken a step she wouldn't be able to reverse.

"You're sure?"

"Yes."

"One last question—did you happen to hear anything during the night? You're staying in the main lodge, right?"

"What would I have heard?"

"That's what I'm asking."

She thought about the screams that had rung through her head, but she'd heard screams before, and they hadn't occurred in real time. "I didn't hear anything. I'm sorry."

"Well, thanks anyway."

"No problem." She walked quickly to the parking lot, feeling the detective's gaze follow her every step. He was suspicious of her—because of her connection to Dylan, possibly, or because he sensed that she'd lied. She would have to be more careful in the future.

As she got into her yellow VW Bug, she couldn't help wondering again what on earth had happened in that cabin. The detective obviously didn't want to say, but it must have been bad, and possibly loud enough for someone to hear.

She hoped she wasn't putting her faith in the wrong person. Dylan had to be innocent. She needed to find him, look into his eyes, hold his hand, see the truth in his soul—if he'd let her.

Although she hadn't spent that much time with him, one thing she knew for sure: Dylan was very private and guarded. He was a man who was used to asking questions, not answering them. She understood that. She had her own emotional walls, walls she had the terrible feeling Dylan could breach—if she let him, but she wasn't about to do that. No one had gotten into her heart in a very long time, and that was the way it was going to stay.

"When will I get the results?" Dylan asked as the lab technician finished taking his blood. He'd already deposited a urine sample, covering all the bases.

"Tomorrow for some of them, a few days or even longer for the rest. DNA can take weeks, depending on the lab's workload."

"DNA," he echoed, his heart skipping a beat.

"That's right," the tech said as she pulled out a cotton-tipped stick. "One last swab."

"Can't you do the test from the blood?"

"Yes, but this works just as well, and we don't have to take more blood."

Damn. Why hadn't he realized that the tests would include DNA? He could have just helped set himself up. He glanced down at his hand. The cut he'd acquired sometime during the night was about an inch long. Had Erica cut him and planted the blood in her cabin? It seemed too devious a plan for someone like her to concoct. She wasn't a rocket scientist. She barely had a high school education. Someone else had to be calling the shots.

After the tech took the swab, she said, "You're good to go."

Dylan stood up and grabbed his coat off a nearby chair before heading out the door. He was relieved to have that over with, but he had no idea what to do next, how to go about defending his innocence when it was becoming clear that someone was going to a lot of trouble to make him look guilty of something.

Catherine was waiting in the hallway. She jumped to her feet, giving him a wary smile. "How's it going?"

"I'm done. It will take some time to get the results. They should prove I was incapacitated last night, too out of it to do whatever they think I did."

She nodded. "I hope that's the way it works out."

He frowned at the doubt in her voice. "You don't sound too confident."

"I'm sorry. I didn't get a lot of sleep last night, and I'm confused by everything that's happened."

"Me, too. Speaking of confused, what the hell happened to you back at the squad car? What were you talking about? Little girl, lots of blood," he reminded her. He'd thought about her comment all the way to the hospital and wondered if it had anything to do with him or with Erica.

"That wasn't about you," she said quickly. "I'm sorry if you thought it was."

"So who was the little girl?"

"It doesn't matter."

"It was you, right?"

"Yes. It was a long time ago, but some memories don't go away."

"What happened?"

"I don't want to talk about it," she said with a dismissive shake of her head.

"But—"

"No buts," she interrupted. "You like to do that— turn the attention away from your own life—but you can't this time."

"Hey, according to you our lives are now intertwined. Which brings me back to the vision you had a few weeks ago. What else did you see?"

"I've already told you what I saw."

"Have you?" he challenged. "I remember that night you read my tea leaves. You were gung ho to tell me my fortune and then you suddenly wanted to stop. Why?"

"It was the colors that surrounded us—dark red like blood, black like death."

Her dramatic words put his nerves back on edge. "So, you saw blood and death in my future, and you didn't think it might be a good idea to stick around when Erica approached me last night?" he asked.

A flash of anger lit Catherine's eyes. "What do you want from me, Dylan? Do you want me to say I made the premonition up? I can do that. I can tell a lie. You're not the first person in my life to make fun of my visions. I gave up trying to convince people a long time ago. I don't really give a damn what you think. And actually I just came down here to say good-bye. I've decided to go home and get on with my life."

She bristled with indignation, her entire body tense, her eyes fiery, her cheeks flushed with red. She was beautiful, and she was pissed. He knew she was two seconds away from walking out the door, and he couldn't let her go.

"I'm sorry," he said, then destroyed his own apology by adding, "But you're not going anywhere. You started this, and you're not walking out in the middle."

"I didn't start anything. Whether I saw you and Erica in a vision has nothing to do with the fact that she approached you last night and allegedly drugged you. She did that on her own."

"There's no 'allegedly' about it," he said sharply. "It happened, and you need to help me figure out why."

"I don't need to do anything."

"Okay, that wasn't the right word."

"Or the right tone," she told him.

He let out a sigh and tipped his head. "I apologize

again. I know you don't have to help me, but I really wish you would."

Indecision danced through her eyes. "I'll consider it. Is Erica your girlfriend?"

"Hell, no, she's not my girlfriend."

"But you had a relationship."

"We'll talk about this later," he said, cutting her off as Deputy Barnes returned. "Are we done?" he asked the officer.

"Looks like it. I can give you a ride to the lodge now," the deputy said.

"Thanks anyway, but my friend will drive me back," Dylan said.

The deputy hesitated and then gave a brisk nod. "All right. Detective Richardson will get in touch with you later today."

"I'm sure he will." Dylan blew out a breath as the deputy left. He needed a little time to think, and he finally had it.

"I'll take you to the lodge; then you're on your own," Catherine said.

"Not so fast," he said as she started down the hall.

She paused, tapping her foot impatiently. "What now?"

"I'm hungry."

"You're hungry?" she echoed, as if she hadn't been expecting such a prosaic response.

"Yes, and I think better after I've eaten. Let's check out the cafeteria."

She hesitated, a frown crossing her lips. "There's a restaurant at the lodge."

"And it will be crawling with cops. I need to catch my breath, get my wits about me. Come on; I'll treat you."

"Fine, but after that I'm done."

"Right." Dylan shrugged back into his coat. As he did so he realized Catherine was staring at his arm. "What's wrong now?"

"You're missing a cuff link," she said, her voice tense.

He glanced down at his sleeve. "It must have come off."

"It did," she agreed, meeting his gaze. "In Erica's cabin."

"How do you know that?" His gut twisted at the certainty in her eyes.

"I walked by her cabin on the way to my car. I assume it was her cabin, because there was yellow tape on the door and the police were going through it. Detective Richardson saw me and asked me if I recognized the cuff link." She paused. "I said I didn't."

"You lied?" he asked, surprised by the admission. "Why?"

"I don't know," she said with a confused shake of her head. "I shouldn't have. Don't you have some friends or family you can call? Surely there were people at the wedding yesterday who would like to help you out."

"The people at the reception were mostly Jake's friends, his coworkers. The few family members who were there left last night."

"Maybe you should call Jake, then."

"On his honeymoon? I don't think so. I've screwed

up a lot of moments in my big brother's life. This isn't going to be another one."

"What about your father?" she asked as they headed down the corridor toward the elevator. "I know you told me your mom left years ago, but couldn't you ask your father for help?"

"My father wouldn't throw water on me if I were on fire," he said. "So it looks like it's just you and me."

She frowned. "For breakfast. Then you're on your own."

Catherine ordered a sizable meal, all healthy items, of course. Her veggie omelet was made of egg whites, accompanied by a bowl of fruit and a cup of green tea, while his pancakes were covered with syrup, and his side of scrambled eggs and bacon was guaranteed to clog his arteries. He topped off his meal with a mug of strong, caffeinated coffee.

As Dylan ate, the food began to take away the queasy feeling in his stomach that was probably the result of whatever drug Erica had given him. He still couldn't quite believe she'd done it. He'd always considered himself a fairly good judge of character, and while he wouldn't have said Erica was a Girl Scout, he hadn't anticipated such a mean streak. Maybe he should have. She'd always looked out for herself. That was the one thing he knew for sure about her.

"Tell me about your relationship with Erica," Catherine said, interrupting his thoughts.

"We didn't have a relationship. We had sex—one night about six weeks ago. That's it."

"How did you meet?"

"I was working on a news story, the murder of a San Francisco socialite, Deborah Ravino, who was also the wife of state senator Joseph Ravino. A man was on trial for the murder, but some things about the case didn't make sense to me. I did some digging and Erica's name came up. Turned out she'd not only had an affair with Joseph Ravino; she could also provide a motive for his wanting to kill his wife. With Erica's help and my story, murder charges were filed against the senator. He's currently in prison awaiting trial. It's been on all the news programs. You must have heard about the case."

"I don't watch the news."

"Excuse me?" he asked in amazement, certain he hadn't heard her correctly. "The news is important. How else do you know what's happening in the world?"

"What does it matter if I know? I can't change anything."

"Of course you can effect change. I helped put the right man in jail by paying attention."

"Well, I'm very glad there are people like you in the world, but it's not my thing."

Her cavalier attitude shocked him. "It should be your thing. It should be everyone's thing."

Her eyes widened at his tone. "I didn't realize your job was so important to you."

"It's not just a job. It's about shining a light on things that need to be seen, not letting the bad guys get away with anything." As he heard the words come out of his mouth, he wanted to take them back. They revealed far too much about him. He picked up his coffee cup and took a sip. The liquid had cooled, but he didn't care. He needed to put some distance between himself and his last comment.

"I never thought about it that way. I should have, because God knows too many people get away with stuff." She let out a sigh. "To be honest, I don't watch the news because it can be so dark. I have . . ." Her voice drifted off as she gazed down at the table. When she looked up at him, he saw shadows in her eyes. "I have so much darkness inside me. I can't take any more in. I'm full."

"Where does it come from?"

"It doesn't matter. It's just there."

Dylan wanted to press for a better answer. He wanted to forget all about his own problems and dive into hers. But he would be using her to avoid what he had to face—his own life. It was a hell of a lot more interesting to dig into other people's problems than his own.

"So back to Erica. You were working on the story together and you ended up in bed. Is that right?" Catherine asked.

"After quite a few celebratory tequila shots."

"That can do it."

"It wasn't a good idea, obviously. But it happened. I didn't think it was that big a deal."

Catherine picked up her cup and sipped her tea, her blue eyes turning speculative. "Maybe it was a bigger deal to Erica."

"Hey, she knew the score. She wasn't some innocent

girl. She'd been having an affair with Ravino, and I'm sure there were many more men in her life."

"Even so, she might have had feelings for you."

"Yeah, that's why she came to Tahoe and drugged me."

Catherine set down her cup and leaned forward in her chair, resting her arms on the table. "What exactly did she say to you? You must have had some idea what she wanted."

"All she said was that she had to talk to me. Frankly I was adding the weeks up in my head and thinking she was about to drop a pregnancy bombshell on me. So when she insisted on going somewhere private, I agreed. That's why I went with her into the woods. I didn't want her to cause a scene at the wedding reception."

"Was she pregnant?"

"She never said she was, but we didn't have a long conversation. She just kept walking, and I was feeling so sick I could barely stumble along, much less get any words out. She said something about it being my turn to pay up. The next thing I knew, I woke up on my back in the forest, and almost twelve hours had passed." He paused, thinking about his missing cuff link. "What else did you see when you went by Erica's cabin?"

"Glass on the ground. The front window was shattered. It appeared as if someone had broken in."

"Or it was made to look that way. And my cuff link was found inside to set me up for something."

"Her disappearance," Catherine finished.

"Exactly, which means I have to find her fast." He

drank the rest of his coffee, adding to the adrenaline rush going through his body. He needed to take action, regain control.

"How are you going to find her?" Catherine asked. "Do you think she went home? She lives in San Francisco, right?"

"Right, but it's doubtful she'd go home, not if she's supposed to be missing."

"What about her family? Where do they live?"

He thought for a moment. "Bakersfield. I know she told me that she hadn't been home in years and was estranged from her parents, so I don't think she'd go there."

"Have you been able to remember anything else that she said to you when you went into the woods last night?"

He'd been racking his brain on that subject ever since he'd woken up. "Erica said she had no choice. She was caught, and it was her only way out. Someone else is involved in whatever is going on. I need to go back to the lodge. I've got files on my laptop from the Ravino case. Maybe a name will jump out at me. That is, if my laptop is still in my room. I don't seem to have my key." He paused, not liking the way Catherine looked at him. Her gaze was so intense. It made him more than a little uncomfortable. "What?" he demanded. "Why are you staring at me like that?"

Instead of answering, she reached across the table and covered his hand with hers. He felt a jolt of electricity. Was it a psychic connection or something more basic, something more sexual? His body was certainly revving up in anticipation. He told himself to get a grip. He was in the middle of a mess that could be traced back to his last one-night stand. He certainly didn't need another.

"Catherine."

"Sh-sh." She closed her eyes.

He thought he would feel relief away from her mesmerizing gaze, but her touch sent waves of heat through his body. His heartbeat quickened and his fingers unconsciously tightened around hers. He had the insane feeling that he could never let her go, that she was going to be very, very important to him. That feeling scared the shit out of him. He was a loner. He liked it that way. He enjoyed women, but he'd never wanted one of them to stay longer than a night or a weekend. And he wasn't going to change now, not for her, not ever.

Still, when Catherine opened her eyes he caught his breath in anticipation of what she would say.

"We're connected," she murmured.

"That's because you're holding my hand." He tried to make a joke out of her statement, to lighten the tension.

"It's more than that." She frowned as if she weren't happy about it either. "It's deeper, much deeper. I just don't know why."

"That's cryptic. Sounds like fortune-teller mumbo jumbo."

She met his gaze head-on. "I know you'd like it to be. Where's your tie, Dylan?"

He started at the abrupt change in subject, then felt

around his neck, realizing his tie was gone. "I must have lost it, or Erica took it off. Maybe it's in her cabin with my cuff link."

Catherine shook her head, her eyes filling with shadows. "It's not in her cabin. It's in water, entwined with something else, something red."

He swallowed hard. "A scarf?"

"Yes. Like the one Erica wore around her neck."

His heart stopped as he gazed into her eyes. "Please don't tell me you saw Erica in the lake."

Chapter 4

"No," Catherine said quickly, not because the question was far-fetched, but because she didn't want to consider the possibility that Erica was dead. Fortunately the brief image in her head had shown only the clothes in the water.

A glitter of relief flashed through Dylan's eyes. "Of course Erica isn't in the lake. She's fine," he muttered. "She's the one who started this game. If her scarf is in the water with my tie, it's because she put them there. And Erica probably broke the window in her cabin to make it look like there was an intruder." He pulled his hand away and reached for his wallet to leave a tip.

Catherine felt a chill as he broke the connection between them, and the sense of disappointment disturbed and surprised her. She was used to being completely on her own. And it was better that way. Emotions in her life only added to her inner turmoil. Any caring, any intimacy with another human being, made the nightmares worse. She'd lost a boyfriend once because of her unnerving dreams—dreams that had stopped shortly after he left. She didn't know if the timing was coincidental, but she suspected not. When she became involved with someone her love made her vulnerable, which was why she needed to keep some distance between herself and Dylan. Because there wasn't just an emotional connection between them; there was also a physical attraction. She might have been living like a nun the past couple of years, but she could still remember what desire felt like, and with Dylan she knew that desire could be dangerous, reckless.

Dylan threw a few dollar bills down on the table. "Are you ready to go? What's wrong now?" His brows knit together in a frown as his gaze raked her face. "Your cheeks are bright red."

"Nothing is wrong." She got to her feet, acutely aware of his gaze.

"I don't get you, Catherine."

"You're not the first one. But you don't have to get me."

"I think I do. You seem to be mixed up in my life. And I like to know the people I'm dealing with. You're a mystery."

"I'm not the mystery you need to figure out."

"I'm not so sure. And right now I don't know who to trust."

"You should hang on to that skepticism."

"Why do you say that?"

"Because I think that whoever is a danger to you is

someone who matters to you," she replied. "It feels very personal."

"If you're suggesting that one of my friends is behind this setup, then—"

"I'm not suggesting anything. I'm just telling you what I feel."

"I'm better with facts than feelings." Dylan turned toward the exit.

"Most men are," she said.

He gave her a look that said he didn't appreciate the generalization. "Let's go back to the lodge. I want to call a friend of mine who's a lawyer. I think I'm going to need one."

Catherine followed Dylan out of the hospital and into the parking lot. It was after nine a.m., and the sun was rising higher in the sky, but there was still a cool morning breeze. She loved the mountains, the crisp, clean air, the tall, towering trees, and the majestic peaks that surrounded them. Even now, in late May, there was still snow on some of the highest points, a reminder that winter was not that long ago. Although for her the darkness of winter was almost a state of mind rather than a time of year. She longed for the carefree days of summer, but she could never seem to escape the dark places in her soul no matter how warm the weather got.

"Do you mind if I drive?" Dylan asked as they headed toward her VW Bug. "I'm not a good passenger."

"There's a big surprise," she said dryly as she tossed

him the keys and walked around to the passenger side. Lucky for Dylan she didn't have control issues; in fact, she'd given up trying to control her life a long time ago. Now she just went along for the ride, no matter how wild it might be—and with Dylan she suspected it was going to get off-the-charts wild.

She fastened her seat belt as Dylan pulled out of the parking lot. Like he did everything else, he drove with impatient, quick, confident movements. Yet, despite his bravado, she knew that his confidence had taken a hit with Erica's unexpected behavior. He was no doubt furious with himself for allowing her to set him up. Now he was trying to regain control of the situation by acting instead of reacting. It was a good tactic. The best defense was a good offense. But Dylan was going to need some ammunition, and what did he have except his word?

"Once the blood tests come back I'll be able to prove I was unconscious while whatever was happening happened," Dylan said, his thoughts following a path parallel to her own.

"That would be helpful," she agreed. "But it will also raise more questions as to why Erica would feel the need to drug you. The detectives are going to dig into your relationship with her. They'll want to know every last detail." She paused. "I must admit I'm curious, too. I know Erica was involved with the man you were researching, but what's her story?" They were just a few miles from the lodge, and Catherine wanted as much information as possible before they were faced with more questions from the police.

"I don't know much about Erica's past. She's a part-time model and used to be a part-time hostess at a private men's club that Senator Ravino frequented. She's a party girl, hits the clubs at night, runs with a fast crowd of rich people. She likes money. She likes men with money. Except when she's had a dozen or so tequila shots; then she'll settle for just about anyone," he added with a self-deprecating shrug.

"I don't think you're just anyone."

"Was that a compliment?"

"You have a mirror. You know what you look like."

"True, but I was talking more about money, not appearances. I make a good living, but I don't have the kind of cash to impress a woman like Erica. She has very expensive tastes, and she knows how to get what she wants, which isn't difficult when it comes to men. She is hot."

"I noticed," Catherine said.

"That's basically what I know about her. When we spoke, it was generally about the case I was working on and her relationship with Joseph Ravino. That was all I was interested in."

"Until you had a dozen tequila shots," she said dryly.

"Right."

"When Erica first sat down at the bar with you, I thought I heard her say that she'd been trying to track you down."

"I did have a few messages from her," he admitted, "but I didn't call her back."

"Why not?"

"Because I was busy."

"Do you ever call women back?"

"On occasion, but this was just sex," Dylan said with a frown. "Look, Erica didn't drug me because she was pissed I didn't call her. There has to be more to it than that. It has to be tied to Ravino. That's all I can think."

"But why would Erica drug you and leave you in the woods? Where does that get her?"

"I suspect that's not all she did, since my cuff link ended up in her cabin. She must have made it look like I assaulted her or something."

"Or something," Catherine echoed.

"You think she's setting me up for murder?"

"Don't you? I can't get rid of the image of your tie and her scarf in the water. If she wanted to set you up and make it look like she was dead, it seems logical that we would find something of hers in the water and something of yours in her cabin, tying you together."

"I'm fairly sure there's blood in that cabin, too, my blood." He held out his hand. "I got this sometime in the night. And the fact that I willingly volunteered for a toxicology screen also allowed the police to request DNA testing, something I should have anticipated."

She stared at the recent cut on his skin. "This is bad, Dylan."

"Tell me about it."

She sat back in her seat, suddenly overwhelmed by the evidence piling up against Dylan. How on earth could he get out of it?

"I need your help, Catherine," he said, uttering the very words she didn't want to hear.

"This situation does not involve me."

"Yes, it does. You said we're connected, remember?"

"We are connected, but I can't help you because you don't believe in my visions, and that's all I have to offer. I'm sure your lawyer friend can give you far more practical assistance than I can. So why should I stick around?"

"Because you should," he said, giving her a quick look. "And if you do, you'll prove to me that you're not involved with Erica's disappearance, that you're not part of the plan."

"I don't have to prove anything to you," she said, annoyed at his ridiculous statement. "I never met Erica before yesterday."

"You predicted her arrival in my life. So either you're lying about knowing her or you used her to fulfill your prediction."

"Or I had a psychic premonition about her, which is what happened," Catherine said firmly. "You can believe me or not, but that doesn't make it untrue."

"If I agree that you had a vision, will you stay for a while and help me sort this out?"

She knew he was giving her premonition lip service to get what he wanted, but she also knew that she wouldn't leave yet. If her nightmares were ever going to stop, maybe she had to take action, get involved, at least until she knew more. "I won't promise to stay forever, but for the time being I'm here," she said slowly.

He gave her a dry smile. "That's usually my line."

"I'll bet it is. You're not big on commitment, are you?"

Dylan turned the car into the parking lot next to the lodge. "Right now I'm very committed to proving my innocence in whatever crime I'm about to be accused of."

The yellow tape had been removed from the front of cabin seven, and a large piece of plywood now covered the broken window. There were no cops in sight, and as they paused in front of the cabin a group of guests on their way out of the lodge were laughing and chatting, seemingly unaware that anything bad had occurred on the property.

"Maybe we imagined it," Catherine muttered. "Everything looks so normal now."

"I'd like to believe that was true," he replied, but the plywood reinforced the fact that something had happened where Erica had been staying. "It's a good sign that the police are gone. Perhaps Erica has resurfaced."

"That would be great," Catherine said.

"Yes, it would, but you don't believe it any more than I do. I was going for the power of positive thinking."

"That sounds more like a feeling," she said with a pointed smile. "I thought you were all about 'the facts and nothing but the facts, ma'am.' "

"I'm a little off my game."

"That's not true. You got right back on your game the minute you woke up in the woods. You had the presence of mind to request drug testing while the drugs might still be present in your system. I doubt I would have done that."

"Even so, I'm still playing catch-up. I'm at least one or two steps behind Erica." He walked up the front steps of the cabin and looked through the window that had not been broken, careful not to touch anything. The last thing he needed was to leave his fingerprints.

There were no lights on inside, and he couldn't make out much, but he could see that the covers on the bed were a mess, a night table and chair were turned on their sides, and there was a lot of stuff strewn about the floor.

Catherine came up next to him. "What do you see?"

"It looks like the room was trashed." He took her hand and pulled her closer to him. "What do you think?"

"I'm not sure. It's awfully dark."

"I thought you could see through the darkness."

She frowned at that. "I'm not Superman. I don't have X-ray vision."

"Sorry, I'm not exactly clear on your powers."

She shook her head in disgust. "I knew you were going to be like this—all skeptical and judgmental. I must have been crazy to consider helping you."

"Wait, I'm sorry. I'm sorry." He gripped her hand tighter as she tried to move away from him. "That was a bad joke. I would appreciate any thoughts you might have. Really. I would."

She let out a sigh and then turned her attention to the cabin. He watched her profile for a long moment, noting the slow flush that spread across her cheeks. He heard the hitch in her breath as her pulse quickened.

Then her fingers squeezed around his, the warmth of her hand sending a rush of heat through his body. He'd initiated the contact, but now he felt a sudden, desperate need to break the current flowing between them. This time Catherine was the one who wasn't letting go.

"Erica was here. She was scared," Catherine said abruptly. "I can feel her . . . fear. She's surprised. As if she's been taken unawares." Catherine turned her gaze on him, shadows filling her eyes. "She's in trouble."

Logically he knew that Catherine hadn't told him one thing she couldn't have surmised by the facts that Erica was gone, the cabin had been ransacked, and the police were looking for her. So why did he feel as if she were seeing something he wasn't? She was just repeating what they already knew. And maybe her pulse had quickened and her cheeks had reddened because she was faking it.

"You have more than Erica to worry about," Catherine added. "Someone else is involved."

"Yeah, that makes sense. I doubt Erica could have come up with this plan on her own. She's not that clever." He paused as Catherine studied the room once more. Her body stiffened, and she gave a little shake of her head, as if she were trying to dislodge something from her mind. He could feel the tension emanating from her.

"I . . . I need to get away from here," she said abruptly, letting go of his hand. She turned quickly and jogged down the steps. She was halfway to the lodge before he caught up with her.

"Wait, Catherine." He grabbed her arm. "What the hell is going on? Is there something you didn't tell me?" He studied her face, seeing the glittering light of fear in her eyes. Was this part of her act? His logical brain did not want to buy into the fact that she had any sort of extrasensory perception, but he had to admit that she looked as though she were feeling something pretty powerful.

She cast a brief look over her shoulder, back at the cabin. "I felt like someone was watching."

"Watching us?" he echoed, searching the area for someone hiding behind a tree or around the side of the building. But they appeared to be completely alone.

"No—Erica," she said.

"What do you mean?"

"It was last night. I could see the moonlight coming in through the open window. Someone was waiting, watching her through that window. I think. I don't know." She shrugged. "I don't want to do this."

"Hey, you can't start and stop. Tell me the rest."

"I don't know the rest. I feel too involved, as if my reality and my dreams are blurring. I'm outside of it, and yet I'm inside of it, too." She took a breath. Disappointment filled her eyes as she stared at him. "You don't believe me."

"It's not a question of belief. I don't know what you're talking about. Inside, outside, what the hell does that mean?"

"It means that for a moment I felt as if I were Erica, and I could see the shadow of a man watching me. I felt her fear, her surprise, her desire to flee. But then a second later I felt as if I were outside, hiding behind that tree across from the cabin, and I was waiting for my chance to get her." Catherine's voice broke off, and she pulled away from him. "I just want to go home. I can't help you. I'm sorry. It's too hard."

"You're not afraid of something being hard," he told her.

"You don't know anything about me."

"I know that two months ago, when Jake and Sarah were in danger, you were brave enough to knock down a man with a baseball bat. You showed more than a little courage in a difficult situation. I was very impressed." To this day he wondered if they would all still be alive if Catherine hadn't been willing to put her life on the line the way she had.

"That was different. I knew what was real and what wasn't—who were the good guys and who were the bad guys. I acted on instinct. But I can't help you if you don't believe me, and I can see in your eyes that you don't. You think I'm conning you or something."

"I'm a logical person. I believe in what I can see."

"Sometimes you have to have faith."

"I lost my faith a long time ago."

"You don't believe in anyone or anything?"

"I trust my brother, Jake, because he's never let me down. He's the only one. And I've certainly never had any experience with the supernatural, so forgive me if it all sounds a little bizarre."

"I understand. You're not the first person to judge me. And I doubt you'll be the last. To be honest, I don't always understand the visions either. So I should just go home and leave you to get on with things. You can do this on your own."

"You're not the kind of woman to run away, Catherine." He didn't know why he felt such a need to keep her with him, but all of his instincts were screaming at him to hang on to her.

"I've been running away my whole life. You have no idea how good I am at it." She met his gaze head-on, and he saw nothing but truth in her eyes.

"Then it's time to stop running." He shifted his feet, searching for the right words. "Dammit, Catherine, you're the one who started this with your prediction about Erica coming into my life. Two women, you said: One is danger; one is salvation. If Erica is danger, then you have to be salvation. You're the only one here who fits the bill."

"You're used to getting your way, aren't you? Don't bother to answer. That was a rhetorical question. I'll say one thing: You're persuasive, and very good at arguing all sides of a discussion."

"So, have I convinced you to stay?"

"For the moment. Then we'll see." She gave him a small smile. "What you don't realize is that by asking me to stick around, you're putting yourself directly in my line of vision, so if you have any secrets don't expect to keep them."

Her words made him uneasy, but he told himself to get over it, because if he didn't believe in her visions then he had nothing to fear. She might be a little more perceptive than most people, but he'd learned a long time ago how to hide what he was thinking or feeling. He could keep her out of his head, and he *would* keep her out, because there was a part of him he couldn't let anyone see.

"So what's next?" Catherine asked.

He was relieved by the question. They were getting back to business, what he did best. "I need to check out my room in the lodge, see if Erica left me any surprises there."

Upon entering the building, Dylan felt like a marked man. The man and woman working the reception desk both gave him long, wary stares. And when he requested another room key, the woman looked very much as if she wanted to say no, but in the end she just handed him a key and asked him to be sure to check out by eleven o'clock.

"I'd like to stay another night," he said.

"I'm sorry, but your room is booked for today," the woman replied. "You'll have to collect your belongings and check out."

Dylan could see the firm resolve in her eyes. Management obviously wanted him out of there as soon as possible. He couldn't blame them. Having a possible murderer or assault suspect staying in the hotel was bad for business.

"I'll go up and pack." He paused. "Has there been any new information on the missing woman? Did the sheriff search the woods?"

The woman hesitated, then shook her head. "I know some people have been looking, but I don't think they found anything."

"That's too bad," he muttered. "Thanks."

"No problem. I hope everything was satisfactory for your stay."

"It was just dandy," Dylan drawled as he walked away. "Apparently I'm presumed guilty until I'm proven innocent," he said to Catherine as they headed across the lobby and got in the elevator. "Management definitely doesn't want me hanging around."

"But the sheriff does. Where will you stay?" She groaned at his pointed smile. "Not with me."

"Hopefully it won't be for long. Once things are cleared up I'll return to San Francisco, and you'll get back to your life."

"What if things aren't settled before tonight?"

"How do you feel about having a roommate?"

"Not thrilled. My room has only one bed, so you'll be sleeping on the floor," she warned.

"If you insist." He grinned as her cheeks flushed. She certainly wore her emotions on her face. He wondered what had gotten her so worked up now. He knew he should leave it alone, but he couldn't help himself. He liked seeing her rattled. He didn't appreciate being the only one off balance. "Is it me you don't trust, Catherine? Or yourself?"

"What? You think I can't resist you?" she asked.

"It's a question."

"A stupid question," she snapped. "Maybe if you weren't always thinking about sex, you wouldn't be in this mess. Did you ever consider that? If you hadn't slept with Erica and avoided her calls, she might not have been inclined to help anyone set you up for murder."

"I told you before, she didn't do this because I didn't call her back. She wasn't in love with me. We weren't having a relationship. We were both on the same page."

"Or so you thought. Never underestimate the fury of a woman scorned. When you tell a woman you're going to call her, you should call her."

"Just for the record, I didn't tell her I would call her." He followed her off the elevator. "I don't make promises I can't keep." He paused. "It sounds like you're speaking from personal experience. Have you missed a few calls over the years?"

"Men can be pigs sometimes."

He smiled at her bluntness. He liked the way Catherine didn't mince words. "Don't tell me you've waited for the phone to ring?" He suspected she had too much pride for that.

"When I was young and stupid," she admitted. "But not anymore."

"You don't have a high opinion of men, do you?"

"Not the ones who have been in my life. I've never met one yet who would stick around when things got tough."

"Maybe you haven't met the right man."

"Are you suggesting that would be you?"

"No," he said quickly, although he had to admit he'd always liked a challenge, and he'd love to prove Catherine wrong. If he wanted to stick, he could. At least, he thought he could. Oh, who the hell was he kidding? He didn't know if he had it in him to stay with anyone. Because it wasn't just the staying part that bothered him; it was all the rest of it—the emotional investment, the intimacy, the sharing of thoughts and feelings, the constant pressure, the incessant need to make someone happy. *Shit!* Who wanted that?

Shaking the distracting thoughts from his mind, he slipped his key card into the lock and opened the door. His room was not at all as he'd left it, which had been neat and in order. He'd arrived at the hotel the day before only an hour before the wedding ceremony and had used the room simply to change his clothes.

So who had messed up his bed, tossing around the covers, the blankets, and the pillows? Who had moved his computer out of its case and onto the desk? Who had unzipped his overnight bag and strewn his clothes on the floor? Someone had been in his room. Why? To search for something or to plant evidence?

"So, are you normally a slob?" Catherine asked.

"I didn't leave the room like this. Someone was in here."

"It appears that way," she agreed. "What were they looking for? Or do you think it was the police who came in here?"

"Doubtful. It would take some time to get a search warrant, and the hotel clerk certainly didn't mention it." Although he did wonder if the hotel had the authority to let the sheriff in without a warrant. That might be possible, since they were the legal owners of the property. "At any rate, the only thing someone might want would be my computer, and it's still here. I'll have to go through my files, see if anything was opened."

"Maybe we should call hotel security and make a report."

Dylan considered her suggestion but quickly dismissed it. The last thing he needed at the moment was to deal with more questions. He wanted to get a handle on what was happening first.

"Nothing was taken, so it would be difficult prove a crime was committed and would probably just focus more attention on me," he replied.

He repacked his overnight bag, slipped his computer back into its leather travel case, and surveyed the room one last time. Just to be extra careful, he opened all the drawers and the closet and even glanced under the bed, hoping not to find anything of Erica's in the room. Once he checked out, the room would certainly be searched. Of course, what he couldn't see were possible fingerprints. "If Erica came in here and touched things, her prints could be all over and would certainly hurt my alibi."

"Just because she was here wouldn't prove you were. And the fact that you got a new key from the manager supports the idea that your key was taken."

"I agree, but I can see how the sheriff might be able to build a circumstantial case against me. Everything that happened last night was plotted out beforehand. Someone took a lot of time and forethought to set me up."

"Maybe we should wipe down the tables and the doorknobs and other surfaces," Catherine said, striding into the bathroom. She grabbed two towels off the rack and tossed one to him as she reentered the room. "At least we can make sure they don't find her prints here."

Dylan nodded. "Good thinking. Have you done this sort of thing before?"

"Maybe," she said, giving him a cryptic smile. "But that's not important now, is it?"

"You're a very interesting woman. I like a good mystery, you know."

"Then you must be loving your life right now."

"I like a good mystery when it doesn't involve me," he amended. "I'd rather be the detective than the victim or the villain."

They worked quickly, wiping off all the furniture and doorknobs; then Dylan tossed the towels in the tub and doused them with water—for what reason he didn't know, except that it seemed like a good finishing touch. When he returned to the room he picked up the phone by the bed and punched the number for the front desk. "I'm checking out of room three oh four," he said when the clerk answered. "I'll leave the key in the room." He gave one last look around as he hung up the phone, remembering the one item he had not located. "Erica must have taken my car keys, unless I lost them in the woods. But I did see my car in the lot when we pulled in, so she didn't take it."

"How will you get home?"

"I'll figure that out later. I guess I'm good to go."

"My room is just down the hall," Catherine said as she opened the door.

Catherine's room was set up the same as his, but her bed was made and everything was in order. Obviously the maid had been in. As Dylan set his bags down on the bed, his gaze caught on the painting displayed on the easel. It was an abstract slash of dark colors that collided with one another in an angry, sinister manner. He'd seen other such paintings at Catherine's beach house and had been struck before by their intensity and passion.

Catherine immediately moved in front of the picture. "Don't look," she said, holding up a hand. "I meant to put it away, but it was still wet when I went downstairs."

"You know that makes it impossible for me *not* to look," he told her. "Besides, I saw the gruesome pictures at your house. I know you have a dark side."

He walked around her to stare at the painting. "When did you do this?"

"Last night. When I wake up from a nightmare I have to paint," she said with a sigh. "It's ugly, isn't it?"

"Definitely not my taste. What did you dream about?"

She shook her head. "I don't remember. I never remember. Sometimes just for a second I hear screams in my head, and then that's it. I wake up feeling a terrifying panic."

"Are the screams female?"

A flicker of doubt sparked in her eyes. "I think so. I never thought about it. But, yes, I believe they're female screams."

"Are you sure last night's screams weren't real? If

something happened to Erica you might have heard her cry out. Her cabin isn't that far away."

"I'm certain it wasn't Erica I heard. The screams were in my head, along with . . ." She stopped talking. "Along with a lot of other crap, nothing that concerns you."

"I'm not so sure about that." He looked back at the picture. Tilting his head, he considered the lines that seemed to stand out, depending on the angle and the light. "It's a face, isn't it?"

"I don't want to talk about it or analyze it," she said quickly.

"Tough, I do. Answer the question."

Catherine frowned, obviously annoyed by the order, but after a moment she said, "I think it's a face, but I'm surprised you can see it."

"Who is it?"

"I don't know."

"I think you do." He gave the portrait several more minutes of consideration, feeling something tickling the back of his brain, some tiny detail that he recognized but couldn't quite figure out. And then it hit him— what appeared to be a tiny gold cross in the center of the chaos of colors. "Erica wore a cross on a necklace," he said, pointing to the tiny gold lines. "I remember thinking that it was an odd choice for a woman who didn't seem to be the religious type." He gazed at Catherine and saw the answer in her eyes. "This is Erica, isn't it?"

"It could be, I guess."

His pulse began to race. "You're not guessing at all. You know it's her."

"I think it is," she admitted. "But usually I don't recognize the faces that I paint. They're strangers. They're not people I think I've ever seen, or if I saw them I didn't notice them. But they all feel like they're calling out to me. As if they're afraid and I'm the only one who can save them. But how can I save them when I don't know who they are?"

He heard the despair in her voice, and even though he didn't completely understand what she was saying, he could see that she was very disturbed by the fact that she couldn't seem to make her visions or her dreams work to help anyone. "This might be your breakthrough. If it's Erica, then you can help her."

"I don't know."

"Don't doubt yourself."

"I can't help it. I've been living with these nightmares for a long time. I don't want to be this way, you know. All my life I just wanted to be normal. But that's not going to happen. So most of the time I try not to look too closely at anything."

"And does that work for you?"

She made a face at him. "Obviously not. Well, let me rephrase that. It works in the daylight, but at night, when my subconscious takes over, I have no control. I'm just along for the ride."

"That must make for some exciting nights."

"That I don't remember in the morning. All I'm left with is another gruesome picture."

"No one is completely normal, Catherine. Everyone

is a little crazy. Trust me; I know. I've covered a lot of crazies in my life. On the scale of nutty, you're not so bad."

"You're just trying to make me feel better."

"I'm trying to make you see that just because you paint your nightmares doesn't mean that you're out of your mind."

"The only difference is that I think my nightmares might be real . . . actually happening in the world. It's difficult to explain, but sometimes I feel like I'm inside the head of someone who is really . . . evil. It scares the hell out of me. For a long time I was afraid that I was sleepwalking, that I was leaving the house and killing people in my dreams. When I was younger I even set up barricades so I could make sure in the morning that I hadn't left."

"And you hadn't," he said, sure that she didn't have a mean bone in her body.

"No, but I still felt like a witness to something I couldn't remember. I used to read the newspapers in the morning after my dreams, wondering if I'd see news of some murder that would trigger a memory in my mind, but there was never anything that seemed familiar."

He wanted to tell her that that was because her dreams weren't real. But she'd probably just interpret that as another slam, and he sensed it wouldn't take much to drive her away. Right now she was the only ally he had. "Why do you think you drew Erica's face, especially the cross? Did you notice it last night when you saw her at the bar?"

"Not consciously." She pressed a hand to her temple, as if he were giving her a headache. "Can we stop talking about this?"

"How often do the nightmares come?"

She sighed. "You're very stubborn."

"So I've been told."

"It depends. Usually when I get them they go on for a couple of days or sometimes weeks. Then they just stop. It seems that the more in touch I am with the people around me, the more likely I am to have the nightmares. It's as if I open up some emotional transmitter and I can't filter out the bad from the good."

"When did they start this last time?"

She bit down on her bottom lip. "The night after I had the vision about you. The nightmares have been getting worse the last two months, intensifying every night. And this is the first picture where I've ever recognized the face. It must mean something."

He ran a hand through his hair, feeling as if he were getting off track. He wasn't going to find the answers to Erica's disappearance in a painting or in Catherine's dreams. He had to get real. "I'm going to call my lawyer." He needed to bring an objective party into the mix, and his longtime friend Mark Singer was a damn good criminal attorney. He would know the best course of action to take.

"That's a good idea," Catherine said with relief, lifting the painting off the easel.

"What are you doing with that?"

"Putting it away. I don't like looking at it." She

slipped the painting into a large portfolio and blew out a breath of relief.

Dylan wished he could set aside his problems as easily. "Mark," he said as his attorney picked up the phone, "I'm in a hell of a lot of trouble."

Chapter 5

While Dylan spoke to his attorney, Catherine tidied up her paints. She felt restless and a little short of breath. Dylan took up a lot of emotional and physical space, and she was so attuned to him that she sensed the tension in his body as if it were her own.

A part of her really wanted to walk away from him, but the fact that she'd drawn Erica's face and that maybe, just maybe, this time she had a chance to actually help someone in her vision made it impossible for her to consider leaving.

Although she had to wonder why she was supposed to help the woman who had drugged Dylan and left him out in the woods all night. Was Erica the victim or the villain? Was she good or was she evil?

As Catherine remembered the fear that had gripped her when she'd looked into Erica's cabin, she suspected that Erica had gotten herself caught in the very trap she was supposed to be setting for Dylan. Catherine felt fairly certain that someone had been watching Erica last night. But who and why? And was Erica really in trouble? Or was her disappearance just part of the plan to set Dylan up?

Catherine glanced over at Dylan as he ended his call. "What did your attorney say?"

"Mark will call the sheriff's office and see what he can find out," Dylan said. "Hopefully they'll give him more information than they gave me. In the meantime I'd like to take a shower. Do you mind? I've been in these clothes way too long."

"Help yourself."

"Would you answer my phone if it rings? I think it will take Mark a while to call back, but I don't want to miss him. His name is Mark Singer."

"Sure," she said, relieved when Dylan grabbed his clothes and entered the bathroom. She needed to catch her breath, figure out what she could do to help, and she could think more clearly with Dylan out of the room.

Returning to the window, she took a moment to absorb the gorgeous view of the mountains and lake. She'd planned to stay in the area and paint for a few days. At least, that was what she'd told herself. Perhaps deep down she'd known all along that she would stay in Tahoe because of Dylan. She'd never admit it aloud, but she hadn't been able to get him out of her head since she'd met him two months earlier. He'd been a prominent star in her daydreams, and painting his portrait had done little to banish him from her mind. She'd told herself it was just a foolish crush or infatuation or an inconvenient attraction, and that it would go away with time, but so far that hadn't happened. When she'd seen him at the wedding, standing next to his brother, looking so ruggedly appealing, her heart had skipped a beat. And it had shocked her to feel that gut-clenching desire. It had also scared her a little.

That was the real reason she'd left Dylan alone with Erica. She'd welcomed the other woman's presence as a good interruption, an opportunity to excuse herself and put some distance between herself and the man she couldn't forget. She knew Dylan wasn't right for her in so many ways.

But perhaps if she hadn't let fear run her off, Dylan wouldn't be in the mess he was in now. Not that she could have possibly anticipated the current turn of events.

As she gazed down at the entrance to the lodge, she saw several men gathering there. They looked like some sort of search-and-rescue team that had come from the woods. They conversed for a few minutes and then got into two separate vehicles and drove away. Obviously they hadn't found Erica, but had they found anything else?

More worry settled in the pit of Catherine's stomach as she let her gaze drift out over the lake, wondering what secrets were hidden in its depths.

As she watched the shimmering blue water it seemed to grow more turbulent, whitecaps and waves developing, shattering its peaceful beauty. The sun disappeared. Dark clouds covered the horizon. Shadows turned the tall trees into terrifying shapes. Shaken, she turned away.

She'd never had nightmares in the daytime before. Was the monster getting closer?

A man parked his car in front of a convenience store just outside Tahoe City and pulled out his cell phone. He was supposed to have reported in several hours ago, but he'd spent half the night searching the woods for that damn woman. He didn't know how she'd gotten away from him, but he would find her, and he would finish the job.

His call was answered on the third ring.

"She got away," he said shortly, hating to admit it, but there was no escaping the facts.

"How did that happen?"

The stone-cold voice reminded him that there was no excuse for failure. "You said she wouldn't be expecting me, that she would be taken by surprise, but she was ready," he complained. "She jumped me before I was halfway through the door."

"You were sloppy to let her hear you coming. I thought you were supposed to be the best."

"I am the best, and next time I'll plan the hit my way." He enjoyed turning the blame around; it took the bad taste of failure out of his mouth and softened the pain in the back of his head where the woman had nailed him with the iron poker from the fireplace. He intended to pay her back for that. Now that he knew what a wildcat she was, it would make the eventual taking that much sweeter. There was nothing like killing a woman. Every time he did it he felt an intense rush of satisfaction, better than sex, better than anything.

"Does anyone know you were there?"

The question drew him back to the present.

"Of course not. I never leave anything behind." Once he'd come to terms with the fact that the woman had escaped, he'd gone back to the cabin and cleaned up his own blood so as not to mix it with the evidence planted in the cabin. Then he'd wiped off the poker and, to be extra careful, had tossed it into the lake. No one could trace it back to him. And no one would ever know he'd been anywhere near the lodge.

"Where is she now?"

"I have a good idea," he said. "Don't worry; I'll find her."

"And you'll kill her as planned. She can't live past tomorrow. You understand that, don't you?"

He understood, all right. If he didn't succeed, not only would he not get his money, he would probably end up dead himself. Kill or be killed. It was the way he'd lived his entire life. And murder . . . well, it was the one thing he was really good at.

Erica Layton would die, but he wouldn't be the one to pay for it. Sometimes life was sweet.

Dylan was tempted to linger in the shower. The hot spray eased the tension in his neck and shoulders, but he forced himself to turn off the water. He didn't have time to waste. The trap was tightening around him, and he needed to find a way out fast. He wondered if this was how Joseph Ravino had felt when he'd realized

Dylan was onto him, when he'd seen the house of lies he'd built begin to crumble. Which also begged the question, was that the purpose for this game—payback?

It would be Ravino's style to use Erica, the very woman who'd betrayed him, to set up someone else. It would be poetic justice. And Erica could be bought—there was no doubt about that. Or she could have been threatened or blackmailed. Erica certainly wouldn't want to end up dead, the way Ravino's wife had. With the senator's connections, even from prison he could be calling the shots. Dylan just needed to figure out the next move before Ravino or Erica made it.

After getting out of the shower, Dylan dried off with a thick terry-cloth towel and threw on a pair of jeans and a long-sleeved T-shirt. It felt good to get out of his suit and back into his normal clothes. His head felt lighter, too. The fuzziness from the drugs was finally wearing off. He was ready to attack the problem head-on.

When he reentered the bedroom Catherine was standing in front of the easel, staring at a blank canvas, a paintbrush in her hand, yet she seemed in no hurry to actually use it. The midday sun streamed through the window, adding a shine to the red highlights in her blond hair, accentuating the curves of her body, her full breasts and the soft sway of her hips.

He felt an unmistakable tingle of desire shoot down his spine that he immediately tried to quell, but his thoughts were already running amok. He wanted to touch her. He wanted to strip off her clothes and trace those curves with his hands and with his mouth. He wanted to see her blue eyes darken with need. He wanted to taste her lips. He wanted to unleash the passion that was brimming inside of her. He'd seen it in her eyes and heard it in her voice.

Catherine was a bundle of intense emotions, and usually he avoided emotional women as if they had the plague, but there was something so intriguing about her that he was tempted to throw caution to the wind. It was a reckless, dangerous attraction that he had for her. He knew that, and he had to push it away. Catherine was far too complicated a woman to get involved with. He couldn't afford to make this any more personal than it already was.

So he counted to ten, took a couple of deep breaths, and tried to get a grip on himself.

Catherine turned her head and caught him staring. Her eyes widened as she read his expression, and he couldn't help wondering how much he was giving away—probably too much. Not that it would take a rocket scientist to figure out what he was thinking, and he already knew Catherine was very perceptive.

"What are you doing?" he asked quickly, hoping to distract her.

"What? Oh." She looked down at the brush in her hand. "I thought I would try to paint, to force something out of my subconscious, but big surprise—nothing happened." She set her brush down. "Your attorney didn't call."

"Well, I'm going to operate on the idea that no news is good news for the moment. I'm sure Mark will be in touch as soon as he knows something." Pulling his laptop out of its case, Dylan set it on the desk. Opening the lid, he hit the power button and waited for it to boot up. "I was thinking in the shower that if Joseph Ravino is behind this frame, he could have easily had one of his people get to Erica and in turn to me."

"So you believe this is about revenge?"

"It sure as hell feels like it. Ravino's friends and family believe I helped send an innocent man to jail by televising inflammatory news reports and fabricating my stories. I didn't, by the way. I got a lot of hate mail right after his arrest." Dylan sat down in the chair. "The man is not only a senator; he's also a philanthropist—oh, yeah, and a murderer."

"That's an odd combination."

"Not if you consider that they're all roles involving power. He's an interesting man, Ravino. He started a cutting-edge software company about fifteen years ago, made a bundle in the stock market. Then he married into blue blood. His wife Deborah's family could trace their roots back to the *Mayflower.* Her family was also twice as rich as Ravino was. The two became a power couple. They were on every society guest list. And once Ravino became a state senator, his personality and his ego got even bigger. I think he began to believe in his own invincibility. He didn't think anyone could touch him. He could have everything exactly the way he wanted."

"Why would he risk it all by killing his wife?"

"For money, perhaps. Ravino's financial holdings took a hit when the stock market collapsed, so he needed Deborah's money, as well as her wifely support for his political goals. Maybe she threatened to divorce him.

She knew about his affairs. She had photographic evidence of the senator and Erica together, and she told Erica she would use it if she had to. She had the weapons to destroy his career. He couldn't let that happen."

"Wouldn't she also destroy herself in the process?"

"Not if she intended to use her weapons only to keep him in the marriage. She might not have anticipated that he would try to kill her."

"Back up a little and tell me more about the murder case," Catherine said as she crossed the room to sit down on a corner of the bed near the desk. "How did you first get involved in it? And what were the details?"

"About a year ago Deborah Ravino was found dead in her very expensive home on Nob Hill in San Francisco. It was believed at first that she accidentally killed herself by quadrupling her Botox injections, which caused muscle paralysis not only in her face but also in her respiratory system. She basically suffocated herself."

"Death by Botox?" Catherine asked, a smile tugging at her lips. "Tell me that wasn't your lead."

"It was," he admitted. "It was too juicy to resist."

"Why would a doctor allow her to have too many injections?"

"Her doctor didn't. Apparently Mrs. Ravino was buying self-injection kits off the Internet because her doctor refused to give her any more, and she was obsessed with her looks."

"It wasn't her who bought the kit, but the senator," Catherine guessed. "Right?"

"That has not yet been proven. Her credit card was used for the purchase. And the only fingerprints found on the syringe were Deborah's. The senator gave a painfully touching interview about his wife's obsession with her looks, remarking how he had always loved her for more than her beauty. I didn't buy the accidental-death explanation, so I looked deeper."

"So you started digging in someone else's sandbox and pissed everyone off. Why am I not surprised?"

He tipped his head in acknowledgment of her point. "That's my job. It doesn't always make me popular, but it does make me good."

"Go on with the story."

"Senator Ravino played the grieving widower very well. He was photographed going to church every Sunday with his elderly parents and his sister and brother-in-law and their kids. He was also seen down at a homeless shelter, serving up soup to the poor. There was something about the guy that didn't feel right to me. He was too good to be true, you know what I mean?"

"I think I do."

"So I started looking into everything about him. I checked out the Metro Club, where he allegedly spent the evening while his wife was killing herself with Botox. The Metro Club is an exclusive and very private men's club in San Francisco that has been around since the early nineteen hundreds, a place where men can be men, discuss politics, et cetera. The club also has a back room where the gentlemen, as they like to call themselves, can spend some time with some very attractive female hostesses. I knew I had to get in there and see what it was all about. Unfortunately you have to be a member to gain access, and I wasn't."

"So what did you do?"

"I used the one connection I had—my father. Although he didn't know I was using him. I stopped by his house when he wasn't home and swiped his membership card. I made a reservation for the two of us for dinner on a night when my father would be out of town. I figured by the time he got back, I would have what I needed."

"So what happened after you got into the club?"

"To make a long story short, I found Erica. She was one of the hostesses. At first she didn't want to talk to me. I could tell she was scared that I was trying to connect her to Ravino. In the end I convinced her that if she knew something, and if her pal Ravino had killed his wife, then she could be in danger, too. After all, a man like Ravino would not want any of his dirty little secrets—and Erica was certainly one of them—to come out. Eventually she broke down and confessed that she and Ravino had been having an affair and that she was afraid she'd slept with a murderer. I convinced her to help me prove it."

"Surely she knew it would put her in danger to reveal something damaging about a state senator."

"I can be very persuasive when I want to be," he said with a shrug.

"I'll bet. I'm surprised you waited until you'd finished the story to go to bed with her."

"I didn't have to use sex to get the information out of her."

"But you would have, right?"

"What are you asking me, Catherine? Wondering just how low I'll go?" he challenged.

"Maybe I am. I don't know you, Dylan. You've asked me to be your partner, your ally. I need to know where your boundaries are."

"I don't have any boundaries." He didn't particularly like the impression she seemed to be forming of him, but he couldn't deny that he could be ruthless in his pursuit of the story. "I do what it takes to get the truth."

"Are there lines you won't cross?"

"I haven't seen any yet."

She tilted her head to one side as she gave him a thoughtful look. "I don't believe you, Dylan. I think you have a conscience, even if you won't admit it. I also believe that you're worried about Erica, not just because of what she did to you last night, but for her own sake."

"I don't know where you'd get that idea. Right now I'd like to wring her neck."

"Fine. You're a tough, ruthless guy—I get it. Let's go back to the Ravino case."

"Erica told me that Deborah had known about the affair because she came and confronted Erica at her apartment. Erica, who thinks very well on her feet, decided to tape the conversation, unbeknownst to Deborah. She thought she might need the tape for some reason. In their conversation Deborah reveals that she told the senator she knew about the affair, that she had photos of him and Erica together, and that she would give them to the press if he didn't stop seeing Erica immediately. She would also divorce him, and under their prenuptial agreement a proven affair would cost him millions. Apparently her reason for going to Erica was to try to gain her cooperation. She offered Erica a sizable chunk of money to cut off contact with the senator."

"Did Erica take it?"

"She was still thinking about it when Mrs. Ravino was killed. The taped conversation, however, gave the senator a motive for murder. But it wasn't enough. There was no proof that the senator injected his wife with too much Botox until I came up with some."

Dylan had a difficult time keeping the boastful note out of his voice. He was damn proud of his accomplishment. "I discovered that when the senator made a trip to Mexico with several other members from the state congress to discuss trade and immigration problems, he also made a side trip to a Mexican doctor who offered up his own version of discounted Botox. With my new information, the coroner's office reran the tissue tests and toxicology screening and discovered that the substance offered by that physician matched what was in Deborah's bloodstream."

"Very impressive," Catherine said. "Since Deborah wasn't in Mexico, then her husband was the one who brought the poison home."

"But that still wasn't enough, because the senator claimed his wife simply asked him to pick up the discounted medication. Unfortunately for him, I discovered a money trail that revealed that the senator had paid the Mexican physician five times the going rate. I also located a female friend of Deborah's who was willing to testify that there was no way Deborah would have used any medication from Mexico, because a friend of theirs had almost died from a diet pill obtained from the same doctor."

"And is that where the senator got his idea?" Catherine asked.

Dylan nodded. "That's my guess."

"It's a pretty good way to kill your wife, because even with all your evidence, it wouldn't be easy to prove beyond a reasonable doubt."

"I agree. It's not a slam dunk, but when you lay everything out the picture is pretty clear as to what happened. Whether or not the DA can get a conviction is still to be determined."

"It certainly sounds like the senator has a good reason to hate you, since he was getting away with murder before you got involved. If he killed his wife, then he probably wouldn't hesitate to kill again. But wouldn't he hate Erica just as much as you—if not more? She betrayed him as well. Why would he use her to set you up? Why wouldn't he set you both up?"

Catherine made a good point. It was something he'd been thinking about as well.

"Maybe that's what he did," Catherine mused, continuing. "Perhaps Erica thought she was setting you up, but in actuality . . ."

"Ravino was setting her up, too," Dylan finished. "If

that's the case, then Erica could be . . . in danger." He couldn't bring himself to use the word *dead*. He hoped to God she was still alive, but he couldn't deny that the facts were leading in the other direction. And if that was the case, it was his fault. He was the one who'd found her, who'd made her talk, who'd told her she'd be safer going to the police with her tape than keeping her mouth shut.

"Dylan, don't go there," Catherine said. "You're not to blame."

"Shit," he swore in annoyance. "Are you reading my mind now?"

"I'm reading your expression. It's obvious you're starting to feel guilty. But you should at least wait until you have your precious facts and see what they add up to."

"Unfortunately, I don't have very many facts," he grumbled.

She paused, tipping her head toward his computer. "What are you looking for now?"

"I'm not sure. First I'd just like to see if anyone has been on my computer or opened any of my files. That might lead me in a specific direction. I also want to refresh my memory on what I know about Erica. If she's still alive and on the run, I need to figure out where she might hide."

"If she was meant to disappear and make it look like murder, she'd have to go far," Catherine said. "She'd have to vanish in a very complete way, no contact with her friends, no use of her credit cards, no trips to her apartment. She would have had to plan her next stop after this before she ever came here."

Catherine's reasoning was right on the money. She wasn't just a quirky psychic painter with a smoking-hot body; she also had a very good brain. And she seemed to understand how people thought. Smart, pretty, and mysterious—a dangerous combination.

"You're going to have to think like Erica," Catherine continued. "Where would you go if you were in her shoes?"

"Probably some remote island in the South Pacific."

Catherine smiled. "That sounds good to me, too."

He grinned back at her. "A few rum drinks with umbrellas in 'em and I could hide out for a while. I'm sure whoever convinced Erica to participate in this plot persuaded her that she could lead a very luxurious life with enough money to make her happy, and all she had to do was put something in my drink and take me into the woods. Easy as pie."

"Then the double cross," Catherine said. "I would have expected that."

"You're smarter than Erica, but to be fair, we don't know that she didn't anticipate the double cross."

"What I felt at her cabin was surprise. Something unexpected happened last night. Someone showed up at her door who wasn't part of the plan."

Catherine's analysis made sense, but he still didn't have any hard facts to back up her theory.

Catherine shook her head, her gaze meeting his. "You're such a skeptic, Dylan. Haven't you ever had an intuition about something, an instinct that you couldn't explain, but it came true?"

"I suppose," he conceded. "Don't take it personally. It's just the way I am." He turned toward his computer, then paused. "Before I do anything else, I want to call Erica."

"Why? She's not going to answer, and won't that raise even more suspicion when the cops get her telephone records, which they might do if she stays missing?"

"Exactly why I should call. I can argue that why would I try to contact her if I knew she was dead?" As he'd expected, Erica's voice mail picked up. He waited for the beep and then said, "Erica, it's Dylan. Hope you're all right. Call me back, would you? I'm very worried about you, and I want to know why you drugged me and left me in the woods."

"You're pretty clever," Catherine commented.

"I've spent a fair amount of time on criminal cases the past year. I've picked up a few things. You seem to know a lot about the police as well, for a woman who lives a quiet life in a seaside town," he said pointedly, knowing there was far more to her past than she'd revealed.

"It's no secret that I grew up in foster care and on the streets. I'm not naive when it comes to law enforcement. Like you, I've picked up a few tricks over the years. What about Erica's work? Her colleagues might know where she would stay if she wasn't at home."

"I'll call them tomorrow. Her modeling agency won't

be open on a Sunday, and she hasn't worked at the Metro Club since the Ravino case broke."

"What about Erica's friends?" Catherine asked as she got to her feet. "Do you know any of them?"

"No."

"Family?"

"We talked mostly about Ravino."

"When you talked," she said dryly.

"I'm not going to try to pretty up my one-night stand, Catherine," he said bluntly. "It was what it was."

"At least you're honest about it," she said with a sigh. "Most men pretend they have deeper intentions when they don't."

"Are you speaking from experience?"

"Perhaps."

"You don't seem the type to have had many casual affairs."

"What type is that?" she asked.

"The easy-come, easy-go kind of woman. Nothing is easy about you, as far as I can tell."

"You don't know me very well."

She was right. He didn't know her, but he wanted to. She was different from anyone he'd ever met, and he was a sucker for secrets. Finding the truth was the driving mantra of his life. He couldn't walk past a mystery without trying to solve it, and Catherine was definitely a puzzle to him.

"Actually," she added, interrupting his thoughts, "I think sex can be easy. It's intimacy that's much more difficult. You can give away your body, disconnect—

but your heart, your mind, that's a whole different thing."

"I wouldn't have thought you'd want one without the other—sex without love, love without intimacy. You have so much . . . You're so . . ." He couldn't find the right words to describe her.

"I have so much what?" she asked, curious.

"Passion. Intensity. Depth. You're emotional. You're sensitive."

"That's why intimacy is more difficult. It takes a lot out of me. It opens me up and makes me vulnerable," she confessed. "And the intensity I have . . . it scares people. No one really wants to see the future, not even when they think they do. You'll be scared one day, too, and you'll leave, and you'll hope to God you never see me again."

"You've already scared me, and I'm still here," he reminded her.

"For the moment. It will get worse, especially when you start to believe in me, which you haven't done yet."

She was right. He still didn't trust her sixth sense, so to speak, but he doubted that would ever happen. "Why are you trying to warn me away?"

"Because you and I . . . we shouldn't get involved." She paused, biting down on her bottom lip, her deep blue gaze fixed on his. "Even if we . . ."

"Even if we what?" he asked, unsettled by the way she was looking at him now—not like a psychic but like a woman, a woman who wanted him. His body hardened as his mind immediately stripped off her clothes. She would not appreciate that he was now imagining her naked, her beautiful breasts filling his hands. Or maybe she already knew what he was thinking. There was knowledge in her eyes, as well as desire.

"Even if we have an attraction. I feel the pull between us," she said simply. "Don't you?"

"Uh, yeah, sure." He cleared his throat. "Are you saying you want to have sex with me?" His body began to sing with anticipation.

She hesitated and then said, "Maybe I do. But not now." She turned quickly and headed toward the door.

"Hey, where are you going? We're in the middle of something, in case you hadn't noticed."

"I'm going for a walk before I do something I regret."

"You wouldn't regret it," he told her.

She smiled. "You're not short on confidence, are you?"

"We'd be good together. Just remember you're the one who ran away, not me. I'm not scared of you."

"Not yet," she murmured before slipping out the door.

Dylan let out a breath as she left the room, feeling frustrated and yet a little relieved that she was gone. He was attracted to her. What man wouldn't be? But, dammit, no matter what he'd told her, the truth was that she did scare him. He liked casual relationships, fun in the sack, nobody saying, *Good-bye,* or *I love you,* or *Don't leave me.* He couldn't give a woman anything more than a good time. And he'd never pretended otherwise.

Intimacy was almost impossible for him. The only person he'd ever cared about was Jake. He'd tried to love his father, but he'd had the love beaten out of him. And his mother . . . well, she hadn't stuck around long enough for anyone to love her. He was just like her, he thought. At least, that was what his father had told him over the years, so much so that he'd come to believe it.

He rolled his head on his shoulders, hearing his joints crack from the tension. He was tired, but there was no time to rest. He had to find Erica. He had to get himself out of this mess before it got worse. But as he focused on his computer he knew that he was in quicksand and sinking fast. He just hoped Catherine hadn't gone far. He suspected he was going to need her help to get out.

Catherine had intended to settle herself in one of the chairs on the outside deck overlooking the lake, but once she got there she was too restless to sit. Bypassing the deck she headed toward the path, the one Dylan had taken with Erica the night before. Maybe she could pick up on something if she followed the same trail.

As she walked, she mentally retraced her conversation with Dylan. She certainly hadn't meant to tell him she wanted to have sex with him. She had a tendency to blurt out her thoughts without editing them first, and this had definitely been one of those times. And her words had been like throwing a red flag in front of a bull. If she hadn't left the room, she and Dylan would probably be rolling around in the sheets right now. That thought gave her libido a nice little jolt.

Despite the fact that she'd told Dylan she thought sex was easy, she knew that sex with Dylan would be anything but easy. He would ask too much of her. He would demand more than she wanted to give.

So she would keep her distance—until she couldn't.

Continuing down the path, she focused her mind on Erica. She'd barely looked at her the night before, but the woman's image was ingrained in her brain. Why had Erica lured Dylan out to these woods? Had she wanted to get him away from the lodge so she could fake her disappearance? Her public appearance in the bar had certainly set the stage for everyone to see her leaving with Dylan.

When the concrete walkway ended, Catherine continued into the woods. Dylan said they'd walked a fair distance from the lodge, so she would keep going, see what else was out here. The lodge and adjacent cabins were the only buildings on the hillside for at least a mile or two in either direction. Part of the appeal lay in the rustic nature of the location. The isolation had certainly made it easier for Erica to get Dylan into an area where no one would see what was going on. Perhaps that was why she hadn't gone to him in San Francisco and instead had waited for the opportunity to get him away from his home turf.

As she hiked Catherine began to grow warm, and she pushed the sleeves of her sweater up to her elbows. The noonday sun was beaming down through the trees. It was a pretty day, the kind of day when summer seemed around the corner, a day when only good things should happen. But as she moved farther into the thick forest, she began to feel nervous. Was she picking up on what had occurred the day before, or were the sudden shadows sparking her active imagination?

The hairs on the back of her neck suddenly stood up. She swung around quickly, expecting to see someone behind her. Had Dylan followed her?

There was no one, and yet she felt as if someone were watching her.

Every sound became acutely loud: the snap of a twig, a rustle in the brush, the sudden squawk of a bird overhead. They were all sounds of nature—or were they?

She put a hand on the trunk of a nearby tree to steady herself. It didn't help. Images flashed through her mind.

The ground was flying by at an amazing pace, as if she were running. She could hear the blood pounding through her veins. Her chest hurt more with each breath of air in the high altitude. She stumbled and fell to the ground, then scrambled back to her feet, desperate to get away. He was coming closer. . . .

But it wasn't her. Those weren't her shoes. And her hands . . . There was a ring on the finger of her right hand, a sparkling opal that was changing colors with the heat of her skin. Who was she? And who was she running from?

The sound of a horn startled her.

The images faded away. She was back to herself again. The sun seemed brighter. The shadows had lightened as well. Her heart began to slow down. The horn came again. Catherine moved closer to the edge of the cliff to investigate the noise. A sharp outcropping of rock fell down to the lake a few hundred yards below.

Two boats were anchored not far offshore. One bore the logo of the coast guard. Someone was in the water, a diver. He held up something red to show to another man on board. Her heart skipped a beat. She knew exactly what it was—Erica's red scarf, the scarf she'd seen around the pretty brunette's neck not only last night, but also in her vision.

Was there a body in the water, too?

Had Erica run through these woods, taken a misstep, and tumbled to her death off the side of the sheer cliff into the cold waters of Lake Tahoe? Or had she been pushed?

Chapter 6

Dylan was immersed in his computer files when his cell phone rang. "Mark, what did you find out?" he asked, hoping for some good news.

"You're in deep shit, buddy," Mark said.

That was not what he wanted to hear. "What do you mean?"

"I spoke to Detective Richardson at the sheriff's office. He said that Erica Layton is still missing and they're extremely concerned about her welfare. A guest in an adjacent cabin reported hearing a woman scream last night. A security guard investigated and discovered that the cabin where Erica was staying had been broken into, and apparently there was evidence of a struggle, including blood evidence, which they are now testing for DNA. Please tell me they're not going to find your DNA at the scene."

"I wish I could, but I have a cut on my hand, which I acquired sometime in the night while I was passed out," Dylan said. "I suspect Erica cut me to plant the blood. It was part of the setup."

"Not the best explanation I've heard."

"It's the truth, and whatever other evidence they have Erica planted as well. The blood tests I took earlier this morning should prove that I was drugged and incapable of hurting anyone."

"Speaking of which, why the hell did you agree to have your blood tested without talking to me first? At the very least we could have stalled until we had a better idea what we were dealing with."

"Yeah, I know. I thought I was going to prove my innocence before the drugs left my system, but I suspect I made things worse. Damn, I hate to be wrong."

"You can't go off half-cocked anymore, Dylan. This is serious."

"Believe me, I'm very aware of just how serious it is. What else did the detective tell you?"

"Not much. They conducted a brief search of the woods but found nothing. They're trying to contact Erica's relatives and friends with the help of the San Francisco Police Department. They plan to launch another search tomorrow if Miss Layton hasn't turned up by then. You need to find her. If she's alive, most of your problems go away."

"Most?" Dylan echoed.

"They could still charge you with assault, breaking and entering, but at least you wouldn't be facing a murder charge."

The idea that he could be arrested for murder sent chills down Dylan's spine. Surely it wouldn't go that far. It couldn't. He was an innocent man. "I can't believe this is happening. I drove up here yesterday for my brother's wedding, and now I'm a suspect in a murder investigation? How is that possible?"

"You do lead an exciting life. I think I should come up there. I know you like to handle things yourself, but this is too big. If you didn't kill this woman, someone is working damn hard to make it look like you did."

"Yes. And for the moment I'm going to stick with the belief that Erica is not dead, that this is just part of the frame. I have to find her and make her talk."

"If someone is framing you for Erica's death," Mark said slowly, "they have extremely good motivation to actually kill her."

Mark had a point. But Erica knew how to look out for herself. At least, Dylan hoped she did.

"I need to take care of a few things here," Mark added, "but I can be in Tahoe by tonight. Don't do or say anything to anyone, Dylan. Just stay put. Keep your mouth shut. I'll be in touch."

It was good advice, but Dylan wasn't sure he could take it. He didn't want to play defense. He had to find a way to turn this game upside down. Slipping his phone back into his pocket, he decided to shut down his computer. It didn't appear to him that anyone had accessed his files, but he couldn't be positive. It didn't make sense that someone would have gone to the trouble of taking out his computer without doing something to it or looking for something, but he couldn't find any obvious evidence.

He had just returned the computer to its case when

Catherine burst into the room. Her breath was coming hard and fast, as if she'd run a few miles. Her hair was tangled, and her cheeks were bright red.

"What's going on?" he asked in alarm.

"They found the scarf," she said. "I took the path you were on last night, and I saw the coast guard and the police searching an area very close to shore."

His chest tightened. "But no body, right?"

"Not that I could see, but I didn't have a great view. This is bad, Dylan. How did they even know to look in the water for her clothing?"

"Someone saw something and called the cops. Or the plan is just continuing to tick away, right on schedule." He paused. "My lawyer thinks they're going to arrest me."

"I do, too." Her gaze clung to his, worry and fear in her eyes.

He made a sudden decision. "I'm not waiting around to find out."

"You shouldn't," Catherine agreed. "You won't be able to fight back if you're in jail."

"Exactly what I was thinking," he muttered, not really surprised they were on the same wavelength. He was starting to get used to the idea that Catherine could almost anticipate what he was going to say before he said it. "Come with me."

"What? Where?"

"Back to San Francisco, for starters."

She hesitated, doubt written across her face. "I don't know, Dylan."

"You said you'd help me," he reminded her.

"Help you find the truth, not evade the police."

He knew she was right. This wasn't her problem; it was his. And he'd always traveled better on his own. But for some reason the idea of cutting her loose disturbed him. "Well, I need to get out of here. You do what you think is best." He couldn't quite believe he was contemplating running out on the cops, but every instinct screamed that he needed to buy himself some time. Everything was moving too fast. The scarf in the lake seemed like another step in a preorchestrated plan to set him up for murder. His tie was probably there, too. If he ran he would definitely look guilty and he could land himself in even worse trouble. It was a risk, but one he had to take. He grabbed the suit he'd worn the night before and stuffed it into his suitcase.

"You should call Jake," Catherine said. "He's your brother. He would want to help."

"I'm not ruining his honeymoon. Nor do I want him involved. He's finally got his life together with Sarah and the baby. He has way too much to lose. I don't."

"Neither do I," she said slowly.

He met her gaze. "Forget it. I shouldn't have asked you to come."

"But you did. And I think I will."

"Why?"

"Do I have to have a reason? You asked me and I accept."

"And I've reconsidered. This isn't your problem, and it could be dangerous."

"I'm coming, Dylan."

"Why would you risk your life to help me?" he questioned.

"Well, I'm hoping I won't be risking my life, but the truth is, I have to see how this plays out. When I was in the woods I connected with Erica again."

"You saw her?"

"In my head," she clarified. "I had another vision. I think it was from last night. Erica was out there in the woods running from someone, then hiding in the trees. She was scared."

"I thought she was in her cabin when someone came after her."

"Maybe she ran into the woods." Catherine pulled her clothes out of the drawers and dragged her suitcase from the closet. "I've been running from my dreams my whole life. I think it's time I chased one down."

"Catherine, if you come with me, you'll be an accessory." He knew he had to state the obvious. She was so caught up in the events going through her head, she wasn't looking at the big picture. "You could be charged, put in jail."

"I've made my decision. I'd like my visions to be worth something good, just once." She paused, taking one last look around the room. "I think I have everything. Should I check out?"

"When did you say you were going to leave?"

"I was planning to stay until Tuesday."

"Then don't check out. I'll pay if you wind up having room charges, but I'd rather not have anyone looking for you yet." He drew in a quick breath. "We'll have to take your car, since I don't have my keys. It's probably better that way anyway. If I leave mine in the lot, it should buy us a little time. Although it won't take much for someone to figure out we're together. The detective already knows we're friends. Still, I'd rather delay the inevitable."

"So you go down the back stairs with the bags and I'll leave through the front," Catherine said. "On the way out, I'll stop at the front desk and tell them I'm interested in taking a boat tour of the lake. I'll make it clear that I'm planning to spend my day on the water, and no one will see me leave with you."

Her words surprised him once again and also reminded him that whatever had happened in her past had taught her how to think ahead, especially when it came to the police. He must have stared at her too long, because her eyebrows pulled together.

"What's wrong? You have an odd look on your face," she said.

"That's admiration. You think very fast on your feet."

"Which is good for you. Speaking of thinking ahead, why do you want to go to San Francisco?" she asked as they turned toward the door. "Won't that be the first place the police look for you?"

"Yes, but if I can get a head start, perhaps I can learn something about Erica that will at least point me in the right direction. I need to find her alive before the cops can prove that I killed her. And I have a feeling it's going to be close."

*   *   *

They were forty-five minutes out of Tahoe but still in the mountains when Dylan pulled out his cell phone and called Mark. He didn't want his friend to make a wasted trip to Tahoe, but he also hadn't wanted to give Mark a chance to talk him out of leaving. Mark's voice mail picked up, and Dylan was relieved. It would be easier to leave a message and not get into explanations.

"Mark, I'm going to find Erica on my own," he said. "I can't sit in Tahoe and wait for the hammer to drop on my head. I'll be in touch. Just hang tight and wait for my call." He hung up and set the phone on the console between the seats. Mark would have a fit when he found out that Dylan had run, and to be honest he was already having second thoughts himself, but it was too late. He wasn't turning back.

"How long will it take to reach San Francisco?" Catherine asked.

"About three more hours." He checked the rearview mirror. It was ridiculous to think the police might already be on his tail. They wouldn't even have the blood tests back from the hospital yet. Nor had Erica been missing for twenty-four hours. He had a little time. He just had to use it wisely.

Unfortunately, he didn't have more than a vague idea of what he would do when he got to the city. He could check out the few places he knew Erica frequented, but she probably wouldn't be there. If she was hiding, she'd go where he couldn't find her. She could be anywhere in the world. If Ravino was behind the plan, he certainly had plenty of money to make sure

Erica disappeared. And if it wasn't Ravino, then who else would use Erica to set him up?

He'd done a lot of stories over the past few years, investigated plenty of crimes, reported on murderers, rapists, burglars, bank robbers. Any one of them could be behind this plan to take him down. But because Erica was involved, it seemed that Ravino was the most likely choice. He was the one person they had in common. However, Dylan didn't want to make the mistake of focusing on one target, only to realize someone had deliberately pointed him in the wrong direction.

"I wish I knew who my enemy was," he muttered, "so I knew who to fight."

"Who else in your life, besides Senator Ravino, would want to torture you like this?" Catherine asked.

"That's what I was just wondering. I have no idea."

"Because it seems to me that a frame for murder is designed to make a person suffer over a long period of time, unlike a bullet to the head, which would kill instantly."

"That's a nice, cheery image."

"Sorry, but it's clear to me that someone hates you, Dylan."

"Yeah, it's pretty obvious to me, too." Her words had brought one person's face to mind, but Dylan dismissed the idea immediately.

Catherine shifted in her seat, and he could feel the heat of her gaze. His hands tightened on the steering wheel. He didn't want her in his head, reading his thoughts. There was a part of himself that he didn't allow anyone to see, a part that had been wounded a long time ago.

"Stop staring at me," he told her.

"I'm making you nervous. But it's not my staring that's really upsetting you. Who hates you, Dylan? It has to be someone close to you," she added. "You should tell me. I might figure it out anyway."

She probably would figure it out. He might not be willing to buy into her psychic power, but he knew she was very perceptive. Finally he said, "There's only one person who I know hates me, and that's my father. But it's ludicrous to think that he would spend any time whatsoever trying to set me up for murder."

"Your *father*? Now I know why you didn't want to tell me."

"Because he's not involved."

"Why do you think he hates you?"

"I don't think it. I know it," he said firmly. "Richard Sanders never pretended to love me. In fact, he beat the crap out of me until I was sixteen years old and could fight back. Then he threw me out of the house, ending what little relationship we had."

"That's horrible."

"It wasn't good," he said through tight lips. He really did not want to talk about his father. "Fortunately I had Jake; otherwise I don't think I would have survived my childhood."

"Jake protected you?"

"As much as he could. He even tried to take the blame a few times, but my father saw through it. He always went after me."

"Was your father physical with Jake, too?"

"I never saw him hit Jake, but he wasn't above manipulating him or finding ways to make him feel bad. But I'd have to say that I was my father's main target. After he kicked me out of the house, I went and lived with Jake. He was going to UC Berkeley at the time and had an apartment with a couple of guys. I slept on the couch and enrolled at the nearest high school and somehow managed to get a diploma. Jake made sure I went to college, too, and he paid for all of it. He worked two jobs, took out loans, all while he was trying to get his own education. I don't know how he did it. He's only three years older than me, but he was more of a surrogate parent than a brother."

"Didn't anyone else in the family try to step in and help you get away from your father?"

"Everyone looked the other way, and Richard Sanders knew how to hit where it wouldn't show. Besides that, he's a rich, socially connected, well-educated man. No one would ever believe he'd use a belt on his kid. I tried to tell a teacher once. She called my father in for a meeting. He said I was a pathological liar. The next thing I knew I was in detention. I didn't bother telling anyone after that."

"I can see why you wouldn't," she agreed.

There was no shock in her voice, just sadness and a weary acceptance, reminding him that Catherine was no stranger to abuse. She'd probably seen worse in her days in the foster-care system. He couldn't help wondering again what her story was, but he doubted she'd tell him. She was as private as he was—as he *usually* was, he silently amended. Around her he was becoming quite the talker.

"I don't know why I told you all that," he said aloud, giving her a quick look. "I don't usually."

"Because you needed to. Don't worry; your secret is safe with me."

"It's not a secret; it's just a part of my life that's over—at least, I thought it was over."

Was it possible that his father was responsible for his latest problems? They hadn't talked in over a year, and that brief conversation had occurred only because they'd happened to pass each other in a restaurant, and Richard hadn't wanted to look bad by snubbing his son in front of his longtime friends.

They lived separate lives now. Jake hadn't even invited their father to his wedding. Neither Jake nor Dylan considered their family to be anyone but the two of them, except their grandmother, when she was lucid enough to know she had grandsons, which was rare these days. And now Jake had his own family in Sarah and their daughter, Caitlyn. He was moving on, and that was the way it was supposed to be. Perhaps this was the perfect time for his father to strike. With Jake away, there was no one to step in and help Dylan, no one else who would point a finger in his father's direction.

"What happened to your mother?" Catherine asked, interrupting his thoughts. "You told me she left when you were a kid, but where is she now?"

"I have no idea. I haven't seen her since I was seven years old. She left us a note saying she was sorry, but she didn't really like being a mother, and she thought we'd be better off with Richard. She never came back to see us, and her name was taboo in my father's household. If I said her name aloud I'd definitely get a beating. So I kept my mouth shut."

"And you never tried to find her?" Catherine asked.

He heard the curious note in her voice and knew it didn't make sense that he'd spent the past decade searching for the truth about other people's lives while ignoring his own. "I've thought about it," he muttered. "That's as far as I've gone."

"Why? You have resources, connections. Why haven't you tried?"

A dozen good reasons crossed his mind, but he spoke the one that was the truth, the plain, simple, unvarnished truth. "Because she left me. She didn't want me or care to know what happened to me. Why should I care about her?" For some reason he couldn't seem to lie to Catherine, although his painful words made him sound like a complete wimp.

"That makes sense."

"It might make sense, but it's a chickenshit way to think," he said, annoyed at himself.

"You're not a coward."

"Aren't I? I'm afraid to find the mother who left me twenty-three years ago. That sounds cowardly to me."

"What does Jake say?"

"He accepts that she's gone. He thinks my father made life difficult for her, and that she had to leave in order to survive. He remembers our parents fighting all the time, and my mother crying. He's far more accepting than I am."

"It seems strange that she wouldn't have taken you with her when she left your dad. She must have known what kind of man she was married to, especially if they were arguing a lot."

"That's what I can't forgive her for," Dylan admitted. "She should have taken us with her."

"Maybe she couldn't. Your father sounds like a bully and a very strong man. She might not have been able to stand up to him."

"He was all that. And to be fair, it's possible he told her she could go, but she wasn't taking us. Although I can't understand why he would have fought to keep me or Jake. He didn't care about being a father any more than she wanted to be a mother. They were two people who should never have had kids." He paused. "It probably would have hurt his reputation too much to lose his family. His standing in the community means everything to him. I'm sure he must have told his friends that my mother was psychotic or something. Hell, maybe he told 'em he put her away in a psychiatric hospital. I doubt he would have ever admitted to anyone that she left him."

"Then he wouldn't set you up for murder," Catherine said. "It wouldn't look good to have his son in jail."

"Exactly. I told you it's not him. But you asked me who hated me enough to want to torture me, and his was the first and only name that popped into my head. So it has to be someone else, most likely Ravino."

"Right."

A few minutes of silence passed between them. Dylan glanced over at Catherine. She stared out the window, lost in thought. He wondered what she was thinking about now, what had drawn the tiny frown lines around the corners of her eyes. She was such a soft person, with beautiful skin, tender lips. There wasn't a hard thing about her. She was all heart and emotion. Once in a while he saw hints of a weary, cynical side, but she still never came off as cold and ruthless, just a little sad at times—like now. He wished he could take away her sadness, carry the burden of her past that she seemed to shoulder like a weary soldier, but he didn't know where the pain came from, and she didn't want to tell him.

Never mind that he'd shared his life story; she was still keeping hers close to the vest. When this was all over, he would find out what she was hiding. He was going to make her talk to him, and maybe there would be some way he could help her. He would definitely owe her.

Catherine suddenly turned her head and caught him staring. A flash of awareness sparked in her eyes, and he felt an immediate response—that damn connection between them that she constantly spoke of. It was definitely there. He felt as if she'd cast a spell over him— not that he believed in spells, but she had some sort of crazy power over him. When he wasn't thinking about saving his ass, he couldn't stop thinking about her and how much he wanted to explore her mouth, kiss the curve of her neck, cup her breasts with his hands, and watch her eyes darken with pleasure.

The way they were darkening now. He was either transparent as hell, or she really could read his mind. It was probably a little of both.

"You should be watching the road," Catherine said.

"You're a lot more interesting than the road."

"So are you."

Damn. Why did she have to admit that? He had to fight to drag his gaze away from hers and concentrate on driving. "You should learn how to lie," he said a moment later, inwardly battling a reckless urge to pull onto the shoulder and see just what else she'd admit to wanting.

"I know how to lie," Catherine replied. "In fact, I can be very good at it."

"How is that possible? You show every damn emotion the second you feel it."

"That's because I'm not trying to hide from you, but I can if you want."

He frowned at her challenging and honest words and knew that was the last thing he wanted. His recent relationships had been filled with games and innuendos and miscommunication, no one saying what they meant, no one acting on their true feelings, no one really trying to make the other person happy. He'd been living a fairly selfish life in regards to women, he thought, experiencing a moment of self-clarity. He'd rationalized by telling himself that if everyone had a good time, what was the harm? But his current situation reminded him that life was short and filled with unexpected events, and he shouldn't be wasting so much time being with people he didn't care about. Not that he cared about Catherine. They'd spent only a few days together, but the odd thing was, he felt as if he knew her better than people he'd spent months with.

"I used to hide what I was feeling," Catherine continued. "Growing up the way I did, I learned that showing tears or letting people know I cared made me weak, vulnerable. I had to fit in. I didn't have a choice. It was sink or swim. I had to be tough. And I had to lie— sometimes to save my life, which I was more than willing to do. But I'm an adult now, and I don't have to pretend anymore. And I guess I've gotten a little rusty at lying."

"You had it rough as a kid."

"Something we have in common."

"I have a feeling your past was worse than mine, but you're not going to tell me, are you?"

"Not now, but I won't say never. As soon as I challenge the universe by making such proclamations, fate usually steps in and shows me how wrong I am to think I can control my destiny," she added lightly.

"I don't believe in fate or destiny. We make our lives what they are. I hate it when people say they must have run out of gas for a reason, as if every little thing that happens in their life is part of some orchestrated plan. Maybe the reason they ran out of gas is because they forgot to fill up the tank."

"I don't think that every little moment in our lives is planned. We make choices that lead to actions and consequences. But I do believe in a higher power; call it God or fate or destiny or whatever. I feel it in my heart and in my head. I'm tuned in to the universe, and you're not, because you're still under the illusion that you're going to control everything."

"Obviously I'm not controlling this situation," he retorted.

"Maybe that's what you're supposed to learn."

"Oh, shit, don't start talking like that. This is not about me learning some lesson."

"It might be. Look, Dylan, I know you don't believe in things you can't see, but how can I not when I see things other people are experiencing? When I feel emotions that aren't mine, when I know what's going to happen before it happens?"

Dylan shook his head. "I can't explain you—or much of anything these days. Maybe it's all a cosmic joke. But I think the universe has some very human helpers, and those are the people I intend to find."

He had barely finished speaking when his cell phone rang. He picked it up from the console, his breath catching in his throat as he saw the number. "Shit!"

"Who is it?"

"Someone is calling me from my apartment, and the only person in the world besides myself who has a key to my place is Jake, and he's in Hawaii. I hope he didn't hear about this mess I'm in and come home. But why would he go to my house?"

Realizing he'd find out more if he just answered the phone, Dylan punched a button and said, "Hello?"

There was a long silence, but he could hear someone's quick, short breaths on the other end of the line. "Who is this, and what the hell are you doing in my apartment?"

"It's me," a woman said.

His heart turned over at the familiar voice. "Erica?" he breathed. "What's going on? What are you trying to do to me?"

"I made a horrible mistake, Dylan. Someone is trying to kill me."

"You made it look like *I* was trying to kill you."

"I had to. I'm sorry. I didn't have a choice."

"Why are you doing this, Erica? Is it Ravino? Does he have some hold over you?"

She didn't answer.

"Erica, talk to me. Whatever trouble you're in, I can help you fix it."

"Oh, God, I have to go," she said, dropping her voice to a hush. "I think someone is coming. I didn't think he'd find me here."

"Who? Erica, dammit, tell me who."

But it was too late. She'd hung up the phone. He couldn't believe he'd lost her again.

"Erica is at your house?" Catherine asked in surprise.

"Yes. She said someone was coming. And then she hung up. She said she was sorry. But she wouldn't say why she was doing it. Fuck!" He hit the redial over and over again, but Erica didn't answer.

"At least we know she's still alive," Catherine offered. "That's something."

"For now," he said grimly. "She said someone was trying to kill her, and that he'd found her again."

Chapter 7

Catherine began to feel uneasy the closer they got to San Francisco. By the time Dylan drove through the tollbooth at the Bay Bridge just before five o'clock that afternoon, every nerve in her body was on edge. The bay seemed to reflect her mood, the dark blue waves shimmering with whitecaps, the result of a strong wind and a bank of cool gray fog sliding in over the far end of the city.

She'd never been to San Francisco, so she didn't know why she had the sense of homecoming. She'd seen photographs of Alcatraz, the island prison in the middle of the bay, as well as pictures of the city, with its downtown skyscrapers, steep hills, and famous cable cars. But that didn't explain the conviction that she'd seen these sights before and that she'd driven across this bridge, heading into the city.

Her mental turmoil grew more chaotic with each passing mile. She gripped the armrest, feeling a desperate need to steady herself. But she couldn't find her center. Dizziness assailed her, and images began to flash through her mind. Her body went from hot to cold. Shivering, she wrapped her arms around her waist, trying to get rid of the sense that she was in terrible danger, but she couldn't stop the terror ripping through her.

"You're shaking. What's wrong?" Dylan asked.

His voice barely registered over the sound of rushing water in her head.

"Catherine," he said in a demanding tone. "What the hell is going on with you?"

"Something bad is happening." It was the same feeling she'd had in the woods, the sense that she was being chased, that she needed to run faster or she wouldn't be able to get away."

"Try to think of something else," Dylan ordered.

"I . . . I can't," she said, her teeth rattling with cold chills.

"Tell me about your art class. Are you still teaching?"

She knew he was trying to change the subject, but the mention of art only drew vivid slashes of color through her mind. She saw black and red again, then a streak of blue, a flash of gold. She felt something hit her chest, and she reached for her neck, wondering why she could feel a chain against her skin when there was nothing there.

"Catherine, answer me," Dylan said. "You have to talk to me. I can't stop the car on the bridge just because you're freaking out. Tell me about your classes."

"They're over until the summer session starts next month," she said tightly. "Oh, God, I can't stand this." She closed her eyes, overwhelmed.

"Don't fight it. Let it in. Tell me what's happening."

"No." She shook her head as she tried desperately to protect herself from the onslaught of emotions.

"What do you see?" Dylan demanded.

"Grass. Trees. A building."

Something that looked like a dome appeared in front of her eyes. A bunch of birds squawked and flew off a pond, as if something evil was coming.

"What kind of building?"

"Arches. Almost like a royal palace or something." *She saw a pillar in front of her. She tried to squeeze behind it. Her heart was pounding against her chest. Footsteps drew closer.*

"What else?"

She couldn't speak. If she said anything he would find her. She had to stay silent, utterly, utterly still. A shadow fell across the ground. She could hear him breathing.

"Catherine, snap out of it."

Dylan's voice shook her out of the moment, and as his hand came down on her leg her eyes flew open. She realized they were no longer on the bridge. Dylan had pulled off at the first exit and stopped the car on a side street. He was half turned in his seat, his eyes filled with concern.

"What is going on with you?" he asked.

She stared at him blankly, his words a blur in her head. Gradually she became aware of her surroundings, cars passing on the street, pedestrians in the crosswalk, the buzz of traffic on the nearby bridge. She wasn't in a dark park, hiding behind a pillar; she was here in the car with Dylan.

"Catherine," Dylan prodded impatiently. "Talk."

"I think I'm connecting with Erica again," she said slowly. "She's here in the city and someone is chasing her."

"Tell me something I don't know," Dylan said in frustration.

"He's very close to finding her."

"Catherine, you have to be more specific. What exactly did you see?"

"A grassy area, water." She thought harder. "A building with a big dome, tall pillars."

His gaze narrowed. "There are a couple of places like that in the city. One is the Palace of Fine Arts; another is the Conservatory of Flowers in Golden Gate Park. It would help to know which one."

"I've never been here before. I've never seen either of those buildings."

"Maybe in a picture. They're well-known tourist attractions."

"I saw the location in my head, not a photograph."

"So which one?"

Blowing out a sigh, she opened her purse and pulled out a memo pad and a pen. Without any more thought, she began to draw. She didn't know what would come out of her head—if it would be as unintelligible as most of her pictures or if it would tell them where Erica was.

In seconds a rough image appeared: a building with tall columns, a dome, a patio, a grassy area surrounding a pond, some sort of waterfall spray, and a flock of birds. She'd shaded one particularly large bird in heavy black—a hawk or a raven perhaps, undeniably a predator—and somewhere hidden behind the pillars was the prey, the shadow of a woman.

She handed Dylan the pad with a shaky hand.

He studied it for a moment and then said, "I think that's the Palace of Fine Arts." He restarted the car. "We might as well check it out. It's by the Golden Gate Bridge and more important, not far from my apartment. If you are somehow channeling Erica, it would make sense that she would be in that area."

"You're starting to believe me," she said, somewhat amazed by the idea.

"I'm not sure I'd go that far, but the Palace is as good a place to start as any other."

Dylan drove across town as quickly as he could, but it was slow going, since the streets were crowded with commuters getting off work. He bypassed the downtown area and sped along the Embarcadero, which edged the various piers and boat docks bordering the bay.

Every now and then he glanced in Catherine's direction. She seemed calmer now, studying the sights with a quiet eye. He had to admit he was relieved. She'd scared the shit out of him when she'd started shaking and sweating as if she were in some sort of trance. The cynical side of him wanted to say she was just acting, making the whole thing up, but if that were the case, she was a hell of a good actress. And in view of their recent discussion about lying, he doubted she was conning him. So, if she wasn't pretending, then maybe she did have some sort of odd telepathy going on with Erica. Whatever—he was in no position to judge or analyze or push her away.

Not that he wanted to push her away. In fact, for a second there he'd been tempted to yank her into his arms. Somehow he'd fought the temptation to touch her, and that was a good thing. Catherine was like a hot wire: If he got too close he would get shocked. But still he couldn't help wondering what it would be like to be inside all that passion and turmoil and energy. Would he feel what she felt? Would he see what she saw? He'd never considered sex any kind of mystical experience, but he had a feeling that with Catherine it would be out of this world.

Clearing his throat, he turned on the radio, needing something to break the silence and the tension rapidly building inside him. He searched for a news station, grateful to hear mundane topics like street closures for Sunday's open-air market and the latest weather and traffic. Being home made him feel stronger, more confident, almost normal. San Francisco was his town. He was playing on his turf now.

"This is a beautiful city," Catherine murmured. "I love the hills and the bay."

"That doesn't surprise me. You live by the beach. You must have an affinity for the water."

"I do, especially the ocean. It just keeps coming in, day after day. There's something comforting about the predictability. You grew up here, right?"

He nodded. "Yeah. I've lived here most of my life, except for the couple of years I spent across the bay with Jake and the three years I was in Sacramento when I first got out of school. For a while I wasn't sure I would come back. In some ways I felt like San Francisco was my father's town, but I decided not to let his presence prevent me from accepting a great job."

"What's that over there?" Catherine asked, pointing to a nearby pier lined with dozens of shops and restaurants as well as street performers and exhibits.

"That's Pier Thirty-nine. It's a tourist attraction: cafés, boutiques, a merry-go-round in the middle. Next to the pier is the Blue and Gold ferry that takes people out on the bay and over to Alcatraz. And coming up on your right is Fisherman's Wharf, one of the city's most famous landmarks. If we had time we could stop and get some crab. They have some of the best seafood in the world right here."

"Sounds good. Maybe after we find Erica we can celebrate."

"I like the way you say *when*, not *if*."

"I'm trying to be optimistic."

"But you're not, are you?"

"I'll feel better when we get to that building."

"It's not far." He stopped at a red light. "You know, I used to ride my bike down here when I was a kid. I hated being at home, so I'd stay out as late as possible, especially on the weekends, when my father would be around. I even learned how to juggle and walk on stilts so I could make some money."

Her eyes widened. "You put out your hat and did a little act?"

"When I was fourteen," he said with a short laugh. "Hey, I was good. The tourists loved me, especially the girls. I made some bucks."

"I'll bet you did. What did you do with all the cash?"

"Saved it for when my dad kicked me out. I knew it would happen. It was inevitable. In fact, it was a relief. Once I got out of his house I felt like a weight had slipped off of me. I was finally free."

"Did your father ever remarry?"

"No, but there were various women in his life over the years. He didn't bring them around the house much. I don't know if he was afraid we'd embarrass him or if he just wanted to keep us separate. In retrospect, I think that was it. He didn't want anyone to see the man he was at home, just the man he was at work and out at parties—the big man. Last year he started seeing a new woman; Rachel Montgomery is her name. I only know that because they've been on the society page of the newspaper a few times. And when I went by the house a few months ago, the housekeeper, Mrs. Rogers, told me that Rachel had moved into the house, so maybe she's the one for him."

"Would that bother you?"

"I don't care one way or the other. Although I hope he treats her decently." Dylan paused as the dome of the Palace of Fine Arts came into view. "Look familiar?" he asked, pointing down the street.

Catherine started and straightened in her seat. "I think that's it."

"Do you feel Erica again?" he asked, not quite sure how to phrase the question.

"No, but I never know when it's going to hit me. It comes when I least expect it. And frankly not usually in the daytime." She took a deep breath. "I'm almost afraid to let my mind wander. I'm not sure what I'll see or if I'll be able to handle it."

"You can do it. You're strong. And if you're really connecting with Erica, then you might be able to save her life."

"I'll do what I can, Dylan. I can't make any promises."

"I never ask for promises, Catherine."

"You wouldn't. Because that way no one disappoints you."

Her sharp words hit home. She was right—again.

Dylan pulled into a parking spot near the grassy field next to the dome. There were a few tourists lingering in the area, including a couple and their young son, who was dipping a toy fishing pole in and out of the lake that ran along one side of the rotunda. The Palace of Fine Arts, with its Greek and Roman architecture, had been built in the nineteen hundreds for the Pan Pacific Expo but now housed the Exploratorium. The beautiful grounds, the sloping lawn, the serene lagoon, the old rotunda with its dome and towering columns were also often used for wedding ceremonies. Dylan had watched two of his friends get married here last year. He could hardly believe he was back now trying to find the woman framing him for murder.

Catherine zipped up her sweater as they got out of the car. The fog was moving farther inland, the thick mist sliding over the top of the building, blocking out the last of the afternoon sun.

"This is definitely the place I saw in my head," Catherine murmured, taking in their surroundings.

He put a hand on her back as he scanned the perimeter. "Let's check it out."

They walked quickly to the rotunda. Once under the dome Catherine paused to look at each of the columns. After a moment's hesitation she crossed to one of them, putting her hand on the cool stone. She took another step and then slid her body into the narrow space between the column and the building. She slipped back out a second later, her breath coming short and fast. "Erica was here, hiding behind that pillar."

"There are people around. Who would try to kill her here?" Dylan pondered. "It's too public."

Catherine stared back at him for a long moment. "Something fell. I remember pulling on a chain around my neck, and . . ." Her voice drifted off as her gaze turned downward.

Dylan saw what she saw a second later: a tiny gold cross lying on the ground, almost hidden in the dark shadows. He recognized it immediately, and his heart skipped a beat. "This is Erica's. She was here." He couldn't keep the amazement out of his voice. He hadn't realized how strong his doubts about Catherine had been until this moment. Erica had been here, and Catherine had somehow seen it in her head. He'd wanted indisputable proof of her telepathy, and now he had it, because he couldn't think of any other way

Catherine could have put Erica in this location. He gazed back at Catherine's face and saw the fire burning in her cheeks, the glittering light in her eyes. "Where is Erica now?"

Catherine shook her head. "I don't know."

He held out his hand, revealing the cross. "Maybe this would help."

She didn't make any move to take the cross from his palm. In fact, she looked as if it were the last thing she wanted to do. "I can't."

"It's a direct link to Erica."

"That's what I'm scared of."

"Then put your hand over mine." He closed his fingers around the cross and waited. "Trust me, Catherine."

She looked him straight in the eye. "Do you trust me?"

"I'm trying," he said. "You have to try, too."

Catherine hesitated another second, then tentatively put her hand over his. He felt a jolt of electricity zing through him. Their gazes met, clashed, clung. He couldn't look away. She couldn't either. This moment was about more than just the cross, more than Erica. It was about whether or not they could count on each other. And it shocked him to know he wanted to be able to count on her. He hadn't felt that way about anyone in a very long time. He was tempted to yank his hand away, but he'd started this, and he had to finish it.

Catherine closed her eyes. "I can feel her heart beating," she whispered. "Fast, short, terrified. She's never been this scared."

Dylan was feeling spooked himself. The cross was growing hot in his hand, burning him with an intense heat. Was he feeling Erica's heartbeat, too, through his connection to Catherine? Or was that his own heart threatening to jump out of his chest?

Catherine opened her eyes and dropped her hand back to her side. Just like that the connection between them broke.

"She's alive—for now." Catherine let out a sigh of relief. "She's not here anymore."

"Did you see where she was?" The cross in his hand was cool now. Had he imagined its heat? *Shit!* What the hell was wrong with him?

"No, but she's hiding. That's all I could feel. I'm sorry. I know that's not very helpful."

"Not really."

"Dylan, I told you that I don't see a road map in my head. I'm not a GPS tracking device. I'm a person who gets feelings that aren't always specific. But I got us here, didn't I?"

"I don't know how you did that."

"You said you were trying to trust me. Were you just bullshitting me so I'd touch the cross?"

"No. I am trying. I'm just pissed off that nothing is working," he said, letting out a sigh. "Sorry if I took it out on you."

"Don't do it again. I'm your partner, and right now you don't have anyone else."

"I know."

Catherine shivered as a wind blew through the rotunda. "It's getting cold."

"Let's go back to the car."

"Then what?"

"My apartment," he said, making a quick decision.

"That's a little risky, isn't it?"

"Erica was there. I need to see if she left me a note or something. It's just a few blocks from here."

They were halfway to the car when Dylan's cell phone rang again. It was his attorney.

"Where the hell are you?" Mark demanded. "I told you to stay put."

"I couldn't do that. I need to find Erica before the police decide to lock me up."

"Then you'd better find her fast, because I just got a call from Detective Richardson, and he's looking for you. He said your car is in the lot, but you checked out of the lodge several hours ago and no one has seen you since. Your best bet is to go back to Tahoe and work this out. I can meet you there. You don't have to do it alone."

"My best bet is to find Erica. I know she's alive. She called me on my cell phone."

"No way. You heard from her?"

"Yes, she said she was sorry."

"That's good news. I'm happy to hear she's alive, but we need more than your word that she called you. What else did she say?"

"That she was in trouble and someone was after her. Then she hung up the phone."

"What does that mean? Who's after her besides you?"

"I suspect whoever is setting me up for her murder wants to make sure she's really dead. And I'm guessing Erica didn't realize that her death was going to be real, not fake."

"This sounds like a damn movie," Mark grumbled.

"Well, I wish I had the script so I could see what was coming next. At any rate, I can't turn myself in until I find Erica."

"Where are you?"

"It's better if you don't know. I don't want to make you an accessory, Mark."

"Dylan, I have to advise you that should the police gather enough evidence to get an arrest warrant, the fact that you ran will make your defense much more difficult."

Dylan knew that everything Mark was saying was true, but he'd made his choice, and he'd have to live with it. "I'll call you when I find Erica."

"Wait. Don't use your cell phone again. It will be too easy to trace."

Mark was right, dammit. Dylan should have thought of that already. The police had probably already figured out he was in San Francisco. "Thanks for the reminder. I'll find a way to get in touch with you."

"The police are looking for you, aren't they?" Catherine asked as he closed his phone.

"They're wondering where I am."

"Mark wants you to go back to Tahoe, doesn't he?"

"Yes, but Erica isn't there. She's in this city, and I'm not leaving until I find her. But maybe you should go, Catherine. This situation is getting worse by the minute.

It's not too late for you to disappear. You can make up a story about me stealing your car, forcing you to come with me. You don't have to do this."

"Oh, please, we are way beyond that, Dylan. I'm in. I'm all the way in." She looked directly into his eyes. "I know Erica is alive, and you didn't kill her. I won't stand by and let an innocent man go to jail."

"I hope you don't regret that decision," Dylan said.

"Me, too."

Chapter 8

Dylan's apartment was on the second floor of a three-story building in the Marina, just a few blocks from the Palace of Fine Arts. When they arrived they found his door wide-open. It appeared that the lock had been broken.

"You'd better wait here," Dylan said, his voice grim. "There could be someone inside."

"There's no one there," Catherine told him, certain as she said the words. "They're gone."

Dylan shot her a quick look. "Well, just to be sure, I'll go first."

She didn't bother to argue. Dylan had to trust his own instincts as well as hers. Despite his suggestion that she wait, she followed him inside. She was curious to see where he lived, if his home fit him. Her first impression was of a masculine yet warm space. In the living room were two soft brown leather couches, a matching reclining chair, and a big-screen plasma TV that took up most of the wall over the fireplace. Against the window was a desk holding a computer as well as a pile of newspapers and a stack of file folders. Dylan obviously brought his work home with him. On the walls were photographs of the city, many of which she suspected had been taken by Sarah. Sarah had also sent her some of her photographs. She was apparently thinking of making her longtime hobby a business.

As Catherine moved around the room she noted the details. The apartment was comfortably messy: an empty cup on the coffee table, a basketball on the floor, a sweatshirt slung over the back of a stool by the kitchen counter. She liked the feel of Dylan's home. It was casual, unpretentious, yet he had all the latest high-tech gadgets. It suited him. And nowhere did she see any sign of a woman's influence. That wasn't surprising. He was a private man, and he liked to control his environment.

It was probably easier to leave if he went home with a woman rather than inviting her here. Not that she needed to be wondering about that part of Dylan's personal life. It was certainly none of her business where he spent his nights, and in whose bed. But, of course, she wondered anyway, because she was ridiculously attracted to the man, and she knew he was not for her. He would rock her entire world, and then he'd go, and she was so tired of saying good-bye to people, especially to someone she wouldn't be able to forget. Dylan definitely fell into that category.

Focus on Erica, she told herself, watching as Dylan disappeared into his bedroom. She needed to try to connect with Erica. The woman had been here in this room. So why couldn't Catherine feel her presence?

It had to be that her mind was too cluttered. Her senses were much too aware of Dylan. She was having trouble letting anything else into her head. She took a deep breath, searching for some tiny hint of perfume lingering in the air, something that would link her to Erica, but nothing clicked.

After a moment she entered Dylan's bedroom, knowing it was probably not the best move but compelled to see where he slept. His king-size bed was unmade, the blankets tossed toward the foot of the bed, but while there were two pillows, only one showed the imprint of a head. Dylan had slept alone the last night he was here. She found that fact strangely comforting.

Dylan shut the window and locked it. "I never leave this window open. I'm going to check the living room again, see if Erica left any clue behind."

Catherine stared at the window for a moment, trying to picture someone climbing out or in, but again her brain refused to cooperate, and her gaze drifted back to the bed. As she focused on the light blue sheets and the soft pillows her pulse quickened, and she was suddenly afraid that the connection she'd been searching for was going to happen now. She knew Dylan and Erica had spent the night together six weeks ago. Had their one-night stand taken place here? The last thing she wanted was to follow Erica into Dylan's bed. She could not stand the idea that she might envision them having sex together. But as much as she wanted to leave the room, she couldn't force herself to move or even gaze away from the bed.

In her mind she could see Dylan sitting on the bed, naked from the waist up, fine golden hairs across his tanned chest. He was waiting for someone. His warm brown eyes sparkled with desire. He waved a beckoning hand and then patted the mattress next to him.

She felt herself drawn to him, the power of his confident smile, his gaze, so intense, so filled with want and need, the same emotions tumbling around inside of her. She didn't want to fight it, yet as she felt herself moving closer, she wondered if she was making a terrible mistake. He wouldn't want her forever, just for tonight.

Maybe that was enough.

It couldn't be wrong, not the way she felt. She would take whatever she could get. She would have no regrets. Nothing in her life had ever lasted forever. Why should this be any different?

She sat down on the bed, placing her palm on his abdomen, the warmth of his skin charging the heat already running through her. He was a beautifully made man with tight, supple, and powerful muscles, a man who could tear her heart apart with one kiss.

He put his hand on the back of her neck, pulling her closer until his breath caressed her cheek. Her heart skipped in anticipation. But he suddenly seemed in no hurry. His fingers curled in her hair; then his lips touched her cheek, setting off a firestorm of emotion, but it wasn't enough, not nearly enough.

Sliding her arms around his back, she turned her head, shamelessly seeking a full-on kiss. As her mouth settled against his, her stomach clenched at the sweet, hot taste. She went back for more, kissing him until she couldn't breathe, her hands moving restlessly down his spine.

Dylan groaned, taking the lead as he tossed her on her back in one quick movement. Her legs tangled in the sheets as he straddled her body. He cupped her face with his hands, then swooped in for another kiss, his tongue sliding inside her mouth, demanding everything she had to give. One of his hands dropped to her breast, kneading the soft flesh, his thumb running across her nipple, making her crazy with desire and very impatient. She'd never felt this way about anyone.

But he was pulling away, his gaze meeting hers. She was afraid he was leaving, but then she saw the seductive smile. "Catherine," he murmured.

The sound of her name sent her reeling. She wasn't seeing Erica and Dylan together. She was seeing—

"Catherine."

Dylan's voice rang out again, and she started in surprise. He wasn't half-naked in bed anymore. He was standing right next to her, fully clothed, his gaze narrowing as he took in her expression. "What did you see? You had another vision, didn't you?"

Her breath came quickly, and she struggled to slow down her racing heart. How on earth was she going to answer that question? She certainly couldn't tell him the truth.

"You saw someone in my bed. Was it Erica?" he persisted. "Were you channeling her again?" His eyes narrowed as his gaze ran across her face. "I'm going to need an answer."

"I thought it was Erica, but it wasn't," she said finally, hoping he would leave it at that. "Did you find anything in the other room? Because if not, I think we should go." She turned to leave, but he caught her by the arm.

"Hold on a second. Don't clam up on me now, Catherine."

"I didn't see anything that will help you," she told him, desperate to get away, but he had a tight grip on her arm.

"Let me be the judge of that. Come on, spill it."

"I saw you in bed with a woman, okay? Are we done?"

"I don't think so." He tilted his head to one side, his gaze thoughtful. "I didn't bring Erica here. I thought you were connected to her."

"I thought I was, too."

"What did the woman look like?"

She stared at him for a long moment. There was a spark in his eyes that told her he was asking a loaded question, a question he already knew the answer to. She wanted to say nothing, but she knew Dylan wouldn't let her go until he'd gotten everything out of her. "I saw us, you and me together. Are you satisfied?"

"I don't know—was I satisfied?" A cocky smile spread across his lips.

"It didn't go that far. We just kissed and stuff." She tried to yank her arm away, but he hung on.

"Stuff?" he echoed. "Like what?"

Her breasts tingled as she remembered the heat of his touch. She cleared her throat, trying to get a grip on her emotions. "I can't remember."

"Liar."

"Just leave it alone."

"You know I never leave anything alone. So you and I are going to go to bed together in the future, right? You said your visions always come true. If you saw us in bed, then—"

"I could have just been imagining it, not seeing a vision from the future." She thought she'd grabbed a great explanation, but as the words came out of her mouth she realized neither scenario worked out well for her. Because she shouldn't have been thinking about him in that way at all.

"You don't have to imagine, you know."

She swallowed hard at the look in his eyes. "Dylan," she said, not sure what else she wanted to say. Should she tell him to stop, to let go, or to pull her closer, to kiss her like he'd kissed her in her vision?

Dylan didn't give her a chance to decide, his mouth descending on hers with passion and purpose. The real thing was so much better than her dream. She opened her mouth to his, their tongues tangling in a dance of heat and desire. The spark that had been smoldering since their first meeting burst into a full blaze as she went fully into his arms. She slipped her hands under his shirt. She wanted to touch him, to taste him, to strip off his clothes. There was nothing else in her mind but him, and she relished the pure focus of her thoughts.

She banished the rolling edges of reason trying to make their way back into her brain, the tiny voice saying this wasn't the right place or the right time. It felt right, dammit. It felt like what she'd been waiting for her whole life. She wanted him. He wanted her.

So why was he pulling away? This wasn't how it was supposed to go.

"Catherine, God, we have to stop." Dylan forced her from him, his chest heaving with rough, ragged breaths.

She stared at him in shock, still dazed from his kiss, unable to comprehend why they were no longer touching.

Dylan dug his hands into his pockets. "We can't do this now."

His words seeped slowly into her brain. Embarrassment came with the realization that she'd completely lost her mind a moment earlier. Of course they couldn't do this now. Erica was missing. Someone was setting Dylan up for murder. What on earth had she been thinking?

She hadn't been thinking. That was the problem. She'd thrown herself at him and made a huge fool of herself. "You're right. I'm sorry."

"Don't apologize, Catherine, and get that damn look off your face. I wanted you, too."

"But you remembered where we were, and I didn't. I got lost in the dream."

"It wasn't a dream. It was real. And it's going to happen between us." He drew in a deep breath. "But not here. Not now."

"No," she agreed. She took a step back. She needed space, air. She needed a new brain. Having sex with Dylan was not on the agenda; nor should it be, not now, not ever, despite the promise he'd just made. He was too much for her. She'd get lost in him, and she'd never find her way out. She tucked her hair behind her ears and shifted her feet. "We should go."

"This isn't over," he said.

"Yes, it is, Dylan. That was a moment of temporary insanity. I won't let it happen again."

"You won't be able to resist, Catherine." He gave her a wicked smile. "Let's just say I had a vision, too."

She was still trying to think of a good reply when Dylan brushed past her. After a moment she followed him into the living room, her heart finally settling into a more normal rhythm, although she was still warm and flushed. She'd never had dream sex in the middle of the day while standing in a man's bedroom, and it disturbed her that she was so connected to Dylan that she could lose track of herself and her surroundings so easily. If Dylan hadn't stopped, she certainly wouldn't have.

Of course, if he'd kept going she'd be feeling calm and satisfied instead of restless and on edge. It thoroughly annoyed her that Dylan was already moving on to the next task, as if what had happened between them were no big deal.

"I found my keys," Dylan said. He stood next to the phone, holding up his key ring. "These were on the floor. I didn't see them when we first came in. I guess that's how Erica got in here. She must have taken them out of my pocket last night when she got my room key. I just wonder why she came. What did she want? What did she think she would find in my apartment? Or was it just a place for her to hide?"

Catherine drew in a deep breath and slowly let it out, forcing her mind back to the situation at hand. "She wouldn't have planned to hide here for long. She would have known the police would eventually get around to searching this place."

"So perhaps she just wanted to make it clear that she was here." He glanced around the room again. "I don't see anything of hers, nothing that she obviously planted, although I haven't gone through every drawer and closet."

"She might not have had time. She left in a hurry. I think we should go, too."

"Let me grab some clothes in case I can't get back here for a while." Dylan moved into the bedroom, returning a few minutes later with a packed sports bag.

"So where are we headed?" she asked as they left his apartment and walked down the stairs. She was relieved to be out of Dylan's house. She didn't want to think any more about what had almost happened between them. She needed to concentrate on what they needed to do to find Erica and get Dylan out of the trouble he was in.

"My grandmother's house," he replied, surprising her.

"Are you serious? We can't go to a family home."

"Relax. It's the perfect place. My grandmother doesn't share my last name. She remarried about ten years ago, and she took her second husband's name. The house belonged to him, so it would take some in-depth investigating to tie her house to me. She also has a car that we can use, since we should probably get yours out of sight."

"This is your grandmother who's in the rest home?" she asked, feeling better about his plan.

"That's right. She has a small house in the Sunset District that no one is using. I have a key, as I occasionally go over there and make sure the cleaning service and gardeners are keeping up with everything."

"What happened to your grandmother's husband?"

"He died about three years ago."

"Are you close to her?"

"Somewhat. She's a good woman. Although it's hard to believe she and my father actually share the same blood. She's generous to a fault. He's a selfish bastard. Her one flaw was that she couldn't see my father for what he was, so I couldn't tell her what he did to me. I tried a few times, but she always turned it around. I guess she couldn't go down that road."

Catherine nodded. A lot of people looked away when it came to abuse. No one wanted to see it or admit that someone they knew could do something so horrible. And despite Dylan's casual manner now, it must have hurt him when he realized that no one was coming to his rescue. At least he'd had his brother.

Dylan stopped the car at a red light and glanced over at her. "On another note, are you hungry?"

Her stomach immediately rumbled in response.

"Now that you mention it, I'm starving. Breakfast was a long time ago."

"There's a very good Italian restaurant not far from my grandmother's house, Antonio's. We can pick something up on our way in."

"That sounds good. What are you going to do about your job, Dylan?"

"I don't have to be at work until Monday. If we haven't found Erica by then I'll take a sick day. I'm just hoping the newsroom doesn't pick up on this story."

"Lake Tahoe is a long way from here."

"Yes, but the prime suspect in the disappearance of a San Francisco woman in Tahoe is KTSF's lead reporter. How's that for a sound bite?"

"Very good. I'm just glad you kept me out of it."

He shot her a pointed look. "I'll try, Catherine, but I can't promise that you'll stay out of it. Before this is through you could very well be an accessory to murder—or worse."

"I don't want to know what 'worse' is," she said.

"But you already do, don't you?"

She hadn't seen a vision, but her gut told her that Erica might not be the only person who was supposed to end up dead.

A half hour later Catherine was distracted from her negative thoughts by their arrival at Dylan's grandmother's house. Set on the corner, the light blue structure shared sidewalls with its neighbor. The house was located about a half mile from the beach, and

Catherine could smell the salty sea air as they got out of the car.

There was an ominous feeling to the sky now. The sun had set, and a heavy mist thickened the air. Catherine felt as if the whole world were closing in on them, the trap tightening with each passing moment. She tried to tell herself that she was being paranoid, letting her imagination get away from her, but the shiver that raised the hairs on the back of her neck was almost never wrong. Something bad was going to happen. She just didn't know when.

Once they were inside the house, Dylan flipped on a small lamp on a table next to the door. "We'll eat in the kitchen," he said. "It's at the back of the house, and it won't be as obvious that anyone is here, although the neighbors are elderly and probably wouldn't notice if there was a party going on."

Dylan's grandmother's house smelled like potpourri, a little bit sweet and kind of sad, Catherine thought as she entered the kitchen. She set the bags of food they'd picked up from Antonio's on a rectangular oak table in the middle of the room. The kitchen was dated, the white cabinets scratched and yellowed, the tile worn, the appliances from a decade ago. The house seemed a little lonely without its owner. "How long has it been since your grandmother lived here?"

"Almost a year. I don't think she'll ever be back. Alzheimer's has her in its grip."

"I'm surprised you've kept the house going, the electricity, the water, the gardener. That must take some money."

"Not that much. My father has power of attorney, and quite frankly, I think he's too busy to care about this place. He's just going to leave things as they are until she dies. He rarely even visits her anymore." Dylan paused. "If you want to eat, go ahead. I'm going to put your car in the garage and move my grandmother's car out to the street."

"Do you want me to help?"

"No, I'll take care of it."

After Dylan left, Catherine set the two foil containers on the table, as well as the bread and butter and packets of Parmesan cheese and hot peppers, but she didn't bother to open them. She felt an intense desire to explore the house. Not sure where the need came from, she decided not to question her instincts but to just follow them.

Moving quietly through the first floor, she peeked into the living and dining rooms. Both were small but impeccably neat, with antique furniture, and lacy doilies on the end tables. A den on the first floor was filled with books and dark furniture: probably a room that had once belonged to the man of the house.

Heading upstairs she discovered two bedrooms and a bath. She entered the master bedroom and turned on the small lamp by the bed, inhaling the lingering scent of lavender that still hung in the air. Across the foot of the bed a floral quilt paid tribute to his grandmother's obvious love of flowers, which were featured in many of the wall hangings as well as the wallpaper trim.

Catherine paused by the bedside table, perusing the

family photographs on display. The one that made her heart skip a beat was of two boys and a man. It was Dylan, Jake, and their father, she realized. Dylan was thin and gangly, not really a boy, not yet a man. He was probably about thirteen in the photo. The man standing in the middle was dressed in a navy blue suit, his face austere, his hand on Jake's shoulder. Dylan stood a foot apart from Jake and his father, as if he didn't think he belonged in the photograph. His expression was somber, almost pleading.

Something inside of her wanted to touch that lonely little boy, take him into her arms, tell him he'd never stand alone again. But she couldn't go back in time, and the man Dylan had become would never admit to being that vulnerable child. She understood his need to be strong now, to take back his life from the bully who had stolen too many years already. But she suspected that his emotional barriers also prevented him from letting anyone in, even someone who might care about him. He wasn't a man who could trust anyone or anything. He certainly didn't trust her—another reason she should not open up her body or her heart to him. Unlike Dylan she'd never been able to lock the emotions away, and they still tormented her.

It had been four years since she'd let herself care about a man, and that man had left her—just like all the others. She was too different, too crazy, too hot, too cold. She'd heard her flaws recited over and over again, until she'd almost started to believe her bad press. But once he'd left she'd realized that she was happier without him. She had her animals for company, and it wasn't the worst thing to live alone in a beautiful cottage on the beach. She had her art, her classes, some friends, good neighbors, people who liked her from afar.

She smiled to herself at that thought. People always liked her from a distance. But when they got closer they realized she was just too much for them. No one could handle her visions or her nightmares or the screams she suddenly let loose in the middle of the night. The truth was that she'd been damaged a long time ago, and no one ever wanted someone who was broken. They wanted perfect, pretty, easy, uncomplicated, and she'd never been any of those things.

"What are you doing?" Dylan asked, startling her.

She set the photograph on the table. "Just looking around," she said, feeling suddenly guilty.

"It's okay. You can look," he said.

"I'm intruding on your grandmother's privacy," she said, knowing it wasn't really his grandmother's life she was interested in, but his.

"My grandmother doesn't know what's going on in the world, much less her own house. Even if she did, she wouldn't care. She didn't have anything to hide."

Catherine wondered if that was true. "Everyone has secrets, Dylan. Some people just hide them better than others."

He gave her a long look. "Are you picking up on something in particular?"

"Just the feeling that we're supposed to be here. That there's something we need to find."

"What could there possibly be in this house that has anything to do with Erica?"

She couldn't explain. "I don't know. Maybe it's something that has to do with you."

Dylan shook his head, letting out a sigh of exasperation. "I'm too tired and hungry to figure that out right now. Let's eat."

"I'll be down in a minute." She was reluctant to leave. She moved over to the desk by the window, aware that Dylan had not left the room. He was watching her. She put her hand on top of the desk, then trailed her fingers down to the second drawer. She opened it and pulled out a photo album.

"Stop," Dylan said abruptly. "You don't need to take a trip down my memory lane."

"I don't, but I think you do."

"Catherine—"

"Dylan, you said you were going to try to trust me." She set the album on the desk and opened it. Most of the early photos were probably of Dylan's grandmother, her generation of family, but as the pages turned the family aged. And suddenly she came to a wedding photograph of a young couple—the same man who was in the photo with Dylan, his father. The man's arm was around his beautiful, blushing bride, a woman who shared Dylan's features, had his brown hair, his golden brown eyes.

She turned to Dylan. She knew he could see the photograph from where he stood in the doorway, his hands on his hips, his features hard and unyielding, unforgiving. "This is your mother, isn't it?"

He didn't move a muscle, and for a moment she didn't think he would speak.

Finally he said, "I didn't realize a picture of her still existed. My father got rid of all the ones in our house the day she left."

"Do you want it?"

"No. I don't need a picture of a woman who left me behind." He put up a hand as she started to speak. "Leave it alone, Catherine. My mother is not part of this."

Catherine's hand grazed the photograph as she started to close the album. A surge of heat swept through her.

A woman cried, her heart breaking in two. Her tears fell in big drops on the sandy wood deck. A pair of child's sandals lay nearby, along with a red bucket and an orange shovel. The porch swing creaked with each sad, painful arc. In the distance the tide came in, bringing with it more regret.

Things would never be the same. She couldn't go back. She couldn't change what had happened. And no one would ever forgive her.

Catherine shut the book and slipped it back into the desk drawer, her heart beating in double time. She must be so tuned in to Dylan that she could feel anyone connected to him, including his long-lost mother. She was almost positive that his mother was the woman she'd seen in her head—maybe not seen, but felt. There had been so much pain in her soul she'd barely been able to breathe. What on earth had happened to destroy what had begun so happily in the wedding photo?

Turning, she caught Dylan staring at her. There was a

battle going on in his eyes. He wanted to know, and yet he didn't. In the end he left, shutting the door behind him, as if he could somehow put a solid barrier between himself and his past. But that was just an illusion. Someday the past would catch up to him, no matter how far he ran.

When she left the room she found Dylan standing in the middle of the hallway. She'd thought he'd be downstairs by now.

"Why did you look in the desk?" he demanded. "Why that drawer? That photo album? That page?"

"I just had a feeling I should."

"My mother is not connected to any of this."

"She's connected to you, and so am I."

He shook his head, anger in his eyes. "I'm not going down that road right now, Catherine. I have enough on my plate. Maybe I'll look for her someday, but not today. She's been gone for twenty-three years. She can stay gone a little longer. From now on my mother is off-limits."

The lingering sound of his mother's sobs filled Catherine's mind. She didn't know if the crying was from years ago or from a more recent period. But one thing she knew for sure was that Dylan's mother had not been happy. She'd suffered for something. Her heart had been broken.

"Damn you," Dylan swore. "Stop thinking about her. I can see it in your face."

"See what?" she challenged.

"That you want to tell me something about my mother. Well, I don't want to hear it. I'll let you know if

I change my mind. Until then, keep your visions to yourself and your mouth shut. Got it?" He didn't wait for her answer. He jogged down the stairs, as if he couldn't get away fast enough, but Catherine knew that she wasn't the one he was running from.

Chapter 9

While he ate dinner Dylan tried to get his parents' wedding photograph out of his mind, but no matter what he'd told Catherine he couldn't stop thinking about it or his mother. Seeing his parents together, in love at the beginning of their lives, had rattled him. He couldn't remember those days. That past wasn't in his memory. And he wasn't sure he wanted it there now.

Why had Catherine been drawn to that particular photo? She'd flipped the pages as if she were seeking exactly that one. A very cynical part of him wondered if she was just part of the setup. Someone could have bought her off as well as Erica.

That plan could have been to have Erica disappear and Catherine torture him with secret visions about his past. Maybe she'd taken him to the Palace of Fine Arts because she knew that was where Erica would leave the cross. She could be working for his enemy while pretending to be his friend.

He picked up his beer and took a large gulp, studying her face in the soft light of the kitchen, and knew that while he didn't want to believe in her or her crazy visions, he did—against all reason, all logic, everything he knew about life and the world. There was something inside of him that told him to accept the fact that Catherine was tuned in to the world in a very special and unique way.

"Just eat," Catherine said. "Stop thinking so much."

"You're making me crazy," he told her. "I really wish you hadn't found that photo. My parents are not a part of this, especially my mother, who has been gone forever."

Catherine set down her fork as she finished her plate of pasta and vegetables. "You don't know who's a part of it. You should keep an open mind. Follow the trail wherever it goes."

"And your sixth sense is supposed to be my conductor?"

"You could say that," she told him with a smile.

"I need to rely on my own eyes, my own instincts," he protested.

"I get that, Dylan. But you might as well use me. I'm here."

She didn't want to know how badly he wanted to use her.

"I didn't mean it that way," she said quickly.

He frowned at how easily she'd read his expression, but then again, it was becoming more and more difficult to keep her out of his mind. "Stop getting into my head," he ordered.

"If you want me to do that, stop thinking all the time about you and me having sex. You're not that good at hiding your thoughts."

"I was before I met you," he complained. "I used to be the best poker player in the neighborhood. When I was sixteen I'd clean up with Jake's friends. No one had a better bluff than me."

"We're not playing cards." She put up a hand. "And if you're thinking about suggesting a quick game of strip poker to test your poker face, think again."

He laughed. "Okay, you are good. Have you ever played strip poker?"

"No, but I'm fairly sure I'd win."

"Why is that?"

"Because I can read people's expressions. And everyone has a tell, something that reveals what they're thinking. My friend Andy, he was a great con artist. He taught me how to look for signs that show someone is nervous or confident or extremely happy about the cards they were dealt. You, for instance, get a little spark in your eyes when you're turned on."

"Really? I must be shooting out fireworks right about now, then," he drawled, enjoying the flush that reddened her cheeks. "And your tell is that your face turns red every time you get excited or scared. Which is it now?"

"You're not turning the tables on me."

"I think I am." He leaned forward, resting his elbows on the table. "You try to be blunt, in my face, but then you back off, as if it's not really your true nature to be so direct. But it is mine."

"It's also your nature to redirect the conversation away from yourself to whoever is sitting across from you."

"Touché."

"And the only reason you're flirting with me is so you won't have to think about that photo that's in the drawer upstairs."

"That's not the only reason. And you know it."

She met his gaze and gave a reluctant nod. "I do know it, but I don't want to get hurt again."

"Again?" he queried, realizing it was the first time she'd volunteered anything about her past romantic life.

"There you go, trying to get into my life when yours is the one we're supposed to be figuring out."

"I wouldn't hurt you, Catherine." Even as he said the words, he wondered if they were true.

"I'm not talking about a physical hurt, Dylan. But I like you, and if I have sex with you I might fall in love with you, and you wouldn't want that. You'd leave. And I've been left many times in my life. I don't want it to happen again. How's that for direct?"

His gut clenched at the image of them together. Catherine wasn't the only one who could envision them in bed together. But he could also see himself leaving, because he didn't do love. He didn't do commitment. He couldn't afford to give up any of his power to another person, especially not a woman who claimed to be able to see into his head.

"So, back to Erica," Catherine said.

He wasn't quite ready to move on, but he could see

by the resolve in her eyes that she was. "Back to Erica," he echoed. But his mind wasn't really on the missing brunette. It was still on Catherine, on what she hadn't told him, and what he knew he needed to ask, even though his every instinct said not to go there. "When you touched the photo album before, you jerked as if you'd seen something."

"I thought you didn't want to talk about your mother."

"Just tell me before I change my mind."

"She was sitting on a porch swing looking out at the ocean. She was crying. She felt tremendous regret, but also a weary resignation that she couldn't change what had happened."

His chest squeezed so tight he could barely catch his breath. "Are you sure it was my mother?" he asked, struggling to get the words out.

"Yes."

He looked away from Catherine's penetrating gaze, trying to absorb what she'd just told him. He couldn't compute what she'd said and what he knew about the past. And a part of him didn't want to let go of the anger he held toward his mother. He didn't want to soften his attitude. He didn't want to think of her as being sad. Maybe she deserved to be unhappy, to have regrets. She'd left her children behind.

"She probably should be crying," he said harshly. "She wasn't exactly mother of the year."

"But you don't really know her story, do you?" Catherine asked, compassion in her eyes.

He wished he could say that he did, but he remembered little about his mother or his life before she left. "I know enough. The facts speak for themselves."

"The facts don't always tell the whole story."

"Why are you defending her? I thought you, of all people, would understand what it's like to grow up without a mother, although you haven't told me what happened to yours. Did she leave you? Did she die? What's her story? What about your father? What happened to him? How did you end up in foster care without anyone?"

Catherine shrank back in her seat with each pounding question. Her face paled under the attack. "Dylan, stop."

"You want to dig into my life, then I'll dig into yours." He felt a twinge of regret as pain fluttered through her eyes. He knew he was taking out his frustration and fear on her, but he couldn't stop himself. She'd brought him to a place he didn't want to be, and he didn't know how to get out.

After a moment Catherine straightened in her chair. She lifted her chin, her eyes refocusing on his. "Nice try. You do know how to go for the jugular, don't you? But I'm not going to stand in as a punching bag for your mother. So stop attacking me. I didn't hurt you. She did."

He let out a sigh. "I'm sorry."

"You should be." She stood up and took her empty food container to the counter. "Do you know where the trash bags are?"

It was such a mundane question and an abrupt

change of subject, it took him a moment to catch up. "Under the sink, if there are any."

She pulled out a white plastic bag and opened it, then dumped her container. Crossing the room, she cleared off the rest of the table and set the bag on the floor. "We should remember to take this out before we leave, since no one may come here for a while."

"Good idea." He paused. "I am sorry. You're right. I jumped on you, and I shouldn't have, but that doesn't change the fact that I'm very curious about your background."

Something wavered in her eyes. "I never talk about my past, not with anyone."

"I'm not just anyone," he told her.

"I know," she admitted. "But right now we have to think about Erica and how to find her." Catherine sat down at the table. "What about Erica's friends? She might have told one of them something."

"I've been thinking about that. One of the other Metro Club hostesses, Joanna, lived next door to Erica. She was probably the closest to her. Although I'm not sure what happened to their relationship after Erica ratted out Ravino. I know the club kicked Erica out. She may have lost her girlfriends there as well. No one likes a snitch."

"Erica risked a lot to talk to you," Catherine commented.

"Because she feared for her life. She thought Ravino could come after her, but in the end I guess she did give up a lot." He was surprised he'd never considered that before. He'd been so intent on getting the story he

hadn't really thought about Erica's involvement beyond what she could do for him. He'd used her to get to
the truth, and the realization left him with a bad taste in
his mouth. Maybe there was more of his father in him
than he'd realized. That disturbing revelation made
him pick up his beer and drain it to the last drop.

"You didn't make her talk," Catherine said.

"Trying to let me off the hook?" he drawled. "Why
don't you say I'm a ruthless, selfish bastard?"

Catherine smiled. "I don't have to, because you just
did. But whatever the reason, Erica did the right thing
by telling the truth. If Senator Ravino killed his wife,
then he deserves to pay. And you should be glad you
got involved. I'm just wondering if the fallout affected
Erica in such a way that she had to go along with this
plan to set you up. Someone has to know what she's
been up to the last two months. I think we should talk
to Joanna."

"I agree. We'll go to Erica's apartment and kill two
birds with one stone."

Catherine frowned. "It's a risk, don't you think?
What if the police are watching her place?"

"Doubtful. Even if they did a drive-by to check on
her, they wouldn't have cause to break in, especially
since she's been gone less than twenty-four hours. I
think we have some time. But if you want to stay here, I
understand."

"Are you kidding me? I'm not staying behind. Where
you go, I go. Besides, if you're thinking of knocking on
Erica's neighbor's door, I might get farther than you. If
Erica suffered repercussions from her snitching, I can't

imagine that you would receive a warm reception from anyone who worked for the Metro Club."

"Good point."

"Thank you," she said with a smile. "And I have another idea. I think you should wear a disguise. You're on television. You're very recognizable, and right now that's the last thing we want. Do you think your grandmother's husband left any clothes behind?"

"I can certainly check," he said, smiling back at her. Catherine was definitely pulling her weight as a partner. He was beginning to wonder why he'd ever liked working alone. "I'll look in the hall closet. You might want to put a hat over that gorgeous hair of yours. It's not exactly forgettable." He saw the glitter of surprise in her eyes. "You don't know how beautiful you are, do you?"

"I'm not . . . not beautiful," she said, stumbling over the words. "I have freckles and pale skin."

"And beautiful breasts and gorgeous eyes and a very nice pair of hips." As he'd expected and hoped, a delicious flush spread across her cheeks. He wondered if the rest of her body would show such heat.

"Stop that," she told him. "You are very bad, Dylan."

"I'd like to be." He laughed at her expression, a mix of curiosity and dismay.

"You're good with the lines, aren't you?"

"I'm good with a lot of things."

She rolled her eyes. "And quite full of yourself—not your most attractive quality. I'm going to look for a disguise. We'll need to find a big hat to fit that enormous head of yours." She got up from her chair and headed into the hallway. She was already rifling through the clothes when he got there.

Dylan wasn't surprised to see that his grandmother had kept not one but a half dozen of her deceased husband's jackets, as well as some baseball caps and fishing hats. She'd always been a pack rat.

Catherine handed him a tan fishing cap and a bulky brown corduroy jacket. She put on one of his grandmother's black peacoats and covered her hair with a blue floral scarf.

"Sexy," he said with a sarcastic grin, as her outfit added twenty pounds to her frame and twenty years to her age. "You're going to look hot when you're old."

"Stop flirting with me, Gramps," she chided.

He laughed, and for a moment the weight he'd been carrying for the past twenty-four hours eased. "At least with these outfits we'll look right at home in my grandmother's fifteen-year-old Ford Taurus."

"Just don't speed. It will ruin the illusion," she told him as they left the house.

"Hey, when I'm old I still plan to be driving in the fast lane," he said as they got into the car. "I'm not going to let anything slow me down." Catherine gave him a thoughtful look. "What did I say now?" he asked, wishing he could read her mind as well as she seemed to read his.

"I was just thinking how I slowed myself down years ago, and how I've been living like a hermit for way too long," she said.

He was surprised by her revelation, and by the fact

that she'd actually given him the opening to ask a personal question. "Why have you been doing that?"

She shrugged. "I don't know."

"Yes, you do. Come on; tell me."

"I guess I thought that if I hid myself away, the dreams wouldn't be able to find me, but they always do. And I'm tired of living in the shadows, afraid to go into the light, afraid to be myself. I haven't been in the fast lane for a very long time. I want to get back there, I think. Well, maybe not all the way to the fast lane, but the second to the slow lane would be a start," she amended.

He smiled and impulsively leaned over and kissed her mouth. He was tempted to linger, to bring her fully awake, but he would need a lot more time to do it right. "I suppose you want to drive now," he said.

"Would you let me?" she asked with a gleam in her eye. "Or would it kill you to be in the passenger seat?"

"It would kill me, but for you I'd do it."

This time Catherine leaned in and kissed him. "Thanks, but I don't need to drive. I just need you to be willing to let me."

"I'll never understand the way women think."

She laughed. "You don't have to. Let's go, old man. We're not getting any younger."

Twenty minutes later Dylan parked down the street from Erica's condo. The new development was in the trendy South of Market area, where a lot of young singles lived. As they left the car Dylan and Catherine strolled arm in arm down the block, as if they were an older couple out for an evening walk. As they passed Erica's front door Catherine looked for any sign of police activity, but there was no yellow tape on the door, no police cruisers nearby, nor were there any lights on inside the condo.

"What do you want to do?" Catherine asked.

"That's Joanna's place," Dylan said, tipping his head toward the condo next to Erica's.

"How do you know that?"

"Research. There's a light on. Hopefully she's home. Are you still up for it?"

"Absolutely." Catherine felt a tingle of excitement at the challenge ahead of her.

"Make sure you push as much as you can. Ask her about Erica's male friends, her finances, visitors to her house, and her family. Don't let her sidestep the questions."

"I won't."

"What exactly are you going to say?"

"I'll figure that out when she answers the door." She could see by Dylan's disgruntled face that he wasn't happy with her answer.

"You have to have a plan of attack," he said. "Maybe I should do it."

"I can handle it. Trust me."

"All right," he said slowly. "I guess I'll wait down at the corner at the Java Hut."

"Order me some tea and maybe some for yourself. You are way too wound up." She gave him a gentle push.

"You and your damn tea," he grumbled as he

stomped off, looking decidedly younger and sprier than his clothing suggested. So much for staying in character.

Deciding it was time to change her look, Catherine pulled off her scarf and her coat, tossing them over one arm as she knocked on Joanna's door. She wanted to look more like a peer of Erica's than her maiden aunt.

A moment later a striking blonde with long legs and big boobs opened the door. She was dressed in a jean miniskirt and a bright red tank top that showed off her cleavage. Dylan would have died and gone to heaven, Catherine thought. He was really going to be sorry he'd given her this job.

"Yes?" the woman asked.

"Are you Joanna?"

"Who wants to know?"

"I'm Catherine, a friend of Erica's," she replied. "I went to high school with her, and I came up from Bakersfield to visit her, but she's not answering the door, and I've been waiting over an hour. I was wondering if you know where she is. She mentioned you were one of her friends."

"Yes," Joanna said, her wary expression softening somewhat. "But I don't know where she is or why she'd have you meet her tonight. She told me she was going out of town when I ran into her the other day. She said she needed a break before the trial starts in a couple of weeks."

"Right, the trial," Catherine echoed. "Erica told me she's been really stressed about that, but she never mentioned leaving town. Where would she have gone?

I'd really like to find her. I'm very concerned about her. She hasn't been herself lately. You don't have a key to her place, do you?"

Joanna stiffened. "I can't let you in. I don't know you."

"Of course you don't," Catherine said with a reassuring smile, realizing she'd moved a bit too fast. "Maybe you could go in and just see if she left any brochures out or reservation confirmations on a notepad or anything like that." She paused, trying to sound like a worried friend. "I guess I could go to the police and ask them. Maybe they could get the key from you."

She could see by the sudden light that passed through Joanna's eyes that the last thing she wanted was the police at her door.

"No, don't do that," Joanna said. "I guess I could check her place. Hang on a second." She walked over to a table in her entryway and took some keys out of a drawer. She pulled her own door shut and then led Catherine to Erica's condo.

Catherine would have preferred to go in alone, but at least she was getting in. That was something. She felt a jolt of adrenaline as Joanna opened the door. With any luck Catherine could find a clue to Erica's whereabouts. Her optimism faded as she took in the state of the apartment, the upturned laundry basket on the living room couch, the open door to the hall closet revealing empty hangers. She had the feeling Erica had packed up and left in a hurry.

She walked over to the couch and picked up a white

jean jacket that had been left behind. An image flashed in her head, taking her back into the past.

She dug through the laundry basket, slipping her hand into the pocket of every pair of pants, every coat. It was gone. Panic ran through her. She couldn't have lost it. Then relief washed away the fear as her fingers closed around the cool metal. She pulled out the key. Attached to the ring was a small piece of paper and the numbers 374. Scribbled in ink were the directions: right after the bridge, left on Falcon, pink flowers in the window box. She would be safe there. No one would find her. She would be free to start again.

Catherine blinked as Joanna's voice sent the image from her mind.

"I found this brochure on her desk," Joanna said.

Catherine turned toward the other woman and took the folder from her hand. It showed a resort in Hawaii. Was that where Erica had gone, number three seven four?

"I'll check the bedroom quickly, and then I really have to go," Joanna said.

While Joanna disappeared into the other room, Catherine moved to the kitchen counter, her gaze settling on the pad by the phone. Erica had jotted down a number, but there was no name attached to it. It could mean nothing, or it could be important. Catherine ripped off the page and stuffed it in the pocket of her jeans. Then she saw Erica's checkbook. Her heart began to pound. Erica's bankbook might show who was paying her. She swiped it off the counter and stuffed it in between the layers of her coat as Joanna returned to the room, shaking her head.

"Nothing else," Joanna said. "She must be in Hawaii."

"I'll give this place a call," Catherine replied as Joanna ushered her to the front door. "Maybe she just forgot to tell me or got the dates of my trip mixed up."

"She's had a lot on her mind," Joanna said. "Frankly I wouldn't be surprised if she never came back here, after what happened. You can't bite the hand that feeds you, especially when it belongs to a senator. Did she tell you what she did?"

"Yes. She got trapped in a bad situation," Catherine said slowly. "She feels terrible about everything that happened."

"She never should have talked to that reporter. She should have kept her mouth shut. I thought she was smarter than that."

"She was afraid she'd be next," Catherine said. "I hope nothing has happened to her now."

For the first time a shadow passed through Joanna's blue eyes. "I hope not, too. But I'm sure she's just lying on a beach somewhere, drinking a margarita and working on her tan." Joanna locked Erica's door behind them. "If Erica comes back I'll tell her you were here."

"Thanks. I'd appreciate it."

Catherine let out a breath of relief as Joanna returned to her condo. She walked down the street quickly, quite satisfied with herself. She'd actually stepped outside of her safe zone and taken a risk, and it felt good. It felt as if she were living again, instead of hiding in the shadows. And it was about damn time.

When she reached the Java Hut she found Dylan pacing impatiently by the front window. "What happened?" he demanded.

"Where's my tea?"

He tipped his head to the cup on the nearby table. "It's probably cold by now. It took you long enough."

"Because I did a good job," she said with a proud smile.

"I saw you got into Erica's condo. How did you manage that?"

"I told Joanna I was worried about Erica. She found this brochure. She said Erica told her she was going on vacation and this is probably where."

Dylan took the flyer from her hand. "Hawaii, huh? I doubt she's managed to get that far, but perhaps that's where she's headed."

"I got a couple of other things." Catherine pulled out Erica's checkbook and saw Dylan's eyes light up. "Not bad, huh?"

"Not bad at all. With her account number I might be able to find a money trail between her and whoever paid her to set me up."

"This was written on a pad by her phone." Catherine handed him the piece of paper. "I don't know who the number belongs to, but maybe it's important." She took a quick breath. "And I had a vision of Erica digging through her pockets for a key. There was a torn piece of paper attached to the ring, and the numbers three, seven, four. There were also some directions: right after the bridge, left on Falcon, pink flowers in the window box," she said, trying to remember every word. "I don't know where the key goes—maybe to a room at the Hawaiian resort." She opened her purse and pulled out her memo pad as she finished speaking. "I'd better write it down before I forget." She quickly jotted down the directions.

"You did good," Dylan said with an impressed nod.

"I know," she said, unable to keep the pleased note out of her voice. "And I think I deserve a reward."

"I already got you your tea."

"I was thinking of something a little more interesting."

"Oh, yeah? Like what?"

She threw her arms around his neck and pressed her mouth against his, letting herself go, savoring the heat of his mouth, the dizzy spin her head took with each kiss. She wanted to go on kissing him for a long time, but the shrill clatter of the cappuccino machine reminded her where she was.

Pulling away, she said, "Thanks," with a breathless smile.

His eyes darkened as his hands gripped her waist. "Why are you thanking me?"

"For letting me do that on my own, when you really wanted to be the one to question Joanna. I finally feel like I'm helping you." She paused. "It's probably difficult for you to believe, but I used to fight for myself when I was a kid. I was pretty scrappy. I don't know what happened to me. I guess I got tired. I lost my way. I started to let the nightmares rule my life. I gave up. But today, in a small way, I took a step toward getting my life back. Because you let me."

"Because you demanded that I let you," he corrected. "I didn't give you anything."

"You're just being nice now."

"By admitting I'm not a generous man?" he asked with a quirk of his brow.

She smiled. "By letting me take all the credit."

"Well, hopefully these clues you found will allow us both to get our lives back."

Chapter 10

Several hours later Dylan's optimism began to fade. The telephone number Catherine had taken from Erica's apartment had rung through to a voice mail, a standard answering-service message, not a personal one. Rather than leave a message, he'd tried to match a name to the number using the Internet, but hadn't had any luck. The Hawaiian resort had no reservation for Erica, so that was a dead end, too.

While Dylan was on the computer, Catherine had gone through Erica's checkbook, jotting down anything that looked intriguing or suspicious. After skimming the entries Dylan couldn't find any clues. The bottom line was that they were no closer to finding Erica.

He sat back in the chair behind his grandmother's desk and stretched his arms high over his head, letting out a weary sigh. Catherine settled back in the chair across from him and yawned, reminding him that they'd both had a hellishly long day.

"You should go to bed," he told her, the innocent suggestion sending an unexpected jolt through his system as his mind quickly flashed forward to Catherine in bed, her beautiful hair spread across the pillow. No matter how many times he tried to distract himself, the chemistry between them continued to sizzle. Well, it would have to slow-cook for a while. He needed to stay focused on finding Erica, and it was already clear to him that one kiss from Catherine would take his head right out of the game.

"I think I will turn in," Catherine said, a brisk note in her voice as she stood up, carefully avoiding his gaze. "I'll use the guest bedroom upstairs. You can have your grandmother's room."

"You don't want to share?" he asked provocatively, knowing he was playing with fire, but unable to resist.

"That would be a bad idea."

"Would it?"

His question hung between them for far too long. He hadn't intended it to be serious . . . or maybe he had.

"Yes," she said finally.

He felt a wave of disappointment, which he quickly masked with a sharp clearing of his throat. "I'll be in here. The couch is fine for me." The last thing he wanted to do was sleep in his grandmother's room, where the damn photo album lay. Nor did he want to be close enough to Catherine to change his mind about staying away from her. A good floor between them couldn't hurt.

"If you hear any screaming in the middle of the night, don't get too alarmed," Catherine said.

"I thought you just heard screams. I didn't realize you did the yelling."

"It works both ways; at least, that's what my last boyfriend said. Apparently I scared the crap out of him a few times. He started leaving right after we made love, so he wouldn't have to actually sleep with me."

"Sounds like a wimp to me."

Catherine shrugged. "He was a professor of art at Cal Poly in San Luis Obispo. He thought I was brilliant in the beginning. He found my gruesome pictures fascinating, but in the end I was just a little too crazy for him."

"His loss."

"Yeah, sure, and don't tell me you've never jumped out of a woman's bed after sex. I bet you do it all the time."

"I'll never tell," he said with a smile.

She smiled back at him. "Fine. Keep your secrets while you can. How long are you going to stay up?"

"A little longer. I keep hoping I'll have a breakthrough. I hate to waste a minute sleeping when who knows what tomorrow will bring. It seems odd that you haven't connected with Erica again."

"I think I tap into her fear. Maybe she's not afraid right now."

"I hope she's found a safe place to hide. I wish she'd call me back, though." His cell phone had remained ominously silent for the past few hours.

"Well, good night." Catherine moved toward the

door, then stopped, turning back to him. "Have you ever been in love?"

"Where did that question come from?" he asked warily.

"I just wondered. Erica was a one-night stand. I'm sure there have been other women. But what about a real relationship?"

"I don't do relationships," he said bluntly.

"Not ever?"

"No. And I don't intend to start."

"Your brother's happy marriage hasn't put you a little more in favor of the idea?"

He shook his head. "I'm not husband or father material."

"How would you know that?"

"I just do. The apple doesn't fall far from the tree."

Her gaze narrowed. "You're not your father."

"His blood runs through my veins. As much as I'd like to believe we're completely different, I don't think we are. Go to bed, Catherine, and stop trying to convince me or yourself that I'm someone I'm not."

She looked like she wanted to argue, but after a moment of internal debate she left the room.

Dylan blew out a breath of relief at her exit and sat back in his chair. Rubbing his eyes, he knew he needed a break from the computer. He got up and stretched out on the couch. Despite his physical exhaustion, his mind spun with unanswered questions, all of them traveling back to the most basic question of all—how the hell had he gotten into this mess? He'd gone from having complete control over his life to having no control whatsoever, from being a respected TV news reporter to being a fugitive on the run, from living by a defined set of beliefs to not knowing what was real and what wasn't. He was starting to sound like Catherine.

And she was another problem. She was really getting to him. He didn't like how easily she read his thoughts or how perceptive she was. He liked being the man of mystery. He preferred being a person whom no one could quite figure out, but Catherine kept challenging him. She didn't buy into his act. She kept making him wonder if he was really who he wanted to be.

Damn her. Shaking his head, he tried to force her face, her body, her touch, her kiss out of his mind. She'd been so proud earlier, so full of joyous satisfaction at having gotten into Erica's house. She'd glowed in a way he'd never seen before. There was a new spark in her dark-blue eyes. She was coming alive. And he couldn't wait to see her go all the way.

But not tonight, he told himself, tempted to go upstairs and take them both for a ride. He knew she wouldn't say no. She might not think it was a good idea, but once they touched each other neither one of them would be thinking anymore.

Letting out a breath, he forced his mind off of Catherine, back to Erica. He brought up Ravino's image, too. He remembered quite clearly the steel glint of anger in the senator's eyes when he'd been arrested, when he'd looked at Dylan and realized a reporter had tracked down some of his biggest secrets. Ravino would love to get even. The only puzzling piece was not only *why*, but also *how* Ravino could get Erica to help him. If they were connected there had to be some proof that they'd spoken. Some phone somewhere had to have recorded that trail, or an e-mail could have been sent, or perhaps Ravino had used an intermediary, someone on the outside, someone who could get to Erica, make a persuasive case.

Of course, the real beauty of the plot would be to kill Erica and frame him, Dylan, for her murder, thereby getting rid of them both.

He should probably go to the jail tomorrow and confront Ravino. Maybe the man would give something away. It was worth a try.

Feeling restless and revved up again, Dylan got up and went back to the desk. But as his fingers hovered over the computer keyboard, his eye was drawn to a photograph of his grandmother and his father on one of the bookshelves across the room. He wondered again if she'd ever known what a bastard her son was, and what she'd known about his mother. He should have asked her at some point over the years, but she'd never brought up the subject, and neither had he. It was as if there were an unspoken rule between them.

He'd never followed any other rules, so why that one? It was interesting that his grandmother had not gotten rid of the photo of his parents at their wedding. Had she forgotten about it? It seemed odd, though, after the fuss his father had made about destroying all evidence of his mother's existence.

On impulse he opened the desk drawers, wondering if his grandmother had kept in touch with his mother over the years. Had they had a secret relationship? He vaguely remembered them laughing together. They'd seemed to get along when he was a little kid. Hadn't they? Or had he just been too young to know?

Shutting the second drawer, he opened the bottom one. He found a manila envelope filled with cards that his grandmother had received over the years: birthday cards, thank-you notes, condolences for when his grandfather had died. And there at the bottom were several childish hand-drawn notes.

His heart quickened at the sight of a stick figure holding a brown teddy bear. Slowly he unfolded the paper and read the message.

Dear Grandma, I feel better now. Thanks for the bear. I love you. Dylan.

He remembered that bear. He had slept with it in his arms for weeks when he'd been in and out of the hospital with some type of infection. He remembered all the needles, the blood tests, the long nights, and his mother, who had never left his side.

He swallowed back an unexpected knot of emotion. She'd brought him ice cream and juice and held his hand when he was scared. She'd lain down next to him in the bed, refusing to leave.

Finally he'd gotten better and gone home. Six months later his mother had left forever.

How had she changed from devotion to complete and utter abandonment in just a few months? What had happened between his parents?

He would have to find out. When this was over he

would get answers to the questions he should have asked a long time ago.

Moving back to the couch he settled down, closing his eyes. His mother's face floated through his brain, her pretty brown hair that always smelled like peaches, her warm brown eyes, and her encouraging smile. It was a long time since he'd seen her image in a picture or in his head. Now he couldn't seem to shake her loose. The floodgates had opened. He remembered other bits and pieces from his early years: running out for hamburgers when his father worked late, snuggling up in bed with his mother and a book, going to the island in the summer, building sand castles and playing in the waves until August turned into September and school started. Those were the good times, he realized, times when it had been just his mother, Jake, and himself.

Sighing, he tried to stop thinking altogether. What he needed now was a clear mind and a good night's sleep. Hopefully when he woke up in the morning, everything would be all right. Erica would turn up. The charges against him would be dropped, and his life would go back to normal.

Yeah, and he still believed in Santa Claus.

She probably should have stayed on the city streets, but she'd thought the tall trees and the thick bushes of the park would offer her protection, a place to hide. Now she realized how desolate the area was at night. There were no phone booths, no people, no businesses to run into. She was completely on her own.

She gasped and stopped abruptly as a shadowy figure came out of the undergrowth. Her heart thudded against her chest. The man walked toward her, one hand outstretched. His clothes were old and torn, and his face was covered with a heavy beard. He wore a baseball cap, and carried a backpack slung over one shoulder. He was probably one of the homeless people who set up camp in the park at night. Or maybe not . . .

"Hey, baby, give me a kiss," he said in a drunken slur.

"Leave me alone." She put up a hand to ward him off, but he kept moving forward.

"I'm just being friendly. Come on now, sweetheart."

Turning, she ran as fast as she could in the other direction, hearing him call after her. She didn't know if he was following her or not, and she was too terrified to look, so she left the sidewalk and moved deeper into the park, looking for a little corner in which to hide. Her side was cramping and her feet were soaked. She desperately needed to find some sanctuary. Branches scraped her bare arms and face, but she kept going. It was so dark in the heavy brush that she could barely see a foot in front of her. Tall trees and fog had completely obliterated the moonlight.

Fortunately she had her hand out in front of her when she ran into a cement wall that rose several stories in the air. She must have hit the side of one of the park buildings. Pausing, she caught her breath and listened. She could hear nothing but her own ragged breathing. Maybe she was safe, at least for the moment.

Leaning back against the cold cement, she pondered her next move, but she didn't know what to do, how to escape. She was out of options.

How had she come to this? Running for her life and all alone? This was not how it was supposed to go. This was Dylan's fault. He'd put her in this situation, and dammit, where the hell was he?

But she couldn't count on him to rescue her. She had to find a way out on her own. She couldn't let things end like this. She'd fought for her life before, and she'd won. She would do it again.

Her heart stopped as a nearby branch snapped in two. A confident male whistle pierced the silent night. Whoever was coming didn't care if she heard him or not. The bushes in front of her slowly parted. Terror ran through her body. There was nowhere left to run.

She screamed and screamed and screamed . . .

Catherine awoke with sweat drenching her body. She sat up straight in bed, disoriented, the terror-filled cries still echoing through her head. She was in Dylan's grandmother's house, she realized. Her gaze moved to the clock. It was two thirty-seven. Something was off.

The door flew open and she put up her hands in defense, letting out a breath when she realized it was Dylan.

"What the hell happened?" he demanded, his eyes wild and worried. "You were yelling your head off."

"A nightmare." She tucked a strand of sweat-dampened hair behind her ear and drew in a shaky breath. As always a restless, relentless energy filled her body, a desperate need to release the fear and darkness inside her. She swung her legs off the bed and stood up. She didn't have her paints set up, but she had to find a way to release her emotions.

"What are you doing?" he asked.

She moved over to her portfolio and pulled out her sketch pad and colored pencils. Sitting cross-legged on the bed she began to draw, her hand flying across the page, constructing lines and angles that came out of her subconscious. She didn't stop until her hand cramped and the pencil fell to the mattress. She set the pad down on the bed and blew out a breath. As she did so she realized Dylan was watching her, and that he'd been standing at the foot of the bed the entire time she'd been drawing.

He leaned over and picked up the pad. "This isn't like your other pictures. It's more distinct, more specific. What is this place?"

Catherine didn't need to look to remember what lines she'd drawn. Dylan was right: She'd remembered more details than she usually did, thick trees and bushes, a shadow of a figure crouched in front of a wall, hiding, fearful. Her heart began to beat faster as reality set in. "I think Erica is in trouble. I heard her screaming."

"Are you sure it was her? You said before that you've had nightmares off and on for most of your life and that you always hear screaming."

"This one was different. Usually I wake up at four forty-four."

"Why?"

"It's just when it usually happens," she said, not willing to tell him exactly what the hour meant to her. It had nothing to do with him, so he didn't need to know.

Dylan glanced at the clock. "That's not for another

two hours. What else do you remember from your dream?"

"Someone was chasing me. I ran into a wall. He kept coming. I could taste the fear in my mouth." She gazed into Dylan's eyes. "Erica is the figure in the drawing. She's trapped."

"In a park, right now, as we speak?" he asked.

"I can't say for sure if it's now, but it was dark in my dream. And the park was spooking her. She realized how isolated she was."

"There are a dozen parks in the city."

"It was big. She was running for a while. She went off the path. The trees were tall and the bushes scratched her arms. She thought she could hide."

Dylan dragged a hand through his hair. "I've got to go to the park."

"You just said you don't know which one."

"The biggest one is Golden Gate Park. It's in the heart of the city, and there are several buildings there."

Catherine didn't want him to leave. She didn't want him to run into the danger that surrounded Erica, but she knew she couldn't stop him. Dylan was a man of action, and even though Erica had wrecked his life, he would still risk his to save her.

"Tell me if there were any other identifying features in your dream, like tennis courts, a lake, paddleboats, a rose garden. . . . Damn, what else is in that park?"

She thought for a moment, but the images were gone from her mind. "Dylan, I think it's too late."

He met her gaze head-on. "Don't say that. Don't tell me Erica is dead. I'm going to look for her." He jogged out of the room. In a few minutes he would be on his way. She had to go with him.

Jumping out of bed, she threw a long sweater over her camisole top and pajama bottoms and slipped her feet into her tennis shoes, then hurried down the stairs. Dylan had put on a sweatshirt and was digging through a desk in the hall.

"What are you looking for?"

He answered by holding up a flashlight. He tested it, and the beam danced off the floor. "Still works. You're coming with me?"

"We're partners. We have to stick together."

"Then let's go."

As they approached his grandmother's car, Catherine took a wary look around. It was the middle of the night and very, very quiet. There was no movement anywhere on the block, no sign of someone sitting in a car watching them. It didn't appear that anyone knew where they were, at least, not yet anyway.

Once inside she quickly locked the doors as Dylan started the engine. She hoped they'd be in time to help Erica. Maybe her vision was of the future, not of the past. That was certainly possible. She tried to hang on to the positive thought, admiring the way Dylan didn't let anything keep him from his goal. He was determined to succeed. Failure was not an option.

She'd grown used to failure, accustomed to disappointment. She hadn't realized until now how low her expectations for herself and others had sunk. But Dylan was setting the bar a little higher, and she was eager to keep up with him.

It was past three thirty in the morning now, and there was little traffic on the city streets. Her nightmare had happened almost an hour ago. Had the dream come in real time? She hoped not.

They entered the park off the Pacific Coast Highway, turning in past an old windmill. As Dylan drove through the twisting streets, Catherine was struck by how enormous Golden Gate Park was. It ran for several miles and encompassed hundreds of acres. There was a stadium, two lakes, a Japanese tea garden, a museum, tennis courts, and a carousel—how on earth could they find Erica? She could be anywhere.

The trees, the shrubs, the plants—they all felt so familiar, but Catherine couldn't bring herself to pinpoint one area over another. They drove for fifteen minutes without speaking a word, each scanning the grounds on their side of the car. They passed several homeless people, some sleeping under the trees, others wandering along the road.

"I don't think I'd want to be here on my own," Catherine murmured.

"Maybe that's why you felt Erica's fear. She could have been afraid of her surroundings, not whoever is trying to get to her."

"That could have been it." Catherine certainly felt uncomfortable now, and she was in a car with the doors locked and Dylan by her side. "This place is creepy. It's dark and deserted. Why would she come here?"

"Hell if I know. If she thought someone was trying to kill her, she should have gone to the police."

Dylan slowed down as a man stumbled across the

road in front of him. He wore a baseball cap, and a backpack hung from one shoulder. Catherine flashed back on her dream.

"I saw him," she said. "He scared her. She ran from him."

"This guy?" Dylan asked. "Are you sure?"

He stopped the car as they watched the man sit down on the side of the road and take a swig out of a bottle. A moment later he lay down on his back. Catherine didn't know if he'd passed out or was just resting. Certainly the man seemed oblivious to the fact that they were watching him.

"What should we do?" she asked, her nerves tingling. She didn't know why she felt so scared, but she really wanted to get out of the park. "Let's go back to the house."

"We haven't found Erica yet. If you saw this guy in your dream, then maybe she's nearby."

"What do you want to do? She was in the bushes. We might not be able to see her from the road."

"You said she was up against a building."

"There are lots of buildings."

Dylan shot her a puzzled look. "Why are you trying to get me out of here?"

"I'm scared," she admitted.

"I won't let anything happen to you. Don't worry. I'll keep you safe."

She wanted to have faith in him, but the need to leave bubbled up inside her. She tried to breathe through her panic as Dylan continued down the road. A moment later the dome of the Conservatory of Flowers came into view. It reminded her of the other dome at the Palace of Fine Arts. Why had Erica chosen to hide herself in these tourist locations? Surely she would have known that the areas would be deserted at night. She must not have had a choice. She couldn't go home. Whoever was after her knew where she lived. She'd already been to Dylan's place and the person had found her there. Whoever was tracking her was very, very good.

Catherine shivered as goose bumps ran down her arms. A second later they saw two police cars, strobe lights turning, and an ambulance. A man pushing a shopping cart stood by the side of the road, watching the activity in the bushes.

Catherine felt suddenly short of breath. In the distance she saw the wall of the museum. She'd been here before—in her dream.

Dylan stopped the car.

"What are you doing?" she asked, grabbing his arm.

"Getting some information." He rolled down his window. "Hey, buddy," he called to the man. He pulled a twenty-dollar bill out of his pocket and waved it at the guy. "I've got a question."

The man ambled over to the car, pushing his cart. His clothes were ragged and worn, and he appeared to have a bunch of recyclable bottles in his cart.

"What do you want?" The man stopped a few feet from the car, giving them a suspicious look.

"What's happening?" Dylan waved his twenty in the air.

"There's a dead girl in there," the man said, his eyes on the money.

"Oh, God," Catherine whispered. "Give him the twenty and let's go."

"Can you describe her?" Dylan asked, ignoring her hand on his arm.

The man gave a noncommittal shrug.

"Dylan, give him the money," she repeated forcefully. "Just do it. Please. And then get us out of here."

Dylan hesitated, then handed the twenty over to the man. "Catherine, I know you're upset, but I have to find out if that's Erica," he said, driving slowly away from the scene. "I'll just park and get out—"

"Dylan, think for a minute," she said, cutting him off. "If you go back there and identify Erica, they're going to want to know who you are. How do you think it will look when they find out you were under suspicion of having killed Erica in Tahoe, and now you happen to show up in the middle of the night right after she's actually been killed?"

"This should prove I didn't do it. It happened here."

"Where you are." She saw her words sink into his brain.

"Damn. I should have thought of that," he muttered.

"Yes."

He hit the gas and drove quickly around the next corner. "I'm usually the logical one. Thanks for saving my ass."

She couldn't speak. Her throat was tight with the certainty that Erica had been killed just a few yards away from them. They were too late. Her vision had been in real time. For the first time in her life she'd tried to chase the nightmare and she'd failed. She might as well have stayed home, hiding her head under the covers. Or maybe if they'd left earlier, right away, if she hadn't taken the time to stop and draw the park . . .

"It's not your fault," Dylan said.

She shook her head and stared out the window, on the verge of breaking down.

"It might not have been her," Dylan added. "There were lots of homeless people in the park. It could have been someone else."

"It wasn't. Oh, God." Another vision was coming into her head, and she didn't want to look. But she couldn't push it away.

One red high heel lay abandoned on the wet grass. The other shoe was still strapped to her foot. Her red toenail polish mixed with the blood dripping down her bare leg. The short dress was hitched up to her hips. The spaghetti straps fell halfway down her arms. Brown hair framed the lifeless, bloodless face, her dark eyes still stamped with the horror of death.

Along with the image came an odd sense of satisfaction, victory, the taste of success. It was a job well-done.

She wasn't in Erica's head anymore. She was in his. She was looking through the eyes of a killer. And she knew he wasn't done yet.

Chapter 11

"Stop!" Catherine screamed.

Dylan hit the brake so quickly she would have struck the windshield if she hadn't been wearing her seat belt.

"What the hell is wrong with you?" he demanded.

She tugged off her seat belt, jumped out of the car, and made it to the edge of the bushes before she threw up. A moment later she felt Dylan's hand on her back as she got rid of the evil, sick taste in her mouth the only way she knew how.

"Are you all right?" he asked when she was done.

She wiped her mouth with the edge of her sleeve, more than a little embarrassed. "I'm okay. I wish you hadn't seen that."

"I've seen worse."

"We can go now."

"Catherine—"

"I just want to get out of here." Maybe if she left the

park she could put some distance between herself and *him*.

Dylan kept his hand on her shoulder as he walked her back to the car. Within minutes they were exiting the park. Catherine blew out a breath of relief at the sight of storefronts and apartment buildings.

"I'm sorry about that," she muttered, afraid to look at Dylan. "And utterly humiliated."

"Don't be. You were thinking about Erica, weren't you?"

She didn't know how to answer the question. She couldn't tell him what she'd seen. It was too horrible, and what was worse was *how* she'd envisioned the scene.

"I don't want to believe it's her," Dylan continued. "If I'd seen her with my own eyes, maybe I could, but right now it just seems impossible. It's unimaginable that she's dead."

"Yeah, I know," she said. But she had seen Erica, and the woman's image was indelibly imprinted on Catherine's brain. She didn't know if she would ever forget Erica's face. Why hadn't she been able to find her before her death? Why hadn't her visions brought her to the park earlier? Catherine felt so angry, so frustrated, so helpless . . . and so dirty. The stench of evil still lingered in her senses. She'd been in his head. She'd felt his joy. God, he was sick. And maybe so was she.

She dug her fingernails into her thighs, feeling the sharp sting of pain. She wanted that pain. She wanted to punish herself or him. Someone deserved to hurt. Someone besides Erica.

Dylan grabbed her hand and wrapped his fingers around hers. He held on tight until they pulled up in front of his grandmother's house. Then he finally let go. They made it into the house without incident, but Catherine couldn't forget the fleeting thought that had run through the killer's mind—that it was time to move on to the next target. Was that target Dylan? Was the danger about to come closer?

Dylan turned on the light in the hall and set the flashlight on the table. Catherine walked into the kitchen and filled a glass with water from the tap. It would be dawn soon, a new day, time to start over—again. She couldn't wait to see the sunrise. Maybe everything would be different in the morning. Perhaps she just thought she was awake when in fact she was in the grip of another nightmare.

But Dylan felt real as he came up behind her and put his arms around her waist. He rested his chin on her head. "Can I help?" he asked.

She shook her head, her throat too tight to speak.

"Let me try." He forced her to turn around, but he didn't let go of her, his hands sliding to her hips. "I could distract you. I have a couple of ideas."

The thought was more than a little tempting, but she felt too . . . dirty. "I need to take a shower."

"What's wrong, Catherine?" His sharp gaze bored into hers. "I'm not as good as you are at reading minds, so you'll have to fill me in."

"I can't tell you."

"Well, now you have to tell me, because I can't stand secrets."

She should have known better than to wave that red flag in front of Dylan.

He pressed a kiss to her forehead. She closed her eyes and wished things were simpler between them. "Don't." She tried to pull away, but he had her trapped between him and the kitchen counter.

"Then talk."

"I saw Erica's body on the ground. The blood from a bullet hole in her forehead dripped down her body. I think he shot her in the heart, too."

He drew in a quick breath. "You saw that in your mind? No wonder you got sick."

"It wasn't just the sight of her," she said, knowing she had to finish it. Dylan needed to know all of it. "I was in his head, the killer's head. I felt his satisfaction at the success of his job. I felt his evil run through me." She was afraid to look into Dylan's eyes, terrified she would see contempt or dislike or revulsion. But he was quiet for so long she finally had to lift her gaze to his. His eyes were thoughtful, speculative, but not condemning. "You don't believe me, do you?" she asked. "After everything I've told you, you still think I'm conning you?" Anger took the place of embarrassment. "How can you think that?"

"Whoa, slow down. You're hitting me with way too many things at once."

She tried to push past him, but his grip on her tightened. "I believe you, okay?"

"You're just saying that."

"I never *just* say anything," he told her. "You should know that about me by now."

"And you should know that I don't lie."

"I do know that. It's hard for me to accept your extrasensory abilities, but I'm trying."

"It doesn't matter if you accept them or not. I'm the one who has to live with them."

"You're not evil," he said.

"No, I'm just crazy."

"So am I."

"Hardly. You're normal and almost damn perfect."

"You *are* rattled if you're calling me perfect now."

"I just wish the visions would let me help someone. It's so frustrating to see people die, and I can't stop anything from happening. Why can't I be tuned in to nice people instead of murderers?" As she asked the question, she realized she knew the answer, and before she could hide her expression Dylan's gaze narrowed.

"You know, don't you?" he said. "You said the visions started when you were a little girl, and the only thing I know about that little girl is that at one point she was surrounded by blood and then taken away in a police cruiser."

"I can't go there, not now. I need to get some sleep, and so do you. It will be morning in a few hours, and God only knows what's coming next." She slipped from his embrace.

"You won't always be able to run from me, Catherine."

His words came after her, but she didn't stop moving until she'd reached the upstairs bedroom. She shut the door and sat down on the bed, trembling from the force of her emotions. Dylan didn't know it, but by running away she'd just done him a huge favor. She might not be able to protect the people in her visions, but she could protect Dylan. The last thing he needed was to get sucked into her nightmare.

"It's done. She's dead," the man said as he kicked his feet onto the coffee table in front of him and leaned back against the couch. He could hear waves crashing on the beach not far from his motel room. The steady beat echoed the now calm thump of his heart. It had been only a short while, but already he missed the adrenaline rush. He could still see her face, her eyes widening with the realization that she was about to die. He wished he could have taken a little longer with her, but she wasn't a pleasure kill. She was a job—a job he'd done well. "The police have already found the body," he continued. "It should be on the news tomorrow."

"It took you long enough."

"I got the job done. That's all that matters."

"Half the job. There's still more to come."

Another murder? He wasn't surprised. The plan had always been fluid. As long as he got paid he didn't care how many other people died. And he'd always liked San Francisco. Not that he stayed anywhere long. He'd lived in too many towns to count, and had been called by a lot of different names. The man he'd once been had vanished years ago, and he didn't miss him one bit.

It bothered him that he was even thinking of that man now. A lifetime had passed since he'd tried to live up to expectations, to fit into a world that wanted to control him. Now he was his own man. He took the jobs he wanted. He called the shots, and he got paid well for what he did.

"When do you want him to die?" he asked.

Silence met his question. Finally the answer came. "I want him to suffer more. I want him to be afraid, to realize there is nowhere to turn, nowhere to run. He's trapped. And soon he will die . . . like everyone else."

There was passionate lust in the voice that gave him his next instructions and the name of his victim. Dylan Sanders had made one hell of an enemy.

Dylan woke a little after nine thirty in the morning. He couldn't remember the last time he'd slept so late, but then again, he'd gotten only about three hours of sleep the night before. He was actually surprised he'd slept at all with so much going through his mind.

Getting up, he jumped in the shower, reviewing what he needed to get done. First things first—strong coffee. He needed caffeine, and he needed it badly. After throwing on some clothes, he headed down the block and picked up coffee, tea, bagels, and the morning newspaper. He also called Mark from a pay phone to update him on what was happening. When he returned to the house all was quiet, so he figured Catherine was still asleep.

He entered the kitchen and turned on the small television set on the counter, eager for his morning news fix. Unfortunately it was just about eleven o'clock on a Sunday morning, and the only news was on the national cable channels. He opened the newspaper, skimming the front-page headlines. There was no report of a murder in Golden Gate Park, which wasn't surprising, since the paper had probably already gone to press before the police arrived at the scene.

Damn. He wanted to know if that woman in the park was Erica. He had some friends on the police force whom he often used to get the news, but he was leery of announcing his presence in the city, especially to the cops. However, he might take a risk and call the station. They'd be preparing the story for the evening news.

He hoped it wasn't Erica in the park, but he was starting to trust Catherine's instincts as much as his own, and she was so certain, how could he doubt her? He was lucky Catherine had been with him last night. He could have made a huge mistake by getting out of the car and putting himself at the scene of the crime. He was still kicking himself for acting on instinct instead of thinking things through. He was usually practical, logical, thoughtful—well, maybe not always. He did have a tendency to act first, think later, but not when the stakes were this high and this personal. He wouldn't make that mistake again.

He glanced up as Catherine entered the kitchen. His stomach clenched at the sight of her. It had been a long time since he'd had such a powerful reaction to a woman. They'd been together almost every minute of the last two days, but a few hours away from her and he almost felt as if he'd missed her. How stupid was that?

Frowning, he picked up his coffee, trying not to look at her, but he couldn't help noticing that she'd taken a shower and changed into a pair of blue jeans and a tank top, both of which molded nicely to her curves. Her reddish blond hair was still damp from her shower, the ends curling around her face. Her blue eyes were bright and sparkling, and he appreciated the absence of fear. She'd recovered from the night before. He wished he could say the same about himself.

"How are you doing?" she asked. "Did you get any sleep?"

"An hour or two. How about you?"

"The same. I must admit I'm always relieved to see the sun come up. Is that tea?" she asked, tipping her head toward one of the paper cups on the table.

"Decaffeinated, some sort of herbal thing."

Her smile broadened. "Thank you. That was thoughtful."

"Yeah, well, I didn't want to hear you complain."

"When have I complained?"

"I'm sure you would have."

"You're in a grumpy mood."

"I am not," he snapped, knowing he was taking his restlessness out on her. He had two choices: yell at her or kiss her, and at the moment yelling was probably safer.

She sat down across from him, took a sip of her tea, and pointed to the newspaper. "Anything about Erica?"

"No. And there's no local news on this morning." He checked his watch. "Although there should be a news break coming up at eleven, with the sound bites for what will be on at five. We've got about ten minutes."

She pulled a bagel out of the bag and covered it with cream cheese, then took a bite. "Mmm, good," she muttered as she swallowed. "I'm always starving in the morning All the dreams, probably. I think I burn up more calories when I'm asleep than when I'm awake." She paused, studying his face. "You wish I hadn't stopped you from barreling into the bushes last night, don't you?"

He shook his head. "No, you were right. I'm just frustrated that I don't know for sure that it was Erica who died. The idea that someone could have really killed her boggles my mind."

"Because up until now you thought it was just a sick game. But it's real."

Catherine was on the money again. The setup, the frame, had seemed like an elaborate hoax, not the foreshadowing of an actual murder. He'd been worried about going to jail, but now he had to wonder if he would get out of this alive—if either of them would. His gaze drifted back to Catherine. He never should have involved her. He'd had no idea what kind of danger he was dragging her into.

Catherine set down her bagel, her eyes darkening with emotion. "Don't worry about me."

"I can't help it. Erica is . . . dead." He finally forced himself to say the word. "We could be next."

"Or whoever is behind this wants you to be charged with a real murder. Maybe they didn't think the circumstantial evidence would be enough. And if that's the case, I suspect that something related to you was left in the park to make sure you can be tied to the crime."

He suspected Catherine was right. But the motivation was what bothered him. "You really think someone just wants me to go to jail? I don't know. Why wouldn't they kill me? They've already killed Erica."

"If they want you to suffer, jail would be worse than death. It would last longer."

"You should go home, back to San Luis Obispo, or stay with some friends."

"I'd spend the whole time worrying about you, and being tormented by nightmares. I'm sticking with you, Dylan."

"It's too dangerous. You need to get out."

"But I'm the conduit. I'm the one who's getting the visions. I know I haven't been very helpful so far, but maybe that will change."

"You might not have the visions anymore. If Erica is gone, then the connection with her is broken."

Catherine considered that for a moment. "I think the connection is with you. That's why I first started getting the dreams after I met you. And besides you, I seem to have a link with the killer. So maybe I'll be able to see him coming at some point. I guess we'll have to wait and see." She paused, tipping her head toward the TV. "Hey, there's the news break."

Dylan pumped up the volume as the weekend news anchor, Blake Howard, forecast the upcoming stories: the latest developments in the Middle East, the details on a murder in Golden Gate Park, and the newest drug to prevent hair loss. "Shit. No name given." Dylan wasn't really surprised. It was early yet, and the police liked to wait until next of kin had been notified.

"At least we know we didn't imagine it," Catherine said.

"I wish we had."

"So, do you know that guy—the one on TV?"

"Blake Howard? Unfortunately, yes."

"Why do you say it like that?"

"Howard is a pretty boy and an idiot. He's a talking head; that's it."

"Tell me what you really think," she said with a smile.

"Hey, you asked."

"Are you jealous of him?"

He snorted at the ridiculous question. "Hardly."

"Don't all news reporters want to sit at the anchor desk? Isn't that your goal?"

Dylan hesitated at the simple question. At one time he would have said yes, but now he wasn't so sure. He'd spent the last ten years chasing one promotion after another, his eye on that top prize, but he hadn't considered exactly how he'd feel about desk duty until recently. "It's certainly the money spot," he conceded. "Actually, Blake is at the lower end of the anchors. What everyone really wants is the five o'clock in the evening weekday newscast at the local station, or the six thirty news for one of the big networks. But I'm afraid I'd get bored waiting for the news to come to me. I like the freedom of chasing down a story, investigating the details, getting out on the streets, talking to the people who are directly affected. I don't know if I want to give that up yet. Plus, I'd have to cut my hair, wear a suit, and suck up to the bosses, and that's not really why I got into the news."

Catherine smiled back at him with complete understanding. "You're a little too rebellious for the anchor desk, huh?"

"I tend to piss people off. I like to get right in their faces and shake 'em up."

"I've noticed," she said dryly.

"Hey, you've done the same to me," he returned. "You've gotten into my head. And I can't shake you loose no matter how hard I try."

She nodded, her gaze meeting his. "We're connected."

He wondered what she'd say if he told her he'd like to be connected in a very physical way, that he wanted to get so close to her that he wouldn't know where he ended and she began. His pulse began to race at the thought of them naked and in bed together. He should never have let her go to bed alone the night before. He should have taken the damn connection between them all the way home.

Catherine glanced away, two fiery spots burning in her cheeks. "It's still not the right time, Dylan."

He knew that. Hell, it would probably never be the right time. So he needed to stop thinking about her in that way.

"So, what's on the schedule for today?" Catherine asked, changing the subject.

"I called Mark from a pay phone at Starbucks to tell him I think Erica may have been killed last night here in the city. He'll check with the Tahoe sheriff's department later this morning and see what's happening there. He's not going to tell them about my suspicions, in case they figure out where he got the information. The last thing I want to do is add another accessory to this crime."

"If it is Erica in the park, then what does Mark think will happen to you?"

"He doesn't like the fact that I'm here in the city at the time of her murder. It may get the Tahoe sheriff's department off my back, but the San Francisco police will surely be interested in me once they learn about the Tahoe incident."

"So you're still going to be the main person of interest?"

"I believe so," he admitted. "And as you suggested, there's probably something in the park that ties Erica to me, too. By leaving Tahoe and coming here I played right into their plan. However, at the moment no one but Mark knows where I am. That could easily change, since I used my cell phone yesterday in San Francisco. We probably have a day or two before the police start putting all the information together and have enough probable cause to get phone records and search and/or arrest warrants. It's all going to move faster now that there's a body."

"It will be difficult to tie the senator to Erica's murder, since he's in jail. How on earth are we going to prove he's the one who's doing this?"

"I wish I knew. What I'd like to do this morning is run down to the station. I taped a lot of my conversations with Erica when I was writing the story. I asked her detailed questions about Ravino's life, who his friends were, who he had dinner with, who he talked to on the phone, who was in his inner circle. Maybe she told me something about herself or Ravino that I've forgotten."

"Isn't it risky to go out in public?"

"Well, since neither Erica nor I has made the news yet, this is my best chance to get the tapes. Once the finger points to me I won't be able to get around freely."

"All right," she said with a nod. "I'll come with you. I'd like to see the inside of a newsroom."

"It's not that exciting," he said.

She grinned as she stood up. "Dylan, with you, every moment is exciting."

He laughed. "You ain't seen nothing yet."

"That's what I'm afraid of."

KTSF was housed in an unassuming three-story building at the edge of downtown San Francisco. The satellite dish on the roof was the only giveaway that they were entering a television station. A security guard checked Dylan in as they entered the underground garage. For a moment Catherine held her breath, wondering if a swarm of police would suddenly descend upon them, but the guard simply raised the gate and waved them through.

They received the same reception from the guard stationed in the first-floor lobby. Dylan was greeted by name and asked how his weekend was going. He responded with a breezy, "Fine," and then they were in the elevator.

"There won't be many people around today, since it's the weekend," he told her.

"I thought the news never stopped."

"It doesn't, but the weekend staff just covers the day's news. During the week we have more people working on long-term investigations, and generally there's more political and business news."

"I never realized that TV newspeople followed stories over a long period of time. I thought it was more about just reporting current events."

"It can be. I've been given a little more latitude to conduct longer investigations, which I enjoy, because there's usually more to any story than what is seen on the surface."

"That's for sure."

They exited on the third floor. After passing a vacant reception desk, they entered the main newsroom, where a couple of people were at work. Some of the desks were out in the open, whereas others were tucked away in cubicles, giving at least the appearance of privacy, although Catherine suspected that just about anything could be heard anywhere in the large room. Along one wall was a display of at least ten different television monitors that were each tuned to a different station. Most were on mute, with the dialogue running in taglines across the bottoms of the screens.

Dylan pointed to several large offices around the perimeter of the room. "The anchors get those," he said. "As do some of the news producers. The main studio is downstairs on the first floor. There's nothing happening there at the moment, but that's where they'll do the five-o'clock newscast. Sales and circulation are on the second floor, as well as accounting, personnel, and the mailroom."

"Isn't that the guy we saw on TV earlier?" Catherine whispered, tipping her head toward a nearby office. She felt a little starstruck by the fact that she was in a television studio, and the handsome morning news anchor was standing about ten feet away talking on the phone. With his slick good looks, dark hair, and blue eyes, Blake Howard could have posed for the cover of *GQ*. "Wow," she muttered. "Now, that's a man who can wear a suit."

Dylan sent her a disgusted look. "Yeah, that's what all the girls say. Howard is all flash, no substance. The guy can't talk without a script and a teleprompter."

"Maybe I can think of better things to do than talk to him," she said with a grin. "Sometimes all you want is flash. Surely you've felt that way on occasion."

"Not about Blake. He's not my type."

"Very funny."

"Damn, he saw me," Dylan said.

"Oh, my God, he's coming over here," she said, nervous at the prospect.

"Of course he's coming over here," Dylan muttered. "You're a woman, and he can't resist the opportunity to schmooze."

Sure enough, Blake was heading their way. He gave Dylan a curt nod and then blessed Catherine with his trademark smile. His teeth were movie-star white, his skin tan, his hair styled. His appearance was perfect: not one blemish on his face, not one hair out of place. He'd probably spent more on his suit than she had on her car.

"Hello, I'm Blake Howard," he said to Catherine, extending his hand.

"Catherine . . . Hilliard," she stammered, feeling a little dazed by the man's smile. "I . . . I just saw you on TV."

His fingers squeezed hers. "So, you're a fan," he said with pleasure.

"She doesn't even live in the area," Dylan cut in. "She can't help you increase your numbers. What's happening today? Any breaking news stories?"

Blake shrugged, his gaze lingering on Catherine as he slowly let go of her hand. "The usual stuff. A couple of murders, a carjacking, a bus accident, the standard Middle East crap."

Catherine was surprised at Blake's lack of respect or even interest in the news. He rattled off devastating incidents with complete disregard for their seriousness. Perhaps he'd read the news so long he was unaffected by it. She could never do his job—or Dylan's, for that matter; she'd get way too involved in every story.

"If you like, I can give you a personal tour of the studio," Blake said to Catherine. "Dylan doesn't know his way around the anchor desk."

"What's to know? There's a desk and a chair and a dummy that sits in it," Dylan shot back.

Blake's eyes glittered with anger, and it seemed he

was searching for a quick comeback, but as the seconds ticked away his face just grew redder and redder. "Well," he sputtered.

Catherine jumped into the breach. "Don't we need to get going?" she said to Dylan, grabbing his arm. "It was wonderful to meet you, Mr. Howard. I'll look forward to seeing you on the news."

"You could do better than Sanders," Blake said, nodding at Dylan again. "He's not going anywhere."

"Except away from you." Dylan shrugged Catherine's hand off his arm and headed across the room at a brisk pace.

"Good heavens. Do you two always snap at each other like that?" Catherine asked, jogging to keep up with him.

"He doesn't like me. I don't like him. Neither one of us loses any sleep over it."

"Why the animosity?"

He gave her a disbelieving look. "He doesn't give a damn about the news. It's a show to him." Dylan frowned. "You fell under his spell just like everyone else. I expected better from you."

"I did not fall under his spell," she protested, knowing it was partly a lie. She had been a bit dazzled by the man, but only for a moment. She'd realized quickly that what Dylan had said was true—without a script, Blake Howard didn't seem to know what to say. "Okay, I know why you don't like Blake, but why doesn't he like you?"

"He thinks I'm after his job. The Ravino story gave me some clout around here. I've been getting special assignments and more airtime ever since then. The next step up for me would be a weekend anchor job."

"But you said you don't want to be an anchor."

"Howard would never believe that. Everyone in news wants to be an anchor."

"Remember when I asked you if you had any enemies . . . ?"

Dylan stopped walking and shook his head at her. "Blake isn't smart enough to set me up."

"Are you sure?"

Irritation flashed through his eyes. "Perhaps you just want it to be Blake so you can spend some time with him, do some hands-on research."

She heard the note of jealousy in his voice, and it shocked the hell out of her. "Yeah, that's it, Dylan. How did you guess?"

"I saw your face. You can't hide anything from me, Catherine."

"Don't be an ass. There's nothing to hide. And you're letting your opinion of Blake cloud your judgment."

"Fine, I'll keep Blake on the list of suspects, but right now he's at the bottom." Dylan started walking again, not stopping until he reached a large desk where a middle-aged bald man was hanging up the phone.

"Sanders, what are you doing here today?" the man asked.

"Hello, Ron," Dylan said with a warm, friendly note in his voice that hadn't been present when he'd spoken with Blake. "I'm showing my friend around. I heard there was a murder in the park last night. Who's on it?"

"Irina left about half an hour ago. She hasn't called in yet."

"Any stats on the victim?"

"Well-dressed Caucasian female in her twenties is all I know."

"Cause of death?"

"Unknown." As Ron finished speaking, he answered the phone again. "News desk. Bill, thanks for calling me back."

"Let's go talk to the fact-checkers," Dylan said to Catherine as Ron continued his conversation. "Irina may have called in to ask them to get background information on the victim."

"Which might bring up your name," Catherine said.

"Hopefully not yet, but I want to know sooner rather than later what the police have. I've been thinking, too, that I've been so caught up in what this means to me that I haven't considered what Erica's death means to Ravino. The case against him could certainly be made weaker without Erica's personal testimony."

"Could that be the point?" Catherine asked, as a new angle suddenly opened up. "Maybe it's not about revenge, but a way for Ravino to get rid of someone who is willing to expose all his secrets."

"It's certainly possible, although Erica already gave her taped conversation with Deborah to the police and made her statement regarding her affair with the senator. The other evidence tying Ravino to the physician who provided the poisoned Botox is much stronger."

"It could still be about revenge on both of you,"

Catherine put in. "Ravino might have made Erica believe that by helping him nail you, she'd be protecting herself from payback."

"When all the while he was planning to kill her."

"Two birds with one shot."

"Hopefully I can convince the police to look into that angle at some point. Certainly Ravino has more motive than I do for wanting Erica dead."

"Did anyone know that you and Erica had an affair?" Catherine asked.

"It wasn't an affair. It was a one-night stand. But I didn't tell anyone. Erica may have. Who knows?"

"I think she must have, because someone had to believe that Erica could get you to do what she wanted."

"Or Ravino just knew that because I'd worked with Erica before, I would trust her enough to go with her into the woods." Dylan pushed open the door to another office. Two of the four desks were occupied. The room was filled with books, computers, and the usual television monitors across one wall. A man and a woman sat in front of their respective computers. The man had on headphones, his fingers flying over the keys. He didn't bother to look up as they entered the room. The woman, however, was quick to turn around.

"Hello, Dylan," she said, a surprised smile on her face. "What are you doing here? I thought you were in Tahoe."

"I just got back. Julie Bristow, this is my friend Catherine Hilliard. Julie is one of the best fact-checkers in the business, Catherine. She's already saved my ass a few times."

Julie pushed her loose glasses back up her nose. "Dylan thinks flattery will get him anywhere."

Despite the fact that she was addressing Catherine, Julie barely glanced in her direction. The slightly plump brunette with her hair pulled back in a tight ponytail seemed entranced by Dylan. Catherine couldn't help wondering if she'd had the same dazed look on her face when Blake Howard had been talking to her.

"Yes!" the young man suddenly shouted, pumping his fist in the air. He must have realized they were there, because he took off his headphones and turned around. "I finally cracked the code."

"Of his computer game," Julie said with annoyance. "He's supposed to be working."

"Hey, I'm on a break. Chill. What's up, dude?"

"Not much, Ryan. This is my friend Catherine. I'm giving her a tour."

"Friend, huh?" Ryan said with a wink. "Wish I had friends who looked like her."

"That might happen if you got out of the video arcade once in a while."

Catherine wasn't surprised to learn that Ryan was a video game freak. He appeared to be in his early twenties, and with his long hair, an earring in his ear, and a couple of tattoos on each arm, he looked like the kind of guy who would be more at home playing videos than checking facts all day long. "Congratulations on cracking the code," Catherine said.

"Thank you. Thank you. I am the best."

Julie rolled her eyes. "He's hopeless," she said.

"I liven this place up," Ryan replied. "Did you take Catherine to the studio yet?"

"No," Dylan answered. "I heard there was a murder last night in the park. Do you have anything on it yet?"

"Irina called in about ten minutes ago and asked us to do a background check on a woman named Erica Layton," Julie said. "I was just about to get started on it."

Catherine's heart skipped a beat at hearing Erica identified as the victim. She'd known it all along, but now it was definite. The pretty brunette she'd seen in the bar with Dylan just two days ago was no longer breathing. It seemed impossible to believe, even though she'd seen her in her head. She'd still been harboring some secret hope that it was all a bad dream.

"What do you know so far?" Dylan asked.

"Not much," Julie replied.

"Did Irina tell you the cause of death?"

"She didn't say, and I didn't ask. Why are you so interested?"

Dylan gave a casual shrug. "I might want to cover it tomorrow."

"You think you're going to take the story away from Irina?" Ryan asked in amazement. "What have you been smoking, dude?"

"Good point," Dylan conceded. "Irina is very territorial," he explained to Catherine. "She doesn't like to share her stories."

"Neither do you," Julie said pointedly. "So what's up?"

"Nothing. Just curious."

"Do you want me to call you later if I find out anything?" Julie asked.

"That would be great."

"No problem. I won't mention it to Irina either," Julie added with a small smile.

"You're a peach. Thanks."

"It was nice to meet you," Catherine said. Ryan nodded and returned to his game. Something fluttered in Julie's eyes, something she quickly tried to hide as she said good-bye and turned back to her computer.

"She likes you," Catherine said as they left the room.

"Who? Julie? I don't think so."

"Oh, come on, Dylan. She couldn't take her eyes off you."

"She's nice, but I don't date my coworkers. Everyone here knows that."

"Knowing you can't have someone doesn't necessarily stop you from wanting them. Didn't you see the way she looked at you?"

"She's just one of those people who stares a lot," he said. "Maybe her vision isn't good; I don't know. She always has those thick glasses on."

"I don't think her eyesight is why she stares." Catherine fell silent as they headed toward Dylan's cubicle. "There are a lot of emotions in this building," she said a moment later. "They're swirling around—anger, jealousy, competitiveness, passion. I can sense them all. It's like a dark, thick cloud. I feel a little short of breath."

Dylan paused, his eyes narrowing. "Are you getting another vision?"

"Not a vision, but goose bumps," she said, holding out her arms to show him.

"TV news is a ruthless business. The stories that come through here can be horrific. Maybe that's what you're picking up on. We're almost done here." He entered his cubicle and immediately began rifling through the drawers. A moment later he pulled out a manila envelope. "Here it is." Opening the envelope, he dumped two tapes onto the desk. "They're still safe. Finally, a break." He put the tapes back into the envelope, then stopped. "What's this?" he muttered, picking up a CD case. "Looks like someone left me a present."

Catherine's nerves began to tighten as Dylan turned on his computer. "Maybe you shouldn't put that in."

"Someone wants me to see whatever is on this CD. And I'm going to look."

"It could be part of the plan. It could be booby-trapped."

His gaze darkened. "It's just a disc. It's not an explosive device. And it could be about one of the other stories I've been working on."

She doubted that, but there was no stopping Dylan.

He slipped the disc into the drive, and a moment later a video began to play. She moved in closer, not sure what they were looking at.

"It's the Metro Club," Dylan said. "I think this is a video from the security camera in the back room of the club."

They watched for several moments. Erica came into view holding two martini glasses. She moved across the room and set them down at a table where two men were in deep conversation.

Dylan sucked in a breath. "Oh, my God."

"Who are they?" she asked.

"That's Ravino on the left," he said, his voice rough. "And the other man is my father."

Chapter 12

Catherine couldn't believe Dylan's words. She squinted at the screen, taking a better look at the men. Ravino was a blond-haired man in his forties. He was lean, and his face was long and angular. Dylan's father's face was square, his shoulders broad like a football player's, his jaw strong and determined. Whatever they were talking about had brought tension to both of their expressions. Then Erica said something, and the men smiled. Ravino got up and followed Erica across the room. They stopped to speak to another man, who had his back to the camera, and then someone walked in front of the group, blocking them all from view.

"Damn," Dylan swore as the video went blank.

"Who was that?" Catherine asked.

"I don't know."

"Play it again."

They watched in silence as the video replayed. When they came to the last bit Dylan hit pause. "That ring looks familiar. Where have I seen that before?" He pointed to the ring on the finger of the man who now had his hand on Erica's back.

Unfortunately he couldn't see anything more than that hand, as someone in the forefront blocked the view. Dylan pressed play again, and the video shut off in exactly the same spot. Dylan played the video three more times, tapping his fingers impatiently on his desk with each run-through. Catherine could see the frustration in his face as he tried to identify other people in the video, but the only one besides Ravino whom he recognized for sure was his father.

She didn't know what it meant, but too many things pointed to Dylan's father to be ignored. The fact that she'd been drawn to the wedding photo at his grandmother's house—even the fact that they were at his grandmother's house—seemed as if it were meant to be. But would Dylan's own father want to see his son put in jail? Given what she knew about the man—his pride, his big reputation—why would he want to risk that to hurt Dylan? Or was his dislike so intense, so strong, that he'd jeopardize it all to send Dylan to jail?

"Why does he hate you so much?" she asked. "You can't tell me you haven't wondered over the years where so much of his animosity comes from."

Dylan hesitated, then shrugged. "I came up with dozens of reasons, but who knows the truth? My father is a perfectionist, a control freak. He couldn't stand a messy room, a spilled cup, any kind of chaos, and I was the kid who always came home with dirt on my shoes and a rip in my clothes. It made him crazy, and Jake was better at following the rules than I was. My father used to say that if I weren't such a stupid fool, he wouldn't have to continually teach me a lesson."

Catherine was sorry she'd asked, seeing the pain in Dylan's eyes. She knew there was never a good reason for abuse, and most abusers justified their actions by claiming it was the victim's fault. Obviously Richard Sanders had done just that. She shivered as Dylan's father's image flashed through her mind again. His features had become indelibly imprinted on her brain, and what she saw was a cold, hard, ruthless man.

"You were right, Catherine. I shouldn't have dismissed my father as a suspect so quickly. I sure would like to know who left me this CD," Dylan said. "Is this supposed to help me? To point me in my father's or someone else's direction?"

She wished she could give him the answers he wanted, but she'd never felt more at a loss for words. Slowly she shook her head. "I don't know, Dylan."

He blew out a breath and threw back his shoulders. "Well, there's only one thing to do." He ejected the disc and slipped it back into the case.

She was almost afraid to ask. "What's that?"

"Talk to my father."

The tape of Ravino and his dad played around and around in Dylan's head as he drove across town to his father's house. He could see the two men hunched over the small table, deep in conversation, and then the way they'd both smiled up at Erica. His father had known Erica, too. Had he also had an affair with her? The thought made him sick to his stomach—that he and his father might have slept with the same woman . . . He was tempted to pull over and throw up, the way Catherine had done the night before. But he didn't have time to be sick. He needed to think. He had to figure out what was going on.

The idea that his father could be involved in his current troubles was mind-blowing, although he had to admit that ever since he'd woken up in the Tahoe woods he'd had the feeling that this particular payback was very personal. His father had hated him forever. The question wasn't really why would he do this, but why wouldn't he? And if he knew Ravino and Erica . . . hell, the three of them could have been in on it together.

But why had someone left him the video? And when had the meeting between his father and Ravino actually occurred—before or after Ravino had killed his wife? He had so many questions. But at least now he had someone else to ask. His father was probably home on a Sunday, in the house Dylan had grown up in. It wasn't where he would have chosen to have a meeting; just going into that house made Dylan feel like a vulnerable kid again. But he reminded himself that he was anything but that. And the only way to win was to take back control of the game.

"You might want to slow down," Catherine suggested as he took a turn on what felt like two wheels. "The last thing we need is to get stopped by the cops for speeding."

He eased his foot off the gas, wondering how his crazy, psychic partner had become the voice of reason, when he'd usually prided himself on acting on facts rather than emotion.

"Do you know what you want to say to your dad?" Catherine asked.

"I'm going to ask him if he's setting me up."

"That's one way to go," she said dryly. "Or you could be more subtle. If you put your father on the defensive right away he won't tell you anything. Why not go in with the question of how he knows Ravino—or Erica? Tell him you saw a video of them together at the Metro Club. That might get him talking about Ravino."

"It's not a bad idea," he said somewhat grudgingly. "But you don't know my father. No matter what I say to him, the conversation will go ballistic within thirty seconds. We've never been able to have a discussion that didn't end in an argument." He glanced over at her. "With Ravino in jail, I knew we needed to link Erica to someone else. I sure as hell didn't think it would be my father."

"Or the link could be any one of the other dozen people who were in the room that night. The video lasted for several minutes," she continued. "Erica and Ravino talked to other people, including that man with the ring that looked familiar to you. Maybe your father wasn't meant to be the focal point of that video."

"Of course he was. Otherwise no one would have given me that disc. They wanted me to see that Ravino and my father knew each other." Dylan stopped at a red light, hitting the steering wheel in frustration. "What makes me crazy is wondering whether going to my father is exactly what they want. I feel like a puppet.

Someone else is pulling the strings, and I just keep dancing to their tune."

"That's a good point. Maybe we shouldn't show up on your father's doorstep."

"I have to. I need to know one way or the other if my father is the puppet master. You'd better come in with me. I might need a witness—or someone to stop me from killing him."

"I'm more worried about someone trying to kill you. Erica is dead, Dylan. You could be next on the list. And if your father hates you . . ."

"That's why I want to take him by surprise. He's not going to shoot me in his own home. Not with his girl-friend around, or his housekeeper."

"I hope you're right."

Dylan turned off the busy commercial streets, driving through a neighborhood of tall, stately homes and mansions. He pulled up in front of a two-story Mediterranean-style villa with an ornate iron fence surrounding the property. He'd often felt like a prisoner behind that fence, and it took everything he had to park the car and turn off the engine. He'd been there only once in the past few years, and the last time was to swipe his father's Metro Club card. He'd deliberately gone at a time when his father would be at work. The housekeeper, Mrs. Rogers, who'd always had a soft spot for him, had let him in on the pretense that he wanted to get some old photos of Jake and himself for the wedding.

His father had probably figured out by now that he'd used his membership to get into the club, and it was possible Mrs. Rogers wouldn't let him in the door. But he had to try. He had to confront his father. And he gave himself a mental kick in the ass for even hesitating. There was nothing Richard Sanders could do to hurt him now. They were both grown men. His father no longer had a physical advantage.

"Beautiful houses often hide ugly secrets, don't they?" Catherine murmured.

"Yes, they do. I want to do this, but . . ."

"I know," she said, an understanding gleam in her eye. "It won't be easy. But you're good at the tough stuff, Dylan. You can do it."

"I don't suppose you have any insight as to what will happen inside?"

"Sorry. I guess we'll both find out at the same time."

"Which is now," he said decisively. "Let's go before I change my mind."

"I've never been very good at meeting the parents," Catherine said as they got out of the car and paused on the sidewalk. "I never know what to say, how to impress them. And what I do say usually comes out wrong and stupid, and I embarrass myself."

"This isn't that kind of meeting, Catherine."

"Are you good at meeting the parents?"

"I don't meet parents. In fact, I don't usually ask if the woman I'm with has parents."

"Really? That's the first question I ask a guy. I guess I always thought one day I'd meet a man with a wonderful family, and they'd become my family, and everything would be good again." She cast him a curious look. "You never thought that way? Never wanted to replace your bad experience with a positive one?"

"Too big a risk that the next experience would turn out just as bad." Dylan started down the path, moving more quickly with each step. She sensed he was gathering strength for the confrontation ahead.

Dylan rang the bell, which pealed loudly through the house. A moment later an older woman opened the front door. She wore black slacks and a white button-down blouse, and her hair was sprinkled with gray. Her dark eyes filled with surprise when she saw Dylan. "Oh, my goodness. What are you doing here?"

"Hello, Mrs. Rogers," Dylan said. "Is my father home?"

"Yes, but he won't want to see you. You have to go." The woman cast a quick look over her shoulder. "He's still upset that you snuck in here a few weeks ago and used his membership card for the Metro Club. He almost fired me for letting you in. I need this job, Dylan. I'm too old to get another one. And your father, for all his faults, pays me well."

"Don't worry. I'll tell him you tried to keep me out." Dylan pushed past the housekeeper. "Where is he? In the den?"

Catherine followed Dylan into the entryway, offering the housekeeper an apologetic smile, but the woman's anxiety was palpable. She twisted her hands together in agitation. "Dylan, this isn't a good time. Your father has been very stressed lately. He's been working long hours, getting telephone calls even after he comes home, holding late-night meetings. It's a busy time for him."

"Why? What's he working on?"

"I don't know. His business."

"Does Senator Ravino ever call here?'

"What the hell is going on?" Dylan's father demanded as he stomped into the entryway, interrupting their conversation.

Even though she'd seen him in the video, Catherine wasn't prepared for the size of the man. He was tall and broad-shouldered and wore a gray cashmere sweater over a pair of black trousers. There was a dark fire of rage in his eyes when his gaze settled on his youngest son. He didn't even glance in Catherine's direction. She felt almost invisible as the energy centered on the two men. Mrs. Rogers slid out of the room, obviously not wanting to be part of the conversation.

Dylan straightened, but he was still a few inches shorter and many pounds lighter than his father. He raised his chin in the air, threw back his shoulders, and said, "I want to know what your connection is to Joseph Ravino."

"That's none of your business," his father replied sharply. "Now get out."

Dylan stood his ground. "Not until you answer my question. I saw a video that shows the two of you together at the Metro Club. You were in an intense conversation."

"We're both members of the club; there's no crime in that. Or are you trying to frame me like you did Ravino?"

Catherine watched Dylan's father, hoping to catch

some sign in his expression that would tell her if he was speaking the truth, if he really thought Dylan had set up the senator. But Richard Sanders was impossible to read, his emotions hidden behind a very cold facade.

"I didn't frame him. Ravino killed his wife. I just helped the police figure it out."

"You think you're some big man now?" Richard challenged. "You're not. You're a worthless piece of shit, and you always have been. Now leave, or I'll call the police and have you thrown out."

"I'll go when I'm ready. Do you know Erica Layton? And I'd suggest you think about your answer before you give it."

Something flickered in the older man's eyes, Catherine thought. Mr. Sanders did know Erica. But how close was their relationship? Did that flash of guilt have to do with Erica's death or something else?

"Erica Layton worked at the Metro Club," Dylan added. "She was a hostess in the back room."

"I know that," Dylan's father replied. "So what?"

"She had an affair with the senator. She revealed his motive for murdering his wife. And now she's . . . disappeared."

"Why should I care? She's nothing to me."

Before Dylan could reply, a very attractive woman came down the stairs. She was dressed in white cropped pants and a button-down pink blouse, her blond hair styled away from her face. His father's girlfriend, Catherine presumed. The woman appeared to be a good fifteen years younger than Richard. She had a cool, classic beauty, the perfect accessory for a rich and successful man. But perhaps Catherine wasn't giving them enough credit. Maybe they actually cared for each other, although it was hard to believe that the hard man standing in front of her was capable of caring for anyone.

"What's going on?" the woman inquired. "You're Dylan, right? I recognize you from the news."

"And you must be Rachel Montgomery," Dylan said.

"How do you know her name?" Dylan's father interrupted.

"I keep up."

"You stay out of my business."

"Richard, maybe we should offer Dylan and his friend something to drink," Rachel said.

For the first time Dylan's father looked in her direction. Faced with the sharp point of his gaze, Catherine felt a sudden desire to flee, but she couldn't leave Dylan alone, not here, not with the bully of his childhood. Instead Catherine moved over to Dylan, slipping her hand into his. She didn't know if he welcomed her support or not, but his fingers tightened around hers and he didn't let go.

"I'm Catherine Hilliard," she said when Dylan couldn't seem to find his way to an introduction.

"Richard Sanders," the man said gruffly. He'd been too well trained not to be polite to a stranger.

Now that he realized she'd witnessed his conversation, he seemed discomfited by her presence. He probably preferred to keep his hateful attitude toward his son a secret.

"Would you like a drink, some coffee?" Rachel asked. "Where on earth is Mrs. Rogers? I'm surprised she didn't offer you anything."

"We're fine," Dylan bit out.

"They're just leaving," Richard added.

"In a minute," Dylan countered. "You want me out of your business, then stay out of mine," he said to his father.

"I don't give a damn about anything that concerns you. Why would I? You were a terrible son, a huge disappointment. Nothing has changed."

Catherine felt her hands clenching into fists as she was assailed with the urge to punch Richard Sanders right in his stuck-up face. "Dylan is not a disappointment," she interjected. "He's an incredible man, and you're lucky to have him as a son. If you don't know that, you're a fool."

Richard spluttered with shock, his face turning red. "How dare you—"

"I dare because this is a good man, and you should see him for who he is."

"So now you've brought a woman to fight your battles for you," Richard said with a sneer in Dylan's direction. "How very impressive."

"At least I have a woman who's willing to stand by me. My mother walked out on you."

"She didn't walk out. I threw her out."

"That's not what you said before," Dylan countered.

"It's what happened."

"Why?" Dylan asked. "Why would you throw her out?"

"That's my business," Richard retorted. "And it was over a long time ago. Now, we're done. Get out."

"I will find out what happened to my mother. Hell, I may even find her and ask her myself," Dylan said. "But first I'm going to figure out how you're connected to Erica Layton and Senator Ravino. If you're involved in Erica's disappearance, you'd better get yourself a lawyer."

"You're the one who will need a lawyer if you come back here, Dylan. As far as I'm concerned, I no longer have two sons. I only have one."

Dylan uttered a harsh, bitter laugh. "Actually, you don't have any. Jake doesn't care about you. He didn't invite you to his wedding. Did you notice that?"

"He invited me. I chose not to come," Richard said. "But you and I—we're through. You're an adult. Live your life and stay out of mine."

Richard turned on his heel and walked down the hall. A moment later a door shut.

"I'm sorry. He's been a little tense lately," Rachel said nervously, darting a quick look after Richard. "I'm sure he didn't mean what he said. He's always talking about how proud he is of his sons."

"Son, maybe," Dylan said. "Why has he been so stressed? What's going on with him?"

"Some problem at work, I guess. He didn't say, but he hasn't been sleeping well."

Catherine wondered if Richard's insomnia had something to do with framing his son for murder.

"Who's the woman you were asking Richard about?" Rachel inquired.

"Erica Layton. Has Richard ever mentioned her?"

Rachel shook her head. "I don't think so. You'd better go before he comes back out here."

"I'll go," Dylan agreed. "You should consider leaving, too. He's not a good man. Sooner or later he'll show you his true colors."

Dylan let his words sink in, then opened the front door and motioned for Catherine to precede him. She muttered a quick good-bye to Rachel and left the house. She could feel Dylan's tension as they walked to the car. She knew he was putting on a front, and he had to be hurting inside. He'd just never admit it.

When they reached the car she gazed back at the house and saw a curtain flutter in a downstairs window. Someone had been watching them leave—Rachel or Dylan's father? Was Richard Sanders as innocent, as uninvolved as he claimed? Or was the recent stress he'd been suffering due to an elaborate plan to get his son out of his life once and for all?

"Are you okay?" Catherine asked. "Maybe I should drive."

"I'm fine. The last thing I want to do is sit in the passenger seat and twiddle my thumbs."

"You could play with the radio," she said lightly.

Dylan didn't crack a smile, just got behind the wheel and slammed the door shut. She took the passenger seat, flipping the locks down once they were inside. Despite Dylan's desire to drive, he made no move to start the car.

"I think he could have done it," he said, his voice bleak. The encounter with his father had taken a lot out of him. It was the one relationship he couldn't fix, couldn't make work no matter how hard he tried. And she suspected that even though he hated his father, there was still a part of him that wanted his father's love, something Dylan would never admit.

"He could have killed Erica—maybe not himself, since he wouldn't want to get his hands dirty, but he could have hired someone to do it," Dylan continued. "He has plenty of money."

"What's his motive?"

"She knew too much about him. Perhaps he's tied to Ravino. They could be working together."

"Or not," Catherine suggested. "I watched your father. He did know Erica. I saw him twitch when you said her name. But he didn't look guilty. He appeared more nervous than anything."

"Because he killed her."

"I don't know, Dylan. I think it's hard for you to judge your father fairly because he's so horrible to you."

"And what the hell were you doing sticking up for me?" Dylan asked, turning to look at her with irritation in his eyes. "I didn't need you to get into the middle of a fight that didn't concern you."

"I couldn't just stand by and let him say those things about you."

"I've heard them before, many times."

"Well, I haven't, and he pissed me off. You're not some worthless piece of shit, Dylan."

"I know that."

"Do you?" she challenged. "Your father has worked awfully hard to convince you otherwise."

"I do," he said, the anger dissipating from his gaze. "It took me a while, but I finally figured out he was the shithead, not me."

"Good. And you should be thanking me, not yelling at me. I could have said a lot more to the man. I was just getting started."

A slow smile spread across Dylan's face. "You're something else, Catherine."

"'Something else' could be good or bad."

"In this case it's good. And you're right—again. Thank you." He paused. "So, did you pick up any other vibes in the house?"

"Your father lied when he told you that Jake invited him to the wedding. I think it bothers him that Jake didn't."

"But he had to save face in front of his girlfriend. I almost feel sorry for her. He's an asshole, and sooner or later she'll figure that out." He started the car and pulled away from the curb. "Just the way my mother did."

"Did you mean what you said about finding her?"

"When this is all over," Dylan said. "I can't let it go any longer. But first I have to figure out what happened to Erica."

"Let's go over what we know," Catherine said. "Assuming Erica didn't anticipate that she was about to be double-crossed, she went to Tahoe with the intention of drugging you and luring you into the woods, which she did. She took your tie and cuff link and cut your hand so she could place evidence in her cabin and also in the lake. But then something went wrong. Someone came to the cabin in the middle of the night and frightened her. She ran, probably hiding in the woods until morning. Then she fled back to San Francisco. Which means she must have had her car." Catherine paused. "Was her car at her condo?"

"I didn't notice it. I wasn't really looking."

"Or the car could be somewhere else in the city. Where else was she?"

"In my apartment; then she went to the Palace of Fine Arts, then Golden Gate Park," Dylan finished. "Why are you worrying about her car?"

"It just seems to me that if she had anything that might lead to whoever she was working with, then it would mostly likely be on her person or in her car, especially since we didn't find anything at her house or yours."

Dylan sent her an approving look. "Good thinking. So we need to find her car. She had a white Jetta; I know that much. It could be in the park. That's the last place she was."

"I think she was on foot in the park," Catherine said. "When I connected with her in my vision she was running and she was tired. I didn't have the sense that she drove there and started walking."

"Then we'll back it up, starting at my apartment. I should have thought of this before."

"You've had a lot on your mind. Don't beat yourself up about it."

"I'm usually better than this."

She knew Dylan set the bar high for himself, but he was only human—not that he'd admit it. They drove across town in silence. As they turned down Dylan's street Catherine studied the parked cars. They were almost at the end of the block when she spotted it. "There it is."

"Finally, a little luck," Dylan said with satisfaction. He pulled into a spot in front of the Jetta.

"Wait," she said as Dylan moved to get out of the car. "There's no one around, is there? No one watching from any of the other cars?" She checked the side-view mirror as Dylan turned in his seat to look behind them. She wasn't just worried about Erica's killer; she was also concerned that the police might be keeping an eye on Dylan's apartment in the hope that he would turn up there.

"I don't see anyone," he said. "But when I get out switch places with me and keep the car running, in case we have to make a quick getaway."

"I'm starting to feel like Bonnie and Clyde."

"Let's hope we don't end up like them," Dylan said as he shut the door.

She crawled over the gearshift and behind the wheel, then watched Dylan's progress through the rearview mirror. He walked right up to the car, paused, looked around, and then checked the doors. A shiver ran through her as she watched him touch the door handle.

She closed her eyes as an image took shape in her mind.

The air was cold. It cut through her dress as she got out of the car. Last night's terror was still fresh in her mind, and she couldn't help but take a look over her shoulder. No one was there. She was safe for the moment. As she reached for her purse her cell phone fell out of the side pocket and slid between the seats. Swearing, she tried to pull it out, but it was wedged in. She'd retrieve it later. She needed to get inside.

Slamming the car door, she walked quickly across the sidewalk to Dylan's apartment building. She was glad now that she'd swiped his keys when she had the chance, although her original intention had been only to make it harder for him to leave Tahoe. She slid the outside door key in with a shaky hand and was relieved when the lock turned. She bounded up the stairs to his apartment, not taking another deep breath until she was inside. Pressing her palms against the back of the door, she stood for a moment to get her bearings.

Now that she was here she wasn't sure what to do. Crossing the room, she picked up the phone and dialed Dylan's cell phone. She had to tell him what was happening. He would be pissed that she'd set him up, but ultimately he'd have to help her. For his sake as well as hers, she had to stay alive.

The phone rang a couple of times. Finally he answered. She started to tell him she was sorry, that she didn't have a choice. Then she heard the front doorknob turn.

Her heart stood still. Someone was trying to break in. It wasn't Dylan. He was on the phone. She hung up, his voice still ringing in her ear. She moved around the room, searching for a way out, but she was on the second floor.

Whoever was after her was going to get her.

She ran into the bedroom, sensing that she didn't have much time. She threw open one of the windows, relieved to see the branches of a tree not far away. If she missed the tree, she could severely hurt herself. But what choice did she have?

She crawled out of the window and jumped toward the tree, her hands slipping on the branch, but she managed to hang on. Then she scrambled down the trunk, dropping to the ground just as she heard a male swear from the floor above her.

She ran through the next yard, pausing when she hit the street. She saw a man come out of Dylan's building. He was between her and her car. Unable to go back, she fled down the block, trying to stay close to the buildings and out of sight. She didn't stop running until she reached the park by the Palace of Fine Arts. She could lose herself in the crowds, the building, the shadows.

"Please, God, don't let him find me," she prayed. But she wondered deep in her heart if anyone was listening. She'd been a fool to believe she was only supposed to pretend to be dead. Her greed had gotten her into this mess, and now she was going to pay.

"Catherine."

Catherine opened her eyes as Dylan's sharp voice penetrated her brain. He'd opened the door on the passenger side, and he was holding a woman's purse.

"I found her bag in the car," he said. "But there's nothing in it except a wallet, a few pens, and some makeup."

She swallowed, trying to bring herself back to reality. "Her cell phone is in the car."

Dylan stared at her for a moment. Then he said, "Where?"

"Between the seats. It fell out of her purse when she reached for your keys."

He took a breath but didn't bother to ask her how she

knew. He jogged back to Erica's car, and she watched him reach between the seats, finally pulling out a hot-pink metallic phone. He was already reading through the numbers when he returned to the car. "Anything else?" he said.

"Nothing that will help you, I don't think. You already know that Erica was in your apartment, and that someone came in after her. She went out the window in your bedroom and ran toward the Palace of Fine Arts."

"You're channeling her again, even though she's dead? Do you think there's a chance that the woman in the park is not her?" Dylan asked.

She immediately cut him off with a wave of her hand, seeing the hopeful glint in his eyes fade. "No, I'm sorry."

"Then where did the vision come from?"

"It was her car. I was watching you, and when you touched the door I suddenly saw her and all the rest."

Dylan sat down in the seat and pulled the door shut, then stared at the cell phone in his hand. "I don't recognize any of these numbers, but I certainly don't mind spending the afternoon calling them. Erica must have had some contact with whoever used her to get to me. That person has to be on this phone. We're getting close, Catherine. I can feel it."

"I hope so. But I don't think we should hang around here."

"I agree. Looks like you finally got the driver's seat. Go down to the corner and turn left. I'll direct you back to my grandmother's house from there."

"Do you think we'll still be safe there?"

He turned on the car radio, flipping through the channels until he got to the news. "As long as we don't hear my name I think we're still okay—for a few hours, anyway."

Catherine shivered as a chill ran through her. She had the distinct feeling they weren't going to have that long.

Chapter 13

Catherine's tension eased as she drove away from Dylan's apartment. Leaving Erica's Jetta behind seemed to break the link between them. Her mind felt light again, yet she couldn't deny a lingering sadness. Her visions had taken her into Erica's head. She had experienced the same fear, the same desperation, and Erica was now dead. She'd lost her battle, and there wasn't a damn thing Catherine could do about it. Erica might have made some huge mistakes, but she certainly hadn't deserved to die.

And it wasn't over. There was still a fight to win, Catherine reminded herself. That was what she had to focus on now. She couldn't do anything to save Erica, but she could help Dylan, and hopefully together they would find Erica's killer and make sure he paid for what he'd done. Erica would have justice, even if she wasn't completely innocent.

Having glimpsed Erica's thoughts, Catherine knew

the woman had been conflicted about what she was doing. Not that that justified her actions, but Erica had obviously felt some pressure to set Dylan up; she'd had some reason to participate, and Catherine suspected that whoever had coerced or invited Erica to participate had known exactly how to manipulate her. That person was very, very clever. She and Dylan were going to have to be smarter.

They had almost reached Dylan's grandmother's house when Catherine spotted a supermarket with a deli. Her stomach rumbled at the thought of food, and she decided to make a quick stop. It was already after one o'clock, and they would need some fuel to keep them going. Dylan looked up from the cell phone when she pulled into the parking lot.

"Groceries," she said simply.

"Want me to go with you?"

"I think I can make it on my own, and your face is the one we're most worried about being seen," she replied.

"I wouldn't be so sure of that. We might see a photo of both of us on the evening news."

She paused, her hand on the door. "The only photo they'd have of me is the one on my driver's license. That's a scary thought."

"Don't flash your license or a credit card in the store. Do you need cash?"

"I have enough. I'll be right back."

It felt surprisingly normal to walk into the market, to be around people who were completing their average, everyday Sunday chores. So much had happened in the past few days, Catherine had begun to feel caught up in a vacuum. Now she could breathe again, give her brain a rest, peruse gossip magazines and listen to the idle conversations of the people waiting in line to check out.

A mother and her young son were in line in front of her. The boy was about four or five years old and was standing in the back of the shopping cart, holding on to the side with tiny, grubby hands. A colorful Band-Aid, decorated with red stars, crossed his forehead, and he was not happy about it. He kept putting his fingers to the Band-Aid. The mother smoothed the golden curls away in a loving, tender gesture. "Don't touch," she said. "We want to keep your skin clean."

Catherine's heart sped up as another voice came into her head, another woman, another child. . . .

The little boy was crying, his knee scraped. The mother knelt down on the deck and placed the Band-Aid over his cut. Then she put her arms around the child and gave him a tight squeeze. Her yellow summer dress blew in the breeze. "It's okay, Dylan. You're all right. Mommy will make it better."

Catherine rocked back on her heels as she realized she'd seen Dylan with his mother, the woman who'd left him so many years ago, who'd abandoned him to his abusive father, the woman Dylan thought hated him. But the woman in her vision had seemed soft and caring, tender and kind. Something was off about Dylan's memories. Or maybe there was something Dylan didn't know about his mother. Catherine sensed that what she'd seen was important in some way. It had been just a brief moment in time, but it meant something. She had to figure out what.

Maybe she'd tapped into his mother because they'd

been at his father's house where so many of Dylan's memories were stored. Or perhaps she was remembering because Dylan was remembering. But that didn't seem likely. Dylan was intent on forgetting his past, not bringing it back.

After checking out of the store she returned to the car to find Dylan on the phone. He hung up with a frown as she set her groceries on the backseat and then slipped behind the wheel.

"Who were you talking to?" she asked.

"Unfortunately, no one. That was the third no answer, no message machine that I called. I thought this phone was going to be more helpful, but so far I've spoken to a woman at a hair salon where Erica went, connected with her wireless company, and reached a pizza place."

"It's funny how those details make her seem less evil, more human, just like us. It's really horrible, what happened to her."

"Yeah," Dylan said in a clipped voice.

"You're not letting yourself feel it, are you?"

He shot her an annoyed look. "What's the point? If I waste time and energy feeling sorry for Erica, I may end up just like her."

She knew he wasn't as callous as he pretended to be. He cared. She'd seen it in his eyes last night when the reality of what had happened to Erica had become clear. But she could understand why he needed to keep his emotions under lock and key, at least for now. Perhaps if he let himself feel too much, he wouldn't be able to go on the way he needed to go on.

Dylan was far more used to compartmentalizing his feelings than she was. As a journalist he had to stay apart from the action. He had to keep a distance between the horror he was reporting and himself. That was what he was doing now. She, on the other hand, felt as if part of her had died the night before. And she felt a sharp edge of pain every time the last image she had of Erica played in her head. She hoped someday she would be able to forget it.

"Erica made a lot of calls in the last two weeks," Dylan said with a sigh.

Catherine started the car and drove out of the parking lot. "Any numbers look familiar?"

"She called my news station three times last week."

"Well, you said she'd tried to call you before she came to Tahoe, so that makes sense."

"The odd thing is, I don't remember getting any messages from her at work. She left messages on my cell and also my home phone but not at work."

"She might not have wanted you to know how many times she was calling, and if you weren't in she just hung up."

"Yeah, you're probably right."

Catherine heard the doubt in his voice. "What are you thinking, Dylan?"

"I'm not sure. I just have a bad feeling. Shit. I'm starting to sound like you."

"You should listen to your feelings," she said, ignoring the jab. "If she didn't call you at the station, who else would she have called?"

"I can't think of anyone." He paused. "Maybe . . .

God, I wonder if Blake Howard is a member of the Metro Club. It would be just like him to belong to an exclusive men's club where he could network with the rich and powerful. If that's true, and he knows Erica—"

"Then he's another connecting link between Erica and all the players we've named so far," Catherine said, with a rush of new excitement. "That would certainly point away from your father. How do we find out if Blake is a member?"

"I'll call his assistant, Rita. She'll know. Even if he is a member, it's a long shot he's behind this. Blake doesn't have that much of a reason to hate me; nor, as I said before, is he that smart."

"Sometimes people play dumb on purpose. It lets them slide under the radar."

"Possibly. I know he's ambitious, and he's also rich. He has some family money backing him. I can't recall him reacting in any particular way to my story on Ravino, although I never asked for his opinion. If he is a Metro Club member, then he probably knew the senator, too, or hoped to." Dylan paused. "You have a good sense of direction. My grandmother's house is on the next block."

"I know. I paid attention when we left."

"You'd make a good reporter, Catherine."

She let out a small laugh. "No way. I could never objectively report the news. I'd get too involved and probably be really depressed most of the time."

"You build up a thick skin over the years. Well, maybe not you," he admitted.

"Thanks."

"It's not an insult."

"Really? I can't imagine that you like emotional women."

"I don't like women who are drama, drama, drama. But that's not you. You're just . . . complicated."

"I'll give you that," she said, as she parked the car in front of his grandmother's house. "And I'll take complicated over crazy any day of the week."

As she stepped out of the car Catherine realized that the neighborhood had come to life since they'd left earlier that morning. Down the street a man watered plants in front of his house. Across the block two kids were playing catch. It was a beautiful sunny Sunday afternoon, the fog lingering on the edge of the horizon but still several hours away from blowing in off the ocean and covering the city.

She followed Dylan up to the house, keeping an eye out for anything unusual, but everything appeared normal. It was doubtful anyone knew where they were, but sooner or later the news about Erica would come out. And certainly Dylan would be a person of interest, if not an outright suspect.

"Do you think you should call your lawyer again?" she asked as they entered the house.

"Mark said he'd e-mail me with news, so I'll check my computer in a minute."

Catherine set the bags of food on the kitchen counter and began unpacking the deli sandwiches she'd picked up. She'd also gotten a rotisserie chicken and some salad makings for dinner. The fewer times they had to leave the house the better.

"Wow," Dylan said as she handed him his turkey-and-ham combo with all the fixings. "I was expecting eggplant with tomatoes on some type of whole-grain bread."

"That's mine," she said with a smile. "How did you guess?"

"I must be picking up on some of your psychic powers."

"That must be it. Speaking of which . . ." She sat down at the table, not sure she wanted to bring up her latest vision, but then again, it could be important, and she might not be able to understand the significance without Dylan.

He set down his sandwich and gave her a wary look. "Why do I get the feeling I'm about to lose my appetite?"

"I was standing in line at the supermarket and there was this mom and her kid in front of me, and the little boy had a Band-Aid on his forehead. I suddenly flashed on another scene. I think it was you and your mother. You had fallen and scraped your knee. She said, 'Don't worry, Dylan. Mommy will make it better.' "

Dylan didn't blink for a long moment, and then he sat back in his chair with a definite shake of his head. "That couldn't have been my mother. She didn't do anything to make my life better."

"You were small, maybe five or six," Catherine said, seeing the echo of pain in his eyes. "I think you were on a deck. It was summer. There was a breeze."

"God." He breathed out. He rested his elbows on the table and put his head in his hands.

She didn't say anything, giving him a moment to re-group. Finally he lifted his head and gazed back at her. "I fell on the pier near our beach house. She put a Band-Aid on my knee. I can't believe I remember that now." He took a breath. "Why would you see that? It doesn't have anything to do with Erica or her killer."

"It has to do with you. Maybe I saw it because we were just in your father's house. Perhaps I was picking up on the vibes there, the lingering ties to your mother, your desire to find out what happened to her."

"My mother hasn't been in that house in twenty-three years."

"But she lived there once, and she's tied to you and to your father. She's also tied to this house. Her photo is upstairs."

"How is your vision supposed to help me?" he challenged. "And you know, it's not like you couldn't have made it up. Every kid skins his knee. Every mother puts on Band-Aids."

She didn't waver in the face of his accusation. He was rattled by his memory, and he'd rather attack her than face what her vision might mean to him. "You remember the incident I described," she said quietly. "And you know somewhere in that thick, stubborn brain of yours that I didn't make it up. We are way past that."

He looked away from her gaze, staring down at his sandwich. After a moment he said, "Even if it was true, so what? Even if she was kind to me back then, even if she cared for a minute, it means nothing to me now. So why should I care about that one moment in time?"

"There had to be other moments, Dylan."

"A few," he conceded. "I got sick after we came back from the beach. I remember being in the hospital for a long time. But eventually I got better, and the next thing I knew she was gone."

"You were in the hospital?" Catherine queried. "You never mentioned that before."

"It's not important. I survived."

"What was wrong with you?"

"I don't remember, some kind of virus or infection. It never came back. I still don't see how your vision is supposed to help me."

"I didn't say it would help you. I just wanted to be up front about it." She knew that Dylan wanted a specific reason for why she'd gotten that brief glimpse into his childhood, but she couldn't give him that. She didn't know herself. "For some reason it's important that you remember her."

"I don't want to remember her," he said, jerking to his feet. "Don't you get it, Catherine? I've spent most of my life trying to forget her. The last thing I want to do is bring her back." He strode toward the door.

"Where are you going? Don't you want to eat?"

"I'm not hungry anymore. I'm going to check my e-mail and review the Metro Club video on my computer." He paused in the doorway. "The past isn't what's important, Catherine. It's the present and the future—the future I do not want to spend in jail. Why don't you concentrate on that for a while and stop trying to piece together my broken family?"

She didn't bother to argue, even though she knew that he was dead wrong. He wouldn't be able to figure out his present or his future until he'd come to terms with his past.

Dylan took the materials he'd gathered at his office into his grandmother's den and set up shop. As his computer booted up on the desk, he paced around the room, restless and angry. He was tired of being the last person to know anything. Even Catherine, with her damn cryptic visions, was a step ahead of him. He needed to find a way to get out in front, to turn the tables. But how could he do that when he had no idea who was pulling the strings in this puppet show?

Was it his father? Was it Ravino? Was it Blake Howard?

He sat down in the desk chair and loaded the video. He played it over and over, scanning every blurry face in the background in search of clues. When he got to the man with his hand on Erica's waist, the ring on the man's finger tugged at his brain. He knew he'd seen that ring before. It was probably Blake's. He wore one of those Ivy League school rings on his left hand, a sign of his importance.

Taking out a piece of paper, he jotted down some names, leaving space under each one. He put Ravino at the top, then his father, then Blake. Who else? He tapped his pencil on the desktop. Then he wrote down Erica. She had an obvious tie to Ravino, a link to his father through the club and possibly Blake. That was one connection he could check out right away. Setting down his pencil, he typed out a quick e-mail to Blake's assistant, Rita Herriman, asking if Blake was a member of the Metro Club. He made it appear as if he were also interested in joining the club and wanted a sponsor. That might get him a direct answer to at least one question. He wanted to ask Rita if Blake had received any phone calls from Erica, but he had to consider how she would view the question when she found out Erica was dead and he was the prime suspect.

How could it hurt? He typed in the question and hit the send button before he could change his mind. Like most newspeople, Rita would no doubt check her messages before the end of the day.

Clicking out of his mail program, he pulled out the tapes of his interviews with Erica, slipped them into his minicassette player, and pushed play. Erica's nervous voice gave him a jolt. It was eerie to hear her speaking and know that she was now dead.

Turning off the tape, he got to his feet and returned to the kitchen. Catherine was reading the newspaper.

"I'm going down to the corner," he told her. "There's a pay phone there. I didn't have any e-mails from Mark, but I want to check in with him."

"Do you want me to come?"

"I'll just be a couple of minutes."

"Be careful," she said, concern in her eyes. "I'm almost afraid to let you out of my sight. It's strange, because I've been living on my own for years, but I'm getting kind of used to having you around."

To his surprise, he felt much the same way. "Don't worry; I'll be back."

* * *

Mark answered on the third ring. "What's up?" Dylan asked.

"I was just about to e-mail you. The woman in the park has been positively identified as Erica Layton. The Lake Tahoe Sheriff's Department is now working with the San Francisco Police Department. They've officially turned over their information to our guys here, including the circumstantial evidence that they have against you."

"That evidence shouldn't mean anything, since Erica didn't die in Tahoe."

"Unfortunately we're going to have to wait for the coroner's report to establish time and date of death, and that she wasn't killed elsewhere and then left in the park. There's more. The drug screen you had done yesterday came back negative."

Dylan couldn't believe what he was hearing. "That's impossible. Erica put something in my drink."

"There are certain drugs that leave the system fairly quickly without a trace. Fortunately DNA will take some time to get back, so if your blood was planted in Erica's Tahoe cabin or here in Golden Gate Park, it will be a few weeks before anyone figures that out. But I have to warn you, Dylan, that the SFPD has requested a search warrant for your house, which means they think they have enough evidence to show probable cause. Once they analyze your phone records, it will be clear that you were here in San Francisco at least near the time of Erica's death."

Dylan's stomach began to churn. He'd been expecting the other shoe to drop, and now it had. He was going to be an official suspect in a murder investigation.

"I talked to a friend of mine in the SFPD," Mark continued. "He told me you should turn yourself in as soon as possible so that they can clear your name."

"They're not going to clear my name; they're going to clear out a cell with my name on it."

"Dylan, Erica is dead. The police may be the least of your worries. Whoever killed her could be coming after you next."

"They want to frame me, not kill me."

"Are you sure about that?"

He wasn't at all sure. He had no real idea what the next move in this game would be. But Erica's murder had certainly upped the ante. Someone was playing for keeps, and depending on who was calling the shots, it wasn't impossible that they also wanted him dead.

"Do you know anything about the way Erica was killed?" he asked.

"She was shot—that's all I know."

"Any evidence at the crime scene?"

"Not that anyone wanted to share with me, but if her murder was part of your setup, then I'm betting something was there to tie you to the crime. I don't think you have a choice, Dylan. You have to turn yourself in."

"Not yet. I need a little more time. But listen, next time you talk to your cop buddy, tell him that there's another person who has a good reason for wanting Erica dead, and that's Joseph Ravino. She helped the police put him in prison. He could easily want revenge, not to mention the fact that it would probably weaken the case against him if she weren't alive to testify about their affair or her conversation with Ravino's wife. Instead of focusing solely on me, they should work that angle."

"I'll pass it along. Unfortunately, Ravino's being in jail means he couldn't have personally committed the crime."

"He didn't personally kill his wife either. He just made sure the Botox she injected into her face would kill her."

"Allegedly," Mark said.

"Well, the one thing I know for sure is that I didn't kill Erica. That means someone else did."

"Aside from the senator, do you have any other ideas?"

Dylan hesitated. "I recently uncovered a link between my father and Ravino. They both socialized at the Metro Club."

"What are you saying? You think your *father* is involved?" Mark asked, amazed. "I know you two don't have a good relationship, but a frame for murder? Your father is an upstanding citizen."

"On the outside he is, but you don't know the real man," Dylan said heavily.

"But murder? Is he capable of that?"

Dylan didn't even hesitate. "Absolutely. I'll be in touch, Mark, and I'll have my computer, so if you need to get hold of me send me a message."

Dylan hung up the phone. He couldn't believe the drug test had come back negative. The noose around his neck was drawing tighter. He didn't know how much longer he'd be free; he had to make use of every second.

"That's it," Dylan said as he finished updating Catherine on his conversation.

"That's a lot," she replied, worry in her eyes.

He tipped his head. "Which means I need to find a way out fast. I'll be in the den."

"Do you want my help?"

"No, there's nothing you can do."

Catherine wasn't surprised he declined her offer. Since she'd shared her vision about his mother, Dylan had cooled toward her. He didn't like that she'd seen that tender moment between him and his mother. It went against the grain. He saw his mother as an evil woman who'd abandoned him, and her vision had poked a hole in his picture. He didn't want to change his attitude. And he didn't want her reading his mind. She should have kept her mouth shut.

Every boyfriend she'd ever had she'd eventually scared away. She'd tried to keep her visions to herself. She'd tried to act normal, like everyone else, but then came the moment when she inadvertently revealed something that was uncomfortable or disturbing. Dylan probably wanted to send her packing. In fact, she wouldn't be surprised if he made the suggestion—but she wasn't going to leave. Whether he believed she could help him or not, she knew she was supposed to be here. And she wasn't going to run from the fear, not anymore. If Dylan could face his problems head-on, then so could she.

With Dylan holed up in the den, she decided to explore his grandmother's house. If she could find any clues to the relationship between Dylan's parents, it might help her understand the family dynamics.

Starting in the kitchen she went through every drawer, trying to open her heart and her brain to the vibrations and the memories. Dylan's grandmother's spirit was still within these walls, a woman who had ties to everyone in the family. Even though she'd never admitted to Dylan that she'd known of her son's abusive attitude toward his grandson, perhaps she had. Perhaps somewhere in this house that knowledge would be evident.

Catherine made her way through each room, eventually ending up once again in the master bedroom. It was the one place in the house that called to her more than any other. She took out the photo album she'd discovered the night before and went through the pictures again, settling on the wedding photograph. Now that she'd seen Dylan's father in person she had a better reference for the differences and similarities between the man in the photograph from thirty-something years ago and the man she'd seen today.

Richard Sanders had his arms around his bride. He looked like someone in love, as did his wife. Dylan's mother was slender and petite, with golden brown hair swept up under a veil. Tiny diamond earrings matched the diamond necklace around her neck. She was a pretty woman with a spark in her eyes that reminded Catherine of Dylan.

Why had she walked away from Dylan and Jake? And just as important, why had she never come back?

Maybe there was no good reason. Catherine had certainly grown up with a lot of kids who'd been deserted by their parents. That wasn't a new story or even an unusual one. So why did she have the feeling that there was something about Dylan's mother that needed to be discovered? It had to exist in her relationship with Richard.

Putting the album aside, Catherine went through the rest of the dresser drawers, striking pay dirt when she got to the last one. It was filled with papers and envelopes and, most important, journals. She pulled out one after another, realizing that Dylan's grandmother had kept diaries her entire life.

She sat down on the floor, leaned her back against the wall, and began to read. The journals began almost sixty years earlier, when his grandmother, Ruth Monroe, had been a little girl. Catherine skimmed through the first book. Apparently Ruth had been born and raised in San Francisco. Her father had run a hardware store. Her mother had been a teacher. Ruth had been the oldest of three children and the only girl, which often made her feel like an outsider, as her brothers were inseparable.

As Catherine continued to read, she began to feel a connection to the little girl telling her life story in bits and pieces. Her heart began to open, and she felt the emotions when Ruth graduated from eighth grade, when she went to high school, had her first kiss, fell in love, lost that love and thought her heart was broken. She followed Dylan's grandmother into her early twenties, to her first job as a receptionist at the *San Francisco*

Herald and her desire to work her way up to reporter, only to continue to be shunted to the society and fashion pages instead of hard news.

Catherine wondered if Dylan knew that his grandmother had shared his passion for journalism. Or maybe he did know, and that was why there was such a closeness between them.

Eventually Dylan's grandmother's ambition was tempered by love. In covering a high-society party, she met and fell in love with Conrad Sanders, the executive vice president of an insurance company. Within a year they were married and expecting a baby, a girl they named Eleanor. Two miscarriages followed Eleanor's birth, and Ruth despaired of ever giving her husband a son.

Catherine wiped her eyes, feeling the woman's sadness and burden as if they were her own. Then she smiled as she flipped through the pages and saw the entry announcing that she was pregnant. Ruth would have her baby boy. And she would name him Richard. Dylan's father had certainly been wanted. And spoiled, according to Ruth, who had chronicled her years as a mother and her guilt at wanting to give everything to the son she had waited so long to have, even at the expense of favoring Richard over Eleanor. Treated in many ways like a little prince, Richard had apparently earned his sense of entitlement at an early age.

As she picked up the next journal, Catherine realized she needed to turn on the lamp. The afternoon had passed and daylight had faded. Checking her watch, she realized it was almost seven. She'd been so wrapped up in the journals she'd lost track of time. The house was certainly quiet. Dylan must still be going over his tapes or working on his computer. Maybe she'd just read one more journal and then go see what he was doing.

The next diary picked up years later, and her pulse quickened as she realized that Ruth was writing about the fact that her precious Richard had asked a woman to marry him. The young woman's name was Olivia Marshall. She was a kindergarten teacher working at her first job. Richard's father, Conrad, was not happy about his son's choice. He thought Richard could have done far better than a teacher who came from a broken home and had not a speck of blue blood in her. But Richard was infatuated with Olivia. He'd even told his mother that Olivia had cast a spell over him. Ruth wrote in her diary that she was secretly thrilled about the match, because she thought Richard needed someone to soften him, to show him another side of life, but at the same time she also worried that Olivia wasn't strong enough to take on her son.

Had Richard broken Olivia's spirit? Was that why she'd run away? Catherine starting flipping pages, realizing that if Ruth had written about everything else, she'd surely written about the breakup of her son's marriage. But the journal ended with the celebration of Jake's birth, years before Richard and Olivia had split up.

Setting the book aside, she dug deeper into the drawer and pulled out two books tied together with a frayed light blue ribbon. As she held the journals, a wave of warmth started in her hand, spreading through her body. Her spine began to tingle. There was something in here, something important. She tried to untie the ribbon, but it was knotted. Anxiety pooled in her stomach. She looked up, wondering why the shadows on the walls were growing bigger. She felt as if something bad were coming. Perhaps she wasn't meant to know. The knot stubbornly eluded her attempts to undo it. She was about to go in search of a pair of scissors when the window shattered.

The blast drove her back against the wall as shards of glass flew across the room.

Shocked by the unexpected attack, she froze, trying to figure out what had happened. Had someone thrown a rock through a window? A baseball? But it was dark outside, and there was no sound of anyone yelling an apology.

"Dylan!" she called in a panic, terrified to take a step.

"Catherine," he yelled back, his footsteps quick as he bounded up the stairs. He ran into the room. "What the hell happened?"

"Something came through the glass."

He started forward. "Wait." She put up her hand. "Don't get too close to the window. It could be a trick, a way to get you in sight."

Dylan squatted down next to the jagged, shattered pieces of glass on the floor. He searched for whatever had broken the window.

"I don't see a rock or a brick or anything," she said.

Dylan glanced at the windowpane and then at her, his gaze worried. "I think someone shot the glass out."

"No," she breathed, putting a hand to her heart. Had whoever shot Erica in the park come after them?

Dylan grabbed her hand and pulled her from the room.

"Where are we going?" she asked as they ran downstairs.

Before he could reply one of the windows burst in the living room; a second later the one next to it suffered the same fate. Yet there was no preceding sound of a shot.

"Why can't I hear a gun?" she asked.

"He must have a silencer," Dylan said grimly as they took cover in the hallway.

"Oh, God," Catherine murmured, more scared than she'd ever been in her life.

"Stay here. I'm going to run to the den, grab my computer, and then we're getting the hell out of here."

"We need to call the police."

"If we do, I'll be arrested."

"It's better than being dead."

"Just wait here. Okay? One problem at a time."

Catherine put her hand against the wall, steeling herself for the sound of another window breaking, but all was quiet, almost too quiet. Her heart pounded against her chest. She had trouble taking a breath. And she felt almost light-headed. But she couldn't pass out. She had to fight for her life.

Think, she told herself. If they were going to make a run for it, she needed her purse, her money. She could live without the rest. Her bag was on a table at the end of the hall. Staying close to the wall, she moved down the corridor on silent feet. She stuffed the journals she still had in her hand into her purse and had just put the strap over her shoulder when the window in the dining room shattered. The scream came out of her mouth without conscious thought.

Dylan rushed out of the den, his computer case in his hands. He looked relieved to see her in one piece. "I told you to stay put."

"I had to get my purse. How are we going to get away? As soon as we try to leave, he'll shoot us. That's probably what he's trying to do right now, flush us out of the house."

"I know, Catherine, but if we don't go, we're sitting ducks."

A second window burst in the dining room. The shooter was playing with them. She blinked back tears of terror.

"The garage," Dylan said. "We'll take your car. We can get into the garage through the kitchen door."

With her heart in her throat, she followed him out to her car. He'd backed it in, so at least they'd be driving forward when he opened the garage door.

Dylan threw his stuff into the backseat while she buckled her seat belt. Then he pushed a button on the side of the garage, jumped into the car, and waited for the door to go up. The next two minutes would be the most dangerous.

"Get down," Dylan told her. "On the floor."

She undid the seat belt and tried to squeeze herself into the space between the seat and the front console. "What about you?"

"I'll be fine. Hang on."

She grabbed the edges of the seat and prayed as Dylan pushed his foot down on the gas and the car shot forward. The window next to her shattered, and she screamed as the car skidded out of the driveway.

Chapter 14

Dylan sped down the street, relieved that that last bullet hadn't hit him or Catherine. He took the turn with a squeal of tires, and as the car straightened out, he glanced in the rearview mirror for headlights. Sure enough, there they were. Was it the shooter or just a random car? He couldn't afford to make the wrong decision. He hit the gas hard again.

Catherine started to wipe the glass off her seat.

"Stay down," he told her tersely. "I think he's following us."

"Can you see him?"

"There's a car, looks like a small truck." Dylan turned right, then left, trying to elude their pursuer, but the vehicle clung to his tail. He saw the silhouette of a man with a cap on his head, but he couldn't get any more detail than that.

Finally he reached the Pacific Coast Highway, a stretch of road that ran along the ocean. There would be more traffic, more cars, which he hoped would prevent the man from taking another shot. Dylan headed north, moving in and out of the lanes as he tried to lose the truck. He passed the Cliff House perched on the edge of the Pacific Ocean, winding his way through the tree-lined roads of the Presidio, finally ending on the approach to the Golden Gate Bridge. There was no way to turn off, and with the bustling traffic on the bridge, Dylan decided leaving San Francisco was his best bet anyway. With the merging of lanes the small truck appeared to be a dozen cars behind them now.

As he left the bridge, reaching the four-lane freeway once again, Dylan pressed the accelerator, hoping to use his small lead to his advantage. With the burst of speed the wind ripped through the missing window, thundering loudly through the car. He glanced over at Catherine, still huddled on the floor. Her head rested on her arms, which were pressed against the edge of the seat. Her hair covered her face, so he couldn't see her expression, but he could see her body shake with each breath she took. He wanted to tell her she could get up now, they were safe, but the area on this side of the bridge was surrounded by empty rolling hills, and if the truck caught up to them now it was possible the shooter would take another drive-by shot. He didn't want Catherine in the line of fire.

For miles he drove, constantly checking the mirror, searching for some sign of the truck. It seemed to have vanished. He wanted to relax, but he couldn't. To date every move he'd thought was the right one had turned out to be wrong. If he'd stayed in Tahoe instead of running back to San Francisco, he wouldn't have been in town when Erica was killed and would have been absolved of the crime. Instead he'd played into the killer's hands. He'd helped to set himself up. What a fool he'd been.

So now what? What was coming next?

Catherine lifted her head, wiped off the remains of the glass from the leather cushion, and climbed back onto the front seat. She let out a weary sigh as she stretched her cramped legs as best she could in the small space. Then she leaned back against the headrest, letting the wind from the broken window blow through her hair.

In the shadows of the night her pale face stood out in sharp relief. Her eyes were huge, wide and scared, but her chin was up, her arms crossed in an almost defiant posture. She wasn't going to quit on him. He could count on her.

The realization hit him hard. He was almost afraid to believe it. Other than Jake, he'd never let himself depend on anyone, and here he was counting on Catherine to stick with him. She certainly didn't have to. She had no obligation to him. She had nothing to gain and everything to lose. But still she'd stayed. Even now she was quiet, going along for the ride, not demanding to be let out at the nearest police precinct.

He was surprised by her loyalty, not sure how to handle it. Did he even want such a commitment from her? What would she expect in return?

Too much, probably. She'd want everything. And he

couldn't offer her that. He was broken inside. He didn't admit that often, not even to himself, but Catherine deserved a whole man, one who hadn't been damaged by his past. She deserved that. She'd had it rough herself, and although he didn't know the extent of her pain, he knew it ran deep.

The next few minutes flew by in silence. He had no words at the moment, and apparently neither did she. They were running for their lives from an enemy they couldn't name. He'd always been able to name the bad guy in every story that he'd covered, from wars to kidnappings to murders, but this time was different.

The problem was, he had no idea how to identify the people in the game, and the farther away he ran, the farther he got from all the players. But he was afraid to stop. So one mile ran into another. He hoped that with distance would come clarity and a chance to regroup and make a plan that would put them on the offensive. Unfortunately the gas gauge on the car told him he was running on empty. He took the next exit. The last thing he wanted to do was run out of gas and end up stranded on the side of the highway.

"Why are you getting off?" Catherine asked in alarm, darting a quick look over her shoulder.

"We're almost out of gas. I haven't seen any sign of the truck in the last hour. I think we lost him at the bridge."

"Are you sure?"

The need in her eyes demanded only one response. "I'm sure. It will be okay, Catherine. We're safe now."

"I know you're humoring me."

"I expected you would," he said with a weary smile. "Where are we?"

"Sonoma County, wine country. I saw a sign for Cloverdale, so we're about an hour or so north of San Francisco."

Dylan pulled into a gas station and turned off the car. His pulse quickened as he opened the door. In the next few minutes they would be extremely vulnerable to any other cars entering the station. He hoped he'd truly lost their tail.

He got out of the car, headed over to the cashier in the minimart, and laid down two twenties. Returning to the car, he inserted the hose into the tank and drew in a deep breath as he gathered himself together. Adrenaline still ran rampant through his body, making it difficult for him to focus. But that was what he needed to do—concentrate and think of a way to save them both.

While the gas was pumping he grabbed the window wiper and walked around to Catherine's side of the car. He scraped away the remaining pieces of glass from the window frame, careful not to get them on her.

"If you hadn't told me to get down, I could have been killed," she said, drawing his gaze to her thankful blue eyes.

"But you got down, and you're all right," he told her, sensing that she needed the confirmation.

"Because of you." She paused. "You're bleeding."

He glanced down at his arm. "Just a scratch from the glass."

"You were lucky the bullet didn't hit you."

"I know."

"If you hadn't taken charge I'd probably still be huddled in the hallway of your grandmother's house, not knowing what to do."

"I doubt that. You were already getting your purse, looking for an escape route. You like to sell yourself short, but I've seen you in action. I know you've got guts."

She gave him a watery smile. "You're being really nice to me."

"Well, don't thank me by crying," he said sharply. "I hate it when women cry."

Catherine shook her head, blinking back her tears. "I never cry. I'm a tough girl."

"You are definitely that." He leaned in the window and kissed her on the lips, thinking he was doing it for her, to give her comfort, to make her feel better, but in truth he was the one who needed the connection, who needed her power, her strength—the strength she so often didn't see in herself. Her lips were soft and sweet under his. He forced himself to pull away, battling a desire to forget about everything and just lose himself in her kiss for the next few hours, days, or weeks.

"I think it's done—the gas," Catherine said, interrupting his thoughts.

He started, realizing he'd been staring at her like an idiot. "Right." Moving back around the car, he took out the hose and replaced the cap. Before returning to the car he took another look around, not seeing any sign of the truck. He opened the door and slid behind the wheel.

"Where are we going now?" Catherine asked, an expectant look in her eyes.

"We have to find somewhere to stay tonight—a motel, I guess. We need to figure out their next move," he said as he turned the key in the ignition.

"Don't you mean *our* next move?"

"I think it's fairly obvious that they're in control of this game," he said, hating to admit it.

"Only it's not a game." Catherine paused. "We should be dead, Dylan. Why aren't we?"

The question had been running around his brain for the last sixty miles. The shooter had played with them, torturing them with anticipation as he decided which window to shoot out next. At any point he could have come in through one of the broken windows and taken them out, but he hadn't. There was only one reason why.

"We weren't supposed to die," Dylan said as he let out the clutch and pulled away from the pumps.

"Why didn't anyone come out of their house to investigate the noise? Or call the police?" Catherine asked. "I don't understand. Didn't anyone hear the windows breaking? The noise was really loud. The whole house shook."

"There must have been a silencer on the gun. I never heard a gunshot, just the glass breaking. It might have sounded louder to us because we were inside. The neighbors are also elderly, probably hard of hearing, and who knows if they were even home."

"I guess," Catherine said doubtfully. "I just can't be-

lieve that we could get shot at in the middle of a resi-
dential neighborhood and no one would come to our
aid."

"People don't like to get involved. As to why we're
not dead, I think the shooter wanted us to know that he
could get to us, that he was close by, waiting, watching.
It was a show of power, and perhaps also a warning."

"About what?"

That was what he didn't know. If Ravino was behind
the attack, what was the purpose of the scare tactics?
It wasn't as if Dylan could stop doing something. He
wasn't continuing to investigate Ravino's case. Everything he'd come up with, he'd already turned over to
the cops. And the trial would continue whether Dylan
was dead or alive. Which brought him back to a more
personal motive: a desire to see him scared and on the
run.

In some ways he was sorry he'd left the house, but
he'd had Catherine to think about, not to mention the
fact that he wasn't egotistical or stupid enough to think
he could win against a man with a gun and the advantage of darkness and surprise. He would have to wait
for another chance to fight. It would come. This game
wasn't close to being over.

"I think the shots were meant to keep us guessing,"
he said aloud. "To knock us off balance, give us something else to think about besides who killed Erica."

"It worked."

"Yes, it did." Dylan paused at the light, then turned
onto the freeway, heading in the northbound direction.

It couldn't hurt to put a few more miles between themselves and the city. He didn't just have the shooter to worry about, but also the police. Although surely having the windows in his grandmother's house shot out would work in his favor and would prove that someone was trying to set him up or was at least involved.

Why hadn't the person orchestrating the setup realized that? Was it a mistake? Had they finally gotten a break? Or had the plan changed?

"I wonder how they found us," Catherine mused. "I hate to bring up your father again, but when we left his house, someone was watching us from the window."

"And we were in my grandmother's car. If my father saw the car then it wouldn't take much for him to figure out where I was," Dylan said, finishing her thought. He tightened his grip on the steering wheel. As much as he'd prefer to believe it was Ravino or even Blake Howard plotting against him, his father's name kept cropping back up. Who else would have been able to figure out where they were? "Well, I have to give the old man credit: If this is his work, he's doing a damn good job. And it would be just like him to want me to suffer before I died."

"It's just one theory, Dylan."

He glanced over at her. "You don't think it's him? You just pointed the finger in his direction."

She shrugged. "I know I did, but it doesn't feel quite right to me."

"Then who do you think it is?"

Catherine thought for a moment. "Someone with a really sick mind. Twisted. Dark. Obsessed."

"You just described my father."

"Really? Always?"

He hated that she was questioning his judgment. She sounded like all the other adults who'd acted as if he were crazy when he dared to mention that things weren't good at home. "I can't believe you doubt me." He couldn't keep the accusation of betrayal from his voice. "I thought you were connected to me. I thought you and I had this psychic link that was honest and true."

"Oh, Dylan, I don't doubt you," she said, the words coming out in a burst of emotion. "Honestly, I don't. I shouldn't have said that. I was just comparing the man we met earlier today to the man I saw in his wedding photo. I was wondering if something had happened to change him. That's all. I know he hurt you badly. I believe what you told me."

"Forget it," he said quickly, brushing off her apology.

"No, I'm not going to forget it. I lived some of what you did, and I know what it's like to feel alone, as if you're in some parallel universe that no one else can see. They think they know your life, but they don't. You're living in hell, but they think it's heaven. Look at me, Dylan."

He cast her a quick glance, seeing the plea in her eyes. Maybe she did understand. Maybe she did get him after all. "I don't know if my father became a monster after my mother left, or if he was always that way," he said. "Since Jake and I were the only people who actually saw the monster, I'll never know. My grandmother, my aunt, my cousins—they didn't see my father for what he was, or at least they were never willing to admit it."

"Are Jake's memories the same as yours?"

"Not exactly," Dylan replied, looking back at the road. "Jake used to say that he thought the divorce made my father bitter and angry, but not all divorced men abuse their kids because they're unhappy. That comes from some other place in the soul."

"Yes, a dark place," she agreed. "Some people are sick, evil."

He had a feeling she wasn't talking about his father anymore. "You can't get Erica's killer out of your mind, can you?"

"I'm trying."

He knew she didn't want to go back to the moment when she'd glimpsed the killer's thoughts, but he felt compelled to take her there. "When you were in the killer's head, did you think you were tapping into the actual shooter, or the person who ordered the hit? Because I think we're dealing with two people."

"The shooter—I was in his head," Catherine answered with certainty. "I saw what he saw. I felt his satisfaction."

"And did you get the sense that he was working for someone else?"

"No, not from anything he thought, but I agree with you that there have to be two people. I just think that at the moment he kills he enjoys it. He's good at it. It's what he does. It's his life."

Catherine's words drew a chill across his body. Dylan glanced over at her profile, seeing the renewed tension in her face. He was sorry he'd brought up the subject. "Don't think about it anymore."

"It's difficult not to. I feel as if there's some clue right in front of me that I'm missing. If I am connected to the shooter, why don't I know who he's working for?"

"Because he didn't give you a clue in his thoughts." Dylan paused, then said, "I'm surprised you didn't sense him tonight, didn't pick up on any vibes that he was watching the house."

She stiffened in her seat. "I did feel uneasy. I thought it was just because it was getting dark. I shrugged it off."

"You shrugged it off," he echoed in surprise. "You can do that? I thought the visions overtook you."

"It was more a feeling than a vision, and I was distracted because I was eager to read the last two journals. I turned on the lamp, thinking I would banish the shadows, and then the window shattered. The shooter must have seen me in the upstairs bedroom. Perhaps he was waiting for the lights to come on, so he could figure out where we were."

"Probably," he said, his mind latching onto an earlier part of her statement. "What journals were you reading?"

"Oh, these," she said, pulling the two books out of her purse. "They're your grandmother's diaries. I had them in my hand when the shooting started. I never put them down."

"What's in them?"

"Actually, I haven't read these books yet, but your grandmother kept journals her entire life. I spent the afternoon reading about her childhood, her family, first love, that sort of thing. I was just getting to the part where you were born when I found these last two books, but I couldn't get them open, and then the window blew, and you know the rest."

Dylan swallowed back a sudden knot of discomfort in his throat. He didn't want to know what his grandmother had written.

"Maybe the journals will give us some insight into your father," Catherine added. "You might find out what your grandmother really thought about your father."

"That he was a prince, no doubt," Dylan said cynically. "She didn't see him as an abusive bully, that's for sure."

"But she did see him as spoiled. She wrote at great length about how saddened she was by the miscarriages she suffered between her daughter Eleanor's birth and your father's birth, and how much she wanted a son. She said that when Richard was born, she couldn't stop herself from spoiling him rotten. She knew it was wrong, but she wanted to give him the world. The older he got, the more he took. She worried when your parents married. She wasn't sure if your mother would be strong enough to handle him." Catherine drew in a breath. "After reading it all, I wonder why your father picked your mother. They were so different. He was an ambitious businessman eager to rise to the top. She was a kindergarten teacher with ordinary parents. What made them want each other?"

"Hell if I know." Dylan put up a hand as Catherine

opened her mouth again. He felt a desperate need to stop her from saying another word. "I don't want to hear any more, Catherine."

"Dylan, I know you don't think the past is important, but—"

"But nothing," he said, cutting her off. "It's my past, and I get to decide what I want to know. Just let me drive. I can't do this right now." He wasn't sure he could ever do it, but he certainly needed to be in a place where he could get away if he had to. Odd that he should think of it that way, as if the past could still hurt him. It was over and done. Wasn't it?

He didn't pretend to have Catherine's psychic abilities, but his own instincts were telling him that he couldn't ignore the fact that Catherine kept bringing his parents back into the present. It had to be because of his father's association with Erica. Dylan just couldn't figure out how his mother entered into it. Maybe it was that Catherine's senses enveloped everything and didn't filter out what wasn't necessary.

He rolled his neck around on his shoulders, hearing the crack of each joint. Everything in his life was a big question mark. Two days ago he would have said he had all the answers. Now he had none. But he did know one thing for sure.

"They made a mistake tonight," he said. "If they wanted us dead they should have done it, because I won't give anyone another chance to kill you or me."

Catherine didn't reply. He didn't know if she believed him or not. And despite his confident words, he had no idea how he was going to back them up.

* * *

Catherine's face was as cold as ice. Her teeth had started to chatter with the ever-present wind blasting through the broken window next to her. She pulled her sweater up over her mouth, but she could still feel the sting of the night air against her cheeks. Her eyes were watering, so she closed them, trying to relax, to find some peaceful place to escape to in her mind, not that her mind had ever given her much peace.

She should be feeling more relaxed by now. They were a hundred miles away from the city, deep into wine country. The police wouldn't be able to find them; nor would the man who was after them. He had to have given up by now. It was only logical to think they were safe for the moment. Unfortunately her instincts always beat down logic, and she couldn't shake the feeling that trouble wasn't far behind.

She wanted to believe that Dylan would protect her. She knew he would try. If it came down to it he'd put himself before her. He was that kind of man: unselfish, courageous. She'd never met anyone like him. She just wished Dylan could see himself for what he was now. In his head he still saw the cowardly child who couldn't escape the bully, the one who did everything wrong and nothing right, the one who felt isolated, lost, and helpless. All the bad things he'd ever heard about himself probably played over and over in his head every night before he went to bed. It was always easier to believe the bad stuff people thought about you than the good. She knew that firsthand.

She wanted to break through his emotional walls,

but they were built strong and sturdy, made to last. Once in a while she slipped through a small break, but then he threw up the barricades and pushed her out.

Dylan was afraid of her, made uncomfortable by what she saw in him. He wasn't the first man she'd terrified with her visions, and she doubted he would be the last, but he was the only one she really wanted to stay. But he would go—eventually. She knew that as surely as she knew anything. Dylan didn't want to be with a woman who could see into his head, who knew where he came from, who had heard all his secrets. She didn't think he'd shared his past with any one of the women he'd dated. He blamed himself for not standing up to his father, for not fighting back, for not being able to win. So he kept that loser hidden behind his big, strong walls.

The man he was today always won, always succeeded. Dylan would someday find a woman who'd add credence to his reputation, someone beautiful and educated and not at all crazy, not at all quirky—not at all like her. He wanted perfection in every part of his life. She didn't blame him for that. She'd yearned for the perfect life, too. But lately she'd begun to realize that she didn't want perfect anymore. She just wanted love, real love, the kind that blossomed with the years, grew stronger with the trials of life, a love that didn't waver in the face of doubt, a love that probably didn't exist in the real world. She'd certainly never seen it. But still she believed in it. What a romantic fool she was.

Letting out a sigh, she tried to redirect her thoughts, think of something else, find some image that wasn't

Dylan or his father or his mother or Erica. She wanted to slip into one of her peaceful paintings—the pretty meadow, the quiet pool, the beach where her dogs liked to run. But those images couldn't take shape in her mind. They were being pushed away by a dark shadow that spread and enveloped everything in its way.

His motel room faced the highway. The cars whirred by, a relentless roar of engines. The orange light from a fast-food restaurant sign blazed through the sagging curtains at the window. The place was a rat hole. He would be able to afford the Ritz after he finished this job, and he was itching to do just that. But not just yet, because the fucking asshole he was working for wanted to play games.

The voice rang through his head again, the cryptic instructions, the odd requests. What the hell was going on? He was a killer, not a game player. When he shot, he shot to kill, not to scare, not to make someone run. But he'd had his orders. And he'd completed his task. Soon he would get to finish the job. The time couldn't come quickly enough for him.

He picked up the phone, punching in the familiar number. "There's two of them, you know. That's double the price if you want them both dead." He listened, his heart soaring at the response. This was going to be sweet. He would trap her. She would know there was no way out, and then she would take her last breath at his command. He couldn't wait. "I understand," he said. "The woman dies first. No problem. No problem at all."

Catherine started, blinking open her eyes, desperate to escape the darkness in her head. She'd seen him again, and he wasn't just after Dylan now. Her heart thudded against her chest. She was next. *The woman dies first.* He'd been talking about her.

"Oh, God," she breathed.

Dylan glanced over at her, his gaze narrowing in alarm. "What's wrong now?"

"He's going to kill me first."

"Who?"

She knew Dylan wanted her to identify the man, but she hadn't seen him. She'd *been* him. She'd felt his delight at the prospect of watching her die. He wanted her cornered, isolated, alone.

Her breath caught in her chest as her mind shot down another haunted corridor in her head, a place she never went, except perhaps in her nightmares, but never when she was awake. She fought to stay in the light, but the shadows sucked her in.

Someone called to her, a voice from a long time ago, his words silky and smooth with evil intent. She clapped her hands over her ears. "No," she said loudly. "Don't. Go away. Stop!"

"Catherine."

She heard Dylan calling to her, but his voice wasn't as strong as the other man's.

"Where are you, little girl? Where are you hiding, sweet pea?"

She held her breath, shrinking into as tight and small a ball as possible. He couldn't find her. He couldn't. She chanted the words over and over again, her gaze catching on the drops of blood staining her toes. She buried her face in her cotton nightgown, smelling her own fear, tasting her own vomit, hearing the screams in her head. If he found her he would kill her, too.

She felt the car swerve, then come to a jolting stop. The seat belt snapped her back into place. Her eyes flew open as Dylan grabbed her hands, pulling them away from her ears so she could hear him.

"Dammit, Catherine," he said forcefully. "Talk to me. Look at me."

Dylan's commands drove the other man back into the recesses of her mind.

She stared at him, her chest heaving as she tried to breathe. Dimly she realized he'd pulled over to the side of the highway.

"What the hell is going on, Catherine? Are you having another vision? Are you connecting with the guy who's trying to kill us?"

She wanted to answer him, but the words wouldn't come. Her present and her past were blurring together. She wanted to escape, but there was no way to leave the terrors of her own mind. She felt very close to the edge of a perilous cliff. All her life she'd wondered if one day she would snap, one day she would break in two, one day she would go to sleep and never wake up. A person could only take so much. And tonight's attack on her life had reminded her of the last time she'd dodged death.

Blinking rapidly, she tried to focus on something real, something right in front of her. She feared she was losing it big-time, and she couldn't help wondering how many more chances she would get before someone succeeded in killing her.

"Catherine, pay attention to me."

Dylan's words made her turn her head. His hands reached again for hers, his warmth cutting through the cold chill.

"You're freezing," he said, rubbing her fingers hard. "I should have stopped before this."

"I'm ... I'm okay," she said finally. One day she would have to face what was in her head, but not today, not now. She wasn't ready. She had too many battles to fight, too many killers to face. She couldn't beat them all at once.

"Can you tell me what you saw?" Dylan asked.

"He's going to kill me first. Then you."

Dylan's eyes widened. "Where? When?"

She shook her head. "I don't know. But he's somewhere out there, and he doesn't seem worried about finding us. How can he know where we're going to be when we don't know?"

"He doesn't know where we are right now. He can't," Dylan told her. "He's not that powerful."

"I think he is—or someone is," she amended. "Someone who's telling him what to do. And that person wants you to watch me die."

He cupped her face with his hands. "That's not going to happen. I swear to God I won't let that happen."

"I know you'll try—" she began.

He cut her off with a shake of his head. "No, I won't just try. I'll succeed. You have to believe in me, Catherine, the way I believe in you."

For the first time she looked into his eyes and saw complete and utter acceptance. He'd told her earlier that he'd lost his faith, but somehow he'd found it in her. She was overwhelmingly touched. And if he could believe, then so could she.

"I do," she whispered. "I do believe in you." She ran her finger along his strong jaw and saw the pulse jump in his neck. "I want to show you how much."

"Catherine." He breathed her name on a note of husky desire.

"Take me somewhere," she said. "Let's stop running just for a little while."

Her head hit the bed two seconds after they entered the motel room.

The reckless energy between them exploded as their mouths met, their tongues tangling together in an impatient dance of need and desire. Catherine didn't want to think anymore. She didn't want to lose herself in the past or the future, just the present—in Dylan's arms. She wanted to feel him on top of her, beneath her, inside of her. She wanted to take his strength, his confidence, his power, and make them her own. She was being selfish, but she didn't care. She needed to take, and he seemed more than willing to give.

Dylan tugged at her shirt, pulling it up and over her head. He tossed it on the bed as his mouth immediately sought the curve of her neck. He sucked her skin between his lips, and she gasped at the sharp tingle that spiraled through her. His mouth moved lower, his tongue tracing the edge of her bra as his fingers played with the front hook. He seemed to take an agonizingly long time to undo the clasp. Finally he opened it, pulling aside the lacy cups. His strong, tanned hand palmed her breast, his thumb grazing her nipple.

She let out a small cry, then wantonly pushed her breast into his hand. His mouth moved lower, his tongue sliding down the valley between her breasts. She felt a line of fire race through her veins. And when his mouth closed over her breast, she pulled his head closer, twisting her fingers in the fine strands of his hair. She sank further into the mattress as he tugged on her nipple with the edge of his teeth. Then his mouth moved lower, laving a sweet trail down to her belly button. He unsnapped her jeans and pulled them off along with her light blue lacy thong.

She felt suddenly exposed, vulnerable, and a little afraid. But as Dylan's eyes met hers, she knew this man wouldn't hurt her. "Trust me," he whispered, and she realized for the first time that he was in her head. He knew what she was thinking, what she wanted, what she needed.

"I do trust you." She sat up, grabbed the edge of his shirt, and helped him off with it.

He reached into his pocket and pulled out a condom, then shucked off his jeans. It shocked her that he had protection with him, so easily within reach, as if he'd been expecting this moment.

Well, why was that so surprising? She'd seen them together in her head. She'd known they'd end up in bed. And he had, too.

He came back to her, covering her body with his. He

put his hand under her head and kissed her with deliberation. She didn't want to go slow. She wanted it hard, fast, wild.

Impatient, she pulled him into the cradle of her hips. He touched her intimately with his fingers, driving her crazy with desire. But she wanted all of him.

Her fingers dug into his hips as he finally thrust into her. He was so big, and she was so tight. He took his time at first, drawing out every movement; then gradually his pace quickened. She urged him on, wanting nothing but the mindless pleasure that was washing over her in huge, caressing waves. The heat that had been building between them since the day they met hit the boiling point.

Her thoughts blurred, her emotions colliding with his. She'd never felt such an intense connection in mind, body, and spirit. They were one. She knew him, and he knew her, in a way that no one else did.

The closeness they shared suddenly worried her. Would the darkness in her head flow to him? She stiffened, suddenly holding back, but Dylan wouldn't let her retreat. He wouldn't let her put her guard up.

"Let it go, Catherine," Dylan urged, each thrust taking her higher, deeper. "I want it all."

He didn't know what he was asking. He didn't know the risk he was taking. But it was too late to stop. They came together, her cries mixing with his. She gave him everything she had.

Dylan rolled over onto his back, a blast of cold air from the air-conditioning drawing the beads of sweat on his chest into goose bumps. Catherine curled up on her side next to him, her head coming to rest in the crook of his shoulder. Her lips touched his skin. The heat of her mouth sent another hot shiver down his spine. He'd thought he'd have her and it would be over. The tension between them would cool. The need to know each other would be satisfied. But he didn't feel satisfaction; he felt restless and on edge.

For a moment a swirl of black energy had flowed between them. He'd felt Catherine's fear, the terror she lived with. It had scared the hell out of him. He hadn't realized the depth of her pain. Even now it overwhelmed him. A sense of powerlessness unlike anything he'd ever experienced assaulted him, as if whatever or whoever she was fighting were too big for both of them. He was assailed by the urge to run—to get as far away from her as possible. He didn't need her shit. He had enough of his own.

He jumped out of bed, giving in to the need to flee. He threw on his clothes, not looking at her until he was dressed, but he could feel her gaze with every passing second. The silence was very, very loud. Finally he turned his head, knowing he couldn't walk out of the room without at least saying something, but what he should say he had no idea.

She was sitting up against the pillows now, the sheet pulled up modestly to her neck. Her hair was a glorious mess of curls. Her lips were soft and well kissed. Her eyes, a deep, dark blue, were filled with shadows. He couldn't read her expression. Or maybe he was afraid to.

"I knew I'd scare you eventually," she murmured, a gleam of disappointment in her eyes.

He hated to think he'd let her down. But, dammit, a man could only take so much. He'd been dodging bullets and cops all day.

But so had she.

He knew he was making excuses, but he couldn't seem to stop. The need to breathe away from her was overwhelming. "I have to get some air. I'm not scared." He was actually terrified.

"Liar."

"Catherine . . ." He started, then stopped, having no idea what he wanted to say. If she could see into his head, then what was the point of making something up?

"Where are you going?" she asked. "We're in the middle of nowhere. You can't just leave."

"There's a soda machine down the hall. Do you want something?"

"No." She looked him directly in the eye. "Usually I can separate my mind from my body so that sex isn't so overwhelming, but this time I couldn't, and . . ." Her voice drifted away as her fingers plucked nervously at the sheet.

"What's inside you, Catherine?" he asked, the words coming out before he could stop them. "What happened to you? Where does the black energy come from?"

Her face paled. "You felt it, too? I was hoping you wouldn't."

Felt it? He'd almost suffocated in the thick, smothering darkness. "Tell me what's behind the pain and the anger and the evil that runs through you."

"I don't know."

"You're the one who's lying now. You can't keep putting me off. You have to tell me your secrets. If not me, then someone. You need to get it out before it consumes you."

"I've tried," she cried, her voice filled with despair. "I'm not lying. I don't know what happened, because I can't remember it. The memory is locked up in my head. And I can't get it out except in little bits and pieces. Because it's . . . it's horrific."

Her words made him want to run, but some deep inner voice told him that would be absolutely the wrong move to make. The evil inside of her wanted her isolated, vulnerable, so it could feed on her insecurity, on her fears. He couldn't leave her alone with her monsters. He couldn't do that to her. In a few steps he was back at the bed, sitting down next to her.

She gazed at him, confusion in her eyes. "I thought you were going."

"Tell me what you do know."

"You don't want me to do that. You're scared now. It will be even worse if you know it all."

He suspected she was right, but he wanted everything out in the open. "I felt it, Catherine. I felt the power of your nightmares. I can't help you fight if I don't know who the enemy is. Who hurt you? Who's hurting you still?"

She stared at him for a long, tense moment. "When I

was six years old, my mother was murdered, and I was the only witness."

He caught his breath at her words. He'd known it would be bad, but he hadn't expected it to be this bad. "Who did it?"

She drew in a deep breath, her eyes blurring with tears. "They said it was my father."

Chapter 15

Dylan's stomach turned over. "Your father killed your mother, and you were there?"

"That's what they said."

"Who's they? Tell me what happened. Start at the beginning."

"I don't know the beginning. I don't have any memories from the time I lived with my parents before that night."

"And that night?" he prodded.

"I remember hiding in a closet. There was blood on my feet, as if I'd run through it. I tried to be really small. I didn't want him to find me. But he kept calling my name, and he said he was coming to get me." She drew in a shaky breath. "Later, I think, I was standing in the kitchen in a puddle of blood. I guess he was gone by then, but I don't know how much time had passed. A policeman put a blanket around me and took me out and put me in the back of the squad car. I didn't want to leave my mother. I remember crying that I didn't want to go, that she needed me, and that she was going to make me pancakes for breakfast. I guess I didn't realize she was dead."

The rawness of her story shocked Dylan. He'd covered murders in his job, but this one was different. This one had happened to Catherine, and he could feel her pain. He wanted to tell her to stop, but now that she'd started she seemed determined to keep going. He had to listen, no matter how uncomfortable he was.

"The rest of that night and the next few days are a blur," she continued. "I know I spoke to the police, social workers, a psychiatrist. They all asked what had happened. Had I heard anything? Had I seen anything? Where was my father? Had my parents been fighting? I couldn't tell them anything. I felt frozen."

"God, Catherine." He leaned over and brushed her hair away from her face, then cupped her head with his hand. "You don't have to go on."

"I do. I've never told anyone about that night—not the other kids in foster care, no one."

Dylan didn't know if he wanted to be her confidant. He was terrified of getting closer. But he could see that she desperately needed to unload the burden she'd been carrying for so long. And he would have to take it. He owed her that much. "I'm listening."

"My father had an alibi, a woman who said she was having an affair with him and that he was in her bed the night my mother was killed. The police, however, didn't believe her or my father. My dad had a history of drug abuse, and he'd been in jail two or three times already for assault. He'd worked odd jobs, and every one of those employers said he had an explosive temper. Plus, there had been a nine-one-one call about six months earlier, when my mother said that my father hit her in the face. She decided not to press charges, so nothing happened." Catherine licked her lips. "You have to understand that this is all stuff people told me later. I was only six years old. I didn't know anything about their relationship, or if I did I couldn't remember it. The police and the district attorney did everything they could to get me to name my father as the murderer, but I couldn't remember. I couldn't say he was for sure." A tear trickled down her cheek and she ruthlessly wiped it away.

"Catherine, I'm so sorry," Dylan breathed, rubbing his thumb along her tight jaw.

"They said he beat her and stabbed her with a kitchen knife twenty-seven times," she continued in a cool voice, as if the horror of it no longer touched her, but Dylan knew that it was there with her every single night. "The police said the violence was unspeakable, and perhaps that's why I couldn't speak it. In the end there wasn't enough evidence to put my father in jail—no murder weapon, no DNA, nothing—so he got off. I had been put into foster care while they were investigating him, and after the charges were dismissed I thought he might come and get me, but he didn't. I never saw him again. I asked the social worker once, and she said that they'd lost track of him, and that after enough time went by, if he didn't show up and they still couldn't locate him, they would terminate his parental rights so I could be adopted. Of course, no one wants to adopt a traumatized little girl whose father was probably a murderer, so that was a moot point."

"I don't understand how your father could have gotten away with the crime. He must have left his fingerprints at the scene, and if it was that bloody, that vicious a fight, I'm surprised there wasn't DNA all over the place."

"His fingerprints were in the house, but he lived there, so that didn't make him the killer. Apparently there wasn't any DNA evidence on her body, because I'm sure they would have done something with it if they'd found it. Although it happened twenty-four years ago, and I don't know what kind of tests they had back then."

"So your dreams . . . they're about that night, aren't they?"

"For a long time they were. I always wake up at four forty-four—I think that's when she died. I believe the screams I hear in my head are those of my mother."

He stared at her for a long moment, wondering if he should push any further, but they'd gone this far. "How do you think you managed to escape?"

"No one knows." She met his gaze, haunting shadows in her eyes. "They found my blanket in the back of a closet in the basement laundry room. That's where I must have been hiding. One of the psychiatrists theorized that if my father was high, he might have forgotten about me or just given up when he couldn't find me." She paused, taking in another breath. "For a long time I thought he'd come back and finish the job."

"He's the monster in your nightmares."

Catherine nodded. "Yes, but as I got older the dreams changed. It wasn't about that night anymore. I didn't hear his voice or see my mother's face. I saw other people getting killed. I heard their pleas for help. Maybe because I was tapped into that particular kind of violence, I don't know. But as I told you before, the nightmares often make no sense at all, and I certainly haven't been able to help anyone because of them. I couldn't stop my mother's murder, and I couldn't stop anyone else's." She paused. "There's something else."

"I'm almost afraid to ask."

"My mother had visions, too. That's what one of the neighbors said. She told me that she heard my father say more than once that there were demons inside of her. The neighbor thought maybe he tried to beat the demons out of her."

Dylan felt sick to his stomach at the image her words brought forth, her innocent mother being brutalized by a monster. And Catherine had seen it all. No wonder she was so filled with darkness, so terrified of what the night would bring. She'd been mentally reliving the murder over and over again, racked with guilt that she hadn't been able to get justice for her mother—a woman who was just like her.

"It's not your fault, Catherine. You can't blame yourself for what happened to your mother."

"Everyone says that," she replied, her voice dull, her eyes bleak. "But I know the truth."

"You couldn't have stopped him from killing her. You were a child, little more than a baby."

"I could have told people what I saw. I could have made him pay for what he did. I could have sent him to jail for the rest of his life."

"I doubt that. The testimony of a six-year-old child wouldn't have been enough to convict him, not without other evidence. You weren't a reliable witness. And there's always the possibility that maybe you didn't see anything. Maybe you were hiding the whole time."

"I've told myself that, too. I don't think it's true." Her voice dropped to a whisper. "I feel in my heart that I know what happened. But I can't seem to release it. It's trapped inside of me."

"Because it's too horrible to remember, that's why. I'm sorry I made you tell me the story. Don't think about it anymore." He wished he could take back the last fifteen minutes and play them over again. He didn't know what to say now, how to begin to comfort her, so he simply put his arms around her. She rested her head on his shoulder and they stayed like that for several long minutes.

Finally she lifted her head and pulled away. "I didn't want to bring you into the darkness with me. I thought we could just have sex and live in the moment. I guess it didn't work out that way."

He gave her a smile. "Maybe it was time for you to stop facing the demons alone."

"I tell myself they're not real. The fears are just in my head, created by my own mind. How can I be afraid of myself? No one is trying to kill me—well, no one *was* trying to kill me before tonight," she amended.

He frowned at the reminder that there was real danger here in the present, danger he had put her in. "I shouldn't have brought you with me."

"It's too late now for regrets." She let out a sigh. "So, go get your soda and I'll get dressed, and we'll focus on your problems instead of mine."

Now that she was telling him to go, perversely he wanted to stay. He wanted to strip off his clothes, crawl back into bed with her, and take another shot at driving the darkness out of her. But he could see by her face that she'd already withdrawn from him, and he wouldn't be getting back into her head or her body anytime soon. He got up and walked over to the door, then paused. "You might not have any regrets, but I do."

"About what?" she asked warily.

"I regret that I ever got out of bed."

"I've never seen anyone get dressed so fast. I think you broke the record. Not much for cuddling, are you?"

"I never have been," he admitted. But it wasn't the cuddling that had made him run; it was the panicked feeling, and the realization that sex with Catherine could never be just sex. And he didn't do complicated. She was absolutely the wrong woman for him. He liked things light and easy, simple, everyone on board with the same game plan. With Catherine everything was raw, deep, and completely unpredictable.

So why wasn't he leaving now? Why wasn't he making it clear that what had happened between them wouldn't happen again? Why was he filled with the desire to ask her for another chance to show that he could stay in bed with her for longer than ten seconds?

"Which is winning?" Catherine asked lightly. "Your head or your body?"

He tipped his head. "I can't hide anything from you, can I?"

"That's what you don't like about me."

"Is it?" he muttered. He turned away. He knew he wasn't fighting his head or his body; he was fighting his heart. But he didn't intend to tell her that. And he hoped to God she wouldn't figure that one out on her own, because if she got past that wall there'd be no stopping her. She'd own him. Hell, maybe she already did.

Catherine let out a breath as Dylan left the room. For a moment she'd thought he was going to get back into bed with her, and she was disappointed that he hadn't. She'd never felt so uninhibited, so wild, so free of restriction, but look where it had gotten her. A few minutes of mind-blowing sex and she'd confessed her entire sordid life story and scared the man to death. Although he'd been wary even before she'd started talking. He'd felt the bad energy when they were together. That was why he'd jumped out of bed so fast. The connection between them had been too intense. She hadn't been able to hide her true self, and Dylan had seen everything.

She wasn't surprised that he'd almost run. She had the genes of a murderer running through her. She had demons in her head. She saw evil in her dreams. Who would ever choose to be a part of that?

Certainly not Dylan. When this was over, when they found whoever was trying to frame him or kill him, he'd go his way and she'd go hers.

Getting out of bed, she put her clothes back on and straightened the covers. She'd barely glanced at the room when they'd first come in, so caught up had she been in a reckless need to get Dylan naked and inside of her. She'd never felt so swept away, so focused on being with a man. Her body still tingled, and there was a sweet ache between her legs that echoed the not-quite-satisfied need inside her. She wanted to make love to Dylan again, more slowly, taking time to savor every taste, every touch, but that probably wouldn't happen now.

Catherine crossed the room and pulled the edge of the curtain aside so she could see out the window. Their room looked down over the parking lot, and her car was parked where they'd left it. She searched the area for a brown truck, but there were only a few other cars, and none that matched the vehicle Dylan had described. They were hours away from the city. They had to be safe here. But the shooter she'd seen in her head had also been in a motel close to a highway. Who knew just how far away he really was? He certainly hadn't seemed concerned or worried about the fact that he'd lost them. Why was that? Had he revealed some clue in his conversation that she'd missed? She strained to remember, but nothing significant came to mind.

Letting the curtain drop, she took the journals out of her purse and sat down on the bed again. She worked the stubborn knot with her fingers until she finally loosened a strand and the ribbon began to unravel. The books slid apart. She opened the first one, nervous anticipation running through her. Something in this journal was important. She'd felt it before, and she felt it even more now. If Dylan's father was involved, then there had to be a clue here.

She couldn't ignore the parallel between Richard Sanders and her own father. Was that where the connection between herself and Dylan originated? Did she feel empathy toward him because of the violence he'd suffered at the hands of his father? Although his father certainly wasn't a murderer—at least, not so far.

The door opened and Dylan reentered the room with a scowl on his face. "You should have put the chain on after me," he scolded.

"You were coming right back."

"We have to be careful, Catherine. Do I really have to tell you that?"

"No." In truth, she'd been so caught up in her memories and the desire to get dressed before Dylan returned that she'd forgotten to lock the door after him. But she wouldn't do it again. He was right: She needed to stay focused. The stakes were getting higher each day, and it wasn't just Dylan's life on the line; it was her own.

Dylan put two sodas down on the dresser and tossed a couple of bags of chips and two candy bars on the bed. "It's not the most nutritious meal, but if you get hungry you won't starve. You can pretend the Cheetos are carrots."

"I don't have that big an imagination."

"When did you become a vegetarian?"

"In my early twenties. I got on this food kick for a while. I thought that if I cut out certain kinds of products I could stop my dreams. It didn't work, but I felt healthier and stronger and more able to deal with the nights, so I just kept it up. However, I do have a weakness for chocolate." She grabbed one of the candy bars and unwrapped it, taking a quick bite of the chocolate-coconut bar. "Mmm, this is one of my favorites."

"I must have read your mind," Dylan said.

She smiled at him, appreciating the light tone. Things had gotten too heavy in the past hour, and they both needed a break.

Dylan sat down in the chair by the table and popped open a can of Coke. He'd barely taken a sip when his cell phone rang. He opened it and read the number. "It's my station."

"Don't answer it."

"I wasn't planning to. But it occurs to me that if I'm not going to use the phone I should get rid of it. I kept it before, thinking Erica might call, but that won't happen now, and I don't want to risk anyone being able to track us through the phone signal. I'll do it tomorrow, when we're on the move again." As he finished speaking the phone started ringing again. "That's my friend Jeff. I'll let it go to voice mail; then I'll turn it off."

Dylan set the phone down on the table. Thirty seconds later it rang again. He checked the number one more time. Then he glanced at his watch. "I know why everyone is calling. The ten-o'clock news just ended."

Catherine's heart skipped a beat. "You think you were on it?"

"I'm guessing yes." He got up and turned on the television set. He flipped through various channels, but there were only a few to choose from, and none was showing the news. He turned off the television and sat back down at the table.

"I wish we knew what was said," Catherine murmured.

Dylan opened up his computer. "I'm glad I brought this along. I can check the Web site for a recap, and if my friends don't reach me by phone I'm sure they'll e-mail." A moment later Dylan let out a low whistle. "Twelve messages—all in the last fifteen minutes."

"Who are they from?" She moved across the room, peering over his shoulder at his in-box.

Dylan clicked on the first message. "This is a reply from Rita, Blake Howard's assistant. I e-mailed her earlier to ask about the Metro Club. Here's what she said: 'Yes, Blake belongs to the Metro Club, but I asked him if he'd be willing to sponsor you and he just laughed. Sorry! Maybe you can find someone else. I just heard that the police want to talk to you about the murder in Golden Gate Park last night. What's going on, Dylan? Are you in trouble?' "

"So, Blake is tied to the Metro Club, Ravino, your father, and Erica," Catherine said, with a surge of excitement.

"Along with a hundred or so other people," Dylan reminded her.

"Yes, but most of them don't dislike you. As far as we know, anyway."

"True. It also appears that the cat is out of the bag

about my connection to Erica." Dylan clicked on the next e-mail. "This one is from Julie Bristow; she's the one you met at the station, the fact-checker: 'Hey, Dylan, I had forgotten that Erica Layton was your source in the Ravino story. Now I know why you were so interested in her murder. But what's up with you being named a person of interest? That's ridiculous. I know you didn't do it. And I'll try to help you prove it. What do you need me to do? I have a friend who's a great PI. I'm sure he'd also be willing to help.' "

"Maybe Julie could find out whether Blake Howard and Erica knew each other," Catherine interjected.

"Good idea." Dylan typed in that question and also asked Julie to see if she could find any information on any of Erica's activities for the past two to three weeks. He clicked down to the next e-mail, which was from Ryan, the other fact-checker.

" 'Dude, you're in deep shit. The cops are interviewing everyone at the station. I had to tell them you were here earlier and asking about Erica. Sorry, man. Let me know if I can help.' "

"Maybe the fact that you were asking for information on Erica's murder will make you appear less of a suspect," Catherine said. She could see by Dylan's cynical expression that he wasn't convinced.

"I'm sure they would chalk that up to me covering my ass."

Catherine glanced back at the computer screen. The next message was from his news producer, expressing concern. Three other friends had also sent supportive messages mixed in with questions. The last message was from Mark.

" 'Dylan, the heat is on. Every news station in the city led off with your photo tonight. I don't know where you are, but you'd better stay low. I don't know if this will help, but a PI friend of mine ran Erica's credit cards for me. She made a trip to Seattle, Washington, about four weeks ago. I don't know if that had to do with you, but I thought I'd mention it. She was also in a lot of financial trouble, heavily in debt, and she was about to lose her condo. She needed cash. She may have sold you out to get it. Let me know what else I can do.' "

"Do you think Erica's trip to Seattle is important?" Catherine asked.

"I can't think why it would be. I don't know anyone in Seattle. I wonder if Ravino has a place there. Something to look into. Maybe Mark can check on that, or find out if she met anyone there." Dylan typed in his questions. "I also want Mark to get someone to go over to my grandmother's house and board up the windows," he added.

"If he tells the police we were shot at, perhaps they'll realize you're not the only one they should be interested in."

"You'd think." Dylan pressed send and sat back in his chair. He looked up at Catherine. "I know you're trying to be an optimist. I appreciate it, even if I can't get on board the happy train with you."

"No one has ever called me a happy train before."

He grinned. "That might have been a reach." He let out a sigh and stretched his arms high over his head. "I know there are a dozen things I should do now, but I can't seem to think of one. Help me out, would you?"

"Okay." She moved around behind him and put her hands on his shoulders. She knew he'd been asking for a suggestion, but she had a better idea. His muscles were in tight, hard knots, and she kneaded them gently but firmly, working to release some of the tension. Her own personal story had undoubtedly put some of those knots there. The least she could do was try to get them out.

"You're good," Dylan muttered, closing his eyes, relaxing his neck. "God, I hope you're not planning to stop anytime soon."

She smiled. "Nope. I can keep going. But let's do this right." She released him and stepped back. "Go over to the bed, take your shirt off, and lie down."

He raised his eyebrow at her. "You're quite the boss all of a sudden. What else do you want me to take off?"

"Nothing," she said, enjoying the return of his cocky smile. "At the moment."

His eyes darkened at her amendment. "Round two?"

"Dylan, I just want to give you a massage. If you ask me more questions, that offer will be off the table."

"My lips are sealed." He took off his shirt and lay down on his stomach on the bed. He rested his head on his arms.

For a moment she just stared at him, delighted by the male feast spread out before her. She didn't know where to start. In fact, she didn't know if she should start, because she might not be able to stop.

Dylan raised his head and squinted at her. "What's the holdup?"

"Nothing." She knelt down next to him and put her hands on his shoulders. She rubbed his muscles gently at first, then worked at the hard knots with as much pressure as she could muster. His murmured appreciation sent a charge through her body. She wanted to please him in so many other ways. But this was just a massage, she told herself, nothing more.

Her hands drifted lower as she attacked the kinks in his mid- and lower back. She loved the feel of his body, the power of his muscles just under his skin. He had a great tan, too, a warm honey brown, paling just below the waistband of his jeans. She ran her finger along the edge of that band, feeling a sudden tightness in her own body, a reckless urge to take this massage a little lower.

Dylan's body stiffened as she ran her hands over his very nice ass, kneading his buttocks through his pants. She wanted to ask him to get rid of his jeans, but she didn't think she could be quite that bold. Or maybe she could. She slid her hands under his body, touching the hot, hard length of him. He was as aroused as she was.

And suddenly the massage was over.

Dylan flipped over onto his back. He grabbed her hand and pressed it back to the bulge in his pants. "Don't be shy," he said, his eyes sparkling, encouraging.

She opened the snap and slid down the zipper. She slipped her hand inside, touching him intimately, wrapping her fingers around his flesh. It wasn't enough. She wanted to see him. She wanted to taste him.

She grabbed the waistband of his jeans and jerked his pants down over his hips, his thighs, his calves, and then Dylan kicked them off. For a moment she just stared at him in pleasure and a bit of amazement. He was a powerfully built man, and for the moment he was all hers. Then she leaned over and took him in her mouth, loving him the way she wanted to. He groaned, threading his hands through her hair.

Finally he pulled her head up and grabbed the hem of her shirt, dragging it over her head in one swift motion. He sat up, his hands colliding with hers as they both reached for the clasp on her bra.

She slid the straps off her shoulders as he put his hands on her breasts. Her nipples tingled against his stroking fingers. She was going up in flames, and she was still wearing half her clothes. She pulled at her jeans, struggling to keep his hands on her while she got rid of her pants.

He smiled at her impatience, his mouth seeking hers as they came together on the bed. Then he lay back down, cupping his hands over her hips as he urged her to straddle him. She leaned over and pressed her lips against his mouth as she moved to take him deep within her.

Over and over he thrust into her, sending ripples of pleasure through her body. She felt his heat everywhere, and it warmed her from the inside out. The orgasm hit her in long, rolling waves that left her gasping for breath. When she finally fell back against the pillows she was amazed at how wonderful she felt, how completely and utterly satisfied.

Dylan rolled over onto his side and threw his arm around her waist, pinning her to the mattress. His lips pressed against the side of her neck, and then he whispered in her ear, "I hope you're not thinking about getting out of this bed anytime soon."

"Not for a minute. What about you?"

"I'm very, very . . . comfortable." His hand crept up from her waist, his palm caressing her breast. "Hmm, this is nice."

"I hope you're not thinking about round three, because you wore me out."

"I can wait—a few minutes, anyway." He lifted his head and gazed into her eyes.

Her heart stopped at the look of not only passion but also tenderness. A tiny part of her wanted to call it love, but she would never say the word out loud. She'd already scared him once today.

"Go to sleep, Catherine. I'm not going anywhere."

She smiled at him and closed her eyes, her mind blessedly blank, and for the first time in a long while she felt safe.

Chapter 16

The sand castle had been built to last, with its turrets and towers and the big moat that would protect the prince and the princess inside, and all of their little children. But it was just an illusion. A large wave hit the shore, rolling along the beach until the white waters swirled over the moat, rushing through the doors and windows, drowning everyone inside.

She couldn't get them out. She couldn't save anyone. A surge of overwhelming grief filled her as she stared at the picture on the wall. The sand castle hadn't lasted past that photograph, nor had the happy family that had built it together. They'd drowned in a sea of lies.

The pain in her heart was palpable; the loss of love, of life, rocketed through her, always ending with the stinging sense of betrayal. So many lies had been told, over and over again. She'd deserved the truth. She'd suffered for the truth. But he'd kept it from her.

Now she knew everything. The pieces had come together.

There were no more secrets . . . well, perhaps just one. And soon, very soon, it would come out.

Catherine blinked her eyes open, the female voice ringing through her head. It took her a moment to remember where she was. The motel room was dark, the only light coming from the digital clock by the bed. It was six o'clock in the morning. She'd made it past four forty-four, but still she'd dreamed.

Who was the woman who felt so betrayed, so sad? Dylan's mother? She'd seen her before in a beach setting. It had to be her. Why did the universe keep showing her Dylan's mother? What was the point?

She glanced over at Dylan, sleeping peacefully on his side. He looked so relaxed, so at ease, but she knew it wouldn't last. When he woke up he would be faced with questions and decisions, and she doubted he had any more ideas than she did on how best to proceed. They needed a clue, a new lead.

Sliding out of bed, she gathered her clothes and went into the bathroom. She took a quick shower, got dressed, and returned to the room. Dylan was still fast asleep. Taking a seat in the chair by the window, she pulled the curtain open just enough to let in some of the early morning light. Then she picked up the first of the two journals and began to read.

The opening pages were all about Dylan's birth, the joy his grandmother had felt upon meeting her second grandson. She wrote about how happy Richard and Olivia were with their small but growing family.

The light grew brighter as Catherine read, absorbing the daily details of Dylan's early life like a sponge.

Reading about his family made her feel closer to him. She smiled when she discovered his first word had been *no*. That didn't surprise her. Dylan had probably been born with a strong sense of his own opinion. He'd always known what he wanted, and he'd always gone after it, sometimes at the risk of infuriating his father, but that had all come later, obviously. Certainly there was no mention of any problems in the family in those first few years—at least, none that his grandmother cared to chronicle.

"What are you doing?"

She looked up in surprise to see that Dylan was awake and looking decidedly sexy and grumpy with his shadowy beard and irritated scowl. "I'm just reading."

"You can't leave my past alone, can you?"

"It won't leave me alone." Closing the book, she got up and sat down next to him on the bed. "I think I dreamed about your mother again. The scene was the same, the background of the beach. Someone was building a sand castle. She felt an overwhelming sense of grief, loss, betrayal. Her family had been shattered."

Dylan's pulse pounded in his neck. "The family broke because of her, Catherine. She left. She didn't stay and fight."

"She wasn't as strong as you are."

Dylan dragged a hand through his hair. He let out a breath. "I wasn't strong either. I didn't leave my father. I didn't run away. I stayed until he kicked me out. Maybe she had more guts to go. I don't know anymore. And I don't know why she's in your head."

"I think the answer must lie in the journal some-where."

He stared at her for a long moment, his scowl deep-ening. "Ravino's not behind this, is he?"

"I don't feel any connection to him," she admitted. "But I've never met him, so perhaps that's why."

"You've never met my mother, yet she seems to come into your head on a regular basis. Why not Ravino?"

"I can't answer that."

"Well, I can. Because he's not the one. It's my father," Dylan said with a resigned shrug. "It has to be him. This is his plan. Maybe he used Erica because he knew she was my source and that she could easily be bought. He's the one who figured out I was at my grand-mother's house. And he didn't kill me because he wasn't ready to have me die yet. There's something else he wants to do to me. Something else he wants me to know, perhaps."

Catherine listened as Dylan unraveled the twisted threads in his head. She didn't disagree with his assess-ment of what had happened so far, but she thought he was missing a critical piece; she just didn't know what it was. When he finally wound down she said, "Are you hungry? I read in the hotel brochure that they have a free continental breakfast. I could go down and get some pastries and tea—coffee for you."

"I don't want you to go anywhere without me. It's too dangerous. Let me get dressed. Then we'll go to-gether."

Dylan got out of bed without any hint of self-consciousness and strode to the bathroom. He was about to shut the door when he stuck his head back out. "Next time don't take your shower without me. I had a few dreams of my own last night, and they involved you and me and some very slippery soap."

Her stomach clenched at the image his words created, and she was almost tempted to strip down and take another shower, but he was already closing the door. It was most likely a good thing, though. It was a new day, and they needed to focus on staying alive.

While Dylan showered she returned to reading. She started to skim, impatient with Ruth's retelling of the minutiae of her life. She'd never known anyone to take such careful note of every conversation, every bad moment, every little thing her kids or husband did to make her happy or sad. And yet on the other hand it was nice to have such a close look at the life of a woman who would probably never be able to tell any of her stories again. In her journal those stories would be forever remembered.

As Catherine flipped through a few more pages, an envelope fell out of the book. Her breath caught in her chest. Instinctively she knew that this was what she'd been looking for.

Before she could open it, Dylan walked out of the bathroom with a towel slung around his hips. He stopped, frowning as his gaze settled on the envelope in her hand. "What's that?"

"I'm not sure. I was just about to look."

Dylan's face tightened. He looked like he wanted to snatch the envelope out of her hand and burn it, but he didn't move, and she gave him credit for staring down his fear.

She pulled out a folded piece of paper and a faded photograph. She gazed at the picture first. It was of a bunch of people sitting under a big beach umbrella. There were four kids—two boys, two girls—two women, and a man. She recognized Dylan's mother from her wedding photograph, and, of course, there was Dylan, towheaded and sunburned, holding a red pail and an orange shovel. "It's you and Jake and your mom at the beach, I guess. I don't know who the other people are."

Dylan didn't step forward or make any attempt to look at the photograph. "What does the note say?"

She glanced down at the handwritten words and began to read aloud: " 'Dear Ruth, The summer is flying by. The boys have grown so much you won't recognize them. They love it here. There are lots of kids their age to play with. I must admit I love it, too. I know you think I'm selfish, leaving my husband every summer, but this place is where I feel safe, happy, and the truth is that Richard and I haven't been getting along for years, and recently our relationship has taken a turn for the worse. I want to make him happy, but it seems impossible. He won't talk to me about what he needs, and I can't seem to guess right. I always make him angry. He doesn't think I'm a good mother or a good wife.

" 'The day before we left, he slapped me. He apologized shortly thereafter, but he told me it was my fault for making him so mad, for not doing things right. Maybe it was my fault, but he shouldn't have struck me. I wasn't sure if I should tell you, and perhaps it's wrong to tell you now. He's your son, and I know you love him, but I'm afraid of what he's becoming. He drinks every night and takes sleeping pills. Ambition consumes him. His small failures make him crazy. His anger knows no bounds. He needs help, and I'm hoping he'll listen to you, even if he won't listen to me. Perhaps you can get him to slow down, to talk to someone before it's too late.

" 'Your loving daughter-in-law, Olivia.' "

Catherine looked up at Dylan. A mix of pain and anger filled his eyes. It had been twenty-three years since he'd heard his mother's words. She couldn't imagine how hard it must be to hear them now.

"So she knew he was a bastard, and she still left us alone with him. Mother of the year." He picked up his clothes and stormed into the bathroom, slamming the door behind him.

Catherine felt his sense of betrayal as keenly as if it were her own. She read through the short letter again, noting the fact that Richard had hit Olivia. His anger had crossed an unforgivable line. Olivia had run to the beach to lick her wounds, to protect her children, and maybe to give Richard some space.

She looked at the date on the letter. Dylan had told her that his mother left when he was seven years old, just before Christmas and shortly after an illness that had put him in the hospital. This letter must have been from the summer before, a few months prior to her departure. Catherine couldn't help wondering if Olivia had actually left voluntarily. Had something else happened to her? Had Richard's abuse escalated?

Catherine's stomach began to churn as she considered the darker possibilities. If Richard Sanders was behind the recent moves against Dylan, then he wasn't afraid to kill. Had he done it once before? Was that why Olivia had never seen her sons again?

Catherine had just slipped the picture and note back into the envelope when Dylan returned, dressed and primed for battle. She'd seen his game face before, and she knew he was now a man on a mission. No more teasing. No more seductive smiles. He was all business.

"I'm going to check my e-mail," he said briskly. "Then I'll go down and get you some breakfast."

"Dylan, don't you think we should talk about the letter?"

"There's nothing to say."

"There's a lot to say."

He sat down in the chair across from her and opened his laptop. "Even if my mother had a reason to leave, she saved herself and not us."

"Dylan, look at me."

He reluctantly met her gaze. "I don't want to hear about any more of your visions of my mother. Let's just table that for now."

"This isn't a vision; it's an opinion, and I'm going to give it to you, because we said we'd be honest and direct with each other, right?" She didn't wait for him to answer. "Have you ever considered the possibility that your mother disappeared at your father's hands, that she didn't leave of her own accord?"

The color left his face, his eyes darkening. "You think he . . . he killed her? Shit! You think he killed her," he repeated. He got to his feet and paced around the small area. "You think that's why she never came back, never sent a card or a Christmas gift."

She didn't answer, because Dylan needed to talk it through himself.

He stopped pacing. "I didn't think of that. I never in my life thought of that. Why? Why was I such an idiot?"

"You were told a story when you were a little boy, a story I'm sure other relatives in the family confirmed—your grandmother, your aunt, cousins. Everyone thought your mother left voluntarily, didn't they?"

"Because they all believed him, the master manipulator. That's why my mother keeps coming into your mind," he added slowly. "She's dead and she wants justice. She wants you to catch him."

Catherine stared back at him, suddenly feeling as off balance as Dylan did. The link between them had tightened with the new information, the mirror of their lives reflecting back upon each other. Her father had killed her mother. Had his father done the same thing? "Oh, my God," she murmured. "It's all on me again. I can't do it. I couldn't do it before, and I can't do it now."

"Not for your mother, but maybe for mine," Dylan said, following her train of thought. "That's why we're connected."

She knew he was right. Her mother had died twenty-four years ago. His mother had vanished twenty-three years ago. They'd been almost exactly the same age when they'd lost their mothers. But the prospect of trying to get justice for Dylan's mother overwhelmed her.

"You can't depend on me. My dreams are unreliable and cryptic and not at all helpful. And we could be on the wrong track here. Your mother might not be dead. She might be living somewhere else, remarried, with other kids. Maybe she's sitting on a beach right now, digging her toes into the sand, sad that she doesn't have you anymore, but not sure how to fix it. When I see her in my dreams she doesn't plead for me to save her."

"Because she's already dead."

"Or she's not," Catherine argued, not sure whom she was trying to convince, herself or him.

"We have to find out. It's time to go back to San Francisco."

"Your father won't tell us anything more. And if we go back there's a good chance you'll get locked up, and we'll never figure this out. Check your e-mail, Dylan. Maybe Mark or someone has come up with something else for us to think about."

"Julie wrote back," Dylan said a moment later. "She says that Blake took a trip with a woman she thinks might have been Erica. They went to Seattle together." He looked up. "That confirms what Mark told me, but I don't get why she would have gone there with Blake." He paused. "I suppose Blake could be involved, too. He could have known my father through the Metro Club. I have to believe that my father is at the heart of this. And the timing with Jake being out of town plays into that. No one would believe my father is a monster, except for him."

"And me," she said quietly, reminding him that even without Jake he wasn't alone.

"And you," he echoed.

She leaned across the table and stole a quick kiss. "Why don't you go get me that breakfast? Some food might bring clarity."

"We've tried everything else."

As Catherine set down the envelope on the table, her gaze tripped over the return address. She'd seen those numbers before. "Dylan, wait," she said, grabbing his arm as he got up. She handed him the envelope. "Three-seven-four Falcon Way. Remember the vision I had at Erica's apartment? She was holding a key and a note with directions to get to an address. The word *Falcon* was there."

"Damn," he muttered, staring down at the address. He lifted his gaze to hers. "That key Erica had was to my mother's beach house on Orcas Island, and those were the directions: right off the bridge, left on Falcon, pink flowers in the window box. Why didn't I realize it before?"

"Are you sure?"

"Yes. And Erica flew to Seattle. From there she could have driven up to Anacortes and gotten the ferry to Orcas Island, where my mother used to take us every summer. That's the beach you keep seeing in your visions."

"But why would Erica go there?" Catherine questioned.

"To meet someone—my father, perhaps? To hide out? Who the hell knows? Maybe Blake went with her, and that's where the three of them concocted this plan. This is the best clue we've had so far."

"We're not going to get breakfast, are we?"

"On the way," he said, packing up his computer. "Grab your stuff. We have a long drive ahead of us. At least we're narrowing down the list of enemies. The only person who knows about that house is my father."

"And your mother," she couldn't help adding. "Don't forget about her."

"You won't let me," he said heavily. "But I can't think about her right now. If she's dead, then she's dead. And if she's not . . . well, we'll have to see what happens."

Chapter 17

The trip to Seattle took fifteen long hours as they made their way over the northern California border, up through Oregon, and finally crossed into Washington State. They stopped to eat twice, filled up the gas tank three times, and learned the words to just about every song on the radio. Catherine drove for a couple of hours, but Dylan did most of the driving, his foot heavy on the gas, his eye on the mirror for any cops. They didn't talk about the past, agreeing to put a moratorium on any more personal revelations until they got off the road. Instead they discussed politics and vacation spots, art, books, movies, music. Dylan was well-read, with opinions on just about everything.

Catherine loved listening to him talk. She liked the enthusiasm he brought to topics he was interested in. He cared about a lot of things. He was involved in the world. He made her want to care, want to defend her positions. He pushed until she pushed back. And in the end she realized she'd shed the cocoon she'd hidden herself inside the past few years. Under Dylan's warm but often challenging gaze she'd blossomed.

She wouldn't be the same person when this was over. And she was glad to say good-bye to the girl who'd been very good at hiding and not so good at living. Life was short. She knew that better than anyone. She had to get on with it. Maybe telling Dylan about her father was the first step in freeing herself from the ties of the past.

She would have liked to have finished reading his grandmother's journals, but the sight of them always seemed to annoy Dylan, and reading in the car tended to make her nauseous, so she decided to save the diaries for later. They had enough to consider as it was.

They reached Seattle at two in the morning. Dylan checked them into another motel, where they promptly collapsed on the bed. Catherine hoped exhaustion would send her into a dreamless sleep, but as she drifted off, a voice came into her head.

"Don't come," the woman said. *"Protect him. Save him. I couldn't. I tried, but I failed. It's not who you think. It's never who you think."*

Catherine opened her eyes and stared at the ceiling, wondering whom the warning had come from. The voice had sounded like Olivia's, Dylan's mother. Was she trying to send them a message? Or was Catherine hearing words from a lifetime ago?

She glanced over at Dylan. He was asleep on his side, his breathing deep and steady, his face turned away from her. She scooted up next to him and put her arm around his waist, snuggling into his back. She would protect him any way she could.

They woke up by eight o'clock the next morning and made the two-hour drive north to Anacortes, where they would catch the ferry to Orcas Island just before noon. The ferry landing was busy, and it took a while to get through the line and on board. After leaving the car on the lower deck, they made their way up to the top deck and looked out at the view.

Catherine had always been a water and beach kind of person, and the vista before her was stunning. She'd never before been to the San Juan Islands, a chain of over a hundred and fifty islands in Puget Sound. She knew that the island they were going to, Orcas Island, was one of the three larger islands, but beyond that she didn't know much, except that Dylan had spent every summer there until his mother had left.

Dylan drew in a deep breath and slowly let it out. "It's strange to be on this boat again. It's been so long. I shouldn't remember anything, but there's a familiarity to the sounds, the smells, the roll of the waves. I feel a sense of excitement, as if I'm going home. That's stupid. The island wasn't home."

"But you were happy there."

"Yes," he admitted. "Summers were awesome— boating, swimming, hiking, picnicking, just running free, wasting hours collecting pebbles on the beach and trying to make them skip across the water."

"It sounds like a lot of fun." In fact, it sounded like more fun than she'd ever had in her childhood. Then again, the good times hadn't lasted that long for Dylan. And the rest of his childhood had been rough.

Dylan put his arm around her shoulders. "The one thing that's different about this trip is you. You weren't with me before."

"I'm with you now," she murmured.

"I'm glad."

His simple words warmed her heart. She never really thought she was helping him much, but maybe in a small way she was. Dylan sneaked a quick kiss and said, "You didn't dream last night. Or if you did I didn't hear you."

"No," she said after a moment. "I didn't dream." She knew he wouldn't want to hear about his mother again, and there was no purpose in telling him. They would find out soon enough whether the island held any answers.

For a few minutes they gazed out at the view. "We might see some whales," Dylan said. "I think this is the season."

"I've never seen a whale up close."

"Then keep your eyes open. Do you want anything to drink?" Dylan asked. "I'm getting some coffee."

"I'm fine, thanks." After he walked away she sat down on a nearby bench. She had a few moments of privacy, and she was itching to read the rest of Dylan's grandmother's journal. Pulling the book out of her purse she skimmed the pages, feeling an intense need to get to the moment when Dylan's mother had left. Perhaps there would be some clue to the breakup of the marriage and where Olivia had gone.

Catherine's heart sped up as she read Ruth's words . . .

I feared it would come to this. I tried to keep Richard away from the hospital, but like a bloodhound he sensed a secret, and he was determined to sniff it out. He didn't understand why Olivia was having private conversations with the doctor, why she was acting so guilty, making calls from a pay phone in the lobby to someone she wouldn't identify, why no one was asking him to donate blood when it appeared that Dylan would need a transfusion. He hadn't wanted Dylan to get blood from a stranger, but in the end Olivia had to tell the truth for Dylan's sake. Richard's blood couldn't save Dylan's life, because Richard was not Dylan's father. Dylan shared a rare blood type with his true biological father. I can't believe I've just written that down. It feels more real now.

Anyway, it seems that Olivia had an affair with another man. And she's lived a lie these past seven years. Now Richard knows the truth, and he's livid. I don't know how he'll ever get past it. He hasn't been home in two days. He can't stand to look at his wife or his child.

My heart breaks for both of them. I am furious that Olivia could do this to my son, could give him such pain, could bring him dishonor. Richard is a man to whom honor is everything. But I also see him for what he is: cold, heartless, a man who can't love anyone as much as he loves himself.

How can I say that about my son? I am racked with guilt. Did I make him this way? Was I responsible for how he turned out?

I knew Olivia was unhappy right after Jake's birth. Richard withdrew from her. He'd wanted a son, and he had

*one, but he didn't really care to raise a child. He left it all to
her, and he couldn't seem to bring himself to want her anymore the way a husband wants a wife. Olivia confided in me
after several glasses of wine one night. It was very awkward.
I know she must have been desperate, to have told me such a
personal thing. I told her to give him time, to pretend all was
well and it would be well. It was advice my mother had given
me, and it had always gotten me through the difficult times in
my own marriage.*

*But Olivia found happiness only in the summers, when
she ran to the beach house her parents had left her in their
will. There on the island she was happy.*

*I suspect it was also there that she met him, the man who
fathered her second child. She wouldn't tell me who he was.
I'm not sure Richard knows either. But he's too angry to listen. He wants her to go, but she can't leave now. Dylan is just
getting better. He needs care, rest, the love of his mother. I
pray that Richard will be able to bring his family back together, to forgive even if he can't forget.*

*I forgive you, Olivia. I just wish I could tell you to your
face, but there are some things a mother can't say aloud to the
woman who betrayed her son. Richard must have all my loyalty.*

Catherine didn't realize she was crying until a tear-
drop hit the page, smearing the blue ink. She closed the
book and lifted her head, staring into Dylan's wary
eyes. He handed her a cup.

"Tea," he said shortly.

She took the cup from his hand, wondering what to
say, how to tell him what she'd learned. Did she even

have the right to tell him? It wasn't her secret. It wasn't her story. But he needed to know. So much now was clear.

"I don't want to hear what you have to say, but you're going to tell me anyway, aren't you?" he asked.

"And I thought I was the only one who could see the future," she said lightly.

He sat down on the bench next to her, stretching out his legs in front of him. He took a sip of his coffee, then set it down on the bench. "Is she dead?"

For a moment she didn't understand the question. "Your mother?"

"Yes. Did my grandmother write that she died—that my father killed her?" His gaze sought hers. "Tell me if it's true."

She shook her head. "No, at least, I didn't get to that part, if it's there. I don't know what happened to her after she left, but I know a little more about why she had to . . . uh . . . go." She stumbled over her words, not sure how to reveal something that would shock Dylan down to his soul.

"Well, something has you rattled. Just say it, Catherine. Whatever it is. Nothing could surprise me anymore."

"I wouldn't be so sure of that."

He frowned, his lips tightening. "Now you're scaring me. It's probably not as bad as I'm starting to imagine."

"It is bad. Okay. Here goes." She drew in a quick breath. "When you were really sick, apparently you needed a blood transfusion, and your father wanted to donate because he didn't want you to have a stranger's blood, but in the end your mother told him that he wasn't a match." She let the words sink in. "That he couldn't give you his blood."

Dylan swallowed hard, his pupils dilating. "Are you saying . . ." He couldn't get out the words.

"He wasn't your real father, Dylan. Richard Sanders is not your biological father." She blew out a breath.

Dylan stared at her in shock. "Are you sure?"

"Your grandmother wrote about when your father found out. It was at the hospital. Your mother confessed that she'd had an affair. I guess she'd been unhappy for a long time, since right after Jake was born. Your father had turned away from her. Your grandmother actually felt sorry for your mother, but she couldn't be disloyal to her son, so she didn't say anything."

"Who is he? Who's my real father?"

"Your grandmother wrote that she didn't know, but I didn't finish the book. It might come out later."

"Then you should keep reading," he said tersely. "I'm going for a walk."

She watched him leave with a heavy heart, wishing she could ease his pain, but he needed time to come to grips with what she'd just told him, if that was even possible. For thirty years he'd known exactly who he was, and now it turned out he was someone completely different.

His father was not his father!

He couldn't believe it, but Catherine's words kept

going around in his head. If it was true, why hadn't Richard ever told him? Or had he?

All their fights, all their yelling matches had ended in the same way, his father screaming, *"You're a worthless piece of shit. You're no son of mine."*

Dylan had never taken the words literally, but now he realized that his father's hate came from a place that was real. His mother had had an affair with another man. His father couldn't live with that. He had to kick her out.

Had he also killed her?

Dylan wouldn't put it past him. He'd seen firsthand the depth of his father's rage, the explosive violence of his temper. His mother had seen it, too. Had his father been abusing her all along? Was that why she had turned to someone else?

And she'd kept it a secret for seven long years.

He stood at the rail, staring out at the water, at the island calling him home. Was that where it had happened? It was the only place his mother had ever gone without her husband. It had to have been there. That was why she'd looked forward to the summers. The island was her safe harbor. Maybe where she'd found love. Although he was cynical enough to believe that it might not have been love; it might have just been sex to cover up the loneliness.

Taking a deep breath, he waited for the anger to come, the pain, the hurt, but all he really felt was confusion and, oddly, relief.

He wasn't related to Richard Sanders. He didn't share his blood. He wasn't his son. Thank God for that.

As the reality sank in he saw everything more clearly, including what was happening now. His father had finally found a way to get rid of him. He'd probably been thinking about it for years, but he couldn't just come out and kill the boy he'd raised and claimed to be his son. He had to find a clever way to make his life miserable. Perhaps seeing his friend the senator go to jail had given Richard an idea. He could make his son suffer the same fate. And to take him down, Richard could use the very woman who had given Dylan his biggest story to date.

Dylan wished that he could turn the ferry around. He wanted to go home. He wanted to face the old man and speak the truth. He wanted to forever break the ties between them. His father would probably tell him he should be grateful that he'd raised him, put a roof over his head, food in his belly, clothes on his back. But Dylan knew that Richard Sanders hadn't done any of those things for him; he'd done them to save his reputation. He'd made sure that no one would ever know that his wife had slept with another man. He'd sent her away to punish her, and he'd tortured Dylan to punish him for the very fact of his birth.

So the question remained—why hadn't his mother tried to save him? She must have known what fate awaited him. Had she simply hoped that his father would do the right thing and raise another man's child? She couldn't have been that big a fool.

And what about his real father? Did he know about Dylan? And if he did, why hadn't he come forward?

Was the man someone his father knew? A friend of

the family? The mailman, the butcher, the next-door neighbor?

Dylan rolled his neck around on his shoulders, wishing he could do more than speculate. He wanted to take action. He wanted to shake the truth out of someone.

"Dylan?"

Catherine's voice was hesitant, unsure. He turned and saw her standing a few feet away. He beckoned her forward. "I'm all right."

"How could you be?"

He smiled, surprising both of them.

"Are you sure you heard what I said earlier?" she queried.

"He's not my father. That's the best news I've received in the past twenty-three years. He's not my father. I can't stop saying it."

"I thought you'd be hurt."

"That I'm not related to a bully? Not for a second. I'm incredibly relieved."

"Well, then I'm glad I told you," she said, smiling back at him. "I can't believe in all the years that passed your grandmother never said anything. Especially when you tried to tell her that your father was hitting you. She must have known why he picked on you and not on Jake. Why didn't she do something? Quite frankly, I'm annoyed with her. If she weren't in a rest home, I'd tell her so."

"I'm sure you would."

"She was a grown woman and you were a child, and she should have protected you, even if it meant turning on her own son."

"I guess she didn't want to see it," Dylan said. "Love is blind."

"Real love isn't blind. It's honest, accepting, generous."

"I don't know what real love is. I sure as hell haven't seen it in my life. And I don't think you have either, have you?"

She hesitated for a second too long. "No, I guess not."

Catherine was lying to him, but he didn't want to call her on it. Like his grandmother, sometimes he preferred to stick his head in the sand. "Well, I don't have the energy or the time to be angry with my grandmother anymore. I can't change the past. However, I would like to know what happened to my mother after she left, and who my real father is. Do you know?"

"No, there was nothing else in the journal. I'm sorry."

Dylan was disappointed, but he would find out what happened before this was all over. He was determined to uncover every last secret. He glanced at the island that was getting bigger as they drew closer. "I have the strangest feeling she's there, and that's why we're on this ferry. You feel it, too, don't you, Catherine?" She looked away from him, a sure sign she didn't want him to see what she was thinking. "What's wrong? What are you trying to hide from me?"

She sighed. "Nothing, really. I think I heard your mother's voice in my dreams last night. She said to stay away, that it's not who you think, it's never who you think. I didn't know what she meant, or really if it was even her. Usually the visions are longer, more vivid;

this was just a voice. It could have been Erica's voice or someone else's. Or it could have just been my imagination."

He didn't know what to make of her latest prophecy, but her words left him uneasy. "It's too late to turn back now."

"Is it? We don't have to get off the boat. We could go back to Anacortes and never set foot on that island."

"You know me better than that. I don't run away. I'm going to face whatever or whoever is on that island if it's the last thing I do."

"Then I will, too," she said, moving over to join him at the rail. "But let's not make it the last thing either one of us does, okay?"

Chapter 18

Thirty minutes later Dylan felt unexpectedly nervous as they got into their car and waited to drive off the ferry. He rarely thought about the past, because it usually pissed him off. Now he had a lot more to consider, and his instincts told him that while he might not find all the answers he was seeking on this island, he would find at least a few. This was where his mother had brought them every summer. They'd spent long days on the beach, summer nights barbecuing. He could hear the sounds of his childhood in his head, the adults talking as the kids roasted marshmallows or chased the dogs into the water. He remembered his mother playing music late into the night while he tried to fall asleep in the twin bed next to his brother.

Sometimes he'd gotten up, crept to the door, and watched his mother rocking back and forth in the porch swing, staring out at the ocean. Sometimes he'd gone out to join her, curling up in her lap while she stroked his hair and told him stories. *God!* An ache settled in his stomach that grew into a knot as he thought about her. He'd pushed all those good times away, but now they were storming back.

And what about those nights when he'd heard a male voice out on the porch, the clink of glasses, soft laughter and whispers? Had his mother had an affair with someone on the island? They'd spent time with several families. There had also been men who worked only in the summers, renting boats, lifeguarding, leading hikes up into the hills. Had one of those men drawn his mother's interest, given her the love and comfort she hadn't found at home?

Dylan wanted to know everything, and he wanted to know it now. Honking his horn impatiently at the car that had stalled in front of him released a little of his tension, but made Catherine roll her eyes.

"It's not that guy's fault." She tipped her head to the teenager who was having trouble getting his car into gear.

"I know, but I'm in a hurry. I want to get to the house."

"Do you think it will look the same?" she asked.

In his heart he thought it would be exactly the same, but his head told him different. Twenty-three years had gone by, and he had no idea what had happened to the house after his mother left. She certainly could have sold it. Or she could have come here to lick her wounds.

"I'm surprised you never considered that your mother might have run here," Catherine said, echoing his thoughts.

He was getting used to having her read his mind. He was beginning to find it somewhat comforting not to have to explain himself all the time. She knew what he knew. "I did consider it," he admitted. "But I never did anything about it. A few months ago, when Jake and Sarah got back together, I told him I was going to look for our mother, that I thought it was time, but then I returned to work and the Ravino case broke, and I put it aside again, like I'd put it aside a hundred times before. A part of me didn't really want to know. I wasn't ready. I don't know if I'm ready now, but here we are."

They found the house easily, right past the bridge, left on Falcon, flowers in the window box. The flowers were yellow daisies now, but Dylan knew he was at the right place. He parked at the curb, taking a minute to absorb the sight before him. The house hadn't changed all that much. It was a simple three-bedroom, one-story pale yellow house that faced a private beach shared by the six other homes in the neighborhood. New paint had been applied sometime in the past five years. The lawn had been mowed recently. Someone was taking care of the property; that was clear.

He didn't feel any emotion until his gaze lit on the porch swing, until in his mind he could see his mother rocking back and forth, one leg tucked under her, one foot tapping the ground. She'd loved to sit on that swing during the daytime, reading a book, glancing up occasionally to watch them playing on the tire swing that hung from a nearby tree. The tire was gone now, and the kids who'd played on it were all grown up.

"Are you getting out?" Catherine asked hesitantly.

He realized he'd been sitting in the car for a while. Maybe he wasn't quite as ready to face his past as he'd thought. "I don't know what I'm worried about," he said.

"You're worried that your mother will answer that door."

"Well, there is that."

"Or worse, that she won't be there, that you still won't know what happened to her."

"Do I even need to speak or can you just keep reading my mind?"

"Some of that was just a guess. Frankly I don't know how you're still functioning after everything you've learned today. I'd probably be in bed, hiding under the covers and hoping it was another bad dream."

"A part of me does hope that," he admitted. "It feels like a dream, being in a place where I was actually happy. There was peace in this house. I can't remember my father ever coming here. I think my mother asked him, but he never had time." He paused, thinking about the clues that had led them here. "Why would my father give Erica a key to this place? And don't tell me it's because he wanted to have an affair with her in this house. That isn't logical. It's far away. It's remote."

"Which would make it ideal for an affair, and I don't have to remind you that we're not dealing with logical people. What's happening to you is not about facts; it's about emotion. It's about love and hate. If your mother betrayed your father here, and you were the result of that betrayal, he might have wanted to punish you in a similar way by sleeping with someone you'd been with."

"That's sick."

"I agree. That doesn't make it untrue."

"Erica wouldn't have slept with both of us." He let out a sigh, knowing that he really had no idea what Erica would have done. "Maybe she would have if the price was right."

"Well, if it's any consolation, he's not your real father."

"That's going to take a while to sink in."

"Do you want me to find out if anyone is home?" Catherine offered.

"No, this is my deal. I'll do it." He got out of the car before he could change his mind, but his steps slowed as he drew closer to the house. It was inevitable that he would eventually get there. He finally had no choice but to ring the bell. He heard it peal through the small house, followed by silence. He felt an intense and immediate letdown. "No one's home. We've come all this way, and no one's here." He shook his head in disgust. "I'm getting in even if I have to break the door down."

"Maybe it won't come to that. There might be an open window." She turned the knob. "Or an open door. It's not locked."

Dylan was surprised. It was too easy. "This isn't right."

"You think it's a trap?"

"It sure as hell could be." He glanced around, considering his options. Was it possible that whoever owned the house now had simply left it open? Were they just down at the beach, out for a bike ride? There was no way to know, and he hadn't come all this way to turn around now. "We might as well check it out. I'll go first." After a momentary hesitation he entered the house, feeling as if he were stepping back in time. Then the feeling passed.

The furniture was different. Gone were the old couch and love seat, replaced by sleek sofas in warm burgundy leather, antique lamps and tables. He didn't recognize one piece. The kitchen had been remodeled with granite countertops and oak cabinets. He opened the refrigerator. It was empty save for a carton of milk, its expiration date today. Someone had been here recently. Who?

He walked over to the bedroom he'd once shared with Jake. A queen-size bed had replaced the twins. A cream-colored comforter covered the mattress. Did the house still even belong to his mother? Or had his father taken it over? He had to have been the one to give Erica the key.

When Dylan returned to the living room he found Catherine rifling through the drawer of a desk. She pulled out a piece of paper, her eyes narrowing.

"What did you find?"

"A rental agreement. It looks like Farrington Realtors handles the vacation rentals for the owner."

"Who is . . . ?" Dylan asked, taking the paper from her hand. He skimmed the memo, which simply recapped the open rental periods, one of which covered the current week, but there was no clue as to who actually owned the house. Was it Richard Sanders? Had he

344 Barbara Freethy

held on to the property all these years? It seemed unimaginable. "Is there anything else in that drawer?"

"A local telephone directory, restaurant menus, local churches, tourist activities," Catherine muttered as she ran through a file folder. As she set it back into the drawer, she pulled out an old newspaper.

Dylan's pulse quickened at the sight of the yellowing paper. "That's from the past."

"Yes," Catherine agreed, her gaze skimming the page. When she looked at Dylan there was pain in her eyes. "Oh, God!"

"What is it?"

She handed him the newspaper. It took him a moment to realize he was looking at the obituaries. A name jumped out at him: *Olivia Sanders.*

Olivia Sanders was dead.

His heart stopped. His breath caught in his chest. He couldn't make a sound.

His mother was dead.

She'd died twenty-three years ago. His gaze fixed on the date. It couldn't have been more than two months after she'd left them. She'd come here, and she'd died here. How? He read through the brief notice, which listed the cause of death as accidental drowning. The notice said that Olivia was survived by her husband and two children. There was nothing else.

How could that have happened? His mother had been an excellent swimmer. She couldn't have drowned. She'd grown up on the island. She'd taught swimming lessons. Something was wrong.

"This can't be right," he said, looking at Catherine.

"I'm sorry, Dylan. I know you wanted to find her alive."

"But she knew how to swim. She wouldn't have drowned."

"Maybe she was on a boat or something, or she got caught in a riptide, had an unexpected cramp."

"Or someone killed her and made it appear as if she had drowned." He waited for Catherine to challenge his words, but her silence told him she was thinking the same thing. He looked into her eyes. "If she never came back, no one would ever challenge his story; no one would ever know the truth about his marriage, or about me."

"Except your real father," she pointed out.

"If he knew. Who's to say my mother told him? He could have been left in the dark. He certainly never came looking for me."

"He had to know if he gave blood when you were sick, if that's when the truth came out."

"Right. So he just didn't want anything to do with me." He shrugged. "Well, I'll think about him later. I have to find out what happened to my mother."

"Dylan," she said, cutting him off, "don't you want to take a minute?"

"To do what?"

"To grieve."

"I already mourned her leaving."

"But it's different now. You know she didn't willingly leave you."

"Yes, she did. Okay, maybe she got kicked out, but she did leave. And she came here."

"But she didn't stay away all this time. She might have intended to come back. She just didn't have the chance."

"We'll never know," he said flatly. "I can't trust this newspaper because too many lies have already been told."

"Do you think someone planted it here?"

"It's certainly not a coincidence that a newspaper from twenty-three years ago is conveniently found in a drawer in an open house. Someone wanted me to see that. It has to be my father. He kept this house and rented it out to make money, because that's what he does."

"Or because he felt some guilt at your mother's death," Catherine interjected.

Dylan immediately shook his head. "Richard Sanders doesn't feel guilt. He doesn't feel anything. He has no heart."

"I'm sure you're right, but you're the logic guy, Dylan, and it isn't logical for your father to hang on to a piece of property that belonged to your mother, a woman he supposedly hated."

"I guess I won't know the answer to that until I confront him, but first things first. If my mother died here, then she's buried on this island. I want to find her grave. I want to see it for myself. I want to make sure this isn't just a fake obituary."

"There's a cemetery on the island?"

"For the longtime residents, yes. It's by the church. We used to walk by it every Sunday. Jake told me that the ghosts would come out and grab me if I was bad."

Catherine smiled. "Nice big brother."

"That was before he knew that I really was the bad kid."

"No, you weren't. Your father hated you for reasons that had nothing to do with you. None of this was ever about you. It was about them—your parents, their messed-up relationship."

"Whatever. I just want to find her grave. I want to see her name written in stone. Only then will I believe she's gone. Otherwise this could all be part of his plan to torture me." Dylan didn't think that was really the case, but he had to make certain of each fact as it came to him. And to be honest, it was easier to concentrate on the facts than the feelings swirling inside him. He'd deal with them later.

As they left the house and walked out to the street, Dylan paused, trying to remember which way the cemetery was. Down the street to the right, he thought. "We can walk. It's not far. Just a couple of blocks."

He'd thought it would be an easy walk, but each step forward took him back in time. He remembered the cracked sidewalk where he'd fallen and broken his little finger, the bushes he'd hidden behind when they'd played hide-and-seek in the twilight hours. He remembered learning how to ride a bike, stopping his downward speed by running onto the lawn of the house at the end of the block.

There had been few rules on the island. Everyone had known one another, left their doors open, shared meals. The kids had run together in a wild pack. He wondered if it was still so idyllic, so close-knit, or if the renters had taken over, turning it into a tourist destination more than a real family neighborhood.

"I want to talk to some of the neighbors when we come back," he said. "Someone might remember my mother and might know more about what really happened to her."

"She died, Dylan. That's what really happened to her."

He frowned at her pragmatic attitude. "Hey, I thought you'd be a little more compassionate."

"I am compassionate, but you can't make a mystery out of everything."

"I'm not doing that. It's possible my father came up here and drowned her. You think that's crazy?"

"I guess not. I just feel as if you're focusing on how she died rather than on the fact that she really is gone, and she's not coming back. That has to bother you."

"I told you, I accepted that a long time ago."

It was obvious she didn't believe him, but she let it go. He wasn't lying, but he wasn't telling the whole truth either. If he gave himself a moment to think about her being dead he'd lose his focus, so he wasn't going to think about it, not right now, anyway.

The graveyard came up quickly. It ran for one long block. Small stones were set in neat rows on the slight rise. It was a peaceful place surrounded by trees, quiet save for the sounds of birds.

He moved through the rows, studying the names, not really recognizing any of them, although some sounded vaguely familiar. Finally, at the top of the hill he found her grave, his mother's name on the simple gray stone, Olivia Sanders, and the dates of her life. There was nothing else. No *loving mother* or *loving wife*. Had his father buried her? Had he even come to the funeral? Or had strangers done the deed?

Finally it sank in.

His mother was dead.

He was never going to see her again. He would never have the chance to talk to her, to hear her side of the story.

His legs weakened. He felt shaky, hot.

Catherine's hand slipped into his. He held on tight, feeling like he might just keel over. He'd thought he was handling it, but apparently he wasn't. Finally the dizziness passed. He drew in several deep breaths and then let go of her hand, embarrassed by his emotional reaction. "I need a minute," he said roughly. "By myself. Do you mind?"

"It's okay to care, Dylan."

"Just wait for me at the end of the road."

"All right. Take whatever time you need."

He didn't know why he'd sent Catherine away. He missed her as soon as she was gone. Now it was just his mother and him, no buffer between them. He felt he should say something, but what? He was normally good at finding the right words, but in this moment he had none. He didn't know what to think. For so many years he'd lived his life believing she'd deserted him. It was hard to let go of that. He didn't even know if he *should* let go of it. She had left. It was just a question of whether or not she would have come back. Now, as he'd told Catherine, they would never know.

Several more minutes passed before he could speak. "I'm sorry," he muttered. "You didn't deserve this. You didn't deserve him, and neither did I." He took a deep breath. "I blamed you for the bad stuff, but I guess you were a victim, too. You didn't come back, but I'm going to believe that you wanted to, and that you would have if you'd had more time." He paused again, staring down at her name on the stone. He knelt down next to the grave, his last words coming out in barely a whisper. "I forgive you, Mom."

He felt a burden slip off his shoulders as he finally let go of all the hate, the bitterness, the rage he'd felt toward her. He still had the same feelings toward his father, but her he could forgive. It was past time to do anything else. And who was he to judge her for the actions she'd taken so many years ago? She'd been a lonely, unhappy woman. He hoped she'd found some joy in her affair; she'd certainly paid a big price for it.

A car door shut; an engine roared. The noise brought his head around. At the end of the lane he saw a car pull away, a man behind the wheel.

Fear suddenly ripped through his heart. Where was Catherine? He'd told her to wait at the end of the road, but she wasn't there.

"Catherine. Where are you?" He ran through the graveyard and down the street, calling her name, but she was gone. Someone had taken her.

Chapter 19

Dylan ran back to the house, jumped into the car, and headed off in the direction of the vehicle he'd seen by the cemetery. As he drove his heart hammered against his chest, desperation washing over him. He never should have told Catherine to leave him alone. He'd put her in a vulnerable position, and someone had taken advantage of his mistake, someone who had been watching him—the shooter, no doubt. He'd tracked them here. Dylan wasn't surprised. Whoever was after them always seemed to know where they were going. He wanted to figure out how, but right now he had more pressing problems. He had to get to Catherine. She must be terrified.

Why hadn't she cried out to him? Why hadn't she screamed, struggled, fought? The man must have come up behind her, caught her off guard. She'd probably been looking at him, worrying about him. *Dammit!*

He'd been so caught up in the past he'd forgotten about the danger that lurked in the present.

He had to think, focus. His hands gripped the steering wheel as he drove across the island, searching for some sign of the car. But the island was huge, with lakes, forests, hills, thousands of acres, and he had no idea where to go.

Where would the killer go?

He was the prime target. Someone wanted *him* dead. So why grab Catherine? Just to get her out of the way first? Or was there another reason? If his father was behind the plan, then what was his ultimate goal? Had his intention always been to bring Dylan to the island where he was conceived and have him die here? That made some sort of poetic sense.

But where had he been conceived? In his mother's house? Somewhere else? How the hell could he figure it out? He didn't even know who his real father was. He'd been seven years old the last time he'd been here. He barely remembered anything.

Or did he? Was the answer locked up in his brain somewhere?

Maybe he should call Jake. Perhaps his brother knew more than he did about his mother and her past relationships on the island, but that would take time, and he didn't have time. He had to get to Catherine. He had to save her. He knew she was counting on him. He could hear her voice in his head, confident that he would find her, that he would save her. They were connected. They were linked.

Damn. That was it. He had to open himself up in a

way he'd never done before, let all the emotions in so he could hear her. Catherine said she couldn't get past his defenses. He had to take them down.

Pulling over to the side of the road, he leaned his head against the steering wheel and closed his eyes, trying to be as quiet as possible. But his own inner voice was too loud, telling him he was an idiot to try to use mental telepathy to solve his problem. He needed to go to the island police, or back to his mother's house or somewhere.

Then he heard her voice again, telling him to listen for a change and stop talking.

Drawing in a deep breath, he focused on Catherine's face, her blue eyes that revealed so much, her sweet lips, the freckles that dotted the tip of her nose.

Tell me where you are. Bring me to you. I know you can do it. Make me believe.

Catherine winced with pain as the car hit another bump in the road and her head struck the roof of the trunk. She didn't know what had happened. She'd been watching Dylan at his mother's grave, and now she was squished into the trunk of a car. Her hands were untied. She didn't have a gag or a blindfold. But as she inhaled she smelled it again: that thick, sweet odor that had covered her nose and mouth so quickly that she couldn't breathe, couldn't scream.

She was in big trouble. She searched in the darkness for some way to open the trunk from the inside, but she couldn't find anything. She stuck her fingers into the thin line of light that streamed into the car, but she couldn't pry open the heavy metal lid. She was trapped, and she was quite possibly going to die.

The realization hit her hard. This wasn't anyone else's nightmare. It was hers. The man who had killed Erica, who had shot out the windows at the house—the man whose evil she'd felt in her soul—was taking her somewhere, and he was going to kill her. She wanted to scream, but she was afraid to draw any more attention to herself. In a moving car would anyone hear her— except him? Did she want him to know she was already awake?

She needed to buy some time, figure out a way to save herself, or at least give Dylan a chance to find her. But how was he going to do that? He wouldn't know where to go, unless he'd seen her get snatched. Even if he had, he'd been on foot. It would have taken him precious minutes to get back to the car. She couldn't count on him to save her.

Well, she'd wanted to get out of her dreams and into the real world, and she'd gotten her wish. But there had to be a way to use her visions to help herself. She closed her eyes and tried to imagine where they were going, what would happen next.

The car stopped for a minute. She held her breath. Had they arrived? A moment later the car started moving again. They'd either been at a traffic light or a stop sign. Had they passed either on their way to the house from the ferry? She couldn't remember.

Panic began to set in despite her best effort to remain calm. She pushed it back. She couldn't let the fear overwhelm her or she'd have no chance of surviving. The car sped up as if they were leaving a more populated area, getting out on the open road. They were going faster now. The person driving knew exactly where he was headed.

A few moments later the car swerved to the right, then to the left in a series of sharp turns. They were on a winding road, noticeably climbing. She could hear the intense whine of the motor, feel the upward tilt. There was a huge mountain on the island. Was that where they were now? And what was going to happen at the end of the trip?

Helplessness engulfed her as she considered the possibilities. Her mind created every possible worst-case scenario. The man might open the trunk and shoot her in the head before she could move. He could wrap her body in the sheet she appeared to be lying on and dump her over the side of the mountain into the water below. She could die without anyone knowing.

"Dylan," she whispered. "You have to find me. I don't think I can do this by myself."

His confident voice came into her head: *I'm coming. Don't give up. Just get me there.*

Get him there? How could she do that?

And then she realized the power she'd always had: the power to enter other people's minds. She'd never tried to use it. She'd always let it use her. She'd been afraid to go into the evil, afraid she'd lose herself there and never come out. But she'd have to take that chance.

Closing her eyes again, she drew in a deep breath. She'd been in the killer's mind before. She just had to get back there. Opening her heart and her mind, she listened. . . .

This was a stupid-ass way to kill someone. A nice clean shot to the head and he could be having lunch by now. She'd be dead, and so would her pal. But, no, he had to play out some ridiculous scenario with so many possibilities for failure. He didn't like it. He'd stayed alive and free this long by following his own instincts. But he needed the cash owed to him, so he'd do what he'd been told—exactly as he'd been told.

He pressed down on the gas, and the car shot forward. The turnout was just ahead. So was the rest . . . the small cottage, the bird feeder on the front deck, the stone chimney, the sweeping vista of the water. It had to happen there, he'd been told, so that was where it would happen.

It wasn't a bad place to die. She was lucky. Well, not that lucky, he thought with a laugh.

Dylan saw an image in his head. A hummingbird danced around a bird feeder that hung on the front porch of a cottage clinging to a cliff on the sea's edge. He saw a stone chimney, a path leading to the water, a long, rickety pier.

His eyes flew open and he started the car. He'd been to that place with his mother many times. They'd gone to visit someone—a man. His breath caught in his throat. Was the man his father? Was he being drawn to the place where it had all begun?

It made sense that there was a method to the madness. The plan had been so well orchestrated up until this point. Why would it change now?

But wasn't he just continuing to march to the beat of someone else's drum? He could be walking into a trap. They could be waiting for him. In fact, he'd bet they *were* waiting for him. He had to be smarter.

Driving down the road, he searched desperately for signposts, memories from his long-ago past. How on earth was he going to find that house on this big island?

Think, he ordered himself. *Make something happen.*

There was a hill that led to the cottage. That narrowed it down. He saw the mountain rising before him like a beacon calling him home. He heard Catherine's voice telling him to turn one way, then the other. Somehow he would find her.

I'm coming, Catherine. Hang on.

The car stopped. The trunk opened a moment later. Catherine blinked, momentarily blinded by the sunlight. She couldn't see much beyond the hand that grabbed her arm and yanked her out of the trunk. She hit the ground, landing on her knees. He hauled her to her feet, his grip tight on the arm he pulled behind her back, facing her away from him.

She strained to see him, but he was standing behind her now, one hand on her arm, the other on the back of her head. She could feel the size and power of him. He was tall, broad, strong, and there was a hint of whiskey on his breath.

"Move," he said, shoving her forward toward a path that went off to the side of a house.

It was the house she'd seen in her head, or his. . . .

This was the place where he was going to kill her. She

stumbled, trying to slow down the inevitable, but he pushed her along.

"I'll shoot you right here if you don't keep going," he growled, his voice low and hard next to her ear.

She recoiled at the sound of that voice, so loud, so intense. Pain shot through her as he gave her arm another vicious twist. At the end of the path they reached the pier. It extended out over the water a good dozen or so feet. It was old, the boards showing signs of weather and age. She tried to look around, to seek help from a neighbor, but there was no other house, no other person anywhere in sight.

She was alone with a killer.

He shoved her onto the pier, taking her right up to the edge. The water was ten feet below, the waves lapping at the columns that supported the dock. It was cold, windy. Her hair blew across her face. She reached up with her free hand to push it back.

"Just tell me why," she said. "Tell me who you're working for. If I'm going to die, I deserve to know who wants me dead."

"Stalling. Women always like to stall," he said.

Something caught in her chest. His voice again—it was so familiar. She'd heard it in her head, but had she also heard it somewhere else, somewhere real? She itched to see his face.

"Just tell me, what's it to you?" she asked. "You're working for someone else. You don't have to protect their secret. I'll be dead, right? What does it matter what I know?"

Squawking birds flew by, two of them diving into the

water. In the sudden commotion he eased his grip on her arm.

Catherine yanked herself away, turning around, facing him head-on.

Her heart thudded to a stop. She couldn't breathe.

It wasn't possible. It couldn't be him.

He stared back at her. He was now pointing a gun at her head. But as he looked at her something in his eyes, his dark eyes, fluttered and caught. He knew her, too.

The moment she'd been dreading her entire life had finally arrived. He'd come back to kill her.

"You," she whispered. "Is it you? Are you really my father?"

"Catherine?" His voice revealed his shock. He hadn't known. Why hadn't he known? "No." He shook his head. His hand wavered slightly, but still he didn't lower the gun. Her back was to the water. He stood between her and the only way off the pier. There was nowhere to run. So she wouldn't try. Instead she would take her moment of truth.

"You killed her, didn't you? You killed my mother and you tried to kill me."

He didn't answer. He didn't have to. She saw the answer in his eyes.

The images from the past suddenly rushed back into her head.

They were fighting, screaming terrible things at each other. He called her mother a witch and a whore. He told her that she was crazy, that the devil was inside her.

She said he was the devil, the one filled with evil. He took out the large kitchen knife. She put up her hands, terror on her face.

"No," she screamed. "Don't do it."

The knife plunged into her chest. Blood spurted every-where. She stared at him in shock. "Die, demons, die," he cried over and over and over again.

Catherine ran. She knocked into the door on her way out. She heard him call her name. She had to hide before he killed her, too.

"You killed my mother," she said again, facing him now with more anger than fear. "She saw you for what you were, and you couldn't stand that."

"You're just like her, aren't you?" he said with a sneer. "I knew you were out there somewhere. I should have gotten rid of you before this."

"How can you talk about me like I'm nothing to you? I'm your child. Your daughter."

"*Her* daughter. Her demon child."

"I have your blood, too."

His fingers tightened around the gun. "This isn't about the past. You're just a job I have to finish."

"This is what you do? You kill people? Did it get eas-ier after you killed her?"

"It was always easy."

Suddenly it made sense. The murders she'd seen in her dreams had been tied to her father. He'd been killing people for the past twenty-four years, people she couldn't save. And now she might not be able to save herself. He was going to win again. She couldn't let him. She had to find a way out.

"I'm good at it," he said. "Everyone dies sometime. I just make it happen sooner."

"Who told you to kill me? Did you know it was me?"

"Actually, I didn't. Not that it matters. But life is funny sometimes."

"You think this is funny?" She shook her head in disbelief. "I know you weren't always like this. You had to have been human sometime. People told me when I was a little girl that it was the drugs that changed you, that you weren't born evil, that somewhere inside was a decent person."

He laughed. "They told you a fairy tale."

She saw the wild light in his eyes and knew that it hadn't all been a fairy tale. "You're high now, aren't you? You feed on the drugs and then you kill and then you get more money to buy more drugs. It's a never-ending circle."

"Pleasure after pleasure," he said, his voice silky. "It's a hell of a way to live, baby girl."

"Don't call me that. Don't stand there and say you're going to kill me and then call me your baby."

"You have a lot to say for someone who's going to die."

"Someday someone will catch you. They'll make you pay," she told him, her anger driving her on. She couldn't think about whether or not she was saying the right thing. She just had to say what she felt.

"No one ever catches me. I'm invincible."

Looking at his face she could see that he believed everything he said. He was the god of his own mind, the ruler of his own world. And she knew without a doubt that, daughter or no daughter, he would take her life. She hated to plead, but she wanted to live more than she wanted to save her pride. "You could let me go. You *should* let me go," she amended. "I'm your child. You owe me that much. You took my mother away. I grew up alone, without anyone."

"You were better off without her."

"When will it stop? You're not a young man anymore. You're . . . old," she said, noting the gray in his hair, the sag in his cheeks, the lines around his eyes. The monster was suddenly beginning to look more human.

His hand shook ever so slightly. "I can still take you out."

Catherine held her breath, her gaze fixed on his finger and the trigger. She could be dead in another second, or—

She didn't have time to finish the thought. A large rock hit her father square on the back of the head. He fell to his knees, the gun hitting the deck with a clatter. She reached for the weapon as Dylan came storming down the pier like a linebacker intent on making the hit of his life. Her father had barely gotten to his feet, blood streaming off the back of his head, when Dylan barreled into his midsection. The force of the tackle took them both to the edge of the pier.

Her father took a swing at Dylan's face, connecting with his nose.

More blood.

Dylan punched back with a roar of fury.

The two men grappled with each other as they skidded off the deck.

Catherine screamed in terror as they lost their footing and went into the water. She ran to the edge, gun in hand. If she could just get a clear shot she would take it.

Wouldn't she?

Doubt flashed through her head. Could she kill her own father?

For Dylan . . . for her mother . . . for all the people her father had ever hurt. She could do it, and she would.

But she couldn't risk hitting Dylan. The men were fighting, fists flying, the water swirling around them, as they each tried to push the other under the water. The waves from their struggle sprayed her face with a fine mist. She wiped her eyes just as they disappeared under the dock. Then she heard a couple of heavy thuds.

Kneeling down, she searched the water, her gut clenching as blood turned the white edges of the waves red. She could no longer hear their battle. It was quiet, very, very quiet.

"Dylan!" she screamed.

He didn't answer. No one did.

Chapter 20

For long, tortured seconds she watched the waves. Where were they? Dammit, she was not going to stand by and let Dylan die. Without any more thought she kicked off her shoes, threw off her sweater, and jumped into the water.

The icy cold stole her breath away, but she dove under the next wave, searching for Dylan.

It was so dark, so deep. She couldn't see anyone. She had lost him. Her heart shattered. She wanted to die herself. But she couldn't give up. It couldn't end like this.

She dove down again, swimming under the pier. Then she saw him sinking into the water facedown, his body limp. He wasn't fighting. He wasn't moving. She grabbed him around the neck and pulled him to the surface. It seemed to take forever to get to shore. She didn't think he was breathing, and the thought terrified her.

"Don't die," she prayed. "Please don't die."

Finally her feet touched sand. She dragged his heavy body out of the water up on the rocks, and rolled him on his back. His lips were turning blue, his face white. She cupped his chin and tilted his head back, trying to remember what she'd ever learned about mouth-to-mouth. She squeezed his nostrils shut and then leaned over and breathed into his mouth—once, twice, short, quick breaths. Pausing, she pulled back and put her finger on the pulse point on his neck. It was slow and weak, but it was there. She pressed on his chest, trying to keep his heart going, then breathed into his mouth again, rotating her movements, not sure whether she was doing it right but trying to find some rhythm.

"Breathe, dammit!" she yelled. "I'm not going to lose you, too."

She put her mouth over his again, willing him to live, focusing on the connection between them, breathing her life into his body.

He jerked, then coughed. She pushed him over onto his side, pounding him on the back as seawater poured out of his mouth. When he finally seemed able to breathe on his own, she crawled around to face him.

He was alive!

She stared into his dazed eyes, noting the gash on his head. He must have hit the edge of the pier when they were fighting and been knocked unconscious.

She sat on her knees and brushed the hair away from his eyes, delighting in the fact that he was alive. He was going to make it.

She loved this man. She loved him more than she'd ever loved anyone in her life.

"Where . . . where is he?" Dylan asked, choking out the words. "Did I kill him? I had my hands on his throat. And then my head must have hit something hard. . . ." Dylan struggled to sit up and look around.

For the first time she remembered her father, the man who'd been intent on killing her. "I don't know. He disappeared under the water. I went after you. I didn't see him anywhere."

Dylan stared at the water for a long moment. She followed his gaze, searching for odd bubbles, a swirl of water, a shadowy monster coming out of the sea. Was he really gone? Was her father dead? Was the man who had haunted her for more than twenty years finally vanquished? She wanted to believe it was over, but she still felt uneasy, uncertain.

Dylan turned his head to look at her, his eyes still conveying his shock. "You saved my life. I would have died if you hadn't come after me."

"You saved my life. He was going to kill me. If you hadn't thrown that rock at his head I'd be dead now."

"I never wanted to hit a target so badly in my life."

Dylan grabbed her by the shoulders and hauled her over to him, kissing her again and again, his mouth impatiently seeking hers, his need to reaffirm that they were both alive echoing through both of them. His fingers dug into her skin as if he were afraid that she'd slip through his fingers, but she wasn't going anywhere. She was going to hold on to him as long as he held on to her. Eventually they had to come up for air. Catherine's heart broke with emotion as she saw the tenderness in Dylan's eyes. He cupped her face with his hands and just looked at her.

"He didn't hurt you, did he?" Dylan asked, his gaze searching.

"No, not in a physical way. I don't really know what happened. He came up behind me at the cemetery. I didn't hear him. He put a cloth over my face. It knocked me out, I guess. The next thing I knew I was in the trunk of his car." She licked her lips. "I was really scared, Dylan. Not like in my dreams. This was real, way too real."

"I know. I've never experienced such terror as that moment when I realized you were gone. I shouldn't have sent you even ten feet away from me. You told me he was coming after you. I should have kept that in my head."

"It's all right. I'm okay. But there's something you don't know about that man."

Dylan's hands dropped to his sides, his gaze narrowing on hers. "What did he tell you? Did he say who hired him? Who wants us dead?"

She shook her head. "I asked, but he didn't answer." Mentally she replayed the scene between them, feeling once again the horror of recognition, the realization that he would kill her, even knowing who she was.

"Catherine," Dylan prodded. "What else?"

"I know why I was connected to him now. I know why I could hear his voice in my head, why I could feel his evil all the way into my soul. That man who was going to kill me was my father."

Dylan's jaw fell open, his eyes widening in amazement, disbelief. "That's . . . that's unbelievable."

"He didn't know it was me," she said quickly. "Not until we got down here to the dock, and he finally looked me in the eye. Before that I was just a job to him. That's what he does. He kills people. All these years . . . all those nightmares . . . all those victims . . . they were his victims. I saw them die. I saw him kill, and I couldn't stop him. I couldn't save anyone, not even my mother." Her eyes filled with tears. "I remembered the night she died, everything—how I crept out of bed when they started yelling, the awful things he said to her. He thought she was crazy. He was high on drugs. He was wild, like an animal, a vicious animal intent on ripping his prey apart. I tried to throw my arms around his leg once, but he shook me off, and after that I just stood there and watched. How could I do that, Dylan? How could I just stand there?"

"Oh, Catherine, you were a little girl." He pulled her into his arms, pressing her face against his chest, stroking her hair. "You did try to stop him, but you couldn't. No one could have."

She wanted to believe him, and in her head she did, but the emotional guilt would run through her veins for a long time to come. "Maybe I wouldn't have succeeded," she admitted. "But I should have tried harder."

He held her away from him so he could look at her. "You tried damn hard to save me, and you did. Think about that, Catherine. Let the past go. It's over. He's dead. He's gone."

"I wish I could be sure he's not going to come out of that water. What if he just swam away?" She could see by Dylan's expression that he'd considered the same possibility.

"I don't think he did. I saw his eyes bug out when I had my hands on his neck. He couldn't get his breath. He was going down."

"But you said you hit something hard. He must have knocked your head into the pillar under the dock. You were unconscious when I jumped in the water. He could have gotten away."

He inclined his head in agreement. "I guess it's possible. But you didn't see him, did you?"

"No. I didn't see him. I just saw blood everywhere."

"I think he's gone, but you don't have to believe me. You know what's in your heart. What do you feel?"

What *did* she feel? She shook her head, not sure she could go there so soon. "I don't know. I'm confused. And I don't really want to try to reach him again."

"Well, that's understandable."

"You finally trust my connections, don't you?" she asked, a little amazed at the idea that Dylan had come around to believing in her so completely. She'd thought that there was a part of her that his logical brain wouldn't ever be able to accept.

"They brought me to you," he said. "I heard you talk to me. You described the house, the bird feeder, the stone chimney."

"Oh, my God. Really? So you're saying you heard voices in your head? You'd better not tell the police that. They'll take you to the loony bin."

"Not voices, your voice." He gave her a slow smile. "Apparently you're not the only one who might be a little psychic, but why don't we keep that between the two of us?" His smile dimmed, his eyes turning more serious. "I also remembered the place from a long time ago. My mother used to come here. I think she met him here, my father. There has to be a meaning to this location. That's all I can think of."

"I wish I could have made my father say who hired him."

"We know, Catherine. It's always been about our fathers and our mothers, and the odd parallels between our lives. I can't believe I'm admitting it, but I'm beginning to see that life isn't just about facts. It's not black and white. It's filled with a million shades of gray and things that don't make sense."

She knew it had taken a lot for Dylan to realize that he didn't have all the answers and that he wasn't in complete control of his life or his destiny. But he was starting to accept his emotions and have faith in what he didn't understand.

For a moment they just sat on the pebbled beach, staring out at the water. She didn't know if Dylan was searching for signs of her father, but she certainly was. He would have had to swim a long way to get out of sight, to be able to come to shore without their seeing him, but it wasn't impossible. Maybe she was the one who needed faith.

"We should go," Dylan said. "But before we leave the island, before we go back to face my father, I want to see if I can find anyone here who can tell me exactly how my mother drowned. Maybe one of the neighbors will know. Some of the people who live on the island have been here for years."

"All right," she agreed. She got to her feet and ran her hands through her wet hair. Her clothes were still dripping, and she leaned over to wring out the edges of her shirt and pants. She retrieved her shoes and sweater from the deck, standing there for a moment to take another sweeping perusal of the area. She drew in a breath and tried to be really quiet. She didn't want to reconnect with her father, but she had to see if she could get to him one last time. Her mind could call up his image. She could see him wrestling with Dylan, falling into the water, but there was nothing else. She couldn't feel him inside of her. Maybe he really was gone.

Dylan shifted in his seat, his soaked jeans sticking uncomfortably to his legs, but being wet was the least of his worries. Despite his confident proclamation that Catherine's father was dead, he wasn't absolutely sure. Nor was he willing to let down his guard in any other way. They'd escaped one bad guy; who knew how many more were waiting in the wings? If there was anything he knew about Richard Sanders, it was that the old man got what he wanted, and he never gave up. But Richard had probably never expected the pro he'd hired to fail. They were both supposed to die on this island, far, far away from Richard's life.

Still, if Richard had wanted to distance himself from the crime, why hadn't he sent them somewhere else, steered them in another direction? Why send them back to a house that he owned? Frowning, Dylan knew something wasn't adding up, but he couldn't figure out what it was.

Hell, maybe the plan had been to kill Catherine and frame Dylan once again. Perhaps he'd never been meant to die, just to be held responsible for the deaths of a bunch of innocent people. It was a sick thought, but his father had to be unbalanced to have lived the lies he'd lived for twenty-plus years.

Not his father, he reminded himself. Richard Sanders was not his father. His ugly, nasty genes did not run through this body. Thank God for that.

Glancing over at Catherine, he realized she was still feeling on edge, because her father—her ugly, nasty father—had tried to kill her. It was amazing that the shooter had turned out to be her father—or maybe it wasn't. Maybe, as Catherine said, the universe had thrown them together for a reason. Whatever the reason, he couldn't imagine how she'd felt facing the man who'd killed her mother. But she certainly hadn't shown fear. When he'd come down the path she'd been standing strong and tall. She hadn't wavered in front of her father. She'd faced him head-on. Dylan was more than a little proud of her. It had to have taken every last ounce of courage she possessed to look her monster in the eye.

Besides being proud, he was also more than a little grateful to her for saving his ass. If she hadn't jumped in the water, pulled him out of Puget Sound, and given him mouth-to-mouth, he'd be swimming with the fishes right now—or worse yet, with her insane father.

They made a good team. It was going to be hard to say good-bye to her.

Why should you say good-bye? a voice inside his head asked.

Because she'll want more than you can give. She'll take everything—your heart, your mind, your soul. You'll never be your own person again. You'll never have complete control over your own life.

But hadn't she already taken everything he had? And hadn't she given him back far more?

She glanced over at him, offering him her beautiful, generous smile. She held out her hand, and he took it.

He didn't have to say good-bye just yet.

After parking the car in front of his mother's house, Catherine and Dylan headed across the street to knock on the door of the nearest neighbor. Dylan had certainly recovered the bounce in his step, Catherine thought, following him a bit more slowly. She still felt uneasy. It probably had to do with the fact that she hadn't really seen her father die, and it was difficult to believe he wasn't going to pop up out of nowhere and finish the job. She tried to push the bad feeling away and concentrate on Dylan. There were so many things he would never know about his mother, but perhaps she could help him at least find the answer to how she'd died.

"I remember I used to play over here with a couple of girls," Dylan said as they approached the blue house with white shutters. "I can't remember their names. I know our parents were friends. We barbecued together

on the weekends. There's a car in the driveway. Hopefully someone is home and can tell me what I need to
know."

Dylan knocked on the door, his rap sending the door
ajar. Apparently it hadn't been closed all the way.

"We can't just go in," she whispered. "It's someone
else's home."

"This is the island; everyone just goes in. The people
are probably at the beach or on a hike. And we won't
find any information out here." He stepped into the living room. Catherine slid in behind him. No one seemed
to have heard them. Nor did anyone appear to be in the
house. The little living room was very neat and very
empty.

Catherine moved farther into the room, her gaze
sweeping over the furniture, the couch, the tables,
the photographs on the mantel. From that distance she
could see two little girls, a mother and a father. She
started across the room, and then stopped abruptly,
the picture on the wall stirring her memory.

*A sand castle with turrets and towers, and a moat to pro-
tect the prince and the princess and all the children inside.
But the waves came and the water swirled through the open
doors and windows, drowning everyone inside.*

She drew in a deep breath and moved closer to get a
better look at the picture. Next to the sand castle stood
two little blond girls and their mother, all wearing
bathing suits. Behind them was their father, a tall man
also in a bathing suit and a bright yellow T-shirt, a big
grin on his face. The man had his arms around all of his
girls, and they looked impossibly proud.

"What are you staring at?" Dylan asked.

"I saw this picture in my head a while ago—yesterday, I think. I thought I was connecting to your mother, but this woman isn't her."

Dylan crossed the room and took the photograph off the mantel. "I think I remember when this was taken. Those were the girls I played with. What were their names? Shannon was the older one, and Julie was the younger one. Yes, Shannon and Julie." Dylan gave her a pleased smile, which quickly faded as he read her expression, as he reviewed what he'd just said in his mind. "No, it can't be." He turned his gaze back to the picture. "My God, Catherine. I think that's Julie Bristow, the woman from my office."

"So you finally remembered me. It's about time."

Catherine swung around as Julie came into the room. Catherine was shocked to see that the woman was in a wheelchair. When she'd met Julie before she'd been sitting at a desk. She'd had no idea that the woman was disabled. There was a blanket over her lap hiding her legs, but there was no hiding the expression of disappointment on her face.

"He didn't kill you," she said, as her gaze settled on Catherine. "I had a feeling he would fail. Dylan always wins. He's the golden boy. He saved you, didn't he?" She turned to Dylan with pure hatred in her eyes. "You're always the hero."

Catherine had thought Julie was in love with Dylan, but now she saw it was the opposite: Julie despised him. She wanted him to suffer. She wanted him dead. She was the one who'd made the plan. The realization hit Catherine hard. They'd been wrong about Dylan's father.

It was Julie. It had always been Julie.

Catherine glanced at Dylan and saw the same shock in his eyes.

"Julie, what's this about?" he demanded. "What's going on?"

"You haven't figured it out yet? I thought you were so smart."

"I know my father isn't my father."

"Very good," she said. "Give the boy a prize."

Dylan stared at her in confusion. "You knew that?"

"Of course I knew."

"I don't get it. You set me up? This is your work? I thought we were friends. Why would you do that to me? Why would you use Erica? Shit! Why would you kill Erica? She was an innocent woman."

"Not so innocent, and she was just the means to an end. I wasn't going to kill her at first, but I knew they wouldn't be able to pin a murder charge on you without a body, so she had to go. I wanted to see you in jail, suffering, trapped. I saw how happy you were when you sent the senator there. Even though he hadn't been convicted yet, you crowed about how he would never be free again. You don't know what it's like not to be free. You need to know. I figured you'd believe the senator was behind the plan to frame you, that you'd never suspect me, and you didn't. I left you that video from the Metro Club so you'd wonder about your father, about Blake. And I told you that Blake had gone to Seattle with Erica so that you'd eventually figure out to come here. Even though you didn't remember me, I thought you might remember coming here. Then I planted your mother's obituary in the drawer of your old house."

"Julie, you're not making sense."

"I'm not making sense? Maybe you're not listening. You never listen. You're far more interested in talking."

"I'm listening now. Tell me the rest."

"When you came to the station the other day I knew you were going to keep running, that it would be difficult to send you to jail, so I had to change the plan. I had to kill you. But first I wanted you to suffer, because dying is easy. It's the rest that's hard." She drew in a quick breath, her eyes filled with the fire of hate. "I wanted you to be afraid of every shadow, every sound, to worry if you would die every time you stepped outside or in front of a window. I wanted you to feel trapped, the way I've been trapped in this chair for the last twenty-three years. And I wanted you to come here, to know the truth before you died. I sent the house key to Erica weeks ago. Originally I was planning to have her come here and leave you a paper trail to follow. But she started asking for more money. She was going to be trouble, so I had to revise a few things."

"You killed her, Julie. Do you even understand that?"

"I didn't pull the trigger."

"You ordered someone else to do it." Dylan paused. "But what did I do to you?" he asked in bemusement. "Why do you hate me so much?"

"Because you were born," she said in a shrill, high voice. "You ruined everything. You made my mother crazy. She found out about you, about my father and your mother." She spit out the words. "Do you finally get it? Our parents had an affair."

Dylan swallowed hard. "Your father is . . ."

"Your father," Julie finished. "And because he couldn't keep his pants up, my mother went insane. She completely lost her mind. She wanted to punish my father. She wanted to destroy everything he had, so she put my sister and me in the car and she drove up to the house where they used to make love. All the way there she ranted about him and her. She said she couldn't leave us with him. He was a bad man. And he had to suffer. He had to pay for what he'd done."

Catherine held her breath as Julie stared at Dylan with wild, crazy eyes. The woman was reliving some horrible moment from her past, and Catherine was almost afraid to hear it. But Julie was going to tell them. She wanted Dylan to know. She'd probably always wanted Dylan to know. That was why she hadn't had him killed before now.

"So my mother drove us off the cliff into the water," Julie said. "She thought we would all die, but guess what? I didn't. I was in terrible pain, but somehow I got out of the car. I tried to open the front door where my sister and mother were, but I couldn't. It was jammed. I could see my mother slumped over the wheel, my sister's hands pressed against the glass, the terror in her eyes as she realized what was happening. I wrapped my hands around the door handle, but the current was too strong. It pulled me away. Eventually I washed up on the shore, my back broken. I was alive, but they were dead. And I would never walk again. Because of you."

Dylan swallowed hard, his face pale. "Julie—"

She cut him off with a wave of her hand. "My father lied to me when I was in the hospital. He told me that I'd imagined my mother's ranting words, that she hadn't tried to kill me, that he hadn't had an affair, that none of it was true. I wanted to believe him. My mother and sister were dead. He was all I had left. But he lied. And last year when he died I found out that he'd bought the house across the street, that he'd wanted to have it because it was where she was happy. I read the truth in the letters your mother had written to him, letters that he couldn't give away because she was the love of his life. I finally realized what had triggered my mother's breakdown. It was you."

"What do you mean?"

"You were sick. You were in the hospital. You needed blood. Your mother kept calling my father because you both had some rare blood type. My father had to tell my mother that he'd betrayed her in order to save you. You're the reason my family broke apart and she tried to kill me. You're the reason I ended up like this. My father saved you, but he didn't save me."

"God, Julie—please. Think. I was a little kid, too," Dylan cried. "I was born. I didn't choose my parents."

"But they always chose you," she said dully. "Over and over again. I knew I had to find you, meet you, make you pay. So I hired a private investigator to track you down. I got a job at the station. I thought for a few days you might recognize me from the past, but you barely glanced at me. You were set on making yourself a superstar. I couldn't stand that your life was so good. It wasn't fair. It just wasn't fair."

Dylan licked his lips. He darted a quick, pleading look at Catherine, but she didn't know how to help him. And she feared that if she got in the middle it would make things worse.

He turned back to Julie. "What about my mother? Do you know what happened to her? Do you know how she died?"

Julie shrugged. "My mother killed her, too. She took her out on the boat one day. She told her she wanted to make peace, be friends again. They were friends, you know, all of them. Then she pushed her off the boat and left her in the middle of the sound. Two days later she drove us off the cliff. It was her final act. She wanted to take everyone my father loved away from him. That was his punishment. And mine."

Julie's words came with a sense of finality, as if she had said everything she intended to say. Catherine started, realizing a split second too late where this was headed.

"Stop!" Julie pulled a gun out from under the blanket on her lap and aimed it at Catherine. "Don't take another step."

"She's not the one you want to kill," Dylan said. "I am."

"But you'd suffer more if you watched her die. You like her; I can tell. I saw the way you looked at her when she came to the office. No one has ever liked me. Who would? I'm in a wheelchair."

Catherine heard the pain as well as the madness in Julie's voice. She knew nothing she could say would change any of it, and she suspected that Julie wanted to hear only from Dylan.

"I won't let you kill her, Julie. I won't let you kill either of us," Dylan said firmly. "I'm fast. I can get to you before you pull the trigger. In two seconds I'll have that gun out of your hand."

Julie stared back at him, weighing his words.

Catherine wasn't sure that Dylan could do what he'd said, but she could see that Julie was wavering. And that was all that mattered.

"You're right. You'd win," Julie said. "You always win. You're the golden boy and I'm just the cripple." Slowly she turned the gun toward her own head.

Dylan took a step forward. Catherine put a hand on his arm, afraid that it was a trick, that Julie could just as easily turn the gun back and shoot one of them.

"I'm tired of fighting you," Julie continued. "I'm tired of fighting the world. It's been a long struggle to survive. I should have died when I was meant to die. That would have been easier."

"No," Dylan said with a definitive shake of his head. "I'm not going to let you kill yourself either."

"You think I'd rather go to prison for murder than die? You're a fool. I've been trapped in this chair forever. I won't roll it into a prison cell."

"Julie, don't," Dylan said one more time. "Think about what you're doing."

"It's too late." Her hand tightened on the gun as she pressed it against her temple.

"Oh, God," Catherine murmured.

Dylan rushed across the room, grabbing for the gun before Julie could pull the trigger. For a moment she struggled, but he was too strong. He pulled the gun out of her hand and stepped back.

"I hate you," Julie said, tears streaming down her face. "I hate you for being alive, and I hate you more for not letting me die."

"I know you do." Dylan's chest heaved with his ragged breath. "But you're my sister. God, Julie, don't you realize that? You're my sister. We're blood. And I won't let you die for what they did. You need help, and I'm going to get it for you."

Julie put her head in her hands, and her racking sobs rent the air as the hatred and grief of a lifetime rolled out of her. Dylan stared down at her as if he didn't know what to do.

Catherine crossed the room, and this time she pulled him into her arms, turning his face away from Julie. "It's not your fault," she said, gazing directly into his eyes. "It's never been your fault. Never. You didn't do this to her."

"No, but they did—my mother and her father. They were both married. They had other families." He shook his head, his jaw tight, as if he were struggling with himself not to break down. "They ruined everything. They ruined her."

"But they're not going to ruin you," Catherine said.

"It was all about our fathers and mothers," he murmured. "You, me, Julie—we were victims of our birth."

"We're not victims anymore. It stops here, Dylan, right now," she said firmly. "It's over. It's all over."

Dylan stood at the rail of the ferry, watching the sun set over Orcas Island as it faded in the distance. It had been forty-eight hours since Julie had put a gun to her head, since his half sister had revealed the depth of her madness and the extent of their parents' betrayal. He hadn't slept for two nights, his mind grappling with the new history that had suddenly been written for him. And during the daylight hours he'd been too busy calling Mark and the various police departments in Washington, California, and Nevada to sort out the mess.

Fortunately Julie had confessed everything to the local police, who had taken her into custody. He was temporarily off the hook. Julie, however, was on her way to the prison ward of a mental hospital. Eventually she would face murder charges for Erica's death, and other assorted charges still to be determined.

As for Catherine's father, his body had washed ashore late last night. He was really dead. Catherine could finally let go of her fear. She was free now, and, Dylan supposed, in an odd way so was he.

Catherine slid down the rail, touching her shoulder to his. Her beautiful hair glistened in the late-afternoon sunshine. "Are you ready to go home?"

It was a simple question, but he didn't have an answer. Where was home? Who was he?

He wasn't a Sanders anymore. Jake was only his half brother, not that that made a difference. Jake would always be an important part of his life. But it might not be the same. Dylan hoped it would, but who knew?

Everyone else was dead, both literally and figuratively. His real parents were gone. He still had to come to grips with the fact that he would never ever know them. He doubted he would ever know Julie either. According to a local psychiatrist, she'd had a psychotic breakdown and had retreated into her head. It was possible she might never come out of it. Apparently her mother's mental illness had been well-known on the island, and the woman had spent years on antidepressants before the episode that had driven her off the edge of sanity and filled her with a desire to kill herself and her children to punish her husband—his real father, Thomas Bristow.

He'd read through some of the letters his parents had written to each other back in the days of their affair, and he knew there had been real love between them. It was small compensation, but it was something.

And the man Dylan had called his father was not going to be in his life ever again. He had yet to tell Richard Sanders that he knew the truth. In fact, Dylan wasn't sure if he'd ever have that conversation. It no longer seemed important. He didn't give a damn about Richard anymore. The man was nothing to him now.

It was strange how he'd accumulated a lot of new people in his life and then lost them again. He was basically alone.

But he didn't have to be alone.

He turned his head and gazed into Catherine's blue

eyes and saw everything he wanted. His past was gone. She was his future.

"Whoa," he said with a smile. "I just had a vision."

"Really? What did you see?"

"You and me having incredible sex together—in bed, in the shower, on the kitchen table, on the desk—"

"On the desk," she interrupted. "Whose desk?"

"The one in our study, the one across from your studio, where you paint beautiful pictures of our children."

Her eyes blurred with tears. "Don't tease, Dylan, not about that."

"You saw it, too, didn't you?" He wasn't joking anymore. And neither was she. "We're connected, Catherine. We always will be. You told me a long time ago that two women would enter my life and one would be my salvation. That's you, and I'm not letting you go."

"I'm crazy," she pointed out.

"You're quirky,"

"I'm a vegetarian. You're a junk-food addict."

"You're emotional. I'm logical. What's your point? Don't you see we're a perfect complement, like mustard and ketchup?" He laughed. "Okay, not the best example, but you know what I mean." His voice softened. "You always know what I mean. I never have to explain myself." He tucked her hair behind her ear. "I'm ready to go home, to you, wherever you want to live, the beachside cottage, San Francisco, somewhere new. . . . I am putting my life in your hands."

"You would trust me with it?" she asked in amazement.

"I would trust you with everything I have. I love you,

Catherine. And you may not believe it, but I've never said that to a woman." Because he'd never been able to feel anyone in his heart. But he felt her with every damn beat. She was in the air that he breathed. She was in his head. She was everywhere he wanted to be.

"Oh, Dylan. I never thought anyone would want me forever. You'd better make sure you really want me, because once I'm in I might never leave."

"I really want you, and I never want you to leave."

Her eyes glistened with happiness. "I love you, too, Dylan. I love the way you brought me out of myself, woke me up, challenged me to live. I feel like a new person, someone who is finally free. I think the nightmares are gone now, because my father is dead. He can't hurt anyone else. And I'm no longer connected to him." She paused. "I wish I could have helped those people he killed. I wish I knew now who they were, so I could bring peace to their families, but the visions I had were so cryptic. I never understood them. I never really saw their faces."

"You have to let it go, Catherine. There's nothing you can do."

"I know. You're right," she said with a sigh. "It will be nice to sleep through the night again."

"Hey, that may not happen every night," he told her. "I can certainly think of other things to do in bed besides sleep."

She smiled. "I'll bet you can. Even if those nightmares are gone, I can't promise that I won't experience other psychic visions."

"They're a part of you. I get that. I'm on board."

"Thank you. What I can promise is this—I'll never lie to you, betray you, or walk away from you."

His heart had never felt so full. Nor had he ever been so scared. He wanted to live up to all her expectations. He wanted to make her happy for the rest of her life. He hoped he could do that. "That's all I want," he said. "And I plan to make sure that any dreams you have involve me." He pressed his lips to hers in a long and promising kiss.

Epilogue

Four months later . . .

Dylan waited at the front of the church, Jake by his side.

"You're a lucky man," Jake said, giving him a little nudge with his elbow. "I still can't believe you went and fell in love while I was out of town, not to mention the fact that you almost got yourself killed. And you never called me. That pissed me off."

"You were on your honeymoon." Dylan paused as he looked out at his friends in the church. "But you're right. I am lucky. Lucky to have found Catherine. Lucky she said yes."

"Well, she hasn't officially said yes," Jake pointed out with a grin. "Ever hear of the runaway bride?"

"Catherine is done running," he said confidently. "And so am I."

"The world's best bachelor bites the dust and takes on the old ball and chain," Jake drawled. "Who could have seen this coming? Well, I guess your wife-to-be could have. You should take her to Vegas, see if she has any insights at the blackjack table."

Dylan laughed. "I already tried that. She's lousy at counting cards. But we had a really good time in the suite with the mirrors on the ceiling."

"I'll bet. I like her. She's good for you," Jake said, a more serious note in his voice. "I think Mom would have liked her, too."

"Yeah," Dylan said, his throat tight with emotion. He'd let go of all the anger he'd had against his mother, and he hoped that somewhere she knew he was finally happy.

"Daddy, Daddy, look." Jake's small daughter, Caitlyn, waved to her father from the front row.

Caitlyn was an honorary flower girl, but since she was only two her mother, Sarah, had walked her down the aisle already, letting Caitlyn throw rose petals wherever she wanted. As a result the left half of the aisle was covered in flowers, with nary a one on the right side. Sarah shushed her daughter while her friend Teresa looked on. Teresa, Sarah, and Catherine had been friends in foster care, and Dylan was happy that the three women had found their way back to a close friendship. Teresa had a new man with her today and seemed to be getting ready to make a trip down the aisle herself. Their circle of friends was rapidly expanding.

The priest stepped forward with a smile. "Are we ready?"

Dylan felt a rush of emotion, a surge of adrenaline as he searched for Catherine. For a moment he wondered where she was, and his stomach took a panicked dive, but then he saw her standing at the back of the church. Everything was right with the world.

He loved her so completely that his heart ached. He'd never thought he'd feel so much for a woman, but Catherine wasn't just anyone—she was his friend, his lover, his partner, his everything.

The music began.

Catherine walked slowly down the aisle in a lacy white dress. She carried a simple bouquet of wildflowers in her hand. She hadn't wanted anyone to give her away. She was giving herself away—to him. He'd never felt so honored.

When she reached his side she flashed him one hell of a smile. His breath caught in his chest. God, she was beautiful.

The priest began to speak. Dylan barely heard the words. He couldn't take his eyes off Catherine. When it came time to make his vows he said them slowly and deliberately, knowing that deep down inside Catherine was still that little orphaned girl who was afraid no one would ever want her forever. But he did and he always would.

They kissed and the audience clapped. As they turned to face their friends Dylan whispered, "I had a vision last night."

Catherine's fingers tightened around his. "Really, what was it?"

"That we were going to live happily ever after."

"Well, you know the thing about visions—they always come true." She paused as they began walking down the aisle. "By the way, I think we should trade in my Volkswagen for a family car."

He stopped abruptly. "You saw a child in our future?" he asked, his voice far too loud.

"No. I saw the stick turn pink," she said with a laugh. "We're going to have a baby, Dylan. You and me— we're going to have the family we always wanted." She cast an embarrassed look at the crowd. "I guess I should have told you that in private."

He grinned. "And later I'll probably say I should have done this in private, too." He leaned in and started a kiss that would last for the rest of his life.

Jake Sanders's lover, Sarah, disappeared
months ago, taking their daughter with her.
When Sarah shows up in a hospital room
without the baby, claiming to remember
nothing, Jake must take action. . . .

Read on for an excerpt to the companion
novel to *Silent Fall*.

SILENT RUN

By Barbara Freethy

Available now

Prologue

Large raindrops streamed against her windshield as she sped along the dark, narrow highway north of Los Angeles. She'd been traveling for over an hour along the wild and beautiful Pacific coastline. She'd passed the busy beach cities of Venice and Santa Monica, the celebrity-studded hills of Malibu and Santa Barbara. Thank God it was a big state. She could start over again, find a safe place to stay, but she had to get there first.

The pair of headlights in her rearview mirror drew closer with each passing mile. Her nerves began to tighten, and goose bumps rose along her arms and the back of her neck. She'd been running too long not to recognize danger. But where had the car come from? She'd been so sure that no one had followed her out of LA. After sixty miles of constantly checking her rearview mirror, she'd begun to relax, but now the fear came rushing back.

It was too dark to see the car behind her, but there

was something about the speed with which it was approaching that made her nervous. She pressed her foot down harder on the gas, clinging to the wheel as gale-force winds blowing in off the ocean rocketed through the car, making the driving even more treacherous.

A few miles later the road veered inland. She looked for a place to exit. Finally she saw a sign for an upcoming turnoff heading into the Santa Ynez Mountains. Maybe with a few twists and turns she could lose the car on her tail, and if her imagination was simply playing tricks on her the car behind her would just continue down the road.

The exit came up fast. She took the turn on two wheels. Five minutes later the pair of headlights was once again directly behind her. There was no mistake: He was coming after her.

She had to get away from him. Adrenaline raced through her bloodstream, giving her courage and strength. She was so tired of running for her life, but she couldn't quit now. She'd probably made a huge mistake by leaving the main highway. There was no traffic on this two-lane road. If he caught her now there would be no one to come to her rescue.

The gap between their cars lessened. He was so close she could see the silhouette of a man in her rearview mirror. He was bearing down on her.

She took the next turn too sharply, her tires sliding on the slick, wet pavement.

Sudden lights coming from the opposite direction blinded her. She hit the brakes hard. The car skidded out of control. She flew across the road, crashed through a wooden barrier, and hurtled down a steep embankment. Rocks splintered the windshield as she threw up her hands in protest and prayer.

When the impact finally came it was crushing, the pain intense. It was too much. All she wanted to do was to sink into oblivion. It was over. She was finished.

But some voice deep inside her screamed at her to stay awake, because if she wasn't dead yet she soon would be.

Chapter 1

The blackness in her mind began to lessen. There was a light behind her eyelids that beckoned and called to her. She was afraid to answer that call, terrified to open her eyes. Maybe it was the white light people talked about, the one to follow when you were dead. But she wasn't dead, was she?

It was just a nightmare, she told herself. She was dreaming; she'd wake up in a minute. But something was wrong. Her bed didn't feel right. The mattress was hard beneath her back. There were odd bells going off in her head. She smelled antiseptic and chlorine bleach. A siren wailed in the distance. Someone was talking to her, a man.

Her stomach clenched with inexplicable fear as she felt a strong hand on her shoulder. Her eyes flew open, and she blinked rapidly, the scene before her confusing.

She wasn't home in her bedroom, as she'd expected. A man in a long white coat stood next to the bed. He appeared to be in his fifties, with salt-and-pepper hair, dark eyes, and a serious expression. He held a clipboard in one hand. A stethoscope hung around his neck, and a pair of glasses rested on his long, narrow nose. Next to him stood a short, plump brunette dressed in blue scrubs, offering a compassionate, encouraging smile that seemed to match the name on her name tag, Rosie.

What was going on? Where was she?

"You're awake," the doctor said, a brisk note in his voice, a gleam of satisfaction in his eyes. "That's good. We were getting concerned about you. You've been unconscious for hours."

Unconscious? She gazed down the length of her body, suddenly aware of the thin blue gown, the hospital identification band on her wrist, the IV strapped to her left arm. And pain—there was pain . . . in her head, her right wrist, and her knees. Her right cheek throbbed. She raised a hand to her temple and was surprised to encounter a bandage. What on earth had happened to her?

"You were in an automobile accident last night," the doctor told her. "You have some injuries, but you're going to be all right. You're at St. Mary's Hospital just outside of Los Olivos in Santa Barbara County. I'm Dr. Carmichael. Do you understand what I'm saying?"

She shook her head, his brisk words jumbling up in her brain, making little to no sense. "Am I dreaming?" she whispered.

"You're not dreaming, but you do have a head injury. It's not unusual to be confused," the doctor replied. He offered her a small, practiced smile that was edged with impatience. "Now, do you feel up to a few questions? Why don't we start with your name?"

She opened her mouth to reply, thinking that was an easy question, until nothing came to mind. Her brain was blank. What was her name? She had to have one. Everyone did. What on earth was wrong with her? She gave a helpless shake of her head. "I'm ... I'm not sure," she murmured, shocked by the realization.

The doctor frowned, his gaze narrowing on her face. "You don't remember your name? What about your address, or where you're from?"

She bit down on her bottom lip, straining to think of the right answers. Numbers danced in her head, but no streets, no cities, no states. A wave of terror rushed through her. She had to be dreaming, lost in a nightmare. She wanted to run, to scream, to wake herself up, but she couldn't do any of those things.

"You don't know, do you?" the nurse interjected.

"I ... I should know. Why don't I know? What's wrong with me? Why can't I remember my name, where I'm from? What's going on?" Her voice rose with each desperate question.

"Your brain suffered a traumatic injury," Dr. Carmichael explained. "It may take some time for you to feel completely back to normal. It's probably nothing to worry about. You just need to rest, let the swelling go down."

His words were meant to be reassuring, but anxiety ran like fire through her veins. She struggled to remember something about herself. Glancing down at her hands she saw the light pink, somewhat chipped polish on her fingernails and wondered how it could be that her own fingers didn't look familiar to her. She wore no rings, no jewelry, not even a watch. Her skin was pale, her arms thin. But she had no idea what her face looked like.

"A mirror," she said abruptly. "Could someone get me a mirror?"

Dr. Carmichael and Rosie exchanged a brief glance, and then he nodded to the nurse, who quickly left the room. "You need to try to stay calm," he said as he jotted something down on his clipboard. "Getting upset won't do you any good."

"I don't know my name. I don't know what I look like." Hysteria bubbled in her throat, and panic made her want to jump out of bed and run . . . but to where, she had no idea. She tried to breathe through the rush of adrenaline. If this was a nightmare, eventually she'd wake up. If it wasn't . . . well, then she'd have to figure out what to do next. . . .

From *USA Today* bestselling author
Barbara Freethy

TAKEN

TAKEN BY A PROMISE…

Kayla Sheridan has longed for love, marriage, and a family.
Now, miraculously, after a whirlwind courtship with the man
of her dreams, she is his wife. But on their wedding night he
vanishes, leaving Kayla with the bitter realization that her
desire has made her an easy mark for deception.

TAKEN BY SURPRISE…

Nick Granville has an ingrained sense of honor and an intense
desire to succeed in building the world's most challenging
high-tech bridges. But when he crosses paths with a ruthless
con man, he's robbed of everything he values, including his
identity. With nothing left to lose, he'll risk any danger to
clear his name and reclaim his life.

TAKING BACK THEIR LIVES…

Thrown together by fate, and endangering their hearts, Kayla
and Nick embark on a desperate journey toward the truth—
to uncover the mysterious motives of an ingenious and
seductive stranger who boasts he can't be caught…and to
reveal the shocking secrets of their own shattered pasts.

**Available wherever books are sold or
at penguin.com**

From the *USA Today* bestselling author of
Taken

PLAYED

Barbara Freethy

Charmingly diabolical con man
Evan Chadwick is back in another blockbuster
romantic suspense novel.

FBI Agent J.T. McIntyre is determined to catch
the thief who conned his father and destroyed
his family. He wants revenge as much as
justice, and he won't let anyone stand in his
way—not even beautiful art historian
Christina Alberti, whose secrets make him
wonder just which side she's on...

**Available wherever books are sold or
at penguin.com**